D0015998

# THE VIEW FROM THE SUMMERHOUSE

# THE VIEW FROM THE SUMMERHOUSE

BARBARA WHITNELL

St. Martin's Press
New York

Library of Congress Cataloging-in-Publication Data

Whitnell, Barbara.
The view from the summerhouse / Barbara Whitnell.
p.     cm.
"A Thomas Dunne book."
ISBN 0-312-11913-5 (hardcover)
1. Family—England—Cornwall—Fiction.   2. Americans—
Travel—England—Cornwall—Fiction.   3. Cornwall
(England)—Fiction.
I. Title.
PR6073.H653V54   1995b
823'.914—dc20       94-48484       CIP

First published in Great Britain by Hodder and Stoughton Ltd.

First U.S. Edition: April 1995
10 9 8 7 6 5 4 3 2 1

*For Bill, with love*

# THE VIEW FROM THE SUMMERHOUSE

# I

David Holt, home at last, sank into his chair beside the window and thankfully rested his head against the cushion. It had always been 'his' chair. Fay had preferred the rocker she'd claimed from the farm in Vermont where her grandparents had lived and died. He had thought, from time to time, of replacing the damned thing – putting it somewhere else; one of the guest bedrooms, maybe, where he didn't have to look at it all the time. He'd never done so, though. Not yet.

By stretching one long leg he was able to nudge the rocker into motion, feeling a gentle sadness at its emptiness. Close on two years now. Time enough, he thought, to have come to terms with her death; and surely he had done so, as much as any happily married man could have done? Despite which there were times like today when the loneliness seemed more than he could bear. Just by turning his head he could see the flowerbeds and the rock-garden and the sweep of lawn, and he closed his eyes to shut out the sight, his throat suddenly tight with the misery of knowing that she wasn't somewhere around the corner, just out of sight, dead-heading the roses or pulling a few weeds.

Earlier in the day when his face felt stiff from smiling at the multitude of plaudits and good wishes he had received, he had thought of the home that awaited him at the end of it all and was cheered by remembrance of its tranquillity. All he wanted, he thought then, was solitude, an absence of heartiness.

Now it seemed he might have been mistaken, for there was, after all, a flat, stale, anti-climactic feel about the afternoon. Perhaps all weekday summer afternoons were like this; how would he know? He looked at his watch. Five thirty. Almost evening, but still two hours earlier than he normally arrived home. Maybe he should have invited some neighbours in for a celebratory drink – or stayed in the city. He could have accepted the Zieglers' invitation to join them at the Met, or gone back to Jim and Dorothy's apartment for dinner. Even gone to a bar and tied one on with Good Old Hank. Heaven knew, they'd all been pressing enough.

They were good friends. The best. Especially Jim. Even if he had gilded the lily somewhat in his speech at the lunchtime jamboree – even if his verbosity had momentarily got the better of him (dammit, 'clear-eyed leader of an initiative both dynamically productive and excitingly inspirational' made him sound more like Billy Graham than the retiring President of an advertising agency. And as for the quotation from Rudyard Kipling's 'If', the less said the better). Still, there was no doubting his sincerity – 90 per cent of it anyway. They went back a long way, he and Jim, and had a high mutual regard for each other. Hobday, Holt Inc. was their joint creation. It had enjoyed an excellent reputation in the past and they were right to be proud of it.

The name would remain, but from now on, in practice, there would be no Holt. And no Hobday, really, since the firm had merged with Honeymans. Jim Hobday was to retain his title of Director of Sales, but everyone knew that the thrusting young Turks from Honeymans would be the driving force.

They, of course, were only too happy to applaud the retiring President today, lifting their glasses and wishing him well – no doubt, thought David, saying to themselves behind their white, executive smiles that, by God, it was about time, it'd seemed like the old boy was never going to quit.

To hell with them! Sixty-five wasn't old. He didn't feel old, anyway – well, not most of the time. The thought of retirement wouldn't have occurred to him if it hadn't been for his instinctive dislike of the new regime, with all its changed objectives and methods. Suddenly he had felt weary of it all – had yearned for change. Much, he thought wryly, as Simon must have felt, which made a nonsense of the caution he had urged upon his son; how he had begged him to think more than twice about throwing up his job on *Commentary* – a prestigious publication, by anyone's standards, which was a great deal more than anyone could say for *Soundings*, the psuedo-arty journal, read by a handful of pseudo-arty poseurs, with whom Simon had now thrown in

8

his lot. He'd needed a break, Simon had said, and *Soundings* would provide it. He was to go to London under their aegis, there to report monthly on the Arts and Drama scene. It paid next to nothing, but would provide him with the necessary work permit.

"It'll be a breeze," Simon had said, brushing aside his father's doubts. "I can write the column with one hand and freelance with the other. Don't worry, Dad, I'm looking forward to it. It'll be an education, give me time to breathe, a bit of space. I just don't like the way *Commentary* is going. It's a different production altogether now Russ Hewlett's taken over. He's determined to make it what he calls more accessible. I call it tacky. It won't do me any harm, Dad, I promise you."

And seemingly it hadn't. David could see that with half an eye, when he went to London at Simon's invitation, several months after he had taken up residence there, for there was no doubt that his son had seemed happier, more relaxed, more at ease with himself. Funny how it had worked out like this; both of them rebelling against the slick and the sleazy at almost the same moment. Two of a kind? Well, maybe. It wasn't, however, a thought he would put into words. He wasn't sure that Simon would think it much of a compliment.

For his part, it wasn't only a distaste for how the business – *his* business – was being run. He had longed for leisure too – leisure to be himself, to stop the daily commuting to the city that he'd undergone for so many years. He gave a short laugh. You've got it now, bud, he thought. All the leisure you can handle.

But even so, he didn't feel old. He still played a mean game of golf; still sailed his boat in Long Island Sound, still had his own teeth. And his own hair. My God, he said silently to Fay's chair, did you get a load of Hank's new weaving job? Pretty damned good, you have to admit. Cost an arm and a leg.

He was cheered, momentarily, by the thought of his own lack of need in this quarter. His hair might be white, but by heaven, it was still plentiful; and then he laughed, amused at the petty vanity. Hair or no hair, he was over the hill. Put out to grass.

Talking of grass, he ought to get the machine out and cut the lawn. Old Jules, who helped around the yard, would do it if he left it long enough, but he was uneasily conscious that Fay would consider its present state a disgrace. Besides, it would do him good to get some air. Well, maybe later. He got up, fetched ice from the refrigerator, poured himself a shot of Jack Daniels.

It wasn't the getting old that bothered him, he mused as he returned to his chair, so much as the rapidity with which the years were flying. Ten years ago at about this time of year he and Fay had been on holiday in Bermuda. Simon had joined them for a few days of the Easter vacation. They had laughed a lot, he remembered, and Fay had worn a cotton skirt patterned with poppies. He could see it now, blowing in the breeze; and could see, too, tanned shoulders banded by narrow white straps, and a wide-brimmed hat. Suddenly he could picture her face quite clearly, which wasn't always the case.

It seemed like yesterday.

He nursed his drink, allowing his thoughts to drift. Twenty-two years ago they'd moved to this house on Long Island. The previous house had been adequate, but this one was more spacious, individual, set apart from its neighbours, with a yard that had scope for lawns and flowerbeds; outward manifestation of Hobday, Holt's success. Fay had loved it. He felt a sudden rush of gratitude to the fates for enabling him to provide it for her, for all of them.

They'd moved in on the day after Simon's eighth birthday. In a hurry to swim in the pool, he'd chipped his tooth on the bottom of it that same day, and had been upset because his mother had fussed about it and wanted to drop everything – all the unpacking and the arranging – to take him to the dentist then and there.

Like yesterday, he thought.

They had both hoped for more children. Today, perhaps, they would have resorted to all kinds of stratagems and devices – would have benefited from the latest technology. Then, they merely accepted the situation with resignation, thankful that their only son was bright and loving, rebelling in due season but basically reasonable, and that they liked as well as loved him. Not that he hadn't, personally, always regretted the lack of a daughter. He would have liked a daughter.

The telephone rang and he reached out to answer it.

"Simon!" His voice soared with delight as he heard his son at the other end. "Great to hear from you. I was just thinking about you."

"Sorry about the noise. I'm at Tom and Katie Barnes's flat-warming party – you remember them, don't you? The couple who came over that day –"

"Sure I remember them. They've moved house? Give them my best."

"Hope you can hear me – I'll have to shout. I tried calling earlier, but I guess you must have been still involved in all the office shenanigans. Thought I'd try now in case you went out later. I just wanted to say I hope everything went OK today."

"It sure did. They gave me a good send-off."

"How are you celebrating your new-found freedom?"

"In my own way, boy – in my own way. Wish you were here, though. The house seems a touch roomy for one old pensioner."

"You're not on your own, are you? I thought you'd be keeping up the revelry."

"No. It's been a pretty tiring day, one way and another."

"Yeah, I guess it has. Still – think of all that freedom ahead of you, Dad."

"Ha! You'll be telling me next that tomorrow is the first day of the rest of my life."

"So it is. You've no cause to be down."

"Who's down? I'm happy as a king." David laughed, to show Simon he was in good spirits. "I'm enjoying just sittin' and whittlin'." This was a family joke, shorthand for total idleness. "Is everything OK with you?"

"Everything's fine. Hey – I had another reason for calling – Holy Cow, the *noise*. Can you hear me? Say, you'll be interested in this. Remember that old guy you met when you were over here in the war? Caleb Carne?"

David's momentary pause, his sudden sharpening of attention, was imperceptible.

"Sure," he said breezily. "How could I forget him? I kind of assumed he'd died a long time ago."

"Well, you kind of assumed wrong. He's coming up for his ninety-fifth birthday next month and since this falls on the fiftieth anniversary of the Battle of Britain when he was at the height of his fame, I've been commissioned to write an in-depth profile for a Sunday supplement. The *Gazette*, no less. How about that? I had to hustle a bit. It's the best assignment I've had for a while, I can tell you – oh, sorry." His voice faded a little. Momentarily, it seemed, he had turned away from the telephone to speak to someone else. "I'm nearly through. Hey, Dad – you there? About Caleb Carne. He's a real hot prospect right now. They've reissued the text of his wartime broadcasts in book form, *The Glory and the Dream* it's called, and it's shot to the top of the best-seller list over here."

"That's amazing."

"Isn't it, though? I thought you might be able to provide me with a few sidelights on his character."

There was silence from David.

"Dad? You still there? I said –"

"Sure. I heard what you said." David's voice was casual. "I was giving it a little thought. No, I can't recall anything of interest. He was an outgoing, hospitable kind of a guy – a touch emotional, I guess. He didn't conform to the usual buttoned-up British stereotype – but there must be plenty of others to tell you that. I only knew him for a short time, you know."

"C'mon, have a heart! You can do better than that, can't you? I only got the job by boasting to the right people about your connection!"

"It was a long time ago, son. Memories fade."

"Sure, I know. And anyway it was the daughters you were interested in, wasn't it? Talking of which, I spoke on the telephone to one of them just a few days ago. The youngest, I gathered."

"Pen," David said, seeing in his mind's eye a skinny, tomboyish figure clutching an armful of daffodils.

"That's it. She lost her husband a good many years ago, and she went back home to look after the old boy when her mother died." A prolonged burst of background laughter made him groan. "Gee, this noise is impossible! I'd better go, Dad – somebody else wants the phone. Look, if you do remember anything interesting about Carne, give me a call, won't you? Or better still, why not come over? You've got all the time in the world now. That crazy Cornish village where he's spent all his life is staging some sort of celebration on the Sunday following his birthday. You might enjoy it – seeing all your old haunts, meeting up with the daughters again. Why don't you think about it?"

"I will," David promised.

And indeed, once the connection had been broken, he found he could think of little else. He showered and changed his business clothes for jeans and a cotton sweater, forcing himself to go out and cut the grass; but his thoughts stubbornly refused to be discarded as easily as his shirt and tie.

Pen. Had she remembered him? Simon hadn't said so; hadn't passed on her good wishes. Perhaps he hadn't even thought to mention his parentage. It wasn't, after all, as if David had ever spoken much about that episode in his life, to his son or to anyone else. He wasn't one to reminisce at length about his war experiences. There had always been too much going on in the present, too much planning to be done for the future.

At the time he had felt nothing but relief when the Cornish interlude was over, even though it had been replaced by the heart-stopping danger of D-day. The consequent terror and elation had successfully blurred all the troubling uncertainty of that terrible night with Carne, all the doubts and suspicions and guilt.

✳     ✳     ✳

He hadn't understood a thing about that night. He'd acted in a kind of trance-like panic; had lain awake afterwards, he remembered now, with his breathing ragged and his heart beating like a trip hammer, sure he had done wrong and would be called to account for it – finding flaws in Caleb Carne's story, making up his mind to tell someone in authority, knowing that he wouldn't.

He liked Carne, admired him, had been made welcome in his home – was in love, dammit, with one of his daughters. He owed him something for that, surely?

But did he trust him? Ah – that was a different matter.

Less than twenty-four hours after leaving Cornwall he had been on his way to the Normandy beaches and other, more immediate concerns had forced themselves upon him. Never, David thought now, had a boy soldier been more relieved to turn his back on any situation. He had wanted to forget, and thankfully had done so. The events of that night were pushed to the back of his mind and eventually had become dream-like, surreal and insubstantial, as indeed had the whole period he had spent in Cornwall. Which was a shame, for there had been – hadn't there? – so much about those months that he might have remembered with pleasure.

Caro and Trish and Pen.

Funny he should have been thinking about the desirability of having daughters when Simon called. He had a sudden memory of a warm spring day, with the sun sparkling on the waves and the whole family gathered in the summerhouse on the cliff where Mrs Carne was silently dispensing tea, taking no part in the volatile, even hilarious conversation that eddied around her.

What was it that caused Caleb to erupt so suddenly, David wondered now? Some impudent, disrespectful remark from one of the girls, he supposed. They made a point of pricking the bubble of his self-importance whenever the chance arose. It was, Pen had assured David on one occasion, their solemn duty to do so, otherwise he would become impossible. As it was, they brought him down to earth and prevented him from taking himself too seriously.

On this particular day he had exploded into simulated wrath, the picture of a man goaded beyond endurance.

"Daughters!" he had yelled, his handsome face ugly with despair. "I'm a man *beset* by daughters – the most be-daughtered man that ever lived, King Lear not excepted! Who will rid me of these pestilential women? What will it take? Tell me –" Rounding on David, he had seized him by the shoulders, eyes blazing with entreaty. "If I press five shillings into your palm – if I volunteer to hold the ladder to the bedroom window – will you do me the favour of eloping with one of them? Maybe more? They come cheaper by the quarter-dozen. Stop laughing, boy – you think I'm joking?"

"I guess I'm not much of a marriage prospect, sir. No secure future, you might say."

And as if, suddenly, Carne had seen the truth of this, the assumed rage left him and he was all kindness, all understanding, the hand on the shoulder now gentle and reassuring.

"You'll be all right, my boy," he'd said softly. "You'll come through. Trust my Celtic intuition."

And surprisingly David had trusted him – which was strange because it had always seemed to him, from the first moment of their meeting, that there was more than a touch of the travelling showman about Caleb Carne, more than a whiff of the bunko booth.

Yet – yet – would his broadcast talks have brought him so much fame if they had not been sincere? The airwaves had a trick of picking up phoniness, revealing the con man in all his threadbare garments.

Listeners had loved Caleb Carne. He had spoken of his native land in a way that could raise a lump in the throat even of an expatriate American – lyrically, yet with deft touches of humour. To the British public, hearing him for the first time on the airwaves just after Dunkirk when everything was dark and without hope, he had come as an inspiration. David, arriving almost four years later, had seen some of the letters that Mrs Carne had preserved for posterity. They had arrived by the sackful – mothers who had lost sons, wives separated from husbands, fire-watchers enduring long, sleepless nights, old people who had seen it all before and wondered if they would live long enough to experience peace once more. The list was almost inexhaustible.

To all, apparently, he had given hope and a determination to endure. He had made them laugh and made them cry, and above all, he had given them something to live for – a vision of the future where all would be at peace, the whole world in harmony.

A dream? Well, perhaps. It was certainly unashamed propaganda, approved by the government – but who could criticise a man who did so much good, stiffened so many sinews? The moment had produced the man, and Caleb Carne was the man. He had gloried in the unexpected acclaim, for until the moment when the world thrilled to his first broadcast he had received only the most modest recognition for the handful of books he had written. Perhaps even that was an overstatement. Pen had lent David one of his pre-war novels and much as he liked reading – much as he liked Caleb Carne himself – he had found it a struggle to finish it, finding the characters two-dimensional and the long patches of purple prose difficult to plough through. There was moreover a sentimentality about it that must, presumably, have appealed to someone, back in the twenties and thirties, but which seemed thoroughly outmoded in the more turbulent world of 1944.

The novels had, however, been written some years before David had come on the scene. By that time the metamorphosis had long taken place, and the little-known novelist had become the established and much-loved broadcaster. David smiled now as he remembered the delight Carne took in his fame, and he smiled more to think of the way his daughters had teased him. Oh yes, he thought now; those girls were something else – and unlike the early days of his marriage to Fay, none of it was a bit like yesterday. It was a different world, light-years away from the here and the now. The David Holt who inhabited this fine but lonely house in the summer of 1990 was a different person from the nineteen-year-old PFC David Holt, US Army, who in 1944 had smiled innocently at Carne's pleas for him to elope with one of the daughters, hoping that he was giving the impression of a man who had never, not in his wildest dreams, entertained any but the purest of thoughts about any of them.

Caro and Trish and Pen. None used more than the diminutives of the gracious names their parents had decreed for them – a practice often deplored by Carne himself.

How impossible it was to think of them as old! Little Pen – a widow? And what of the others? They would be for ever young in his memory, for ever slim and vital and unpredictable. He'd never understood them, never quite known what to make of them, just known that they dazzled and bewitched and enthralled him. And maddened him, just as they maddened their father.

How strange it was that Simon had come within their orbit – thought not, on reflection, so extraordinary, given that his work was in the field of literature and drama. Caleb Carne, breaking new ground in 1940, had been acclaimed as a master of both. His discourses were, it was said at the time and apparently was being said again, literary gems; his delivery of them masterly.

Should he go back to Cornwall, as Simon had suggested? He had avoided it so far, though he had been to Britain many times since those wartime days. The avoidance had not been deliberate – or at least, until now the possibility that it might have been had not occurred to him; events, rather, had dictated his movements – business commitments in London and Manchester, and the fact that Fay had relations in Scotland.

Only now, as memories came flooding back, did he wonder if, after all, there had been some subliminal reason that had prevented him returning to the scene of his youthful indiscretions.

Indiscretions? He laughed ruefully as the word occurred to him. Thus did age remove the intensity and the drama from past events. He would have put it more strongly at the time. No, he thought. I'm not going back. It wouldn't do.

Not even to learn the full story?

No, no. It wouldn't do. Old secrets were better left buried, forgotten. Let Simon write his bland and laudatory profile untroubled by his father's disturbing memories. And let Pen remain a schoolgirl, and Caro a tragedy queen, and Trish a ravishing heart-breaker, forever young.

Impatient with himself for his backward-looking thoughts he went outside and tackled the long grass. You see this? he said to Fay. I'm beginning my retirement as I mean to go on.

It wasn't such a chore, really; in fact he was so lost in thought that he was surprised how quickly he was through. With the machine put away he went inside once more, washed his hands at the kitchen sink and peered inside the refrigerator to find the meal that his housekeeper had left ready to put into the microwave.

No more memories, he thought, idly watching the dish as it rotated. Enough was enough. Infuriating as the cliché might be, tomorrow was, very truly, the first day of the rest of his life, and he had more to do with it than brood about the mistakes of the past. For weeks he'd been meaning to mend the fence at the far end of the yard. Tomorrow he'd make a start. Then he'd go down to the Club for lunch, take the boat out for a sail. Meantime the news was on television in five minutes. He wanted to catch it, see what was going on in the Middle East. It didn't look good . . .

But it *would* be satisfying to know the full story of those far-off days. Was it possible, after so long? He remembered Simon's injunction to think about it.

"That's what I'll do," he said to himself, obeying the bleeps of the microwave and opening the door to extract his meal. "I'll think about it."

\*  \*  \*

The house on the headland beyond the fishing village of Porthlivick was accustomed to storms. Since the reign of Queen Victoria,

Roscarrow had stood facing the sea, its tall front windows and gothic gables overlooking the beach that lay beneath it, its grey stones weathering and darkening with each year that passed.

The spell of hot weather had broken at last. Thunder and lightning split the sky, and Pen lay, sleepless, listening to the wind tearing in from the sea, knowing that she would have to get up to jam the window and stop its rattling. It had always rattled at the slightest provocation. She wondered briefly if the recent improvement in her father's fortunes might at last mean that double glazing was a possibility.

Don't hold your breath, she warned herself with amused resignation. He hated change. Even the acquisition of a new sink and double drainer in the kitchen had been a major battle, despite the fact that the previous one was crazed and discoloured and guaranteed to break the back of anyone unfortunate enough to work at it. You could understand it, of course. He'd never had any money to spare, even in the days of his fame. Since the failure of his post-war novels his only income had resulted from local journalism, boosted for the past thirty years by his retirement pension.

Her own pension didn't amount to a great deal either, though it was she who paid for help in the house since it soon became clear that she would have no life of her own if she did not. It meant that there was little over for much in the way of refurbishment, and parsimony in such matters had become a way of life. No doubt she would have to go on jamming the window with the folded postcard that she kept on the sill for the purpose. It was a view of Antibes sent by Trish two years ago, just after she'd gone to live there. All right for some, Pen thought, as she always did on these occasions – but again the tone was amused and bore no trace of envy. Antibes seemed as right for Trish as Trish was for Antibes; and, come to that, as Pen was for Porthlivick, which had been her home for so long that she couldn't imagine living anywhere else.

The kitchen door was banging, echoing through the house. She sighed and climbed resignedly out of bed. She'd have to do the rounds – check that her father was still sleeping peacefully, go downstairs to deal with the door. She needed no lights. She knew every stair, every corner of this house. Roscarrow had been her home all her life, except for the years of her marriage to the young doctor when she had lived in the village. She had been born, in fact, in the room where her father now slept – undisturbed, she discovered, by the sudden storm, leading her to think that his hearing must, after all, be deteriorating. So far she had suspected that his deafness was highly selective, only in operation when he chose.

Back in bed after her foray downstairs, she found to her annoyance that any inclination to sleep had left her, despite the fact that the drama of the storm had abated as suddenly as it had started, settling down into a steady downpour. The thoughts she had done her best to ignore all day had surfaced and refused to go away. Scenes from the past unrolled before her like a costume drama on television; and all because of the phone call from David's son.

Though he had mentioned his name at the beginning of the conversation she hadn't taken it in properly and it certainly hadn't dawned on her, not for one moment, that this American might be related to the young soldier she had known so many years before. She had forgotten – actually forgotten! – that David's name was Holt. Imagine telling her fifteen-year-old self that; imagine her fifteen-year-old self believing it! It was only after the conversation was over and the arrangements made that Simon had said:

"I believe you once knew my father, back in the war."

"Did I? Oh –" Suddenly the penny had dropped. "You mean – you mean *David*? Of *course*! David Holt!" Astonishment silenced her for a moment. "Good gracious," she said faintly at last. "How is he?"

"He's fine," Simon told her. "He's about to retire. Sadly, my mother died a couple of years ago –"

"Oh, I'm so very sorry."

"I'll get you up to date with all the news when we meet."

"I shall look forward to that. Can I offer you a bed? The village tends to be crowded this time of year."

"That's kind of you, but there's really no need. I managed to get a room at the Anchor."

"Well, if you're sure . . . the Anchor's nothing grand, but it's clean and comfortable. I'll see you on Wednesday, then."

She hadn't, she realised afterwards, sent her good wishes to David, or her condolences or anything. Her brain had somehow ceased functioning properly, half-stunned by the thought that she was in touch with him again, even if only at a distance – which was illogical, to say the least. She had carried no torch for him during the intervening years, had not yearned for what might have been; would have said, in fact, that she had little memory of those few short months, so much had happened since.

Why, then, this feeling of – of what? Excitement? Nostalgia? Embarrassment? No, not that; not any more. She found she could now stand back and remember the gaucheries of her youth with a kind of affectionate indulgence, as if some shy stranger was responsible for them.

But there was, she recognised to her amused exasperation, a residue of – caring? And annoyance? No, not exactly annoyance. Hurt feelings, then; which really was ridiculous because she didn't approve of hurt feelings. She'd always maintained that they were demeaning and a waste of time, as well as nearly always unjustified.

"I'll come to tell you goodbye before we leave," David had said. She had been intrigued by the Americanism which, like all his speech, had added to his glamour. But he hadn't come. Or written. He knew how she felt about him, must have known she would be anxious, but he'd done nothing to let her know if he was alive or dead. He could have sent a line, surely? After all, they'd been good friends. It was she who had invited him to the house, she who'd seen him first.

Oh, go to sleep, she told herself crossly. Was there ever a woman more stupid? As if any of it mattered now. Even so, it was impossible to stop the film rolling, rolling . . .

\*    \*    \*

He was there, just inside the lych-gate, as she walked up to the church with her arms full of daffodils, that early spring of 1944.

Porthlivick hummed with the influx of the American soldiers who had set up a kind of tented village on Bow Beach – a long, duny stretch of sand about two miles to the west – where they engaged in mysterious manoeuvres with strange-looking amphibious vessels. Every night the GIs, as she learned to call them, would gather in Porthlivick in groups, along the quay, in the square, outside the pubs, whistling at the girls and offering sweets to the children. Candies, they called them.

Pen, the least extrovert of the three Carne girls, found them inimical, perhaps because they were always in packs, like hunting dogs; she walked quickly past them, head down, not looking in their direction. And yet, at the same time, they fascinated her. Hollywood films had taught her all she knew of America. It was a country where High School students put on musical shows of astonishing brilliance, where everyone owned huge cars and refrigerators, where women had shiny blonde hair and walked around in high-heeled shoes and full make-up, even in the kitchen, even first thing in the morning. They actually went to bed with their make-up on! And as for the men – well, they were all handsome and amusing and romantic.

Some of the Americans she saw were short and swarthy, but they were in the minority. Many claimed to be film stars, and some of them looked as if they might be. In any case there was no denying they were an attractive, exotic bunch. Maybe the uniform had something to do with it, for they were of so much better quality than those worn by British soldiers that even the enlisted men looked like officers. No wonder they'd turned all the girls' heads, and no wonder she was overwhelmed with shyness whenever she came anywhere near them. Not that they ever whistled at her. She was too thin, too scraggy, too immature.

"Where's the fire, baby?" one had called out the other day as, head down, she had headed briskly up the hill away from the square. She had flicked a small, embarrassed smile in his direction as she hurried on; but saw that already his attention had been diverted to Doreen Laity who was walking behind her. Doreen was a form below her at school and a full year younger, but had a bosom and permed hair and always applied lipstick in the bus that brought the Porthlivick youth home from the Grammar School in St Jory, the market town six miles away.

Now, seeing the soldier in the churchyard, she was quite certain that he would speak to her. Her heart beat a little faster as she wondered wildly what she would say in reply. It would be just *like* her not to be able to string two articulate words together. Sure enough, he opened the gate for her and held it politely as she passed through.

"Say, those are beautiful," he said, with a nod at the daffodils.

"Yes." She smiled at him nervously. He appeared younger than most of the GIs, and had a nice smile – friendly, not frightening.

She was aware that she ought, really, to make some kind of an effort. It was, after all, her country. She was the hostess, as it were.

"I'm – I'm going to put them in the church. Arrange them, I mean. In vases." Her voice sounded strange in her ears, breathy and hesitant and childish. *Idiot*, she thought. Where else would you put flowers?

"My Mom does that, back home." He fell into step beside her as she walked up the path to the church door. "I've been looking at the tombstones. Some are real old, aren't they? Look – 1790." He crouched down beside one that was close to the path, tracing the inscription with his finger. "Josiah Nan-kiv-*ell*."

"Nan*kiv*ell," Pen corrected him. Then, fearing that she had sounded offensively schoolma'amish, rattled breathlessy on: "There are loads of Nankivells in Porthlivick. The really old graves are round the other side, only they're so old you can't see the dates on them any more. And there are some even older inside, under the flagstones."

"Is it OK if I come in and see them?"

"Of course. The church is always open."

He held the door for her and she went in ahead of him, marching straight to the vestry, not looking back to see what he was doing. All the time she was dealing with the flowers, however, she was conscious of him prowling around the church. She could hear the odd footstep, a scrape of a shoe; but for the most part there was silence.

Maybe he's gone, she thought, when the silence seemed to have continued for some time. She didn't know whether to be glad or sorry. She'd hated the thought of his seeing her ham-fisted efforts with the daffodils, for she was only deputising for Trish who had quite a knack for flower arranging; and she was quite sure that he would despise her social ineptitude. On the other hand, she wanted to hear his voice again. It was exciting to hear the accent, foreign but familiar, and the phrases heard so often at the pictures.

There was no sign of him when she came out bearing the huge brass vase that was to go by the chancel steps. He's gone, she thought, feeling a surprisingly sharp pang of loss. Just as well, really. She would probably have said something daft, made a fool of herself –

She heard the sound of footsteps and turned in surprise to see that he hadn't gone at all but was still there, moving out of the shadows where, it seemed, he had been occupying himself by reading the names on the war memorial.

"Those are great," he said, coming down the aisle towards her.

A pale sun filtering through a stained-glass window seemed to bathe him in a golden light. He's *beautiful*, she thought, suddenly breathless; and she turned abruptly, bending down to fiddle with the flowers.

"I'm hopeless, actually," she said, her voice cold with shyness. "Trish, my sister, was supposed to do it, but she was out late last night and wouldn't get up."

"Well, they look really pretty to me. They kind of light up the place, don't they?"

"There's another vase in the vestry." Pen went past him, not looking at him. Uncomfortably she became aware that he was following her.

"Can I carry it for you?" He didn't wait for an answer but went past her and picked up the vase. "Where does it go?"

"Just under the altar. Thank you," she added, remembering her manners, but only just. She knew she sounded ungracious, but she didn't want him to think – well, she didn't know quite what she didn't want him to think, but it would be awful if he imagined that she thought that he thought – not that he would, of course –

It was all too complicated, and floundering helplessly, not knowing quite what she was trying to express, she left it. Just beside the vestry door, as she trailed behind him back to the body of the church, she caught sight of herself in the small mirror installed by the vicar for last-minute grooming. Oh, why couldn't she look more like Trish or Caro – or even like Doreen Laity, instead of being thin and childish, with her straight hair tucked behind her ears? He probably thought she was about twelve, instead of nearly sixteen. Well, fifteen and a half anyway.

"They smell good," he said, over his shoulder. "We have them in our orchard this time of year. My Mom always cuts them and brings them into the house."

"Where do you come from?"

"Massachusetts. A town called Hannville."

She couldn't see his face, but there was something in his voice that made her think that he would, at that moment, give much to be back there.

"Is it nice?" she asked as he set down the vase and turned to smile at her.

"Hannville?" He gave a breath of laughter. "It's just a place, I guess. Not big, not small. My dad runs the town newspaper."

"Really?" Forgetting to be shy, Pen looked at him properly. "My dad's a writer too. And a broadcaster. He's called Caleb Carne."

"Oh. I guess I should have heard of him."

"No, of course not. Why should you?" Pen dismissed such an idea without ceremony. Her father's fame, she had found, was sometimes a bit of a liability. "I must go and clear up in the vestry," she said.

"Sure. Can I help?" He didn't wait for an answer, but once more followed behind her. "Say, this place is really great, isn't it? It kind of smells of history – and who the heck are those people on that tomb over there, lying side by side, with ruffs around their necks? That's Elizabethan costume, isn't it?"

"Oh, they're the Teales. Sir Walter and Lady Alice. There are still Teales in Dever Manor in the middle of Dever Wood, down in the valley. Don't you love the little dog at their feet?"

She spoke more easily now, her shyness almost forgotten. He seemed friendly, easy to talk to, and she tended to warm towards anyone who liked the Teales. She had woven stories about them for as long as she could remember.

"Are your ancestors buried here?" he asked, as she swept up pieces of daffodil stalks.

"Some of them. My mother's family was Chapel, so all her lot are in the cemetery across the lane." She put the broom away and turned to look at him again. There was no doubting his interest. "Would you like to see my great-great-grandparents' tombstone?" she asked him.

"Sure," he said.

"It's *disgusting*," she confided, her eyes blazing with sudden passion. "My sisters and I absolutely hate it."

"Why?" He was laughing a little, amused at her vehemence, and once more she was struck by his extreme good looks. He

24

had fair hair and a clear complexion, and his smile was – well, it was *lovely*. She'd never seen such white teeth. He looked, she thought, a bit like one of the students in the film about the musical show. She couldn't wait to tell Trish about him. It jolly well served her right. Maybe it would teach her not to loll in bed letting other people do her dirty work.

"I'll show you. Come on."

Pen led the way out of the church, turning off the path and crossing the wet grass beneath which the burghers of Porthlivick lay.

"It's over here," she said. "Caro says we ought to paint rude words on it."

Together they stood before it.

"It looks perfectly normal to me," said the American. "What's so bad about it?"

"Read it," Pen said. He did as he was told.

" 'Sacred to the memory of Annie Carne, dutiful wife, born 1800, died 1839.

'Also Caleb Howard Carne, husband of the above, who passed into eternal rest 3rd January 1868.

> 'His life's work was nobly done
> His children numbered twelve and one.' "

The American saw the point at once.

"Wow," he said. "Poor Annie sure was dutiful. She doesn't get a lot of credit for the thirteen children, does she?"

"She was only thirty-nine when she died," Pen pointed out. "Say she got married at eighteen, she must have had a baby every eighteen months, or thereabouts. Caro worked it out."

"I guess big families weren't so unusual in those days. Still, maybe if Caleb Howard Carne had performed a little less nobly and rested a bit more often, Annie might have lasted longer."

Pen suddenly found herself blushing scarlet, embarrassed at the turn the conversation was taking. What would he think? It was one thing to discuss Caleb Howard's activities with Trish and Caro; quite another with an unknown American soldier, however sympathetic.

He turned to her, holding out his hand.

"Hey," he said. "It's time we were introduced. I'm David Holt. What do I call you?"

"Pen." Pen took the proffered hand. "It's Penelope, really, but no one calls me that."

"Hi, Pen. Good to know you."

He really did sound just like the student in the film, and he seemed every bit as nice, with his talk about Mom and the orchard and the daffodils in Massachusetts, not to mention his ready sympathy for Annie. He didn't seem at all threatening, like so many of the others.

And he seemed fascinated by the age of everything. He was full of questions about the origins of the church, delighted by the message of thanks from Charles I for assistance in the Civil War which, as in so many Cornish churches, was to be found over the door. Were battles fought near by, he wanted to know? And who exactly was St Finbar, the patron saint of the church and presumably of the village?

"My father could tell you everything," Pen said, more conscious by the minute of the gaps in her own knowledge. "You ought to meet him. He's called after Caleb Howard, but he's much nicer."

"Say, that'd be great. I'd love to meet him."

"Well –" Pen paused, considering. Her father, she felt sure, would enjoy talking to the young American. He loved meeting new people and liked nothing more than to talk about the history of Porthlivick. It was her mother who might be the stumbling block. Strangers made her nervous, made her seem unwelcoming, but if Father approved, then she would too. It was worth a risk.

"Look," she went on, taking a deep breath. "Come to tea tomorrow. My father went up to London a few days ago, but he'll be back tonight. He sort of goes up and down a lot. To London, I mean."

There she went again, talking total rubbish. What would he think?

"Well, gee, thanks," he said, apparently not thinking anything very untoward. "That's real nice of you. I'd like that."

He looked pleased, Pen saw, as if he really meant it. Maybe he was just exactly what he seemed; a homesick young soldier who was glad to be invited to someone's house for tea. She gave him directions; said she would look out for him about four o'clock, and as she set off along the lane in the direction of home she felt elated that she'd taken the bull by the horns and found the courage to issue the invitation. What a feather in her cap, to be the one to introduce such a handsome American to the family!

But by the time she reached Roscarrow the feeling of euphoria had evaporated. He would have forgotten or thought better of it by tomorrow, most probably. Or be on duty. And if he did come, he wouldn't be bothered to speak to her. Not with Trish in the same room. There were times, and this was one of them, when she felt quite sure that no one ever would.

✻    ✻    ✻

"Sorry," Simon Holt said to the woman hovering close to him. "I hope I didn't tie up the phone too long."

"No, no. It's perfectly all right."

Who was she? Katie's mother, maybe – though somehow this seemed unlikely. Katie's athletic beauty was of the outdoor kind, scrubbed and wholesome. This dainty, painted lady, on the other hand, seemed to have used every artifice known to man to enhance her faded prettiness. And who could blame her? She must, Simon thought, have been a knock-out in her day.

For a moment she hesitated as if nerving herself to speak, one claw-like, enamel-tipped hand playing with the triple strand of pearls that circled her neck.

"I have to phone about my little dog," she confided breathlessly. "I've never left him before, you see."

Simon smiled at her with polite sympathy, and as he made his way towards the kitchen where Tom had set up the bar, he wondered who she was and how she came to be there. Her age – sixtyish, he judged – and her dress, composed as it was of a series of floating panels in peach chiffon – set her apart from the majority of the guests. If not Katie's mother, then she had to be some other relative. Hard to explain her any other way. Tom lectured on Post-Modernist literature and Katie was a sculptor. Their associates tended towards the young, the unconventional and the avant-garde, among whom peach chiffon and a triple string of pearls appeared to have no place.

It was later, long after he had forgotten her, that he felt a tug on his sleeve and turned to find her next to him. He had for some time been pinned to the wall by an intense girl with greasy hair and an ethnic kind of dress, a red-hot feminist of the type who attributed to all men no thought that did not denigrate women, no motive towards them other than the most heinous, and who did not hesitate to expound her beliefs at length, in hectoring tones. Of all the girls in all of London, Simon was thinking drearily, I have to end up with this one. The lady of the telephone might be knocking sixty, but even her arrival gladdened his heart and he greeted her as evidence of divine intervention.

"Why, hallo again," he said, as if she were an old friend.

"Please forgive me." She had a fluttery little voice that added to the impression of helpless femininity. "I hate to break in, but I wonder – *might* I have a word?"

"Sure!" Simon eased himself away from the wall. "You'll excuse me, won't you?" he said to his previous companion; adding, polite to the last: "It's been good talking to you."

He smiled down at the older woman, wondering, in passing, if her dog could possibly be one of those small, silvery animals – Yorkshire terriers, were they? If so, it definitely gave credence to the theory that owners grew to resemble their pets. Her carefully teased, ash-blonde hair hung in wisps over her eyes and there was a muzzle-like look to her miniature mouth and chin.

"Say, can I get you a drink?" Simon asked her. "I'm Simon Holt, by the way."

"I know." She gave him a coquettish little smile. "I asked Katie. I'm Polly Godwin." A delicate hand was extended for him to shake. "Another glass of wine would be simply lovely. White, please."

"Sure," Simon said again.

He battled his way to the bar and back again, to find on his return that she had retired to a quiet corner, somehow managing to find two free chairs which she had pulled together in close proximity.

"Isn't this a lovely party?" she said, rewarding him with one of her fluttery little smiles as he handed her the glass of wine and sat down beside her. "But so noisy! I thought it would be easier to talk here."

"Do you know Tom and Katie well?" Simon was feeling his way, totally unable to guess what she wanted with him. "I figured maybe you were a relation."

"Oh, no, no, nothing like that. I'm just a friend." She smiled again and took a small, ladylike sip of her wine. "They are such fun, aren't they, Tom and Katie? They were my closest neighbours in Chiswick, and I was devastated when they decided to move to Hammersmith. I ran into them in Sainsbury's, you know, and couldn't help teasing them about all the bottles in their trolley."

She went on to recount, with an arch smile and a wagging finger, how she had joked about the likelihood of their drinking themselves to death; and how Tom had said they were having a flat-warming party; and how Katie had *at once* invited her, without a moment's hesitation.

"Wasn't it utterly sweet of her?" she said. "I don't actually go out much at night because I hate taking a mini-cab home, all on my own – honestly, you can't trust anyone these days, can you? – but my daughter very kindly said she would come and pick me up. There's a PTA meeting at the school where she teaches, you see, and a meeting afterwards to talk about – oh, I don't know! Whatever teachers talk about when they get together. Anyway, she said it would probably keep her quite late. She teaches at the West London Collegiate – I expect you've heard of it. It's one of London's most prestigious day schools. It used to be boys only, but they've taken girls into the sixth form now. Of course, being American you would think that quite natural, but I'm not so sure it's a good thing –"

"It seems to work quite well in our neck of the woods," Simon said, wondering where this was leading.

"The headmaster thinks the world of her." Mrs Godwin twittered on as if he hadn't spoken. "Laura – my daughter – is head of English and Drama, and frightfully enthusiastic about everything. A terrific asset. You should have seen her production of *A Midsummer Night's Dream*! It really was quite extraordinary. She really got the best out of those children."

Simon nodded and smiled, and smiled and nodded.

"Was there something particular you wanted to talk to me about?" he asked at last.

She bit her lip and hesitated a moment before leaning towards him in a confidential manner, opening her eyes wide.

"Now you're going to think me very bold," she said, lowering her voice to a whisper. "But I hope you'll forgive me. I couldn't help overhearing you mention Caleb Carne when you were talking

29

on the phone, and I've been wanting to speak to you ever since. May I ask what your interest is?"

"I'm writing a piece about his life." She had all of Simon's attention now. "Why, Mrs Godwin? Did you – do you know him, by any chance? You would remember his broadcasts, of course."

"Oh, *really!*" She laughed, pouting roguishly, enhancing the muzzle effect. "How very ungallant of you. Well, I can't pretend I didn't hear them, but I don't remember them very well. I was awfully young during the war. I remember *him*, though. Vividly. Such a larger-than-life character – such charm –"

"You actually knew him?" Simon sat up straighter, conscious of a feeling of dawning excitement, a kind of certainty that she would tell him something of importance, that he and she had been brought together for this very purpose. Such serendipity had happened before; it seemed one of the magical, incomprehensible rules of the game that such things happened from time to time. Synchronicity, Arthur Koestler called it, and sometimes it worked. "That's wonderful! I'd be glad of any insights –"

Mrs Godwin's attention momentarily wandered as their hostess passed across her line of vision.

"Isn't that a *frightfully* pretty dress that Katie's wearing? Such a clever girl! She made it herself –"

"Oh, really? Yes, it's great. About Caleb Carne, Mrs Godwin. I'd be fascinated to know what your connection is with him."

"Well –" She gave a small, knowing smile. "The connection actually was with my mother. Carne and my mother were very, very good friends, Mr Holt." Her voice was heavy with meaning. "In fact, more than friends."

"Lovers, you mean?"

Mrs Godwin shrugged her shoulders.

"I told you, I was just a child. I only knew that he was a constant visitor in our home." Her expression, however, said otherwise.

"I always understood that he was a devoted family man. He had – *has* – three daughters –"

"Quite," she said. "It would have been the finish of him if there'd been a whisper of scandal. People weren't so broadminded then as they are now – and of course he was at the height of his fame. A celebrity, they'd call him these days." She paused for a moment, then gave a tight, bitter little smile. "Make no mistake, in spite of everything I adored my mother. She was very talented – a wonderful, wonderful woman in many ways, but there's no doubt she was rather like some of these people here tonight." She looked about her, her gaze lingering on this group and that. "Unconventional," she went on. "Bohemian, one might say." She paused again, head on one side as if in thought. "You know," she went on as if struck by a revelation. "That could well be the reason I have such a good rapport with Tom and Katie and all you young people. I understand where you're coming from, as they say today."

"So you're telling me that secretly Caleb Carne and your mother were lovers?" he said.

"Well, with hindsight, I can't help thinking that it was highly probable."

"Highly probable." Simon repeated the words thoughtfully, his excitement waning rapidly.

Highly probable wasn't good enough. The whole thing could be a figment of this woman's imagination, for all he knew, and in any case it was no part of his brief to dish the dirt on the old man. So what if he did have an *affaire*? Unless it had some influence on his work, of course. But even then –

"What do you mean, in spite of everything?" he went on, suddenly remembering the expression she had used regarding her mother. "In spite of what?"

"I don't wish to speak ill of the dead –"

"Caleb Carne isn't dead."

"But my mother is, Mr Holt."

"In what way was she talented?"

"She was like you, a journalist. Freelance. Stella Morel, her name was. She was quite well known in her time. She was one of the few women journalists reporting the Spanish Civil War! And then she worked for the BBC –"

"Was that where she met Carne?"

For a moment Mrs Godwin hesitated.

"I'm not altogether sure," she admitted at last. "I don't think so. I confess to being rather vague about that. She didn't stay there for long. It was during the war that they became, well, friendly – and I wasn't living at home then. You see, Mr Holt, it has to be said that the war rather suited my mother. I was – always had been – something of an encumbrance. She was delighted to have the excuse of probable air raids to send me away. I was really brought up by some dear country people in Wales until such time as I was old enough for boarding school, so I was hardly *au fait* with what was going on here. But I saw quite enough to know that Carne and my mother were very close indeed."

"Did they live together?"

"Oh, no!" Mrs Godwin sounded shocked. "Nothing like that. I mean, people didn't."

"No. Well, thank you, Mrs Godwin." He smiled at her, but he felt no optimism now, no certainty that she could be of any help. "I suppose it was possible that they could have been – as they say – 'just good friends'?"

She gave a tinkling little laugh that seemed to express amusement tinged with pity, as if simple friendship between the sexes was nothing more than a chimera and no one but a simpleton would think otherwise.

"If you believe that, Mr Holt," she said, tapping him lightly on the knee. "Then you'll believe anything!"

"Mother –" Simon looked up at the sound of a new voice and scrambled to his feet. A girl stood before them. She was dressed in something plain and sleeveless, in a shade of brown that made him think of autumn leaves. Her dark hair was tied behind her and spangled with the summer rain that was falling outside. "I'm sorry to rush you. I'm double-parked –"

Mrs Godwin pouted prettily.

"Oh Laura, darling, it's frightfully early!"

"Actually, I'm late. You said come at eleven, but I couldn't get away –"

"Oh, darling – I'm having such an interesting chat with Mr Holt. This is my daughter, Laura, Mr Holt."

"Glad to know you," Simon said.

She was, he saw, nothing like her mother. She was tall, for one thing, with a confident, direct gaze. Maybe all that her mother had said about her was true. She looked exactly the kind of girl that people might, very likely, think the world of. He could even imagine doing so himself.

"Hallo." She smiled back at him, but it was a brief, cold smile, and meant nothing. Immediately she turned to her mother again. "Honestly, I can't leave the car where it is. I really am sorry. It's almost half past, so I thought you'd be cursing me. I'm sure Mr Holt will forgive you if you rush off."

"Well, if you must," Simon said. "But to be honest I'd much rather you didn't. Can't I get you a drink?" Laura looked at him again, this time even more coldly. She had clear hazel eyes, he noted; more green than brown with thick, dark lashes, and they held the unambiguous message that flirtatious gambits were not appreciated. "Your mother and I were finding a lot to talk about," he went on hastily. He fumbled for a card. "Look, Mrs Godwin, you can always find me here if you remember anything of interest."

"About what?" Laura's question was incisive, almost accusing.

"Caleb Carne. I'm a journalist, and I'm writing a profile of him –"

"Oh, *Mother*!" Laura's voice expressed amused irritation. "Mr Holt, she's been dining out on Caleb Carne ever since he suddenly became famous again – just because she met him two or three times during the war."

"Don't talk over my head." Mrs Godwin, on her feet now, was irritated too. "You know quite well he and your grandmother had a – a *relationship*. I can't bear that expression," she added, turning to Simon, "But I suppose it describes the situation."

"But you weren't there, were you?" Laura said in milder tones. "You were in Wales. You don't know anything for sure. Do come, Mother – unless you want to pay for getting me unclamped. Goodbye, Mr Holt."

"Ms Godwin." Equally formal, hamming it up a little, Simon bowed in her direction. Laura looked unamused.

"Actually, the name's Rossi," she said.

So she was married. Well, Simon thought, as she bore her mother away. You win some, you lose some. She didn't, actually, seem a barrel of laughs anyway; but he saw, as mother and daughter took their leave of Tom and Katie, that Laura had suddenly come alive, sparkling with interest and amusement at something Katie was saying to her.

Pity, he thought. Something told him she would have been worth knowing, a challenge worth accepting, and he was conscious of a pang of regret as she left the room. But it only lasted a moment.

\*       \*       \*

I should have been nicer to that Holt chap, Laura thought guiltily as, having left her mother in Chiswick, she drove back to her flat in Notting Hill. He'd really done nothing to deserve the chilly treatment she'd meted out, except make it clear by his expression that he thought her attractive; which, after all, wasn't exactly a hanging offence.

She hadn't been in the best of moods when she arrived at the party, that was the truth of it. Brian Crathorne, head of Science, and his crony-in-chief, Lance Packer, had been more than usually patronising to the female members of staff, making their resentment of their presence more obvious than ever. They had both objected to the admission of girls to the sixth form, and even more to the small feminine presence in their staff room. They were, however, helpless against the combined will of the headmaster and the school governors, and took their revenge by using every opportunity to demoralise any female, staff or student, who crossed their paths.

She shouldn't have let them get to her. They were nerds, she told herself savagely; nerds with attitude, thankfully unrepresentative, and as such she had no valid excuse for being so short with Whatsisname Holt, who had, after all, been harmless and not at all nerdish. In fact he had nice, intelligent eyes and a humorous kind of mouth. Attractive, really. Certainly her mother seemed to think so.

And that was another thing. It wasn't only Crathorne and Packer that made her mad. It was seeing her mother across the room being her roguish, flirtatious little self. A lifetime of wrong choices, subservience, betrayals, hadn't, apparently, dampened her enthusiasm for the opposite sex in any way. Seeing the manner in which she had clutched the unknown young man's sleeve with her tiny, predatory hand, eyelashes fluttering, lips pouting in a winsome manner, had produced the usual reaction in Laura – a reaction magnified a thousand times by her knowledge of the method used by her mother to con her way into the party in the first place. Tom and Katie would never have dreamed of asking her if she hadn't put them in such an awkward position in the supermarket. Knowing this, Laura felt a helpless embarrassment allied to an almost irresistible desire to seize her manipulative mother by the scruff of the neck and frog-march her from the vicinity of her latest unfortunate victim.

So what else is new? she thought now. The guy was big enough to stand up for himself. It wasn't the first time she'd felt this way and it wouldn't be the last. But what had her mother told him about Caleb Carne? She couldn't have said much. She didn't know much.

Not like me, Laura thought, as she slowed down to make the turn at the traffic lights. Not like me.

# II

Simon noticed the difference the moment he stepped off the train
at St Jory. The air was soft and people seemed to move at a
different rate, as if the world were spinning on its axis at a slower
pace; or perhaps it wasn't spinning at all, but merely ambling round,
stopping every now and again to smell the flowers.

And speaking of the smell, surely it was fresher, even there on
the station, as if the breeze were gently wafting the scent of the
countryside towards him? He felt a million miles away from
the steamy London streets and the stench of car exhausts. It
took him back to his youth when he and his parents used
to go up to Vermont to visit his mother's folks – made him
feel that it was too long since he'd had a breath of country
air in his lungs, and regret that he'd only arranged to be
away from London for one night.

He took a taxi to Porthlivick. The rain that had fallen during
the past few days had cleared away once more, and now the
sun shone from a cloudless sky. They drove through hilly fields
and woodlands towards the sea that glinted in the distance; and
when it seemed that the road would continue on and on until
waves were lapping over the wheels of the car, it turned sharp
right, parallel to a wide beach bordered with coarse, sandy grass
on which were parked fifty or more trailers. Caravans, he must
remember to call them. People were swimming, families playing on
the beach.

The taxi driver, garrulous from the first, jerked his head in its
direction.

"Thass where you Yanks was to in the war," he said. "Bow
Beach, 'tis called."

"Yeah?" Simon sat forward and peered out. "My Dad was there."

"He was, was he? Well, 'tis all different now. Not quite the 'eight of the season, but very near. Next week, 'tis school holidays, and you won't be able to put a pin between them."

It was the past, however, that interested Simon.

"They must have made quite an impact, the Americans," he said, trying to imagine it. "I mean, this is a pretty small place, isn't it? An invasion of GIs must have been cataclysmic."

"They made an impact on the girls, I'll tell ee that!" The taxi driver chortled salaciously. "Devils with the women, they was. Oversexed, overpaid and over 'ere, our boys used to say. I was only a little tacker at the time, but I remember it well. Me and my mates, we used to track 'em over the cliffs, wriggling along in the grass, spying on 'em. Great fun, 'twas. Added to my education, you might say."

"I bet."

The road left the beach behind and climbed uphill; but in another few minutes they had turned towards the coast again and there, below them, was the small fishing port of Porthlivick, apparently drowsing in the sunshine of early evening. Simon drew in his breath, conscious of a sudden shaft of delight at the beauty of it. The harbour itself was divided into two, encircled by the protective arms of the quays, the fishing boats moored, for the most part, within the inner harbour. On the steep cliffs above, houses rose, tier upon tier, washed in pale colours.

The view was lost as they changed direction again and descended more steeply, and in a few moments they were running into a small square where the Anchor Inn occupied almost the whole of one side. As he paid off the taxi and stood looking about him, Simon found himself smiling a little, picturing his father as a young man standing here on this same spot, one of the invading multitude described by the taxi driver. Had he been a devil with the women? It was possible, he reflected. Likely, in fact. Simon had seen photographs of him in uniform, and there was no doubt he'd been a damned good-looking guy.

On the other hand he had been young, unsophisticated, a small-town boy, born of small-town parents, whose social life had centered round church and school and drug-store. He had enlisted immediately after graduating from High School; University had come later.

Any knowledge of the world outside Hannville, Massachusetts would have come from books, for he'd always been a reader – had come from a reading family. Simon could dimly remember the book-filled house a little out of town where his Holt grandparents had lived.

He'd liked the sound of Mrs Hambly's voice on the telephone – Pen, as his father called her. She'd come over as warm and welcoming, though he had the distinct feeling that she'd had a bit of a shock when he announced his father's identity. What had gone on all those years ago? His father had never appeared to attribute any importance to his Cornish posting, mentioning it rarely and then only in passing, but he would bet his bottom dollar that there was a story there somewhere.

But, he reminded himself, it was Caleb Carne's story he was after. Once inside the cramped little room where he was ushered by the landlady of the inn – presumably the Ruby Saunders who was declared over the front door as being licensed to sell beer, wines and spirits – he sat down on the bed with its slippery gold eiderdown and leafed through the notes provided by Mandy, the earnest research assistant provided by the *Gazette*. They gave the basic facts of Carne's life.

He had been born in Porthlivick at No. 3 Quay Street on 15th September 1895, and had lived in humble circumstances, battling against the odds to gain a scholarship to Oxford. Who had influenced him in his boyhood? Someone must have done. His mother? Father? Teacher?

At Oxford he had performed well, achieving a first class honours degree which he might have expected to lead to great things in the academic world; however, only two years after his graduation, during which time he had remained at Christ Church as a don, the First World War interrupted his career and he joined the Army with the rank of Second Lieutenant.

He was posted to France and served at Neuve Chapelle and the Somme, where he suffered a wounded knee which rendered him unfit for further active service. He returned to Britain for treatment, and during his convalescence he married Emily Trevail of Porthlivick, a girl he had known all his life.

He was promoted to Lieutenant and posted to Woolwich Barracks, after which he was again promoted, to Captain, and sent to Paris where he stayed for the rest of the war, engaged in activities that were described as 'administrative' but were generally assumed to have more to do with Intelligence.

In 1919 he left the Army and returned to Oxford where he lived with Emily in a small house off the Banbury Road and lectured in Medieval Literature for four years, during this time publishing several pamphlets on Celtic influences in literature, ancient and modern. No trace could now be found of them.

What had made him leave it all and come back to Cornwall in 1923? Simple homesickness? His wife, perhaps? Maybe she had been ill at ease in Oxford society and had persuaded him to return to the south-west. Whatever the reason, he had come home and had written those appalling novels. If he'd been searching for inspiration in Porthlivick, Simon thought, then he'd been short-changed.

It was pointless to speculate. He made a few notes regarding possible lines of questioning, then, suddenly conscious of hunger – hardly surprising, since he'd skipped lunch – he went out into the village where, in a café opposite the pub, he ate a plate of the best fish and chips he had ever tasted.

The long summer evening was perceptibly fading as he found the road that led from the square to the quay. There was a warm, still feeling about the narrow streets; a concentration of colour. Holiday-makers sauntered along, bare shoulders red from the sun, eating ice-creams, stopping to peer in the windows of art galleries and gift shops. Seagulls were screaming overhead. It was in this street that Carne had lived as a child, Simon reminded himself, though it would have been different then. Except for the seagulls, of course.

He found No. 3 without difficulty. It was a narrow dwelling, in a terrace of others exactly the same. No doubt it had been mean enough in the days of Carne's youth, but he guessed its appearance had changed considerably in more recent years. Someone had tarted it up. There were new bull's-eye windows, a bright yellow door with a brass dolphin knocker, a hanging basket of geraniums and lobelias. The light wasn't good enough to take a picture, but he made a mental note to return the following morning.

On the quay itself, he found there was still considerable activity. Seats, thoughtfully placed in sheltered spots, were filled with those enjoying the last rays of the sun. Others strolled to the end of the quay and back. A gang of teenagers clustered around a bollard shrieked with laughter at the witticisms of a tall dark boy in a baseball cap, worn back to front. Leader of the pack, Simon thought; every town has one.

Weatherbeaten men in sweaters and sea-boots, strangely alike at first glance, were occupied with nets and lobster pots, moving majestically about their boats with controlled efficiency, like cooks in a kitchen. Others worked on their engines; and as they worked, they called to each other in accents that Simon found impenetrable. No doubt they would be putting to sea very soon; they were waiting, perhaps, for the tide to turn.

Some looked up at him as he stood above them on the quay, and smiled and nodded towards him. Kindly men, he thought. Times were hard for fishermen, everyone knew that, but in spite of it there seemed a serenity about this brotherhood. Had Caleb Carne's inspirational broadcasts been influenced by men such as these? It seemed more than likely.

The light was definitely fading now. Simon walked on to the end of the quay and leaned on the harbour wall, looking across the bay to the headland that thrust its bony finger into the sea, waves creaming against the granite rocks that tumbled from it. It looked majestic, he thought, and also rather threatening, as if to warn passing ships that they came close only at their peril. After a moment's thought he realised that this must be the headland where Carne lived in his house called Roscarrow. Perhaps that was it, that solid, grey stone building with windows that glinted in the evening sun. Yes – surely it must be. There were no other houses of any size in the area, though a huddle of roofs and a church tower to its landward side meant that it was not totally isolated.

He turned and, with his back to the wall, looked up at the houses that climbed the hill on the other side of the harbour. Street lights came on as he watched, and there were lights too from uncurtained windows. Not a particularly sentimental man, Simon nevertheless found himself imagining the emotions of storm-tossed sailors approaching such potent symbols of home and safety. He could well appreciate how hearts would lighten and spirits soar.

Surely there was no need to wonder further what had brought Carne home from Oxford, or what had lifted him beyond the mediocre standard of his previous work to craft the talks that had made him famous? The answer was here, in all this beauty. How could anyone think otherwise?

*   *   *

Pen knocked briefly at the bedroom door and, her hands occupied with the breakfast tray, a copy of *The Times* under her arm, pushed it open with her elbow. Her father was propped high on his pillows, but his eyes remained shut.

"Room service," she called softly. "Good morning." She saw his eyelids flutter and came into the room. "I hate to say it," she went on. "But you were absolutely right about three down. It *was* 'bastion'."

"Of course it was." Caleb Carne still declined to open his eyes or even to smile.

"Darling, I hate to hurry you but you must wake up." Pen put the tray down on a bed-table, pulling it closer to her father. "Today's the day, you know."

"The day for what?"

At last he turned his head on the pillow and looked at her with his old man's eyes, red-rimmed, the blue faded. Even these days they were capable of sparkling with enthusiasm, but not now. Her heart sank a little. She knew that expression well. He was playing the pathetic card, making capital of the fact that he was old and feeble and not long for this world. She didn't blame him; merely wished he had chosen some other day for it.

"Oh Father, you know! Simon Holt is coming to interview you." She leant over to pour his tea. "Come on, now," she said coaxingly. "The toast is really thin, just how you like it, and I opened a new jar of your special marmalade."

He closed his eyes again.

"I don't like being interviewed." His voice quavered piteously.

"Yes, you do. You love it! It's a chance to talk about yourself to an entirely new audience, with nothing better to do but make notes of your pearls of wisdom."

"Tell him to come another day."

"I can't do that." Behind the gentle raillery Pen's voice became fractionally more bracing. "He's come all the way from London to see you. Anyway, he's David's son. It'll be interesting to meet him, won't it? Come on – let me hoist you up a bit."

Sighing heavily, Carne allowed himself to be pulled into a more upright sitting position and looked without enthusiasm at the breakfast before him. Tea and toast and marmalade. It was always the same, because Pen knew from long experience that even the simplest variation would meet with objections. He eyed it today, however, as if it came as an unwelcome surprise, before, with another sigh, picking up the teacup and taking a few dispirited sips.

"David who?" he asked, after a moment.

"David Holt. You remember, darling – that young American soldier who was here during the war. Trish's boy-friend. We were talking about him last night. You liked him a lot."

Carne put the cup down and sank back against the pillows, half-closing his eyes, his handsome, high-bridged nose pointing to heaven, his mouth downturned with displeasure.

"Oh, I did, did I? Damned if I can remember. I had a rotten night," he went on peevishly. "I don't feel like seeing anyone today."

"You'll feel better when you've had your breakfast." Pen bent and kissed his cheek. "If you've got all you need, I'll go and have mine and get myself dolled up a bit. Shall I put the radio on for you? Fred's just arrived, so he'll be up soon to get you ready."

Fred Pawley was a retired hospital porter who came each day to bath the old man and get him dressed, combining these duties with those of gardener and general handyman. He was a sprightly, good-humoured seventy-year-old, and Pen couldn't imagine what her life would be like without him – or, for that matter, without his wife, Dolly, who came three days a week to help in the house and was usually willing to stay with Caleb in the evening if the occasion demanded it, thus freeing Pen for something of a life of her own.

Of course he could remember David, she thought with exasperated amusement as she sipped her own breakfast coffee. Why, only last night he was reminiscing about him, saying how odd it was that he could recall those wartime days as clearly as if it were yesterday when sometimes he couldn't remember if he'd had his lunch or not. He was, she felt sure, only doing it to be aggravating – but who, really, could blame him? Once he'd had a little circle of friends he could invite to the house or sit with in the snug at the

Anchor, but now all were gone and he, who loved nothing better than to gossip and laugh and entertain, was left with no audience apart from Fred and Dolly and herself, and any of her friends who happened to come to the house. His life had narrowed down to almost nothing, *The Times* crossword, certain radio programmes and the odd spurt of arrogance or rebellion his only amusement. He had never enjoyed television very much, and found it too much of a strain on his failing eyesight to watch now.

All the more reason, one might think, for him to welcome the appearance of Simon Holt and this chance to talk about his life – and Pen had no real doubts that, when the time came, he would be as forthcoming and irresistible as ever, the old charmer, wooing his listeners with all the old skill. It merely amused him to see how far he could go before she grew impatient.

Meantime there was her own part to consider. Simon was due at eleven o'clock and was to stay to lunch. The fish pie – easily digestible, with due concern for her father's capricious stomach, but with added prawns to make it special enough for a guest – was already made and put in the fridge to be browned later, while she had made the ice-cream several days ago from blackcurrants picked from the garden. Was it, she wondered now, all too delicate, too much like invalid cookery, to please a young and healthy male? There was time to make an apple pie –

Oh, nonsense! She was annoyed with herself for fussing. She was getting old and losing confidence, that was the trouble. She'd got out of the way of cooking for more than two. There was absolutely no need to worry. It was all delicious – and there was always that lovely bit of Stilton if Simon should still be hungry after the ice-cream. Together with one of the bottles of wine that Trish had brought over from France last time she came home, it made a meal that anyone could enjoy.

It was foolish to get in a state simply because this young man was David's son and would, perhaps, report on the visit to his father; because that was the main reason for this stupid attack of nerves, she had no doubt. Did you ever hear of anything so daft? She asked the question of herself, as she brushed and combed her hair, pulling it back in its usual knot high at the back of her head. She'd done it that way for years, and was mildly pleased that, unexpectedly, it had now become quite trendy, though trends were not something that bothered her. Years ago she had decided on a style for herself, both in hair and dress, and had stuck to it. Greying hair and changing fashions had altered nothing.

At least, she thought as she zipped up her skirt, Simon could report that she hadn't lost her figure – a thought which made her smile because, truth to tell, she'd never had much of a figure to lose. Thin as a board she'd been when David last saw her, and thin as a board she was now. The only difference was that instead of wearing her sister's discarded dresses, she now chose clothes that flattered her; full skirts with neat waists, plain blouses, sweaters and draped scarves, usually in autumnal colours, russet and terracotta, apricot and cinnamon. She had a good eye for colour and knew what did most for her rather sallow skin and brown eyes. She painted a little, mainly pretty pictures of Porthlivick, which sold well in the local shops. It was hardly what she had dreamed of when she had gone to Art College, but it was enough to satisfy her now. She had long ago come to terms with the limits of her artistic ability and these days was modestly delighted that she was able to make a steady, if barely discernible, income.

The sudden and unwonted attack of nervousness had passed by the time Simon arrived. He, still bemused by the beauty he could see all around him, turned from his study of the distant view of Porthlivick as she answered his ring at the front door.

"Simon!" Pen held out her hand to welcome him. "It's good to meet you. My father's been looking forward so much to talking to you. He's in the summerhouse – across the garden and down the steps. He loves to sit there on a day like this. I'll take you down."

She felt like crossing her fingers behind her back as she spoke. She had installed her father in his favourite chair in his favourite position, panama hat on his head, cushion at his back, spectacles and binoculars on the table beside him, *The Times* crossword at hand, book at his elbow; but he was still, at the last viewing, sighing heavily and muttering about 'representatives of the gutter press thrusting themselves where they're not wanted'.

"The *Gazette* is hardly the gutter press," she had pointed out. "You read it yourself! Anyway, he sounded nice. After all, he's David's son. He's bound to be nice."

45

"David, David." Querulously he had flapped his hand at her. "What did we know of David, after all? I can barely remember him."

Well, at least he had admitted to having some glimmer of a recollection – which was a degree better than having none at all, Pen comforted herself. She was sure – well, almost sure – that he would rise to the occasion when Simon actually appeared.

Her first impression of the visitor was favourable anyway. He was by no means as handsome as his father, but he had a likeable, long-jawed face and a friendly smile. His grey eyes seemed to survey her with a curiosity equal to her own; because of David? Or because he was about to interview Caleb Carne?

Probably the latter, she thought. He didn't look as young as his voice had led her to believe. There was a toughness about him, as if, while prepared to be sociable, he was here on business. How foolish of her to have regarded him as some kind of emissary from David – to think that either of them cared a jot about the old days. A tremor of nervousness returned and to her annoyance she said the first thing that came into her head.

"You're not very much like your father, are you?" Even as she spoke she recognised the banality of it.

"I guess not." He smiled at her as together they walked down a wide path. On each side of the house were soaring rhododendron bushes growing in large and unkempt clumps, but here, to the front, the view of the sea was unobstructed. "He's much better looking! I'm supposed to look like my grandfather on my mother's side."

"I was so sorry to hear about your mother's death. How is your father coping?"

"Quite well. He puts up a good front, anyway, though I've never thought retirement a particularly good idea. I don't want him sitting around brooding. They were very close."

"Poor David! You will give him all my sympathy, won't you? Tell him –" she broke off, hesitated. "Well, just say that I've been there and I understand how he must feel. I'm longing to hear all about him," she went on, her voice taking on a more cheerful note. "Perhaps later, after lunch, we can have a chat, if you're not in too great a hurry. My father always goes up to his room for a rest in the afternoon."

46

"That'll be great. I know Dad'll want to hear all your news too. My train doesn't leave until six. The taxi's coming to the pub for me around five fifteen."

"That's good. D'you know, I brought your father down this path to the summerhouse the very first time he came to see us? It wasn't as warm as it is today, though. It was before we'd opened it up, I seem to remember."

"He mentioned how beautiful it was here, but he didn't tell me the half of it. It's an incredible situation for a house."

"Yes, isn't it? You can go through that far hedge and out on to the headland. I ought to take you there too. It's very spectacular – a sheer drop to the rocks below."

"It's kind of strange to think that Dad knew this place."

"It hasn't really changed much, except for this path. And the summerhouse itself, of course. That's been totally rebuilt – the other one was made of wood and quietly disintegrated about twenty years ago. There were steps here in David's time, but we converted them into a slope just as far as the summerhouse so that it was easier for Father to manage. He does love the place so – he likes to come and sit down here at the first hint of warmth. Here we are!"

They had achieved a kind of plateau where the summerhouse stood, its back wall flat against the rock. The roof was of slate and the front of it consisted almost entirely of sliding glass doors, now drawn back to give the old man inside an uninterrupted view of the small cove in front of him.

"So here you are at last," he greeted them in his reedy, old man's voice. He was smiling, Pen was thankful to see. "I was beginning to think that Pen was determined to keep you to herself."

"Go on with you! We only stopped a moment to look at the view." Pen smiled back, giving an inward sigh of relief. He had, it seemed, decided to be sociable after all. It was going to be all right. "Father, this is Simon. David's son."

"My dear boy –"

Caleb Carne made as if to stand up, but quickly Simon moved across and took the proffered hand to forestall him.

"Please don't get up, sir. I'm very honoured that you've agreed to see me."

"Why, it's the very least we could do, isn't it, Pen? We were all very fond of David. Pen, darling, why don't you bring us some coffee? We've a lot to talk about, this young feller and I."

"I was about to," Pen said, leaving them with a grin in Simon's direction – a mischievous look of complicity that made her look suddenly younger.

"We've been looking forward to seeing you," Carne went on. "Reminding each other of all the happy times we had when your father was a constant visitor here. He was quite one of the family, you know. I expect he's told you all about us."

"Well, he's certainly told me how hospitable you were; he's not the kind of armchair warrior that keeps harping on about the war, though."

"Ha!" Carne raised both hands from the arms of his chair and laughed delightedly. "I never thought he would be! He was much too interested in everything that was around him. My God, what bores they are, aren't they, those men who fight every battle all over again – 'When I was at Sidi Barrani', and so on." He chuckled again. "The poverty of their post-war lives must be indescribable."

"I imagine that isn't something that can be said for your life, Mr Carne."

"Oh, oh!" Carne lifted his arms again, but this time in a gesture of resignation. "Have we come to that already? My life and times, eh? Well, where do we begin?" He cocked an eye at Simon who had put a small tape-recorder on the table between them. "Is that strictly necessary, my boy?"

"Well, it's a great help. You don't mind, do you, sir?"

Carne puffed out his lips as if considering the matter. What an incredible guy, Simon thought as he waited for the verdict. It was quite impossible to believe that he was coming up to his ninety-fifth birthday. He was a big man with an even bigger presence – something of a dandy, Simon guessed, with his yellow waistcoat under a fawn corduroy jacket and a pale-yellow bow tie. Age had made him bald and given him liver-spots and a somewhat pendulous lower lip, but even so it was easy to see that he must have been a fine-looking man. He had good bones, with prominent cheekbones and a jutting, well-shaped nose – bones that Pen had inherited. Simon, unable to avoid speculating on his father's far-off involvement with her, guessed that she'd never

48

been pretty, but there was a liveliness about her face that must, even so, have made her attractive. She still looked pretty good to him.

"Oh, very well, if you must use it." Carne leaned towards Simon with a confidential smile. "I plead guilty to vanity! They used to tell me that my voice could charm the birds from the trees. Well, I don't know about that, but I do know that it's a poor thing now, nothing more than an old man's ineffectual piping. I hate to hear it – and hate others to hear it."

"It's fine," Simon assured him. "Just forget about the recorder, and tell me about your early life here."

"Ah – first the coffee!" Pen had returned bearing a tray. "Thank you, my dear. It smells delicious – and some of your wonderful scones too. You must try these, my boy."

Pen poured the coffee and handed it round, delighted to hear that her father had launched into tales of his poverty-stricken schooldays and early manhood with fluency and humour and unabated vivacity. Discreetly she left him to it, happy now to retire to the kitchen to drink her own coffee in the company of Dolly and Fred. The old spell-binder had come alive, pulled off the magic once more, just as she had hoped.

Simon listened with delight. Carne's description of the women and children of Porthlivick waiting on the cliff looking for the shoals of pilchards, and running back to their men with a cry of 'heva, heva, heva' made the whole scene spring to life; he could see it, smell it, hear the voices; and there were tales too of past jokes and past companions that made Carne laugh until he was forced to mop his eyes with the green and yellow paisely handkerchief that drooped from his top pocket.

"It couldn't have been the norm for a boy of your background to go to University," Simon said at last. "Who would you say influenced you?"

"My mother," Carne said without hesitation. "She was always ambitious for me. I owe everything to her."

"Was she a Porthlivick woman?"

"Oh, no. She was from Somerset. She came down here as a young teacher in 1890, the year that the Porthlivick school was opened. Seventeen, she was. You can see the date still, carved in the stone over the door. She and my father married three years later."

49

"I see."

"She knew that life didn't have to be as most people lived it. She was determined that it would be different for me."

"Did you have brothers and sisters?"

Carne shook his head.

"Alas, no. Perhaps it was as well, under the circumstances. My father died young, you see. He drowned. He was a fisherman, as I believe I told you."

"And your mother didn't remarry?"

"Never. She made a little money by giving music lessons, but apart from that she devoted herself to me." He paused, on his lips a faint, reminiscent smile. "We were all in all to each other," he added softly.

"Was she the reason you returned to Cornwall in 1923?"

"Not altogether – it was a combination of circumstances. I took a fancy to write novels and I thought I would come back here to do so. And *then*, just as if the fates were giving us their blessing, this house suddenly became available to rent. I'd roamed all over this headland as a boy, always loved it, always longed to live in it. The thought of actually doing so was irresistible. At the same time there were elections to the Town Council for which friends persuaded me to stand. I had a dream of serving – but alas, it was not to be."

He paused for a moment his eyes turned towards the view but focused on the past. His mouth tightened now, and turned down as if he were tasting something sour. Clearly his defeat had indeed been a bitter one.

"There were people in the village who resented me," he said with a shaking voice, turning to look at Simon with eyes that were growing moist as he remembered and resented afresh the malice of long ago. "Cruel, foul things were said about me, scurrilous tales put about; the typically jealous reaction, I am afraid, of the ignorant who see one of their number rising in life."

"Well, things are sure different now. This forthcoming celebration proves how much they think of you."

"What? Oh, that!" He appeared to dismiss the prospect with disdain. He gave a short, mirthless heave of the shoulders. "A lot of water has flowed under many bridges since those days, my boy. There aren't many left who remember my defeat. My wife felt it

50

badly. She, perhaps, was my main reason for coming home. She was the best of women – no man could have wished for a more loyal and devoted wife, but she never took to Oxford life, poor dear. She miscarried twice during our years there and she became obsessed with the notion that only if she came back to Cornwall would she succeed in having a family."

"Perhaps she was right?" Simon suggested.

"Perhaps she was. Only a year after we moved in here Caro was born – then Trish, then Pen. So all was well and we lived happily ever after."

"So you stayed down here, writing your novels until the war came. What prompted the broadcasts?"

He paused again, stared out of the window, cleared his throat.

"A deep love of my country," he went on after a moment, his voice full of emotion once more. "And a sincere conviction that we were fighting for everything we hold dear. I hope that doesn't sound too sentimental, too sententious? Perhaps it does. I know I've been accused of sentimentality in my novels and I plead guilty to the charge. It's the Celt in me, you see; tears and laughter alike come easily to us. It's in our nature. As for patriotism, my generation, perhaps, was more prone to it than many, for we were able to remember how much we had invested in the First World War. Anything less than total commitment somehow seemed a betrayal of our comrades who were left in Flanders."

"You were wounded yourself, I believe."

"I was, I was. And feel it still. I walk with a slight limp and always have. At the time, I confess to you, I felt nothing but relief that I had a 'Blighty' – for your information, my boy, that was a wound that necessitated returning to England. They were much coveted, I assure you!" He chuckled, mischievously reminiscent. "Yes, home I came. And afterwards was sent to Paris."

"It's rumoured, sir," Simon said, "that you worked in Intelligence"

Carne looked delighted, but enigmatic. He beetled his brows and twisted his mouth in a teasing smile.

"Well now, well now," he said. "Intelligence, eh? You see me as a kind of early – what's that fellow? James Bond, eh?"

Simon laughed with him.

"It doesn't take such an almighty leap of the imagination, sir."

"I played my part. I'm not prepared to say more."

"Even now?"

"Even now. I've not been released from any oaths of secrecy, as far as I'm aware. No – what I know will die with me. I was simply a cog in a wheel. Many others were far more important."

"You've not thought of writing down your memories of those days?"

Carne drew in his breath sharply and shook his head.

"No, no. I've always prided myself on being a man of honour, my boy. Let others speak if they wish. I shall stay silent."

Simon let it hang for a moment, but saw little could be gained from pressing him.

"Returning to World War II," he said. "You worked, I believe in the Ministry of Information –"

"In the Home Propaganda Section. Perfectly poised, as you will see, to step into broadcasting, but never, of course, did I imagine the reception my poor efforts would receive. It was quite overwhelming! Pen will let you see some of the letters people wrote to me. She's kept them all, somewhere –"

"I'd love to see them. And any photographs too, from those early days. Tell me – that first broadcast, the one about patriotism – I've heard the recording and seen the text. I must say there's something about its very simplicity that's moving, given the atmosphere of those times. Professionally it must have signalled a whole new career for you. I'm presuming the reception of it was the thing that sparked off your entire change of direction?"

Slowly Carne nodded.

"Much was, as you say, in the timing. But yes – it appeared to strike a chord. I shall never forget that first time in the studio! It was the most extraordinary experience –"

He was off again. Near disasters and monumental blunders, his mobbing at the hands of admiring dinner-ladies at a British Restaurant, the invitation to lunch with Winston Churchill; an audience even, with the King. All were recounted with self-deprecating humour and undiminished vitality. Ninety-five, Simon thought again, almost with disbelief. If I have half that vitality at the same age –

It seemed almost brutal to rein him in a little and bring him to the years after the war, but Simon finally succeeded in doing so with as much tact as he could muster; for it had to be acknowledged that his post-war work had been a disappointment to his public and had signalled an end to all the acclaim. Memories of his wartime fame were still fresh when his first two post-war books were published and they sold reasonably well in the shops. The critics, however, were damning, and his third post-war novel flopped. He published no more. For a while he was in demand as an after-dinner speaker in the south-west, and his presence was constantly requested to open war museums or exhibitions of wartime paintings; but then the years passed and he grew older. Such invitations diminished in number and then stopped altogether.

"What I don't understand is why you didn't go on broadcasting?" Simon said. "You were a natural! I can't imagine why the BBC let you go."

For a moment Carne made no answer, but lifted his head and stared out of the window towards the sea.

"It was my decision," he said bleakly after a long pause. Simon waited. Carne did not elaborate, however. The pause lengthened, became embarrassingly long, but Simon hesitated to fill it for there was a hint in Carne's manner that there was more to come. In the event, he merely sighed and whispered the words again, and then once more, this time his voice no more than a thread of sound. "My decision; my decision."

It was the first awkward, downbeat moment – the first time that Simon had found himself at something of a loss. He knew he should pursue this line of questioning in the interests of good journalism, but it was clear that Carne, not surprisingly, was beginning to tire. His voice reflected it, and he sighed as he leaned his head wearily against the back of his chair. It would have been inhuman to press him.

"Well, you've sure been rediscovered now," Simon said.

"Ha!" Carne gave a short laugh, the merest shadow of his former high spirits. "I think everyone thought I was dead. Well, now they've wheeled me out again."

"We'll stop there," Simon said, feeling a pang of contrition that he had gone so far. Suddenly the old man's strength seemed totally depleted – and who could wonder at it? From the first he had dominated the interview with the kind of energy that could have proved a strain on a far younger man.

"He's one hell of a guy," Simon said to Pen when, after the lunch which had proved more than adequate, she returned from helping her father to his room for his usual siesta.

"Yes." Pen smiled in agreement. "Shall we take our coffee down to the summerhouse again? We can take this selection of father's fan letters too. It'll be cooler and more pleasant there now that the sun's moved round. No, no –" she fended him off as he attempted to take the box-file from her. "You carry the tray. I can manage this."

He did so, and watched her with interest as she poured the coffee. An attractive woman, he thought again. And so were the other sisters, if the photographs on the mantelpiece in the dining-room were anything to go by. Which reminded him to ask for a photograph of Carne as a young man, preferably with his family. Pen promised to look some out.

"There's one rather sweet and solemn one taken at his graduation – I think I have it upstairs. And there's a wedding picture, of course, and one or two of all of us together."

"That would be great. I haven't seen a picture of your mother."

"She was a handsome woman."

"She must have been very proud when your father became so famous."

Pen smiled her thoughts.

"Oh, indeed she was; but then she was proud of him long before he became famous. She adored him. I don't think she ever got over her astonishment that he actually deigned to marry her."

"I got the impression it was a very happy marriage. Was I right?"

Pen looked at him for a moment without speaking.

"Do you know," she said at last, "I really have no idea! I feel terribly guilty these days when I think about my mother. We none of us knew her very well when we were children, odd as that sounds. She was a reserved, undemonstrative woman – rather taciturn, not one to show her feelings openly. I became closer to her after I married and I realised then that she did love us in her way, but I honestly can't remember any occasion when she actually said so, or showed her affection. We were, I think, always very much aware that the three of us came a poor second in her affections."

Simon thought, not for the first time, of Stella Morel. If Caleb Carne had indeed indulged in a love affair in London, it seemed unlikely that any whisper of it would have reached Cornwall. But one never knew.

"They must have spent a good deal of time away from each other during the war," he said, probing gently.

"He came home as often as he could, which is a great deal more than many men were able to do, and towards the end of the war he spent more and more time here. His broadcast talks were less frequent by then, and apparently his work at the Ministry of Information was finished. To be honest, I don't think I ever knew the ins and outs of it all – or if I did, I've forgotten! It was all so long ago. All I can remember is that by the time your father was in the picture, he was spending more time here than in London."

"Which must have pleased your mother."

"Indeed it did – though even for him there wasn't any open display of affection. She rushed to satisfy his every whim and used to get furious with us if we upset him in any way, but it was her eyes that really reflected the way she felt about him. They were very dark and deep-set, and they followed him around and seemed to glow when she looked at him."

"Your father said she wasn't happy in Oxford."

"She was out of her element – and, I think, hated sharing him with others who were more on his intellectual level than she could hope to be. She was a village girl, you see, who never grew beyond the village. She had no self-esteem. It was rather sad, because she had a lot to offer – strictly between us, I think Father has much to answer for. If he'd made the effort he could have brought her out of her shell, given her some sense of her own worth. I'm afraid she was an unhappy, complicated woman whom none of us understood. She suffered a nervous breakdown at one time –"

She paused, glanced at him as if conscious that she was saying too much. Then she smiled.

"You know, Simon," she went on, "your father was sweet to her – I've just remembered! She was so difficult to talk to that most of our friends took the easy way out and ignored her – and who, really, could blame them? But David always took notice of her and brought her little presents and made her smile. She was fond of him."

"That sounds like Dad."

Again, Simon thought of introducing the name of Stella Morel into the conversation, but this time he dismissed the idea completely, sure that Pen would know nothing. It was irrelevant, anyway, and better forgotten.

"About the letters," Pen said, bringing him back to more immediate concerns. "You can take them back with you, if you like. Or have a look through and take the ones you want. I would ask you to send them back as soon as possible, though. My father treasures them very highly."

"I'm sure he does. I'll just look through now and maybe take some names and addresses. I thought maybe I'd try to contact some of the writers – get them to say how they felt at the time."

Pen looked doubtful.

"It's an awful long time ago, and some of them were pretty old then. Still, no harm in trying."

For a moment there was silence between them, but there was no awkwardness in it. Simon felt, strangely, as if he had known Pen Hambly for a long time. Because of his father's connection? That hardly made sense; but still there was something that made him feel at home here. Perhaps it was the sheer beauty of the place.

The room where they sat seemed suspended in a vast bowl of light; a space filled with the sea's glittering immensity. Even from this position, a halfway house to the cove beneath, the rocky cliffs looked difficult to climb. From beneath, Simon thought, they must indeed be daunting. The tide, receding from them, had left a small strip of golden sand.

"Did you ever succeed in climbing those cliffs?" he asked. "I bet you tried!"

"Only once. We soon learned a very healthy respect for them, I can tell you."

"It's a wonderful place to grow up in," he said. "A beach all to yourself!"

"It was rather idyllic." Pen smiled, remembering the good things. "We had a little boat – just a sailing dinghy – that was moored down below. There's still a rusty iron ring set into the steps, but alas, no boat any more."

"Did you have it when my father was here?" Simon asked. "He loves boats."

"Oh, yes, we did. At least –" Pen frowned, struggling to remember. "We certainly owned it then, but it was too early in the year for us to have it in the water, I think. No, that can't be true. How one forgets! I remember now, we went on a picnic to a cove just south of Porthlivick, and the weather was gorgeous."

How could she have forgotten? That was the day when Trish and David had quarrelled; a day that had started out well but had ended in discord. The day she had told David she would remember for ever – but that was earlier, before the quarrel with Trish, when he and she had gone exploring and everything had been peaceful and she had been so happy.

"Was all your childhood spent here?" Simon asked.

"Yes. I was born here. We all were."

"It must have been a great contrast to the kind of place your father lived in as a child."

"Apparently it was always his dream to live here one day."

"He told me."

"He rented at first, and then, years later, the owners decided to sell, and of course he had first refusal."

"Did his mother live with you?"

Pen gave a sudden, surprised laugh.

"His mother? Certainly not!"

"He spoke of her very fondly."

"Did he? Well, yes – he always reckons he wouldn't have got anywhere without her. She made him stick at his books, no doubt about it. He didn't dare do anything else! She was an extraordinarily formidable woman, my grandmother – the archetypal, interfering, disapproving mother-in-law and even Father saw that having her to live here would have been too much for Mother to bear. Or any of us, come to that. I don't think the question arose, really, as she went on living in the little cottage in the village and managed to look after herself until she died quite suddenly just after the war. We girls were terrified of her. She often came to Sunday lunch, and it was amazing how we all managed to find urgent occupations elsewhere the minute lunch was over."

"Do you know anything about his connections with Intelligence?"

Pen laughed again.

"Only that we teased him unmercifully about beautiful spies. I really can't help you on that – in fact I was never sure how much was true and how much fantasy – I strongly suspect the latter. It was all a bit of a joke, and if he played any part at all then I'm sure it was a minor one."

"You've been very helpful."

"Can we please talk about your father now? I'm longing to hear his news. What did he do with his life, after all?"

They talked throughout the afternoon, without strain and with increasing friendliness. The ease between them delighted Pen. He was David's son, all right, with all the same natural charm and good humour and, apparently, a consuming interest in his companion of the moment. Now, as then, it was a beguiling mix.

At last she looked at her watch, and got to her feet.

"Father will be ready to come down for his tea now," she said. "I must go and help him. Why don't you take the opportunity to look through the letters?"

"I'll do that," Simon said. "And – and thanks, Mrs Hambly. Thanks for everything."

She looked at him for a moment with an expression on her face he found hard to read.

"It's been a pleasure," she said.

# III

**P**en leaned from her bedroom window to take a last look at the night sky and to breathe in the sweet, soft air. Simon would be nearing London by this time. Would she ever see him again? The thought that she might not brought with it an inexplicable sense of loss.

He might have been my son, she thought; and for the first time for many years she felt the agonising pain of her barren womb, the screaming emptiness. It was a pain she thought she had come to terms with a long time ago, and it would pass, she knew that. She couldn't wish her life any different. She had loved Philip and had happily married him – for better, for worse; in sickness and in health. That there was more sickness than health was bad luck, that's all – if such a mild phrase could begin to describe three years in a Japanese prisoner of war camp. He'd never really recovered from the experience, but she'd known the risks when she made her vows. The war had been over for four years by the time they were married.

Their childlessness had always been more difficult for him than for her, for he felt responsible and had taken on her grief as well as his own. She had struggled to hide her sadness, to appear philosophical. No one in the whole world, she told him, had everything they wanted. Just think how lucky they were! They had each other and they had a wonderful life in a wonderful place. No commuting, no city streets, a job that he found intensely satisfying.

He wasn't taken in, though. Of course he wasn't! He knew her too well, was far too sensitive. But then all the sickness and privation of his war years finally caught up with him, and the pain of Pen's childlessness was swallowed in the far greater pain of knowing that she was losing him.

So long ago, she thought as she listened to the distant hush-hush of the waves. She had been a widow now for twenty-three years; five years longer than she had been a wife. Trish always said that she should have married again – which was easy enough to say. There had been men in her life, but marriage, for one reason or another, had never been an option; and then there was her father. Someone had to look after him and she was the obvious choice.

Trish couldn't have done it. She wouldn't have lasted five minutes and was honest enough to admit it. She was fond of her father but she had no patience – and, as Pen knew only too well, one needed patience. By the end of a week at Roscarrow, Trish's need to get away was overpowering and obvious to all.

Apart from anything else, she hated country life – and in addition, there was Raoul, husband number three, to consider; the Lounge Lizard, as Caleb called him. Pen found the soubriquet remarkably apt. There was something undeniably reptilian about his smile, and his cold, muddy, hooded eyes. She had never taken to her French brother-in-law's brand of bogus charm, and though she always expressed polite regrets she was secretly delighted that he never accompanied his wife when she came home. Still, he and Trish seemed to rub along happily enough, which was all that mattered.

As for Caro, there had never been any question of her looking after Father – rightly, in Pen's view, for though she had sufficient room to accommodate him in her great house in Harrogate, she had more than enough to cope with, with a husband and four children. Seventeen years ago when their mother had died and the question of his care had arisen, Caro's children had been teenagers, their future careers, their loves, their day-to-day problems of all-consuming importance. Any further pressure on her would have been unfair – and anyway, though fences had been mended, distant quarrels apparently forgotten, the relationship between Caro and Caleb had always been an uneasy one.

Pen didn't mind, didn't feel resentful. She and Caleb had always got on well together. They made each other laugh, enjoyed the same things. She was able to cut through his pretensions, bring him down to earth. She knew his faults, but she loved him just the same. She would have said she was utterly contented with her lot, until suddenly there was that pain again, that foolish, primeval longing, no less severe now she was well past child-bearing age. Worse, perhaps.

She would let the peace of the night seep into her bones and restore her, she thought now. It would; it always did. And anyway, she was being ridiculous. Simon could never have been her son. She might have loved David, but he had never been in love with her, and had never pretended to be so. It had all been a fantasy, an impressionable girl's dream, forgotten long ago. It was only this strange and unexpected appearance of his son that had brought it all to mind . . .

\*    \*    \*

Her announcement of the invitation and David's acceptance of it had met with luke-warm response. She had expected nothing more from her mother; her father, when he knew of it, would be glad and welcoming, she felt certain, and would generate enough warmth to compensate for Mother's deficiencies in this respect. However, she had certainly expected more enthusiasm from Trish and Caro. Instead Caro had hardly reacted at all, merely saying in an off-hand way that she wouldn't be in. She had arranged to go to the Wilkins's for tea, she told them. Ken and Molly Wilkins ran a market garden on the St Jory road where Caro worked six days a week. She'd wanted, at one time, to join the Land Army, but had settled for the Wilkins's instead. At least she was able to live at home and enjoy the luxury of good food and hot baths.

"I've got other plans too," Trish said. "I've promised to cycle over to Pansy's house to talk about bridesmaids' dresses."

Pansy was her great friend who worked with her in the library at St Jory. She was to marry her sailor sweetheart on his next leave, and there was much to discuss with Trish who had been asked to be chief bridesmaid.

"Anyway, I don't suppose he'll come," she went on, when Pen protested. "Honestly, Pen, why should he?"

Who'd want to have tea with a skinny kid like you? That was what she meant, Pen knew, even if she didn't say it.

"You'll be sorry," she said. "He's awfully good-looking. You should see him, Trish."

"Some other time," Trish said, off-handedly. Good-looking Americans, she implied, were no novelty to her.

Pen didn't know whether to be glad or sorry. She longed to show David off to her sisters, but at least now she would have him to herself, and maybe she could take him to the headland, or down to the little beach. On the other hand, it was terrifying to think of having to entertain him on her own. He might think she had tricked him. After all, he knew she had two older sisters; maybe he'd only accepted the invitation *because* she had two older sisters!

It had been easy enough at the church because they had the graves to talk about, but what would they discuss at their next meeting? Her panic grew the more she thought about it. He would feel cheated, she felt certain. Maybe it would be all for the best if he didn't come after all – but it was only necessary for this gloomy possibility to cross her mind for her to feel sick with disappointment. He was so nice, not a bit like the frightening sort of American who wolf-whistled at the girls, and she loved hearing the way he spoke and the expressions he used. He seemed younger, less cocky, more ordinary. No, not ordinary, that was quite the wrong word. Normal, then. But that didn't express it, either.

Oh, please God, she prayed fervently as she knelt in her pew that Sunday morning. Make him come, and make it all right.

The family had walked to church together. It was a bright, blustery day towards the end of March, with all the spring flowers dipping and nodding in the garden and white horses on the waves in the bay. Pen had knelt and stood up and sat down, had sung the hymns and made the responses, but she might have been on another planet for all she had heard of the service. She was thinking all the time of David. Her desire to see him again had taken root and grown since the previous day, and in her memory his glamour increased with every passing moment. She stared at her vase of daffodils (now definitely lop-sided) and thought of him – of how he had looked and smiled when he stood at the chancel steps, and how the light through the stained-glass window had made him appear like some kind of knight in search of the Holy Grail.

On the way out she had lingered a moment to touch the cold marble of the Teales' tomb and caress the little dog, just for luck;

and as she turned to continue towards the door she saw Caro looking over her shoulder in the direction of the pew where the Yeos habitually sat. They were there today: Walter Yeo and his wife, Florence; Hilda Yeo, the gaunt, wild-eyed wife of Henry, Walter's brother, now away up-country somewhere in a safe desk job (which was, the whole of Porthlivick agreed, just *like* him!). And, at the end, Alan, son of Walter and Florence, home on leave from the Navy and wearing a smart new Petty Officer's uniform.

Pen's heart sank. Surely, she thought with dismay, that business with Alan and Caro wasn't going to start up all over again. It was months since she had mentioned his name and it was generally assumed that she had long forgotten him; but now, seeing her face, Pen couldn't help wondering. Surreptitiously she turned to look at Alan and saw, her heart sinking still further, that he was looking at Caro with much the same kind of expression.

Her father hated the Yeos. All hell had been let loose when it was discovered, a year or two back, that Alan and Caro had been meeting, going to dances and for walks and heaven alone knew what else.

On the whole Pen was on their side – not, personally, that she considered Alan Yeo worth making a fuss about. He was thin and dark with deep-set eyes and a long nose and would, Trish said, undoubtedly look just like his Uncle Henry, known to the girls as The Walking Skeleton, when he was forty. Still, it was the principal of the thing. Whatever Father had against the Yeos as a family was ancient history, nothing whatever to do with Alan, who was amiable enough despite his looks. On the other hand, was anything worth putting him in the sort of state he'd got into last year? Never could she remember so much unpleasantness in the whole of her life; so much shouting and tears and temper and ultimatums.

Caro had appeared to cave in in the face of days and days of argument and the silent, weighty reproach of her mother. Anyway, she couldn't go out with Alan any more for he was back at sea – where, no one knew. Pen hoped that the whole thing had died a natural death. After all, Caro had had loads of boy-friends in the past, and none had lasted very long.

63

There was no reason to think that Alan Yeo would be any different; but since intercepting that look Pen wasn't so sure any more – in fact she felt suddenly certain that Caro had no intention of going to the Wilkins's to tea; why should she, when she saw them every day of the week? That was just an excuse. She was going out with Alan.

Well, Pen thought, she just hoped no one else had twigged. She didn't want anything to spoil David's visit – if he actually turned up, of course. Oh, he had to, he had to! She had, by this time, come to the definite conclusion that she would die if he didn't.

She was all ready half an hour before he was due. For once she felt reasonably grown up in a tartan kilt discarded by Trish, and an emerald-green, high-necked sweater which was absolutely brand new, knitted by her mother especially for her. She'd washed her hair and swept it up a bit at the sides, borrowing some hair grips from Trish to keep it in place. And while at Trish's dressing-table she borrowed some face powder too. She contemplated a touch of lipstick but couldn't bear to think of the amused – and in her mother's case, disapproving – comments it might excite.

On the dot of four she heard the ring of the front door bell, and ran downstairs to answer it, her stomach fluttering with nervousness – but everything was all right, her father was already there. He'd been in the garden and had come round the side of the house to see David on the steps, and they had come in together, Father talking in his usual friendly way, putting the visitor at ease. He shone at that sort of thing. Nobody, Pen thought, could possibly feel strange or out of things when he was around. Except Alan Yeo, of course.

"My – my sisters are both out." Pen, stuttering a little, was anxious to make this clear right from the start so that he shouldn't expect anyone more exciting to put in an appearance.

"That's a shame," David said; but he smiled at her as he spoke, and didn't look as if he minded at all. "It's great to see you again, though."

"I don't suppose tea will be for another hour or so," Caleb said. "We can have a good talk then, David. Pen tells me you're seeking enlightenment on Porthlivick history – but for the moment, why don't you take advantage of the sunshine and let Pen show you the beach?"

Pen looked at David.

"Would you like that? We don't have to, if you'd rather not."

"Can't think of anything I'd like better."

"I'll get my coat."

It had to be the old school raincoat. It was either that or her best one, which would be ridiculous. Or opting to freeze, which would be even more ridiculous, because in spite of the sun the wind was cold. Oh, what did it matter? Suddenly she wasn't nervous any more, but was deliriously happy because David had come and was every bit as nice as he had seemed – nice and normal and unthreatening, and even more handsome than she had remembered. What's more, he seemed pleased to see her, and she had him all to herself for a whole hour.

She led him past the summer-house which the family used a lot during the warm weather, but which was all shut up now. The path to the beach was steep and grew even steeper until it was no more than ladder-like steps attached to the rocks. Beside them, the cliff was shored up with a concrete skim. An iron ring was set into the concrete.

"Is that for a boat?" David asked.

"Yes. Only a little one. It's laid up for the winter, but I suppose we'll be getting it in the water soon."

"Do you sail?" David pursued.

"Well, sort of." It wasn't, in fact, an activity that Pen enjoyed very much. "Do you?" she asked.

"Sure. I love it."

"Oh, so do I."

Pen was glad neither of her sisters was around to hear her utter such an outrageous lie. She should, she supposed, feel ashamed, but in fact she felt defiant. Maybe this year she *would* love it! People changed, after all. Perhaps if she *tried* a bit more, she would like it better.

The tide was going out, leaving the small cove without mark or footprint, the sand newly washed, a trail of shiny seaweed along its edge.

"This is terrific," David said, just standing and looking at it. "Do you have it all to yourselves?"

"Yes. There's no other way down. The harbour isn't very far away – only across those high rocks, but they're just unclimbable."

"Wouldn't it be great if we found footsteps, coming the other way?"

"Man Friday?" Pen suggested.

"Who else?"

"Maybe the ghost of Uther Pendragon – except that ghosts don't leave footsteps."

"Who's he?"

"He was a King of Cornwall. Father will tell you." Pen leapt down the last few steps. "Come and see the cave. It's a bit disappointing actually, because from the opening it looks as if it's going to be a proper, smuggler-type thing, but it's not at all. It's hardly big enough to hide half an ounce of baccy, never mind the 'laces for a lady and letters for a spy'."

"Come again?"

"Don't you know it? It's Kipling – all about smugglers."

"Tell me!"

She recited a verse and was pleased to see that he listened. Properly. So many people didn't.

"I like that," he said; and repeated, in a dramatic whisper: "'Watch the wall, my darling, as the gentlemen go by.' That's great!"

"Tell me some American poetry," Pen said, and David leapt immediately to the top of a small rock and struck a dramatic pose.

"'What seas, what shores, what grey rocks and what islands –'" he began.

"That's *cheating*." Pen was laughing, delighted that she had caught him out. "You can't fool me! That's T.S. Eliot. He's English."

"He was born in St Louis, Missouri."

"I don't believe you. He's as English as I am."

"Whaddya bet?"

"A million pounds."

"Done!"

"Father will know."

"That's fine by me. I hope you've got a million pounds."

"I hope *you* have."

"C'mon, let's climb."

66

"I've tried to paint this view hundreds and hundreds of times, but it's awfully hard to do the sea properly," Pen said when they were perched on a flat rock above the beach. She had firmly refused to go any further. She had tried it before, and had learned her limitations the hard way.

"Hey – you're an artist?"

She coloured to the roots of her hair, suddenly afraid he'd think she'd been showing off, instead of desperately casting around for something to fill the silence.

"No, of course not. Not really. I just mess about with paints and things. I'd like to go to Art College, though, when I leave school."

"So what else do you do with yourself, besides paint and read poetry?"

"Oh, I read all sorts of things. Do you like reading?"

"I sure do."

"I bet there aren't many GIs on Bow Beach who could quote T.S. Eliot."

David laughed.

"Er – no. Maybe not. Not many that would let on, anyway. It's kinda nice to be civilised for a bit. My Dad would approve – he's nuts about poetry."

"Are you going to work on his newspaper when you get back?"

"Maybe. I don't know. I have to go to college first."

"Have you got any brothers and sisters?"

"Sure, one of each. A kid sister about your age called Cathy, and a little brother called Joe. He's only ten."

Pen didn't think much of being mentioned in the same breath as a kid sister and declined to pursue the subject.

"Tell me about Hannville," she said. He laughed.

"There's nothing to tell. Nothing ever happens there."

"What does your father print in his paper, then?"

"OK, OK. People are born and they marry and die, and there are rows about whether we should have a new school or a new sewerage system, and if it's right for Edna May Becker to open a stationery store on the corner of Main Street when Herb Murphy has carried stationery for the past fifty years in his bookshop just three doors along, and is it really true that Patrick O'Hegarty's Olds. has been parked outside Mrs Blum's house three nights in a row, and Mr Blum out of town –"

"He doesn't print that?"

David laughed and shook his head.

"No, of course he doesn't. I'm just trying to tell you that it's a small town with small concerns. Not a lot different than Porthlivick, I guess."

"Different than! Is that what you say?"

"Yeah. Don't you?"

"No. We say different *from*, and opposite *to*. Don't you think that's interesting? Who started it? I wonder what else is different – I mean besides the accent."

"I don't have an accent," David protested. "It's you that have the accent."

Pen laughed and gave him a playful push. It was, she thought, as if he were someone she had known for years, a schoolfriend or a cousin; except that he was more glamorous, of course. All her fears about the afternoon had been quite unnecessary. There had hardly been any awkward pauses, which, for her, was little short of miraculous.

"Porthlivick is pretty small," she said, returning to his original comment. She paused for a moment and bit her lip. "Promise not to tell, David, but I'm worried about Caro."

"Your sister?"

"Yes. The oldest one. I think she's out with Alan Yeo – he's a sailor, home on leave. Dad could so easily get to hear about it."

"Why shouldn't she be out with him?"

Pen explained about the rows of last year and her father's total prohibition on the slightest contact with any Yeos, past, present or future.

"He doesn't get angry very often," she said. "But when he does – boy, you really know about it!"

"It sounds like the Montagues and Capulets," David said. "What's he got against these people?"

"I don't know, exactly – just some quarrel that goes back years and years. Silly, unimportant, ancient stuff, like Dad being bullied at school and losing an election because Walter Yeo spread lies. Stuff like that."

"How old's your sister?"

"Caro? She's twenty. Twenty-one at the end of May."

"Well, I'm only nineteen, and I'm considered old enough to die for my country. I guess at twenty she's old enough to go out with whoever she wants to."

Pen stared at him. The awful possibility of his dying for his country had wiped everything from her mind; she felt strangely hollow inside.

"But you won't, will you?" she said after a moment. He grinned at her.

"Certainly not," he said. "I aim to die of old age. Come on –" As if seeking to dispel the sudden gloom that seemed to have overtaken her, he stood up. "Isn't it time we got back?" he asked. "I guess this tea business is a kind of ritual, isn't it? It sounds so British. Will there be cucumber sandwiches?"

"Like in *The Importance of Being Earnest*? I shouldn't think so. More yeast buns and strawberry jam, I should imagine. And I believe there's a sponge cake."

David was silent as he turned and offered his hand to help her down the last, awkward rock. Normally she would have jumped down without a thought, but she rather liked the sensation of being treated like a lady.

"You know," he said. "I feel bad about this. We're told not to eat your food."

Pen looked outraged.

"Why? There's nothing wrong with it."

David laughed so much that he had to lean against the cliff to support himself.

"If looks could kill," he said at last. "I didn't mean that, you dope! I meant that we've been told that you don't have any to spare."

"Oh –" Pen gave a small, shamefaced giggle. "Sorry! Don't worry about it – we haven't gone hungry yet. We always have yeast buns and a cake for Sunday tea. It's not so bad with five ration books and the odd perk from the place where Caro works. Chickens, and eggs and things. Come on – race you to the steps."

Over tea, Pen hardly spoke but was content to sit back and let her father take over once the T.S. Eliot question was settled. The poet, Caleb assured them, had indeed been born in Missouri but had taken British nationality some time in the twenties; so David readily agreed that they owed each other a million pounds.

"I really don't have it about my person," he said solemnly. "But I'll be happy to forget it if you will."

"Well –" Pen pretended to consider it. "It's against my principles to welsh on a deal, but OK. This once." And laughing, they shook hands on it.

Throughout tea Mrs Carne sat in her usual silence, devoting herself to passing plates and filling cups. David had, politely, tried to draw her into the conversation, but without a great deal of success – not, Pen thought, that anyone had much chance against her father who was on top of his form. He certainly had a way of making history come alive! David, it was easy to see, was both intrigued and amused by him, showing just the right amount of deference to warm his heart, asking questions and making comments that kept him in full flow. Finally, however, with obvious regret, he looked at his watch and said he had to leave.

"I want to thank you for a wonderful afternoon," he said as he got to his feet. "It was a great tea, Mrs Carne –"

Silently, Emily Carne inclined her head; but she smiled, Pen noted. She looked pleased, as if she wouldn't object if David were to come again.

"We've been delighted to meet you, my boy," Carne said.

"I've enjoyed hearing your stories, sir. And going down on the beach, and everything. I just had the best time."

"Come again." Carne rose from his chair and put a fatherly arm around his shoulder. "We'd like that, wouldn't we, Pen?"

"Oh yes," Pen said. "Come any time, David."

"Well, thanks. I'll do that." David smiled at her and her heart turned over. She just couldn't believe that it had all gone so well.

There was, at that moment, the sound of the front door slamming, and a voice calling from the hall.

"Coo-ee, I'm home!" It was Trish, back from tea with Pansy. "Honestly, you'll never guess –" She stopped short as she swirled with her usual verve into the room and saw David standing in the middle of it, clearly about to leave. She was shorter than Pen, and almost as slim, but much to her younger sister's envy she had a superb figure which went in and out in all the right places. The wind had whipped colour into her cheeks, and just then, with her brown eyes sparkling with animation, her dark curls flying about her, she looked stunning. There was, Pen thought, no other word to describe her.

She always attracted wolf-whistles from the packs of Americans in the square, and this particular American, Pen could see at a glance, would have whistled too, if circumstances had allowed and if he could have summoned sufficient breath to do so. He looked, however, as if he had stopped breathing altogether; as if he couldn't believe his eyes; as if Trish was the answer to all his prayers.

"Hallo. You must be David." Smiling, accepting his unspoken admiration as if it were no more than her due, Trish held out her hand. "I'm Trish. I'm so sorry I wasn't here earlier – and now you're just about to leave! What an awful shame."

David, who had seemed so relaxed and self-confident, cleared his throat and appeared to swallow with difficulty.

"Yeah," he said. "It's too bad. I wish I didn't have to go, but I'm on duty tonight. Still –" he looked towards Mrs Carne and smiled at her. "I've been told I can come again. I'll sure look forward to that."

"Me too." Trish tilted her head and slanted a provocative smile towards him. "Next time I'll make sure I'm in."

David dragged his eyes away from her to thank everyone all over again, and Pen stepped up smartly to see him to the door. *Damned* if I'm going to let Trish muscle in, she thought. She knows what she can do with her squinty-eyed, sexy smiles.

"I hope you really do come again, David," she said, as they approached the front door.

"Oh, I sure will. You can count on that. Thanks again."

"Thank *you*. It – it was fun down on the beach, wasn't it?"

"Sure it was. I haven't had so much fun for a long, long time."

So there, Trish Carne, Pen thought. He's my friend and it's me he likes, and me he'll be coming to see.

And then he spoiled it all.

"You're a good kid, Pen," he said. And with a smile and a casual salute he was off down the drive.

\*　　\*　　\*

71

Simon was back in London by ten thirty. The journey had passed pleasantly enough. He'd had a leisurely dinner and sat afterwards over coffee and a brandy pondering the events of the day.

Maybe he should have mentioned Stella Morel, just in case. It might have got some reaction. Mandy had looked out some of the articles she had written for the *Gazette*, and having read them Simon had decided that she must have been an interesting lady. She had written with insight and authority about affairs of the day and had been a champion of the underdog and a supporter of causes, particularly women's causes. Anyone, however, less like the militant feminist who had addressed him at such length at the party would be hard to find; or, for that matter, anyone less like her daughter, Polly Godwin. Stella Morel's writings were full of verve and wit. Some of her pieces had made him laugh out loud. It was easy to see that she could well have been a most attractive woman.

On the whole he was glad he'd said nothing, though he was uneasily aware that he could be accused of an unusual lack of professionalism. Maybe he'd been too subjective, too sympathetic towards Carne and his daughter. Well, so be it. It was probably a load of bullshit anyway. Mrs Godwin hadn't impressed him. She seemed just the sort of woman to say anything that might add a little excitement to an otherwise excruciatingly dull life; hadn't her daughter implied as much?

Besides, what was the point? Caleb Carne may well have been a philanderer – with Stella Morel and heaven alone knew how many others. Given his vitality and his undoubted good looks it was by no means unimaginable. But unless it had materially affected his work there was absolutely nothing to be gained by muck-raking at this late stage. He hadn't been commissioned to write that kind of article. Anyway, he had only three thousand words to play with. Readers might be more interested if he followed up the Intelligence angle.

He couldn't help being curious, though. What a guy, he thought again. What a performer! Sentences formed themselves in his head: 'Today,' he would begin his article, 'in a tiny church perched on a Cornish clifftop, the villagers of Porthlivick will gather to honour a broadcaster who some say did more to raise morale during the Second World War than any other man alive, Winston Churchill not excepted.'

He'd go on then to a few quotes from the letters: 'Just when hope was lost, I turned the knob on my wireless and heard your voice', etc., etc., etc. Then, maybe, he'd cut to the idyllic situation of Roscarrow and the inspirational view from the summerhouse where so many of the talks had, presumably, been crafted; after which he would cut to Carne's early life; the village school, the ambitious mother, the struggle to get to Oxford; his service in the First World War; the development of the ethos, in short, that inspired the famous talks.

Was it all, then, to be laudatory? He frowned, and unseeingly gazed from the carriage window at the fields and woodland that flashed past outside. How was he going to handle Carne's disappointing career post-war? He should have pressed him about that, he thought. He wasn't usually such a soft touch when it came to interviewing people. Come to think of it, his father's wartime link with Carne had been something of a distraction; better far if he had come to the story cold, a total outsider.

Lost in thought, his arrival at Paddington took him by surprise. He took the tube to South Kensington and walked down Pelham Street to the Fulham Road. He was housed, he was the first to admit, above his station. A friend of his father's, an executive in the oil industry, had a flat in Kensington which he kept for his frequent visits to London while based in New York. Now, however, business had taken him to the Far East for a couple of years and he offered Simon the chance to live in his London apartment for next to nothing, on the understanding that he would give it up at a moment's notice should circumstances change. It was an offer he couldn't possibly afford to refuse.

The balcony which led from the large living-room looked out over a small, railing-enclosed square to which only residents were permitted a key. There were a few formal flowerbeds in the middle of it, but at this level he could only see the branches of the chestnut trees, the leaves looking now over-bright and oddly artificial in the light of the street lamps.

It was very hot in spite of the lateness of the hour. He opened the two long windows as wide as they would go, but there was no breeze to stir the flimsy curtains, nor any hint of one. All was still and airless and stale, and for a moment he thought of Porthlivick and the summerhouse and the gulls wheeling and dipping in the sky above the little beach and wondered why he'd been in such a hurry to come back to the city. Because I had to, he answered himself; and resignedly turned away from the square with its tantalising reminder of other, greener places, to sort his mail and check his Answerphone. There was a message from a computer firm in Fulham letting him know that his printer had been repaired and was ready for collection, followed by one from the editor of a magazine to say that he'd had new thoughts about the article on the Youth Theatre. Would Simon get in touch a.s.a.p.?

There then followed a kind of gasping noise, and a nervous clearing of the throat.

"Oh dear," a voice said. "Oh, it's one of these things. I'm not sure – I mean, I'm not very good –" Further clearing of the throat. "It's Polly Godwin," the voice went on. "I suddenly remembered something that might be of interest. Perhaps you'd ring me. Oh –" This last gasp came as Simon felt sure she had gone. "I'd better give you the number."

She did so, and Simon wrote it down, without a great deal of hope. Still, every avenue ought to be explored, every stone dutifully turned. He'd give her a ring in the morning. She might, conceivably, have a snippet of information to shed light on Carne's state of mind after the war.

He unpacked his toilet things, threw dirty laundry into the basket, made himself a mug of coffee; and all the time he was aware of a nagging feeling of disquiet, the reason for which eluded him. It was something to do with Carne, though; he felt sure of that.

He took his coffee through to the living-room and sat down with it, switching on the tape recorder as he did so.

"Is that really necessary, my boy?"

He smiled as he heard Carne's voice. It brought back the sight of him – the dapper appearance, the charming expression, the laughter. One hell of a guy, he thought. But as the tape ran its course the smile died, and when it was finished, he sat without moving, deep in thought.

He'd been right to describe Carne as a performer. That's what it had been, the whole thing. He was no nearer knowing anything of substance about the real Caleb Carne than he had been before making the journey to Cornwall.

Had the old guy meant to conceal so much? And if so, how clever of him to talk about his childhood and his wife and his family and his life in general with such apparent frankness and yet reveal so little.

"You're slipping, my boy," Simon said to himself, imitating Carne. "You let him get away with it."

\* \* \*

Polly Godwin was out when he tried to ring her next morning; and when, after going out to collect the printer, he tried again with more success, he was sufficiently unwise to mention that it was his second attempt, thus provoking a long and involved explanation.

"Oh dear, I'm *so* sorry!" Mrs Godwin was as breathless and over-emphatic as ever. "I just had to rush out to Sainsbury's. I thought I'd make a cake, you see, because I have a friend coming to tea, and I quite forgot that I used the last of my eggs the day before –"

"You said you'd thought of something that might interest me," Simon reminded her gently.

"Yes – isn't it odd how things just pop into your mind? When we were talking the other night at the party – *wasn't* it fun, by the way? I was sorry when Laura arrived and swept me away. Such a reversal of roles! It seems no time at all since I was pacing the floor wondering when she was going to get back from some frightful disco or other – I mean, you hear such dreadful things, don't you? Being a parent is no easy thing these days, Mr Holt."

"I guess it never has been," Simon said. "What was it you wanted –"

"Oh yes, the box! I can't imagine why I didn't remember it when we were talking. My mother lived in this house, you see, and when she died she left the contents to Laura and the house to me. That was five years ago. Laura already had her little flat.

She took a few pieces of furniture that she needed, but the rest of my mother's stuff just stayed where it was. I didn't have very much of my own, you see. I've moved around quite a lot, haven't collected many possessions –"

"So what about the box, Mrs Godwin?" Simon congratulated himself on the evenness of his voice.

"There were these papers, you see, in a drawer of a chest upstairs in an attic room. I decided it would go very nicely in my bedroom – the chest, I mean – so I just cleared the papers out and dumped them in a box. I forgot all about them until now."

"You're telling me," Simon said slowly, wondering if he had any reason to get excited all over again, "that you have all your mother's papers stashed away?"

"That's *right!*" Mrs Godwin's voice was bright and congratulatory, as if she was surprised that he had caught on so quickly. "Well, not all. Just some of them. There were other, more recent ones, in the desk that Laura took – these are really quite old. I don't think she could have thrown anything away, ever. I even saw a ration book and her wartime identity card."

"And was there anything else?" Simon asked. "Anything pertaining to Caleb Carne, I mean?" Mrs Godwin gave a trilling laugh.

"Oh my dear, there might be. I only looked in a very casual sort of a way – there were some rather sweet photographs of me as a baby, but I really didn't bother to look any further. I *meant* to, but the whole thing went right out of my head. Until now. Then I suddenly thought of you, and I wondered –"

"I'd love to see what's there." Simon thought, on the whole, that he wouldn't get hopeful; on the other hand, who could tell? If Carne had been as friendly with Stella Morel as Mrs Godwin implied, there might conceivably be something among her papers that could shed a new light on his work – particularly on the contrast between the broadcasts and the novels that had come before and after. His failure to pursue this line with Carne still nagged at him.

"Then come and see me." The flirtatious note was back in Polly Godwin's voice. "We could have a bite of lunch."

"Oh really, there's no need –"

"Come at twelve. It won't be much! Just a little drinkie and a snack."

"That's most kind –"

"I'm about fifteen minutes' walk from Turnham Green Station, if you're coming by train, 10 Pomfret Road; out of the station, turn right, keep on to the end of the road, turn left and right again. You can't possibly miss it."

"Twelve o'clock, then," said Simon.

For some reason he had envisaged a shoe box, but instead, when at last Polly Godwin ushered him upstairs to the attic floor of the terrace house in Pomfret Road, he found a tea-chest all of three feet high and two feet across, almost full of leaflets and cards and paper and heaven alone knew what, all dumped in a jumble, one on top of the other. Even without touching any of it, he saw a yellowed theatre programme for *Strike a New Note*, starring Sid Field – whoever he might be. Further perfunctory investigation revealed a bank statement dated October 1945, a letter in a crabbed hand written on cheap, lined paper from an address in Wales, also yellowing about the edges, and a Ministry of Food leaflet about Digging for Victory. On top was the previously mentioned ration book.

"That letter was from the woman I lived with when I was evacuated," Mrs Godwin said. "I told you that my mother sent me away –"

"Yes, you did." Simon smiled at her, hoping to forestall a reprise. "I guess she was glad to know you were safe."

Mrs Godwin's pretty little face took on a cynical expression, as she played with the ears of the small dog she held in her arms. It was not a Yorkshire terrier, as Simon had imagined, but a miniature poodle, introduced as Fifi, with a vicious mouth and hate-filled eyes. She was forced to hold her, since she appeared to have taken a dislike to Simon and had yapped and harried his ankles from the moment of arrival.

"There are lots of other things there," she went on. "All kinds of typescripts and letters and photographs."

"Diaries?" Simon asked hopefully.

"Not that I saw – but you never know. There were a few notebooks. They might tell you something."

"Maybe. It would be very time-consuming to go through the whole box in detail." And, he added to himself, would probably at the end of it prove unproductive. The sheer volume of papers was daunting, blunting his original enthusiasm.

"You could take it home and examine it at your leisure, if you wanted to," Mrs Godwin said.

"That's very kind. On second thoughts, though, I'm not entirely sure –"

"I thought," she went on, not looking at him, still apparently totally absorbed in stroking the dog, "that you might be willing to pay –"

"*Pay?*" Simon looked at her in astonishment. "What on earth for?"

"Well, I just thought – I mean, newspapers do pay for information, don't they?"

"But Mrs Godwin –" She looked up at that, and fluttered her eyelashes.

"Polly, *please!*"

"Polly, then. You haven't given me any information yet. Anyway, I honestly don't think that at this late stage anyone is going to be terribly interested, even if your mother did have an *affaire* with Caleb Carne. It's not going to be that sort of article."

"You were quick enough to come," Polly pointed out, with justification.

"I didn't entirely realise what the papers consisted of, or how many there were. There seems a great deal of –" trivia, he was going to say, but realised in time that Polly would probably be mortally offended by this description. "Personal data," he finished weakly.

"So you're not interested?"

Simon struggled with indecision. He certainly wasn't going to offer her any money for a pig in a poke like this; as it was, if he took it back to the apartment he'd need to take a taxi, which would cost a fortune. He had a good mind to thank her warmly and beat a retreat. On the other hand, there was that nagging consciousness that so far he had failed to put his finger on the key to Caleb Carne. Without dragging anyone into disrepute, there might conceivably be something he could use. Who could tell?

"Look," he said at last. "I'm just a freelance – I can't pay you some enormous sum for the privilege of looking through all of this when it might not be the slightest use to me. But for some reason – sheer nosiness, I guess – I'd like to do it. Will you trust me? If I find anything here about Caleb Carne that I can make use of, then I swear I'll get you some kind of payment, one way or another."

"That's rather vague."

"Yeah, I know." Simon smiled at her in apology. "Well, it's the best I can do, I'm afraid. I know it's asking a lot. I'd give you a receipt, of course. Put it down in writing."

She bit her lip and became engrossed in the dog again, seeming for the moment undecided what to say next; then she looked up and gave him a provocative smile and a little push on his arm.

"I'll make a bargain with you," she said. "If you find anything you can use, you can stand me dinner. Somewhere really super. How about that?"

"Deal," said Simon, smiling back.

The taxi home was even more expensive than he had expected, and by the time he had staggered upstairs with the box he was quite sure he had been all kinds of a fool to bother with it. He dumped it thankfully on the floor by the side of his desk, and for a moment he stood looking at it, hands on his hips. How the hell was he to set about it? If it were to be of any use at all he would have to go through it minutely, sheet by sheet. He'd just have to start at the top and work down, making a pile of any personal things – letters, and so on – and another of impersonal documents such as the Digging for Victory leaf-let and the theatre programme.

For the moment, however, he had other matters to attend to. There was the Youth Theatre article, for one thing; he'd phoned the magazine editor and received his new instructions. Then there was his regular monthly column for the paper back home giving up-to-date news about the arts scene in London. He'd done his research, made his notes; all he had to do now was to write it.

He worked throughout the afternoon, then went to the Groucho Club for a drink and a chance to hear the latest media gossip. It was after eight by the time he arrived back home again, intending to have a quick meal and make a start on looking through the box.

He was just reaching his hand towards the freezer with a view to finding something both filling and microwavable when the entry phone in the hall buzzed, signalling that someone was downstairs and wished to see him. It proved to be Laura Rossi, who was, by the sound of it, very angry indeed.

"I believe you have some property of mine," she said crisply, in a voice that brooked no denial.

"You'd better come up."

Simon pressed the button and waited. He didn't have to wait long. Laura must have run up the stairs two at a time, so quickly after the announcement of her presence came the ring at his doorbell. He opened the door and found her there, panting a little, her cheeks pink, but whether with fury or exertion he couldn't tell.

"Hi!" he said, smiling at her. "Come right in."

"You bet I will." She stormed past him into the hall. "I've come to collect what belongs to me. I must say I think you've behaved despicably."

"What?" He was too taken aback to register anything other than astonishment at this attack.

"Don't sound so surprised. Don't you think it's despicable to bribe a foolish woman to give you access to private papers?"

"*Bribe?*" Simon gave an astounded laugh. "I think you've got your wires crossed, Ms Rossi. Look – why don't you come in and let me give you a drink. Let's talk this thing over –"

"No, thank you." She stood with her arms folded, glaring at him. "You can't soft-soap me like you soft-soaped my mother."

"No one's soft-soaping anyone, I promise you. Your mother rang me and offered me the chance to look at some of your grandmother's papers, and I accepted. That's the plain, unvarnished truth. It'll all go back to her in due course."

Laura was clearly unmollified, but Simon detected a flicker of those hazel eyes that seemed to say she was slightly less sure of her ground. For a second she looked at him, lips pressed angrily together.

"Maybe it will," she said. "But not till you've had your grubby little hands on it!"

"Hey!" His voice was soft, but there was an edge of annoyance to it. "Hold it right there. If you want the dam' box, take it. I only brought it home because your mother was so insistent.

I'm far from certain it's any use to me, and I sure don't need this hassle. It's in there."

He jerked his head towards the living-room, and she swept past without giving him a glance, halting for a moment as she crossed the threshold as if surprised by her surroundings. For a second she looked around her; at the impressionist prints on the walls, the Chinese rugs, the Liberty print curtains, the expensive reproduction furniture.

"How very *Homes and Gardens*," she remarked. "I expected something less conventional. Working for the gutter press must pay surprisingly well."

"Oh sure, I'm loaded. The box is over there, if you want it. Help yourself."

The size of it seemed as much of a surprise to her as it had been to him, and for a second she contemplated it silently.

"Very funny," she said flatly at last. "Perhaps you'll be kind enough to bring it down to my car."

"The hell I will," Simon said.

Deadlock. They stared at each other challengingly. She was still, Simon thought, conscious of regret, his kind of girl – feisty and full of life. The shape and the size and the look of her were right too. Words being his business, he looked for the one that would adequately describe her, and found it without difficulty. Vital, he thought. That was it. Her thick, dark hair crackled with vitality; her eyes and skin glowed with it. Even her nose – perhaps too long and dominant for beauty, added character to a face that already reflected energy and strength. He wondered briefly if he was ever likely to meet her when she wasn't annoyed about something; and whether Mr Rossi was man enough to cope with her. Incidentally, where was Mr Rossi?

Her eyes held his; then, suddenly, without warning, the fight seemed to go out of her.

"Oh, God," she said, sitting down heavily in the armchair that was right behind her. She covered her face with her hands for a moment, before lifting her head and looking at him once more. "Look, I'm sorry," she said. "I was rude."

"You could say that." He wasn't ready, yet, to be totally mollified.

"I was very angry."

"*No!* That's a surprise!"

"Is it true my mother contacted you? You didn't ring up and offer a bribe?"

"Well -" Simon hesitated for a moment, feeling a pang of sympathy for Mrs Godwin who, he felt, must come a poor second in any battle of wills with her formidable daughter. Then self-preservation took over. "No, I didn't," he said. "She asked me for some kind of payment and we settled on dinner. But only if I found something of interest about Caleb Carne. I probably won't."

"I'm sure you won't. Those papers are my property. They're absolutely nothing to do with my mother, and I still want them back. There's nothing there that could possibly be of interest to you."

"You've examined them?"

"Well -" she shrugged her shoulders. "Not exactly. Not in detail. But it's just trivial stuff, you can see that with half an eye."

"Why are you so bothered about it, then?"

"That's my grandmother's private life in there, and I'm not having a stranger pry into it."

Simon looked at her thoughtfully.

"OK," he said. "And of course I'll help you down with the box."

"Thanks. Look, I'm sorry I tore into you like that. It's just that -" she shrugged helplessly. "I know it sounds awfully unfilial, but my mother makes me madder than anyone else in the entire universe. I love her. I'd do anything for her. But the fact remains—"

Simon smiled at her, amused but sympathetic.

"It can happen. What do you say we have that drink now? Chianti Classico suit you?"

It only took a moment for her to consider it.

"Well - OK. Chianti's fine. Thanks."

He went to the kitchen, but was back in a few moments, a glass in each hand. He gave her one, then sat down in the chair opposite hers.

"Cheers." He lifted his glass towards her and drank, his eyes still on her. There was silence between them. Perversely, having decided not to bother with the papers, her opposition to his possession of them had awoken his curiosity again. A charm offensive might pay off. Mr Rossi or no Mr Rossi, he would ply her with a few drinks; maybe suggest dinner. All, it went without saying, in the interest of research.

And then, inwardly, he laughed. He liked Laura Rossi, and found the challenge she offered the most exciting thing he'd come across for a long, long time. Her smile was exciting too. He'd never seen anything quite like it. It altered the shape of her face, made her chin more pointed, revealed a slight indentation in her lower left cheek that was wholly enchanting.

Research? Who was he kidding?

# IV

Simon could tell, from the moment he'd mentioned his interview with Carne, that Laura was far from indifferent about the man; which seemed strange when, from her own admission, she'd never met him.

"I don't know what you've got against him," he said. "Do you know something I don't?"

They had moved from his flat to Tonino's, the Italian restaurant not fifty yards away that did its best, summer and winter, to look as if it were set in the heart of Naples. Tonight, with tables set amid potted orange trees in the cobbled side alley and the heat of the summer day still heavy upon them, the illusion was more valid than usual.

"What did you really think of him?" she asked at last, not answering his question.

"I told you. I liked him. It was impossible not to. He's an attractive, entertaining kind of guy. He has a certain –" he waved his hand vaguely. "Charisma, I guess. I don't know what you'd call it."

Laura looked down at the menu she held in her hands, but not before Simon had noted the small smile and the derisive glint in her eye that seemed to say she suspected some laddish conspiracy and despised it on principle.

It had seemed a natural progression, this move to the restaurant. Laura had refused another glass of wine since she was driving, but even so conversation had thrived. His job, her job, his surprising, if temporary ownership of the flat, his father's meeting with Carne during the war – all this and more had occupied them happily until it was acknowledged that neither of them had eaten that evening. Simon's invitation to dinner was accepted with only the smallest of hesitations on Laura's part. He had offered the use of his phone in case she wanted to let anyone know her movements, but she had declined – so presumably Mr Rossi wasn't waiting at home, pacing the floor, tasty casserole in the oven. He had already checked that she wasn't wearing a wedding ring – but that, he thought, meant little in these emancipated days. He'd been caught that way before.

"Is their fettucini good?" she asked, apparently dismissing Caleb Carne as a subject for conversation.

"Excellent. Come on – level with me. Why are you so prejudiced against him?"

"Carne?" She gave a short laugh, putting the menu to one side. "Have you read that book everyone's raving about? The text of his wartime talks? It's pure schmaltz!"

"Oh, c'mon, now. I can't agree with that altogether. Maybe there's a sentimentality about it that wouldn't catch on today, but you can't judge it by today's standards. Some of the language is beautiful – poetic, even. I'd go so far as to say it had heroic resonances. Maybe you should re-read it."

"Maybe I should." Laura, however, clearly remained unconvinced. "I confess I only glanced at it in a bookshop, but it didn't appeal. OK, I'm prejudiced, I admit it. I tried one of his early novels once. It was quite the worst thing I've ever read!"

"*The Glory and the Dream* is something else. Believe me!"

"It's such a pretentious title."

"You're looking at it with 1990 eyes. Can't you imagine how it might have touched a chord in 1940."

"When we Stood Alone?" She gave the words a mocking twist. "OK," she went on after a moment. "I grant that the talks must have had a relevance then that they don't have now; what I don't like is the way people are drooling over them all over again. It's a retrograde step, like the resurgence of the Fascist party –"

"Oh, come *on*!"

"No, really. I believe this utterly. It's time we stopped fighting the war, re-running *Colditz* and *The Guns of Navarone* on the telly, glorifying all that gung-ho-ness. Thousands upon thousands died in the war, the poor bastards. What good does reliving it do them? We ought to put it all behind us and concentrate on the future. Besides –" She paused, took a sip of water.

"Besides?"

"I can't take Carne seriously. All that gentle wisdom and high-mindedness, when he was such a bastard in his private life –"

"Hey! Now we're getting somewhere. What do you know about his private life?"

"Enough. It doesn't matter, it's nothing to do with his work, I promise. Look, I just feel that shedding nostalgic tears over Carne's outpourings is somehow unhealthy – it's typical of something maudlin in the British psyche, pure self-indulgence. I'll have the fettucini," she said in the same fierce voice, as a hovering waiter came nearer. "With the cream and salmon sauce," she added. She laughed a little shamefacedly as she caught Simon's eye. "Well, OK, I'm not totally against self-indulgence."

"I'm relieved to hear it. I think you should forget your prejudices and actually listen to the talks," Simon went on after the waiter had taken their order and disappeared. "The tape's not out commercially yet, but I've got an advance copy. When you hear Carne's delivery of his own words, I'll bet any money you feel differently. Believe me, he was great."

She laughed suddenly.

"OK. I'll withhold judgement."

For a moment Simon said nothing, studying her expression as if wondering how far he could push her.

"Were Carne and your grandmother lovers?" he asked, without warning. "Is that how you know about his private life?" She looked at him, cold once more.

"Does it matter?" Her face, Simon decided, seemed accustomed to fierceness; maybe that imperious nose had something to do with it. But her smile, when it appeared, was brilliant, all-embracing, that small indentation wholly delightful. He wished, fervently, that he could say something that would inspire it to appear again. "Well?" she prompted him.

"Only if it sheds light on Carne's work. I admit I'm puzzled by him. I agree with you absolutely about the pre-war novels."

Laura pulled a face.

"I just couldn't finish the one I started. Couldn't get beyond Chapter Four! What a load of over-written, sententious, moralistic rubbish."

"I'll go along with that."

"And what a chauvinist! His female characters are all coy little wimps – the 'good' ones, that is. Only the baddies have any guts. It shows what he really thought about a woman's place."

"All this from four chapters?"

"I'm not wrong, am I?"

"Not essentially," Simon admitted. "Though I understand he had a certain following. I guess he must have done, to get the books published at all. It's amazing, isn't it? Obscurity before the talks, obscurity afterwards – only during the war did he fulfil his potential. I guess you could call it the Andy Warhol syndrome. He'd found his metier and for a few short years was famous. Were his perceptions heightened by war? Or did the love of a good woman make all the difference?"

She said nothing in response to this. It was almost as if she had hardly heard him. She rested her chin in her hand, elbow on the table, and regarded him closely, a faint line between her brows. Simon, sensing her irresolution, pressed home his advantage.

"So am I right to think your grandmother might have influenced him? Your mother seems convinced they were more than friends."

"My mother knows nothing."

"But you do? Look, this is off the record, strictly for my own satisfaction. I'm not going to destroy anyone's reputation, believe me; it's not that sort of article. It's just that I can't help being curious about the old guy now that I've met him."

"You swear it? You're not going to quote me?"

"Absolutely not."

"I don't know why I should trust you." She continued to look at him searchingly; then she sighed. "I suppose I've already given the game away. The answer's yes, they were lovers, but I swear I'll kill you if you print it. It was a secret she kept all her life. She and Carne met some time in the early part of the war and, according to Stella, fell in love more or less at first sight. Amazing, eh? I was with Stella a lot in her final illness, and she talked to me about all sorts of things she'd never mentioned before. She told me that Carne was the only man she'd ever really loved. That's when I read his book – well, tried to, anyway. I could never understand how she could feel that way about a man who wrote so badly."

Simon laughed explosively.

"For heaven's sake, sexual attraction isn't a reward for good behaviour. It's there or it isn't. I'm telling you, worthy or not, Carne must have been an attractive guy." He broke off as their food was served. "Mm, this is good," he said, tucking into his tagliatelli with appreciation. "Is yours OK? You can always rely on good old Tonino. Tell me," he went on after a few moments' application to the food. "What kind of a woman was your grandmother?"

Laura looked down while she pushed the fettucini about her plate. Her eyelashes were like two dark fans against the creamy-peach shade of her cheek.

"What sort of a woman?" She repeated the question thoughtfully, raising her eyes to his. If she noticed the closeness of his regard, the warmth of his expression, by no flicker of emotion did she reveal it. "One hell of a woman. That sort. Worth ten of Caleb Carne, I can tell you. She was wise and kind and tough and understanding. You wouldn't believe how I miss her still."

"I like what I've read of her work."

"You've seen it?" Laura looked astonished and Simon had the distinct feeling that this piece of thoroughness had caused him to rise in her estimation.

"Some of it. It wasn't too difficult to find," he said. "She wrote for the *Sunday Gazette*, you know."

"Of course I know. Is that the paper –"

"That I'm preparing this article for? The very same. The Magazine section, anyway."

"I didn't realise. You didn't say. Well –" Laura was silent for a moment. "Well," she began again, aware that Simon was looking at her with a mocking amusement. "I take back all I said about the gutter press. Funny it should be the same paper. It was more radical in Stella's time than it is now."

"Why did she leave the BBC?"

"She was only there briefly, just before the war. She went over to France in the early thirties, just for the hell of it, and married a Frenchman called Jean Morel. He was an artist and a Communist – Communist first and artist second, in fact." She broke off and laughed. "You're not going to believe all this. It sounds too Ernest Hemingway-ish for words!"

"Go on. I'm fascinated."

"Well, their life was all very Rive Gauche. They married and starved in a garret, living on what Stella could earn as a writer because Morel sure as hell didn't earn anything. Then Polly was born – Paulette, she was christened – and after a while they went to live with Jean's parents in Lille because they just couldn't have survived otherwise. This lasted some years, with the marriage under terrific strain, mainly because Morel still spent a lot of time in Paris on political business. Stella stayed in Lille with Polly, hating every minute.

"Then, when the Spanish Civil War broke out, Morel announced he was off to fight. Stella left Polly with her grandmother and went too, partly because she was bored out of her skull, but also because she saw it as a final throw to save the marriage. She wasn't accredited to any particular paper, but she sent back reports and was published in several. Jean was killed in the bombing of Madrid. When it was all over, Stella returned to Lille, but by this time everyone there was fearful that there would be a war with Germany; her mother-in-law was convinced of it, apparently, and urged her to take Polly home to England. So that's what she did, and that's when she worked for the BBC. She'd never been a Communist herself – she was leftish, but not anywhere near that far left – but after she'd been at Broadcasting House for a few months someone realised that she'd been married to a fully paid-up member of the party and questions were asked. She was required to give all kinds of undertakings about not getting involved in politics – in those Reithian days the BBC was terribly careful about that sort of thing – and it got under her skin. She had quite a row with them – said 'Sod 'em all' and upped and left."

"Why is your mother so resentful of Stella?"

"You may well ask. I've never understood it."

"She was sent away during the war –"

Laura looked exasperated, as if this was a remark she had heard too often.

"To a place where she was safe, not to say pampered. Most city children were evacuated to the country to total strangers. Stella busted a gut to find this farm in Wales run by a childless couple who'd always wanted a pretty little girl of their own. I think that was part of the trouble. They spoiled Polly rotten by all accounts – obeyed her lightest whim, made her feel Queen of the May.

Inevitably, Stella had to come the heavy parent from time to time when she came back home. Look –" Earnestly, Laura leaned a little closer. "What else could Stella do but send her away? She was a single parent, she had to earn enough for both of them, and everyone expected London to be annihilated. Polly knows that, really. It's only half the story."

The other half, she told him, was the simple fact that Polly and Stella had nothing in common, no way of communication.

"You wouldn't dream they were mother and daughter. They never understood each other; just didn't speak the same language. Stella was a professional to her fingertips, dedicated to her work and the various causes she espoused. Polly was frivolous and flighty." She laughed. "Still is!"

"How come Stella told you about Carne but didn't tell Polly?"

"I told you – they were never close. I suppose it was natural that it was all kept secret while Polly was very young. It's not, really, the kind of thing a mother would talk to a small daughter about, is it? Then later – well, the last thing Stella wanted was to appear unprincipled or immoral, not to Polly. She was in quite enough trouble without any encouragement from her mother. Stella and I – well, we were always close. She told me about him in an unguarded moment in the middle of the night when she was quite ill. I told you, I spent a lot of time with her at that stage. We'd sit and drink tea and talk about everything under the sun. I sort of felt she was talking to herself rather than to me."

"Polly got wind of it, though."

"It's all guesswork. She overheard something once when she was a child, but she doesn't know anything for sure. I don't imagine anyone does except me. And now you. Well, I suppose close friends of Stella's must have known, but it was a well-guarded secret. Any whisper of it back in the 1940s would have finished Carne."

"Stella never remarried? After the war, I mean. After Carne."

"No. Oh, she had her chances, I'm sure. She was always old to me, of course – I mean, grandmothers are, aren't they? But even so, I knew, right from my earliest days, that she had – something. It sounds like the something you said Carne has. I don't know how to describe it any better than you could, but it was there, all right. She was so attractive, even when she was old. She had such a joyful nature – so much vitality."

The word stopped Simon in his tracks. Were they alike, then, grandmother and granddaughter? It seemed possible.

"But your mother didn't appreciate it?" he said after a moment.

"No. Stella was an independent person, with strongly held opinions, particularly on women's rights. Fifty years earlier she would have been a suffragette. Fifty years on, she might have been a founder member of *Spare Rib*!"

Simon gave a grunt of laughter.

"I agree she doesn't sound too much like Polly," he said.

"No." Laura laughed too. "Polly can't envisage life without a man to cling to. The problem is that she clings to quite hopeless specimens; she never seems to learn."

Polly had made a disastrous early marriage, Laura told him. Divorce had followed; then marriage to an older man with a string of grocery shops from which, eventually, she fled with an Italian waiter.

"Luigi Rossi. My sainted father. They never married, but I was given his name – I suppose for appearances' sake. They lived together as man and wife for a year or two. He wasn't altogether unlike that chap over there." She indicated the handsome young waiter pouring wine at the next table, with a nod. "I've seen a photograph and believe me, he looked like an angel – which didn't stop him hot-footing it back to Italy the moment he got tired of life with Polly."

Simon fastened on the one piece of information that had caught his attention.

"You're not married, then?"

"Heavens, no! What gave you that idea?"

"Your name isn't Godwin –"

"So you thought I might have a Luigi of my own stashed away somewhere?" She laughed at him as if the thought amused her. "That'll be the day! If I ever marry, it won't be an Italian. They tend to have old-fashioned, Carne-like views about a woman's place."

"Where does Mr Godwin come in?" Simon asked her.

"Believe me, my mother's life story is boringly repetitive," Laura said. "She was left penniless after my father decamped. She was forced to get a job, and I ended up spending long periods with my grandmother while Polly worked as a housekeeper to various gentlemen. Mr Godwin was the last."

"So they married and lived happily ever after?"

"They married, that's true, but not happily. Oh no, not happily. Mr Godwin, not to put too fine a point upon it, was a bastard. Oh, he seemed reasonable enough to start with; well-mannered, the perfect gentleman, public school, the right accent. She thought he would keep us both in comfort, but as usual she'd picked a wrong 'un. He had ways of making both our lives a misery that don't bear repeating. Believe me, he was cruel and miserly and utterly hateful. It's a long story and I won't bore you with it, but the result was that at the age of fourteen I went back to Stella, and lived with her until I went to University."

"And Polly?"

"She put up with Godwin for another nine years, before he finally had a stroke and died. She didn't want to miss out on the fortune he assured her she'd inherit – but once he'd popped his clogs, it transpired that he didn't own the house he'd promised to her, and he'd been living on capital for years. It turned out he owed thousands and there was practically nothing left for Polly, after all her years of virtual slavery. She went to live with Stella then. Stella was old and none too well by that time, and was glad of someone to look after her. I think she thought that even at that late date, she and Polly might reach some kind of rapprochement."

"And did they?"

"Not really. Even now Polly still trots out the old complaints about being abandoned as a child. Still, Stella left the Chiswick house and enough money for her to invest to give her a small income. She'd be in a bad way without it. Can you wonder," she added after a pause, "that I'm the independent sort? No one in my family has a very good track record when it comes to men, even Stella; and as for my mother – well, she's the kind of woman who never learns. She's for ever urging marriage on me, and worries herself to death about my lack of prospects. She honestly thinks, poor soul, that life without a man is no life at all. Believe me, I've learned my lesson well – take good care of yourself, because it's more than likely no one else will."

"Mm." A mouthful of tagliatelli gave Simon ample excuse for not commenting further on this remark. He was, in fact, a little ashamed of his pang of regret at this dismissal of the man-as-hunter concept.

"This food is wonderful," Laura said; but there seemed to be a glint in her eye, as if she knew exactly what he was thinking and was amused by it.

"You never told me why you're so down on Carne," Simon said, hastily changing the subject. "I would have thought, since you admire your grandmother so much –"

"Oh, she was in *lerve*." Laura drew out the word, laughing at him. "You can't trust anyone's judgement in that state. Even Stella's."

"I can understand the attraction."

Laura gave a short, dismissive snort of laughter.

"Don't you see? He was a prize shit, dishonest with both his women. He played the usual married man's game. All during the war, when he was doing his broadcasting, he travelled up and down from Cornwall to London. Apparently he had a *pied à terre* in Hammersmith and used to stay for days at a time. Maybe he comes from a long line of sailors with a wife in every port. He had a wife at each end of the railway line, anyway. He strung Stella along – said he would leave his wife, that there was nothing between them any more and they had stayed together because of the children. But now the children had grown up, more or less, so there was nothing to keep him. She believed him, she told me. For month after month, year after year, she believed all his excuses and his promises; but then, suddenly, he broke it off. He said his wife was ill and he couldn't leave her, that she needed him, etc., etc."

"And that was it?"

"That was it. She didn't see him again. He severed his connection with the BBC and didn't come to London any more. She never heard another word, but she loved him until the day she died."

"Everybody loved him," Simon said. "I managed to contact a few out of the hundreds who wrote to him and they all said more or less the same. He gave them the courage to carry on – made them feel all the sacrifices were worthwhile."

"He was such a *nice* man." Laura's voice was loaded with sarcasm. "It was his stock-in-trade."

"They took a risk, didn't they, he and your grandmother? Tell me, what did she do in the war? Just keep on writing?"

"Not at all. I told you her life was unbelievable! Because of the years she'd spent in France and her command of the language, she was recruited by the SOE – the Special Operations Executive – to work at the office in London, helping to select and train agents that were later dropped over France."

"My God! It's her story I should be writing!"

"Don't you dare!" Laura's reply was immediate, and she blushed a little as Simon looked at her with amused understanding.

"You're going to do it yourself?"

She sighed and smiled rather ruefully.

"One day," she said. "I've already made a start, but somehow –" She broke off, shrugged her shoulders. "It's not so easy, is it? In her old age Stella wrote down lots of notes for the autobiography she thought she might write one day – all about Spain, and the SOE, so I've got the facts –"

"The facts about Carne?" Simon broke in.

"No more than she told me, which is what I've told you." She paused, frowning. Then she shook her head defeatedly. "What I've written sounds flat, somehow. It doesn't bring her to life in any way. I suppose I knew her as well as anyone, but even so I'm finding it hard to pin her down, make her seem real. Maybe that's the difference between an amateur and a professional."

"Everyone starts somewhere."

"I know. I'll do it some day – in fact I intend to have a real blitz on it in these coming holidays."

"Good for you. I'm sure you'll make it. Laura – about the papers in that box. Are you still adamant I shouldn't see them?"

She sat back and shook her head, laughing at his persistence.

"I can't imagine why you should want to."

There was that little indentation of the cheek again. I bet, Simon thought, she'd hate it to be described as a dimple. Carne's heroines in the much-despised novels tended to have dimples.

"Curiosity, I guess," he said after a moment's silent appreciation. "And a feeling I ought to leave no stone unturned. Carne's such an enigma. Maybe it would give a little background material. Clues about the wartime days, other friends – I don't honestly know until I find it. Maybe we could go through it together."

"I can't do anything for at least a week." Laura dabbed at her lips with the napkin and Simon recognised, with a pang, that the evening was almost over. "I'm going on a school trip to Paris

95

tomorrow." She sighed, as if the prospect failed to charm her, and looked at her watch. "I ought to get home. I've still a million things to do."

"Paris," said Simon, "is no place to go with a bunch of kids." He wanted, suddenly, nothing more than to be there with her, strolling beside the Seine, sitting at a pavement café.

"You're telling me!" Laura's agreement was heartfelt, but she retracted it almost at once. "Actually it won't be so bad. It's just a small crowd with a particular interest in art and the theatre. We're going to the Comédie Française and the Louvre, among other places. I'm quite looking forward to it, really. They're a lively lot."

"You like your job?"

"Yes, I do, in spite of a few male chauvinists on the staff. I think I'll call them Carnists from now on. The West London Collegiate is a pretty special sort of a place, with a really enthusiastic headmaster. The parents are supportive too. We're privileged, I can't deny."

"So are they," he said, meaning it. "To have you. Will you call me when you get back?"

"Yes, I will." The reply came without any hesitation.

"And the box?" This time she paused for a moment.

"Keep it," she said at last. "For now, anyway. Something tells me that Stella wouldn't mind you looking through it, just so long as you don't use anything you find there without asking me first."

"I won't," Simon promised. "You can trust me."

"Yes," she said. "Yes, I believe I can."

Simon felt as if she had handed him a priceless gift.

\* \* \*

"Hi! This is Simon Holt. Sorry I'm not around right now, but if you leave your name and number I'll get back to you."

Bloody Answerphone! Silently David swore to himself. He'd wanted a chat; had felt suddenly lonely, cut off.

"Dad here, Simon. Where are you?" He made his voice sound cheerful. "Living it up somewhere, I guess. Well, boys will be boys. There's no real news to report. I'm fine. Putting in a lot of sailing and golf. And fishing. Spent the day with old George. Didn't catch a thing, but we set the world to rights. Say, what does Saddam Hussein think he's up to? I don't like the look of it at all.

"I didn't call to talk about him, though. I've been thinking about coming over to see you, like you said. Can't come until towards the end of August, on account of your Aunt Cathy's fortieth wedding anniversary; they're planning a big party. Would it fit in with your plans if I came then? Give me a call some time. Hope everything's OK, and work's going well. Guess that about wraps it up. Bye now."

David replaced the receiver. Idly, hands in pockets, he sauntered to the open windows and stared out at the garden, frowning a little. It didn't look right somehow. Despite his spasmodic attention and the weekly visits of old Jules, it was beginning to have a vaguely unsatisfactory appearance. There were gaps in the beds that he'd left unfilled, annuals that should have been rooted out and replaced. He was only beginning to appreciate the unstinting and constant attention that Fay must have paid to it.

Nothing stayed the same, he thought gloomily. Take Answerphones. They were useful, of course. Modern technology was undoubtedly a wonderful thing, but to him using one always seemed, somehow, the equivalent of putting a message in a bottle and hurling it into the sea. You could never be absolutely certain that the recipient would act on today's message – or would even receive it at all. Who was to say that there wouldn't be some kind of a blip that would wipe it altogether?

He might be showing his age, but in his view there was nothing that would ever replace the written word. Did youngsters write love letters any more? Shame on them if they didn't; but on the other hand, maybe he'd always been too ready to commit himself to paper. He'd written to Fay one hour after parting from her that first time they'd met; Christmas, it had been, with Vermont under snow, and emotions heightened by all the beauty and the excitement.

Crazy, romantic fool! They ought to put that on his gravestone. Still, that time it had worked out all right. More than all right. Not like the time in Cornwall, when, come to think of it, he'd wanted to write just the same sort of letter . . .

\*     \*     \*

He'd started composing it in his head on the way home from Roscarrow, his emotions in more of a turmoil than he could ever remember. This was love; there was no mistake. There'd been other girls, way back to Sally Anne Morgan. She had been his very first date, when he was only thirteen. He'd taken her to the movies to see Fred Astaire and Ginger Rogers in *Top Hat* and bought her a bag of popcorn. Whatever, come to think of it, had become of Sally Anne Morgan?

Then came girls at proms, girls who played tennis, girls in backs of cars. There was one girl, a blonde who sang with the Hannville High School Harmonettes. Diane, her name was. She'd said she would write, but she hadn't done so and he hadn't really minded too much.

From time to time he'd fancied himself in love, but he knew now that he hadn't known the meaning of the word. Never, never in the history of the world could anyone have felt like he was feeling now. There surely could never be, anywhere, a girl like Trish – a girl so utterly, sublimely, devastatingly beautiful. The US Army could never appreciate the effort needed – surely above and beyond the call of duty? – to say goodbye and leave her, when all he wanted was to stay and gaze at that glowing face. It was all he could do, even now, not to turn back for another look. But he couldn't, of course. Even if there were not the small matter of guard duty to perform, the Carne family would think him mad. *She* would think him mad.

Duty consisted of standing around, patrolling the beach at intervals. It was, perhaps, fortunate that there were no enemy aliens about to take advantage of his distraction, for one thing was certain – he wouldn't have noticed an entire platoon of them marching towards him with fixed bayonets, so bemused was he by the memory of Trish.

He thought of the fineness of her skin with the faint flush upon it, and her dark, glowing eyes. Spanish eyes? Mr Carne had said something about Spanish sailors visiting Cornwall some time in the historic past. No doubt they'd left their mark – and Trish was the result. Beautiful Trish.

He thought of those breathtaking curves, and her smile, with its hint of a secret shared, its promise of intimacy. Or was he letting his imagination run away with him? Why should a girl like that, a girl with a figure that made him ache with longing – that would make any man ache with longing – look twice at him? His mood swung between elation and despair as he plodded up and down the beach.

He could hear the sound of a radio coming from a nearby tent. Someone was singing 'As Time Goes By'.

> You must remember this,
> A kiss is still a kiss,
> A sigh is just a sigh.

He hadn't kissed her yet; perhaps he never would. Yet the sound of the song made him feel weak with loss, just as if he had kissed her and held her and been torn from her. It was, after all, the only possible outcome. None of them knew how long they were here for, but it couldn't be long. Just a handful of weeks, no more. It wouldn't do to waste any time.

Oblivious of the cold wind that had sprung up, he laid plans. It came to him in a blinding flash that the smart thing to do would be to write not to Trish but to Mrs Carne to thank her for her hospitality. He'd say what a pleasure it was to be with a family again, and that he hoped she wouldn't be too dismayed if he took their invitation seriously and stopped by when he was next off duty, which would be on Wednesday, after the evening meal. This, he felt, would be a particularly tactful touch, likely to win approval. He didn't want to antagonise Mrs Carne by inviting himself to eat with them; there was something in her dark watchfulness which made him think she might be easy to antagonise.

After he came off duty he wrote several versions of the letter before finding one that seemed to convey all he wished to say. It wasn't, after all, possible to say 'please make sure that Trish is in on Wednesday night', so he confined himself to a pious hope that this time he might meet all the family and prayed earnestly that Trish would take the hint.

Wednesday was fine all day, the sea as blue and calm as if it were high summer, though there was still a nip in the air. He went through all his duties and drills with his mind miles away, invoking the Sergeant's wrathful scorn and unending ribaldry from his comrades. That evening Chuck Stein, his biggest buddie, with him all the way from the Reception Centre on Long Island, sat on his cot and looked at him curiously as he changed from fatigues into a clean shirt and best uniform.

"You got a date?" he asked.

"Could be."

"Say, who is she? Not that blonde floosie in the pub? Hey, didn't I tell you she was all set to roll over –"

"*Not* that blonde floosie in the pub. She's all yours, feller. See you around."

The road was winding and steep, but the knocking of David's heart had more to do with the prospect of seeing Trish than any physical strain. He had thought of little else since the previous Sunday; had experienced delight and shame in almost equal measure at the wildness of his fantasies. Technically he was no virgin; but spiritually, he knew now, last summer's experimental fumblings in the back of his father's Dodge with Diane were empty and meaningless compared with the delight that awaited him – oh please, please, God, let it await him! – in Trish's arms. This was the kind of love that poets wrote about, *real* love, sacramental love, not to be spoken of in the same breath as the lust that had responded to Diane's clear invitation with such enthusiasm.

"Good evening, my boy."

The sight of his goddess's father stepping out from a gap in the hedge took him by surprise, jerking him back to the present, and for a moment he stood and gaped as if he couldn't remember the identity of this large, handsome, smiling man, clad in a suit of hairy, greenish tweed.

"G – good evening, sir," he stuttered, a little breathlessly. He felt hot and embarrassed, as if his thoughts were spread out for all to see. Carne appeared to notice nothing, however.

"Well met, my boy," he said with jocular enthusiasm. "We weren't sure if you would come via the road or the cliff path, so I took a chance and covered a bit of both."

"I hope it's OK for me to visit."

"My dear chap, we're delighted to see you – many thanks for your charming letter, by the way. My wife was delighted. I thought this was a wonderful opportunity to waylay you before it gets dark, and show you a marvellous piece of history that all too many people pass by. I'll take a bet with you that no one in your camp has ever heard of Caer Pras."

"No, sir," David said glumly, falling into step beside him. "I guess you're right."

He had no one to blame but himself, he thought, as they crossed the road to where the track led across a field where cows, now presumably retired to the milking shed, had clearly trodden before them. He'd shown all that wide-eyed interest in local history, asked questions, egged the old boy on. Partly, it had to be admitted, to make a good impression, but mainly because at the time – pre his sighting of Trish – there had been room in his mind for such things. Now they were totally irrelevant. Why should he care about this bit of English history he was being dragged to see, when Trish was back at the house?

They crossed another empty, steeply sloping field, before arriving at their destination.

"You'll think it a strange name, no doubt," Carne said, panting a little after scrambling over a ditch and climbing up a bank. "This was once a moat. Caer means 'fort' in the old Cornish language, you see, and Pras means 'meadow'. Hence, the Fort in the Meadow. There's no trace of it left, except this deep circular trench, but the site is interesting, don't you agree? It's the highest point for miles. Look at the view it commands – the whole of the bay is stretched out before you from the Dodman and beyond right over to Fowey; and if you turn around, you have an unrestricted view inland for mile upon mile. And of course from the walls the range of vision would have been even greater."

"Yes." David cleared this throat, conscious that his response had been half-hearted. Quarter-hearted. "How – er – how old was the fort, sir?"

It was an incautious question, eagerly seized upon by Carne. Excavations, he said, had proved that there was a village on the site before the time of the Roman conquest. Pottery shards had been found. Beads. That kind of thing. And over *here* it was suggested that huts had been built – rectangular, made of wood and wattle –

until a later wave of inhabitants had dug the trench and constructed a circular fort made of wood.

Full of enthusiasm which in other times might have ignited an equal interest in his listener, Carne sprang about the site, flinging an arm out in one direction to illustrate the size of the walls, in another to point out the path of the Royalist troops who occupied it briefly, shortly before its total demise; at intervals David nodded defeatedly. How old was Carne, he wondered? In his forties, he guessed. Not so old, anyway, as his own father, who was fifty-five. There was, it had to be admitted, something engaging about all this enthusiasm; on the other hand, wouldn't you think he'd *know* that it was his daughters – well, one of his daughters – that David had come to see? It seemed to show a lack of sensitivity; but then maybe famous men were like that. He'd gathered at their previous meeting that Mr Carne was pretty famous, though he was still rather vague about his activities.

He was conscious as never before of the passing of time. The light was fading fast, and Trish would surely be going out for the evening. Why wouldn't she? A girl like that would have no need to kick her heels at home, waiting for a visitor who didn't arrive until the night was half over. Wasn't there anything he could say or do to make her father get the hell out of here?

On the other hand, the last thing he wanted to do was to alienate Trish's dad. Resignedly he sighed inwardly, and made an effort to ask intelligent questions. The old guy meant well, he reminded himself. He could cheerfully throttle him, but he undoubtedly had the best of intentions.

"Pen loves it up here," Carne said, interrupting his flow of information to stand with his head thrown back, handsome nose pointed skywards as he sniffed the air, hair lifting in the wind. "She would have come with me, but she had schoolwork to do. A geography exam on the morrow. Look at it, boy. Can earth have anything to show more fair?"

David was conscious of a spasm of irritation. Why couldn't he say 'tomorrow' like everyone else? Why did he have to be so theatrical?

Hardly had the word occurred to him when, as if in confirmation and to his acute embarrassment, Carne squared his shoulders, half-raised a hand, and launched into a speech from

Shakespeare's *Richard II*: 'This royal throne of kings, this scepter'd isle' right the way down to 'This blessed plot, this earth, this realm, this England.' The words were delivered in a passionate, throbbing voice and seemed to go on for ever. Holy Cow, David thought, moving uneasily. And they say the British are inhibited!

"Forgive my Celtic fervour," Carne said when the speech was over, turning towards him to clasp his shoulder, tears glinting in his eyes. "I embarrassed you. I'm nothing but an old ham, that's the truth of it. My girls will tell you."

At this engaging confession, David felt a surprising rush of amused sympathy for Carne, even affection. You couldn't help liking the guy, in spite of everything, he thought – as indeed he was to think many times in the future.

"It – it was mighty moving, sir," he said, comfortingly mendacious.

"Well, I always find it so, I must admit. Yes, Pen would have loved it here tonight."

"What about your other daughters?" David asked. "Are they interested in history?"

"Not unduly."

This remark seemed to give no leeway for supplementary questions, at least none that David could think of. He only hoped that his relief was sufficiently concealed when at last the chill of evening and the encroaching darkness prompted his host to suggest turning for home.

There was no sign of any of the daughters as he was shown into the sitting-room where Mrs Carne was listening to the radio and knitting something unspecified, made of khaki wool. She greeted David gravely, her heavy face almost without expression, inclining her head as if she were a queen receiving due homage. Her eyes were like plums, dark and opaque.

David didn't know what to make of her. He should have brought her something, he thought wildly. A present. Candies. Why hadn't he *thought*? It seemed the obvious move now – but then again, he wasn't at all sure that Mrs Carne was the candy type.

"It sure is beautiful around here," he said, feeling that some remark of a social nature was called for. The needles continued to flash as she nodded.

"I have always thought so," she said. "I remember when I was young –"

She said no more, but smiled at him; and he saw that it was a smile of great sweetness, lightening her face so that it was possible to see that she might have been quite pretty, once.

"Come along, come along, I'll take you to see the girls," Mr Carne said, putting a hand on his shoulder. He led him to another room at the end of a passage, and threw open the door. "Enter the Roscarrow Zenana – what the girls get up to here, one can only surmise, but I imagine that eye of newt and toe of frog come into it somewhere."

Trish was sitting beside a popping gas fire, sewing. She looked up and laughed.

"Honestly, Father! You do say such terrible things. What will David think?"

David, at that moment, was incapable of coherent thought of any kind. He couldn't believe that there she was, at last, looking as wonderful as ever in a dark skirt and pink blouse. He couldn't think of anything to say, either; the thoughts and dreams and fantasies he had experienced since their first meeting effectively tied his tongue and he despised himself for his village-idiot grin, his dipping head and mumbled greetings. What would she think of him? No doubt perfectly accustomed to creating havoc in the hearts of every man who looked at her, she seemed amused at his nervousness.

"Take care of him," Carne said as he left the room. "He needs – what do you GIs call it? Rest and Recreation, that's it. He's had his dose of education and now he requires some entertainment. I leave him in your capable hands."

"Did – did you like Caer Plas?"

It was Pen speaking, putting the question in a small, shy voice. He had barely registered her presence; now he turned to see that she was standing beside a table to his left, pausing in the act of stuffing books into a school bag. A sewing machine occupied a space on the other side of the table and an ancient piano stood against one wall. This room was not one he had seen on his last visit; it seemed to be some kind of work room, furnished rather haphazardly with things that looked as if they might have been discarded from other parts of the house. The heavy curtains, already drawn across the windows because of blackout restrictions, were a kind of snuff-brown, with lighter stripes running from top to bottom where they had, perhaps for many years prior to the war, remained in folds.

"Hi, there! Good to see you, Pen." That was better, he thought. He sounded more natural. Maybe even *too* hearty. "It was great – sure is chock-full of history."

"I knew you'd like it." Pen was smiling at him, her eyes shining. She seemed to grow in confidence, and came a little closer. "It's one of my favourite places. I just wish I could have come too, but I've got a geography exam tomorrow."

"So your father told me. That's too bad."

"I don't mind learning about places, but I can't seem to get the hang of winds and currents. I tend to draw arrows at random and hope for the best."

"A policy that will get you nowhere," said Trish, looking up from her sewing with a smile of complicity at David as if some deeper meaning lay behind her words. It was her practice to do this, David was to learn as the weeks went on. "Aren't you going to offer your guest a chair, Pen?"

"Yes, do sit down, David." Pen seemed struck by shyness again, but rallied as he made for the chair opposite Trish. "No, no, not that one," she said, darting forward. "Sorry. The leg tends to fall off. It looks all right, but it isn't. Better have this cane one. It sags a bit but it won't let you down. Sorry," she said again, a little breathlessly."

"That's OK. It's fine. Don't worry."

"Would you like some tea? I was just going to make some, really."

"Bring the seed cake," Trish called after her as, not waiting for a reply, Pen headed towards the door.

Tea and seed cake, David thought. Well, you couldn't say he wasn't experiencing British life in the raw. More importantly, he was alone with Trish; it was maddening, therefore, that he didn't know what to say.

"We must all seem terribly unsophisticated to you," Trish said, coming to his rescue. She gave him one of her provocative smiles. "We've never been anywhere."

"Nor have I. Well, not until I came to England. It's really great here; just a bit different, that's all."

"What sort of things are different?"

For a moment he could think of nothing except the lack of central heating – the lack of warmth generally. It had, for instance, felt clammily cold in the passage, and even in this room no one could call it cosy. This, however, seemed a somewhat negative point to raise, not likely to cement friendship.

"Well," he said after a second's thought, "the automobiles are different, I guess."

It seemed such an inane thing to say; not at all what he had imagined when he fantasised about being alone with Trish. He swallowed with difficulty, took a breath. There must be *something* he could say that was at least halfway intelligent.

"What do you find to do in Porthlivick?" he asked – and could have bitten his tongue out. The question sounded patronising; as if Porthlivick was a hick town with nothing to offer. Which, of course, in a way it was –

"Oh, just ordinary things," she said, without any apparent offence having been taken. "I go into St Jory every day on the bus and work in the library, and sometimes I stay in and go to the pictures, or maybe a dance –"

David didn't so much listen as watch the shape of her mouth, the incredibly beautiful way the edges tilted upwards when she spoke. She was still talking when Pen returned with the tea, breaking the spell.

"Shall I put a record on?" Pen asked when they'd finished eating and drinking. She hadn't, throughout, had much to say; she was, David thought, considerably more subdued than she had been on his previous visit. Maybe it was the thought of the geography exam.

"Great idea," he said. Now that his smile was turned on her, Pen seemed to perk up a little.

"Trish bought a new Spike Jones the other day –"

"For heaven's *sake*, Pen." Trish gave an exasperated laugh. "I'm not in the mood! If anything is calculated to kill conversation stone dead, then it's Spike Jones. Try Glenn Miller."

"You like Glenn Miller?" David asked, as Pen went towards the gramophone.

"Adore him. We always listen to the American Forces show." Trish was silent for a moment, picking up her needlework once more. "Tell me," she went on, flashing a sly and smiling glance in his direction, "were you really enraptured with Caer Plas?"

"On any other occasion I might have been." David's voice was soft. "Tonight I couldn't wait to get here. I – I wasn't sure you'd be at home."

"I had this dress to finish."

"It's pretty."

"I hope it'll be all right. The colour's nice, but this material is difficult to handle. It's part of an old evening dress my mother had years ago. I can't imagine her wearing this colour, can you? I *desperately* needed something new for the dance on Saturday, but didn't have enough coupons to buy anything."

"Gee –" David was speechless at the thought of so much skill and ingenuity. It wasn't something he would have expected from a girl like Trish. It made her seem – well, wholesome and worthwhile, the kind of girl his mother would approve of. He wanted to shower her with beautiful dresses – take her to Jordan Marsh, tell her to choose anything. One day he would; he'd make money, spend it all on her.

The strains of 'Moonlight Serenade' flooded the room, and as if it said all the things he couldn't find the words for, he looked at her. For a moment, a smile as mysterious as the Mona Lisa's on her lips, she returned his look before demurely returning to her sewing.

"Isn't the view wonderful at Caer Plas?" Pen was back again, coming to perch on the chair with the wonky leg. "I don't much like going with Father, though. He will prance about so."

"He's very enthusiastic."

"He's like that about everything. He always has been."

"Oh, he's much worse now," Trish said. "It's all the adulation wot does it – everyone falling over themselves to tell him how marvellous he is."

"What kind of books does he write?" David asked.

"*Did* he write. He doesn't any more, thank heaven, now that he does this broadcasting thing."

"Trish, *honestly!*" Pen was quite pink with outrage. "His books weren't all that bad."

"You hated *The Yearning Heart*. You know you did."

"Only because of that terrible girl Edwina. She yearned too jolly much to my mind. I was *glad* when she died."

"I was hoping they'd all die," Trish said. "You know, like the last act of *Hamlet*. It was one of the soppiest stories I've ever read."

"Don't be so disloyal."

"I'm just being honest. David asked what kind of books Father wrote, so I told him. Mind you, a certain class of batty spinster seems to like him, if the library is anything to go by."

"You ought to be ashamed, Trish."

"Oh, I am, I am." Trish shot another amused, provocative glance in David's direction. "I'm the worst person in the world, bar none. Truly, David, I have all sorts of vices."

"What – what exactly are these broadcasts?" David felt it was time to move the conversation on.

"He gives pep-talks," Trish said, before Pen could answer.

"There's more to them than that. They're *lovely*, David. Honestly. The programme's called *The Glory and the Dream* – that's a quotation from Wordsworth – *Intimations of Immortality*. He just talks about England and how it's worth fighting for, and about all kinds of funny things that happen and how wonderful people are deep down, and how a better world will be built after the war that's worthy of them, not like it was before. He broadcasts on a Friday night, after the six o'clock news, and he has thousands and thousands of listeners. Lots of them write to him."

"Chin up, stiff upper lip." Trish did her best to obey these commands, and collapsed into giggles. "Don't mind us, David. We tease him unmercifully, but really we're awfully proud. The talks are good. Sometimes they're quite funny. Record's stopped, Pen."

"What now, then?"

"Can't think. Let's have a look." Trish got up and flung the dress on the table with an air of subdued excitement, as if she had other, more urgent things on her mind. She swooped over to the gramophone. "What shall it be? Do you like dancing, David?"

"Yeah, I guess so." He hadn't really thought about actually liking or not liking dancing. It was a means to an end, that was all. Then it dawned on him that she might be asking him to dance here, tonight. "Yeah, I like it a lot," he said with more enthusiasm.

"What about this then?" It was the bouncier rhythm of 'Don't Sit Under the Apple Tree' that was the choice this time, and Trish danced over to him, holding out her arms. "Roll up the rug, Pen. Come on, David, let's see what you can do."

This was more than he had hoped for. He felt like whooping with joy as he answered the invitation, suiting his steps to hers, growing in confidence, flinging her away from him, pulling her back. They laughed as they danced. Outwardly it was all good fun; the undercurrents, however, were more exciting. They looked into each other's eyes, so conscious of each other that desire vibrated in the air between them.

David knew, with certainty, that heaven could never be better than this. She was *glorious*, answering every pull of his hand, every movement of his feet with a lightness that seemed intuitive. The silky hair bounced on her shoulders in time to the music. They might, he thought, have been dancing together for years. Didn't it just prove they were meant for each other?

Dimly he was conscious of Pen watching them; and it was she who lifted the arm off the record when it came to an end. Trish and David stood still, laughing, panting, hands on each other's shoulders, still removed from the everyday world all about them.

"That was great," he said. "What now?"

Trish looked over her shoulder to where Pen stood beside the gramophone. David's conscience smote him a little, she looked so thin and forlorn. The sight brought him back to reality.

"Do you like dancing, Pen?" he asked her.

"She doesn't know a foxtrot from a Dashing White Sergeant," Trish said.

"I can do a waltz, and a quickstep," Pen answered, on the defensive.

"Pen's clever," Trish said. "And artistic. But she can't dance."

"I *can!*" Pen had flushed with annoyance.

"Put on 'String of Pearls', there's a pet," Trish said. "I fancy a slow foxtrot, now I think about it."

David knew he should insist on dancing with Pen; common politeness demanded it. But how could he resist Trish, when he had longed for her so? Especially how could he resist holding her and dancing to this wonderfully dreamy, smoochy music. You couldn't jitterbug to 'String of Pearls'; it was cheek to cheek stuff. How could he reject her, even temporarily?

He couldn't, that was the truth of it. The guilt didn't last long, once his arm was around her, her hand clasped in his. He nestled it against his left shoulder, like a small, delicate bird he wanted to keep safe. She smelled sweet and flowery and her cheek was soft. Pen was forgotten – Pen, and all the world outside this room. The war could rage on, bombs rain from the sky; only this had any importance.

He wasn't aware of the door opening. He only knew that the music stopped with shocking abruptness; and when he looked up he saw that there was someone else in the room; a girl dressed in trousers and a plain sweater, her dark hair framing a face that looked distinctly angry.

Caro, he thought. This had to be Caro.

"Sorry to interrupt the charming little snog," she said bitingly. "I simply wanted to enquire what selfish toad hogged all the hot water. I suppose it was our own, home-grown sex-pot." She glared at Trish. "You knew damned well I was going to work late tonight, packing caulis. How could you, Trish? My God, if you did some real, physical work for a change instead of drooping around trying to look like a Hollywood starlet, batting your eyelashes all over the place –"

"Do you *mind*, Caro? We have company. David, meet my charming big sister, Caro. She's not often as revolting as this."

"Hi," David said, feeling at a disadvantage, as if the pursuit Caro had interrupted was far more intimate than a simple dance.

"Such an honour to have you Americans here." Caro's voice was bitingly sarcastic.

"Well, thank you." He knew she didn't mean it, but couldn't think what else to say.

"Caro, may I suggest," Trish said sweetly, "a pan of hot water and a good, stand up wash? It might make you a little nicer to be near."

Caro glared at her for a moment, and then went out, slamming the door and muttering under her breath, the exact wording of her remarks inaudible but clearly not meant to be complimentary.

"That was a pretty rotten thing to do, Trish," Pen said when she had gone. "How would you like it if you'd been working on the land all day –"

"Oh, hark at Miss Goody-Two-Shoes! I've been working all day too, and books can be just as dirty as cauliflowers. I wanted to look my best for David."

She turned and smiled at him, and his heart turned over. This, then, was true happiness. Who would have believed, when stomping about that goddammed field being lectured on English history, that he could have felt like this before the evening ended? He swallowed painfully, his throat suddenly dry.

"I guess I ought to go soon." His voice sounded hoarse.

"There's a full moon out there," Trish said. "I'll show you the cliff path. It's quicker than the road."

"Do take care not to fall over and dash yourself to pieces on the rocks, won't you?" Pen said savagely. "We'd all miss you so much." She flung out of the room and the door banged for the second time in five minutes. David barely noticed it. The only reality was this beautiful girl who stood with her hand in his.

"Trish – oh, Trish" he said. It was the first time he had uttered her name aloud, and it seemed a significant moment. "You're just the loveliest thing. Just the loveliest."

Trish smiled, complacently, provocatively.

"Let's go," she said softly.

\*  \*  \*

Laura kissed Simon on the cheek as she said goodbye; briefly, one friend to another. It was enough to send him bounding up the stairs to the flat in high good humour.

The red light on his Answerphone was flashing. He pressed the playback button and listened to his father's message.

"Sorry I missed you, Dad, but it was in a good cause," he said out loud.

There was a second call, this one totally unexpected, from John Greeley, someone he had worked with on *Commentary*. It was full of his customary obscenities, but boiled down to the information that he'd just flown in from New York, was staying at the Inn on the Park, wanted to see Simon urgently but would be tied up with meetings all the following day, flying to Geneva the day after.

"If you're in before midnight, come over," he said. "I won't be ready to hit the sack for hours yet."

It was still only ten thirty; early by Greeley's standards. He had been on the Editorial Staff of the magazine and had stayed on the staff despite disenchantment. Simon couldn't imagine what the urgency was all about, but it would be interesting to hear all the gossip. Without hesitation he re-set the Answerphone and went out again, down to the street where the pavement was still warm, the walls of buildings discharged their own heat and the air hummed with the beat of a city whose life-blood throbbed more feverishly than ever, now that night had come.

# V

John Greeley had come with a message from the owners of *Commentary*. They wondered how Simon would feel if he were asked to go back. Just if, mind you. Greeley's brief had been to contact him to gauge his reaction, kick the idea around, for it appeared that Russ Hewlett's style of editorship did not, after all, attract undiluted approval. On the contrary; he was on the skids, according to Greeley. Conrad Kern, a man of principles and integrity for whom everyone had great respect, was tipped for the top job, and he it was who had floated the idea that Simon should be appointed as Arts Editor, no less.

Simon was both astonished and elated by the suggestion; and he remained so in the hours that followed, even though he had kept his head with Greeley and stated his terms clearly and unequivocally. It was all far from settled. There was a Board Meeting some time in the future, decisions to be discussed, terms arranged. Meantime he continued to work on his various projects, at times not even certain that he could bear to leave London. For all its dirt and disarray, its dossers in shop doorways, its cold and its damp (well, not now at the beginning of August 1990 with the whole country in the grip of a heat-wave, but most of the time), he had begun to feel settled here. There was something stimulating about living in a foreign capital, about being part of a place but not of it.

And then, of course, there was Laura, still in Paris. Crazy, of course, to make her part of the equation, but somehow he couldn't help it; it was as if some primeval instinct told him that she would be important in his life.

Halfway through the week he had received a postcard from her depicting Raphael's masterpiece, *St Michael Conquering Satan*.

Whether this had any particular significance remained obscure; was he meant to see himself as either of these characters – and if so, which one? He had no idea of the answer to this, but in any case was rather more interested in the message on the obverse:

Apologies all round. Bought *The G. and the D* at Heathrow and re-read with open mind. Still can't say it's my type of read, but I See What You Mean: it packs quite a punch (in a schmaltzy kind of way!). Easy to see why he succeeded in 1940. Perhaps less easy to understand now – but who can account for public taste? (cf. The Edwardian Diary of You Know Who). Life is hectic and I'm exhausted, but enjoyably so. Just off to Versailles. See you.

Pleasant as it was to have his literary judgement at least partially vindicated, it was perhaps the last two words that pleased him most of all.

Meantime there was work to do, the *Soundings* column to collate, the Carne feature to polish. He was less than satisfied with what he had written so far, had rewritten the opening paragraph many times over. So much seemed a mystery. A man who had come from such a lowly background to achieve a first class honours degree at Oxford might surely have been expected to show more evidence of scholarship than Carne had done? And why, having found his *métier* during the war, had he turned his back on it so comprehensively? He must, surely, have known that his novels would never sustain the acclaim of his wartime talks – not, that is, unless they were radically different from the ones he produced pre-war; which they had signally failed to be. It was all rather strange, and frustrating.

It was after midnight, the end of a blazing week and still hot. Simon fetched a cold beer from the fridge, took a long pull, then returned to his desk to stare without enthusiasm at the display screen. The text was too anodyne, too insipid, failing in some elusive way to get over the colourful and entertaining aspect of Carne's character.

Maybe the sound of Carne's voice would inspire him. He slotted the tape into the tape recorder and slumped into one of his decoratively chintzy chairs, beer can in hand, listening once more to the now familiar tones.

It was a seductive voice. Simon, not entirely at home in placing regional accents, nevertheless recognised that though undoubtedly educated, it was not entirely of the establishment but carried a soft, west-country burr that seemed to say that this was a man of the people, a man who could be trusted, a simple man without guile. In this, the first of his 'chats' as he called them, he was musing on the subject of patriotism:

You don't think about it, do you? It's there, like a long-standing marriage; or like the love of a mother for her child, a child for its mother – taken for granted – not spoken of, perhaps, as often as it should be.

And like that mother or that child, we complain about it from time to time. We say our country is unfeeling and unfair.

Often we're right. It isn't perfect. But let a stranger raise a hand against it and we draw together in love and loyalty, full of defensive pride and anger and determination – for this is *our* country, and for all its faults it is beautiful beyond compare, even more dear to our hearts now that it's wounded and bleeding.

Maybe Laura was right, Simon thought; well partly right. It was pretty sentimental stuff. There was, however, a simplicity about it that was moving, given the spirit of the time – and not all the talks were so solemn. Most of them were gently humorous, full of charm. Was that typical of the Celt, he wondered? For Carne had mentioned several times how important his Cornish roots were to him.

What else had been important to him? Shaped him? Simon's eyes fell on the box of papers that still stood in the corner of the room, and he continued to look at it broodingly. The few documents he had extracted so far had been irrelevent, of an entirely domestic nature, interesting only as any trivia from a bygone age takes on significance. He'd been too busy to delve further. Now he strolled over to it thoughtfully, still holding his beer can, the tape running its course. Carne had arrived, Simon noted with part of his mind, at the 'tempered in the fire' passage which he had always found moving. He'd heard it all before; could almost repeat it word for word.

He didn't have a thing to lose by checking the papers more thoroughly. There just might be something that would give him some kind of a slant. Idly, one-handed, he stirred the contents once more, picked out a photograph. Polly as a child – and Laura had been right to describe her as a pretty little girl. She was lovely; she looked like an advertisement for Pears Soap.

He dumped the first few layers of assorted papers on the floor. There were more photographs; Polly again, at the seaside with a woman who must surely be Stella – and he saw he had been right, too, to think that Laura must resemble her grandmother. There was that eager, vital look that he found so attractive.

It spurred him to greater efforts. He put down the beer can and using both hands, stooped to lift out a larger pile of papers, mostly typescripts of newspaper articles. He scanned them quickly, put them on one side. There were yellowed cuttings, too, from all kinds of publications – research material, he guessed. Things torn out of papers because they might be of use one day. He'd done it himself often enough.

His attention was caught by the appearance of a notebook that had been concealed until this moment. It was thin and limp-covered, an exercise book of the kind that could be bought, even now, for only a few pence in Woolworths. It was probably a cash book, he thought; or perhaps a jotter for random ideas that might turn into articles at a later date.

He had not the slightest premonition that it would prove to be a diary. It was far too flimsy, far too temporary a receptacle for the thoughts and doings of a respected journalist; but a diary it was, and he was conscious once more of that magical, instinctive stirring of excitement. The tape fell silent as he turned the pages:

I am not a diarist by instinct or inclination [Stella had written on 4th September 1939] but times change and we must change with them. Returned from Wales on Saturday having left Polly feeding hens in company with the delightful Mrs Evans. It was I who wept – but not, thank God, until safely on the train. It seems a mother's lot to feel guilty, but I think I feel as little guilty as possible under the circumstances. Mrs E. is warm and loving – a little, pink-cheeked, cottage-loaf kind of woman, who is overjoyed to have the privilege of looking after my Poll.

Jane came over on Sat. night ostensibly to ensure I did not brood over the empty nest but in reality to drink my wine. Not entirely true! We both drank my wine. Dutch courage? Maybe. We talked endlessly about the war, and how this time it would be different, with so many more civilians involved. 'Remember Guernica,' Jane said dolefully, and I could only agree that this was undoubtedly the bench-mark we could expect for the future. I felt less bad (as opposed to actually *better*) about Poll. She'll be safe on her Welsh hillside.

J. stayed the night in P's little bed and we listened to the PM's broadcast together yesterday morning. He sounded tired and defeated. We, by contrast, experienced a feeling of relief that the die was cast after so many years of knowing that the Fascist threat loomed ever larger.

The immediate sounding of the air raid warning made the heart beat faster, but nothing happened and it proved to be a false alarm. After the All Clear we walked over to the Kayes' house at Stamford Brook where, as expected, quite a crowd had foregathered, each avidly recounting their own personal emotions at the turn of events; Magda, dramatic in flowing black garments, as if in mourning. Victor, smoking constantly, haggard and urbane. Jock Fraser, as trenchantly witty as ever, plus several friends from the writing world. We laughed a lot but recognised it as gallows humour. Something tells me there will be much of it in the months (years?) to come. The general consensus, at the end of it all, was that we, the scribbling classes, must surely be uniquely empowered to do something useful. At the end of the first day of the war I am not certain what this might turn out to be. Meantime it is, as they said in the last unpleasantness, Business as Usual.

Simon, coming to the end of the first entry, expelled his breath slowly, unable to believe his luck. The book wasn't very thick; whatever her intentions, she couldn't have kept up her diary-writing activities throughout the war, unless there were further volumes, so far undiscovered. He'd have to look through the box again, but he was pretty sure he would have seen them, had any more been present.

Even so, he might have got lucky. She and Carne met early in the war, Laura said; he might, possibly, figure even in this truncated journal. In any case, this was a fascinating document, and one that would interest Laura if she were serious about writing that biography.

He forgot the time and the heat and all the disappointment in his work that had weighed him down earlier, and delightedly read on.

\*   \*   \*

He rang his father the following day.

"You think I should still come?" David asked him. "What does Saddam Hussein think he's up to? Something tells me we could be at war sooner than anyone thinks."

"Saddam can't take on the US, surely? He'll see sense. Anyway, life goes on as normal here."

He caught an echo of Stella's diary. Business as Usual. What else?

"Everyone I know is cancelling flights to Europe –"

"All the more space for you. Say, am I talking to the guy who was in the Normandy landings?"

David chuckled.

"I was only asking. Sure I'm coming. I intend booking a flight on the 28th, if that suits you."

"Suits me fine. I'm dashing up to Scotland mid-month for the beginning of the Edinburgh Festival, but I'll be back by then."

"How's the Carne article progressing?"

"Not bad. I've found some new material that might be helpful."

"Oh?" Surely, Simon thought, he was imagining that sudden note of – what? More personal concern? "What kind of material?"

"The diaries of a woman he is said to have had an *affaire* with."

"How in the world did you get hold of those?"

"Too complicated to explain. I'll tell all when I see you."

"So long as you didn't come by them dishonestly."

"You know me better than that."

David chuckled again.

"Son, I know all about journalists. I grew up with one, remember?"

"Sure I remember. It's kind of funny – this lady was a journalist too. Stella Morel. Did you ever hear the name mentioned in the Carne household?"

"Not that I recall. I was thinking back the other night, trying to remember things that might help you, though, and I suddenly thought of Carne's mother. She was one fierce lady, I can tell you. It's my guess she had a lot of influence on him."

"Yeah, Pen mentioned her."

"I don't know much about psychology, but it wouldn't surprise me if she accounted for a great many things."

"Oh?" Simon's antennae were quivering. "Like what?"

"We-ell –" David drew out the word, considering. "I remember the girls saying that when he was a boy he was scared stiff of her and desperate to win her approval, and that really nothing had changed. That kind of fitted in with what I knew of him. He seemed desperate to succeed, desperate to be liked."

"Yeah, I kind of got that impression too. But –" Simon hesitated, considering in his turn. "It doesn't add up, Dad. Having made an unsuccessful bid for fame with his crappy novels, he then actually hits the jackpot with his wartime talks. *Then* what happens? Just when anyone might think he was on the brink of a starry post-war career, he goes back to crappy novels and no one ever hears of him again. Crazy, isn't it?"

"Mm. Sure seems like it."

"You're certain you never heard of Stella Morel?"

"Positive."

"He never spoke about the life he lived in London?"

"Not to me. But then, why would he?"

"I guess he had good reason for being cagey."

"Maybe he had."

\*    \*    \*

Cagey, David mused, thinking over the conversation afterwards. It wasn't a word he would have thought of using to describe Caleb

Carne. Affable, genial, exhibitionist; unpredictable, even. All these things, perhaps, but never cagey.

Never any sign of it, anyway, in the way he welcomed the young American into his home and into his life. He was almost embarrassingly fulsome, in fact, finding all kinds of things to remark on favourably – David's interest in literature and history; his ability to quote the odd verse of poetry; his manners; even his appearance. All were praised, until he too became the target of the girls' teasing. 'Daddy's little blue-eyed boy' they called him, but he didn't mind it too much. He gave as good as he got, and it made him feel at home, one of the family.

He found so much approval extraordinary, the most extraordinary thing of all being that Carne showed no sign of suspicion that the so called 'walks' that David and Trish took along the cliff and through Dever Woods were made for any purpose other than the serious study of nature.

Well, maybe he was right, David thought now. I sure learned a lot about nature. About Trish's nature, anyway.

She knew all the secluded, hidden spots where they could lie together, locked in each other's arms, exploring all the secret delights of mouth and tongue. She permitted – even encouraged – him to unbutton her dress, to fondle her firm and silky breasts, only occasionally uttering the ritual disclaimers:

"Oh, you mustn't, you mustn't! I don't know what you must think of me, David. What *do* you think of me?"

"I'm crazy about you, you know that."

"Do I? How do I know you're not just using me?"

He remembered one day; early May, he guessed, with the sun making it unseasonably warm. There was a haze of bluebells under the trees and a few late primroses on the bank where he lay on his back, looking up at the cloudless sky through a lattice of fresh green beech leaves. They'd known each other for four weeks; perhaps a little more.

At her question he'd raised his head and looked at her in astonishment.

"*Using* you! For God's sake, Trish, you won't let me anywhere near you!"

"How can you say that?" She'd turned and pushed him back to the ground, kissing him, her sweet-smelling hair dangling down to touch his face until he groaned with desire and pulled her closer.

"You won't let me love you properly," he whispered at last. "Why not, Trish? You say you love me."

She sat up then and primly buttoned her dress, her hair hanging forward so that her face was hidden.

"I'm not that sort of a girl. There are plenty who are, if that's what you want."

"You're crazy!" Half-sitting up, he pulled her to face him. "It's you I love and you I want."

"Well!" She was teasing him now, lips compressed in a smile of mock-severity. "Want will have to be your master, my lad."

He closed his eyes, fighting the desire to shake her, slap her, take her by force; a desire so strong that it frightened him. But all he did was bite his lip, shake his head. He lay down again, not looking at her.

"God knows what makes you tick," he said. "Sometimes I think you don't give a damn about me."

"Oh Davey, sweet Davey." She was cooing at him now in the kind of baby voice she used sometimes, leaning over him once more, covering his face with kisses. "Be nice to your little Trishy who loves you to pieces."

Was that the day they had returned to Roscarrow to find the family gathered in the summerhouse for tea? The day when Carne had cried to heaven to be relieved of his pestilential daughters? It might have been; if not that day, then one very like it, for by this time the summerhouse was open and in use, and tea in this little *maison perchée* a daily ritual, unless it was raining.

It didn't rain much during those weeks; or if it did, he couldn't remember it. Looking back, David could only remember the scene in front of the summerhouse bathed in sunshine, the sea sparkling blue, with gentle waves lapping the rocks and the small, curved beach beneath them. Sometimes they would see distant figures walking along the cliffs on the other side of the cove. They would stop and look down and move on, daunted by the steep cliff and the jagged rocks. And the Carne family would sit and watch them, sipping their tea, privileged and in possession.

"Run along, my children," Trish used to say sweetly, in a voice inaudible to the walkers. "This is a Very Famous Person's hideaway, not meant for the likes of you."

"For," Pen might add, "though you might think this Very Famous Person is doing nothing but scoffing splits and cream, he is in fact thinking Beautiful Thoughts and must not be disturbed under any circumstances."

The boat was in use now too; the *Lady Sal* it was called, though no one seemed to know who Lady Sal was.

"That's what the name was when we bought her," Caro said. "Dad rather liked it, so we kept it; it made him feel piratical and rather rakish."

Caro was the one who loved sailing. The *Lady Sal* was a simple sailing dinghy without a jib, a single-hander which she – more of a loner than her sisters – often took out on her own, now that the evenings were longer. David had seen her on the water from time to time, beating back home, the sea stained pink and gold by the setting sun.

The fine weather held and Pen, thought by the other sisters to be able to twist their father round her little finger, was deputed to use her powers of persuasion to get his permission to forgo church the following Sunday.

"We must take David to Merrick Beach while the sun shines, mustn't we?" she said, using the most effective argument she could think of. "It would be a crying shame if it rained the rest of the summer, and he'd never been there. Oh, do *admit*, father – he must see it!"

Her father so admitted, and the expedition was arranged. David, arriving at the appointed time, was greeted by a flushed and excited Pen, who rushed to let him in.

"Oh, thank *heaven* it's still fine," she said. "I prayed and prayed for good weather – without a lot of hope, really, because I thought God might be a bit miffed we weren't going to church."

"I guess He had other things on his mind," David said, laughing at her in an affectionate kind of way. He looked beyond her to where Trish had emerged from the kitchen. "Hi, honey," he said, on a different note, feeling, as always when confronted by the sight of her, as if a blow had been delivered to his solar plexus.

Since there were no parents about, he kissed her; Pen, unnoticed, watched for a moment before turning suddenly to return to the kitchen where she and Trish were assembling a picnic.

Caro was already down on the beach readying the *Lady Sal* for the short trip. David was pleased at the thought of it, even though it meant that he wouldn't be having Trish to himself. He had always loved sailing; and though the *Lady Sal* was the simplest kind of vessel known to man, still it was better than nothing. It floated.

Anxious to make himself useful, he cast off his tunic and tie, rolled up his sleeves and went to see what help he could offer Caro, but he found, on arrival at the bottom of the steps, that he was too late to be of much practical use; the *Lady Sal* was already rigged.

"I came to help, but you've done everything," he said to Caro.

"Well, it's not exactly a four-masted schooner, is it?" She was smiling at him, more friendly than he had ever known her. Ever since that first encounter with her, he'd felt wary of her, not wholly at ease. He had never, in fact, been in her company without some or all the rest of the family being present. She seemed to him remote and rather solemn, as if her hard physical work sapped her energy. It seemed now that she too had been aware of constraint.

"Look," she said, her face turned away from him as she crouched down to push a coiled rope into a locker. "That first evening you came to the house. I'm sorry I was so rude."

"That's OK. You were tired, I guess."

"Yes, I was." She straightened up and sighed, pushing her hair away from her eyes. "I often am, as a matter of fact."

"You work hard –"

"You're telling me! Sometimes I feel so exhausted I could die. But it's not just that. It's not knowing –"

"What?" David prompted as she lapsed into silence. He was sitting on the bottom step, and after a moment she stepped out of the boat and sat beside him.

"It's Alan," she said. "My sailor. He's in the north Atlantic somewhere and I can't stop worrying about him." She was looking down into the green, waveless depths of the water between the steps and the boat as she spoke, one finger rubbing at the rough stonework. Then she sighed and seemed to shake herself. "Oh David, I'm sorry! I ought to be ashamed of myself. It's no worse for me than anyone else, I know, but I seem to have been worrying for ever. Sometimes I feel I could die from that, too."

"It must be tough for you. I'm sorry, Caro."

"Oh, I'm just having a low spot. I'll be better soon. It's just that he's been in almost from the beginning, and he's had so many near misses and lucky escapes. He was in an open boat for three days once, without food or water."

"That's terrible!"

"Yes, well . . . I'm lucky, really – he was home not too long ago. And now you lot are in it, maybe the war won't last much longer. It can't, can it? Things are going really well in Italy, and the Russians are clearing the Jerries out of the Crimea, and soon there'll be an invasion of Europe. At least, I imagine that's what all the fun and games on Bow Beach is all about. When's it going to be?"

"You imagine they tell the likes of me?" David laughed at the notion.

"No, I suppose not. Look, you won't repeat what I said about Alan, will you? Not to my parents, anyway. Father's forbidden me to see him or write to him or anything."

"But you do, just the same."

"Of course. He writes when he can, care of the Wilkins's, where I work."

"Pen told me Mr Carne has some grudge against his family."

"That's right. Daft, isn't it? None of it has anything to do with Alan and me."

"It was about some election, she said."

Caro opened her mouth as if to elaborate on this, then smiled hopelessly and shook her head.

"There's more to it than that, but it's a long story," she said.

"Well, don't worry. I won't say a word."

She gave him a quick, sideways glance; rather shy and self-conscious. She looked a little like Pen, he thought, but prettier. In fact this new, more relaxed Caro was quite a girl, now that he actually concentrated on her. She had a great figure and a classic kind of beauty – chiselled features seemed the appropriate description. She sure looked a knock-out in a fresh, outdoor-girl kind of way in the navy slacks and white shirt she had donned for this excursion.

"I wonder if you'll be here for my twenty-first?" she said.

"When is it?"

"24th May.

David smiled and shook his head.

"Lap of the gods," he said. "Say, do you enjoy all that hard work you do? Digging and all that? You look kind of frail for it."

"Frail?" She laughed at that. "Oh, I'm a lot tougher than I look. It's OK; well, it's OK this time of the year, anyway. I hate the early mornings in winter."

"Don't blame you. What made you decide to do it?"

Caro laughed.

"Sheer masochism, I expect. No, that's not true. I enjoy it, in a strange kind of way. I like being involved with growing things. Maybe it's because I've got farming genes in my blood. My mother comes from an agricultural background."

"I never knew that. She – doesn't have much to say, does she?"

"No. She's a deep one, is Mother. She likes you, you know."

"Does she?" David felt unexpectedly gratified at this. "You amaze me!"

"You're nice to her. You take the trouble to talk to her."

"My Mom would kill me if I didn't mind my manners. It's kind of difficult, though, when she's so –" he broke off, searching for the word. "So darned *quiet*," he said. "So kind of watchful. I don't know what she's thinking. She looks at me like she's a judge and I'm being tried for some ghastly crime."

"She's harmless, honestly. Sometimes I think she's a throw-back to poor Annie, wife of the unspeakable Caleb –"

"Of 'Life's Work Nobly Done' fame? I know about him. Pen showed me the gravestone."

"There are times when I could shake her, I don't mind telling you. A woman ought to have a mind of her own, not think everything her husband tells her to think. Not that I want her to take against people like Father does, and get blazing mad, and lose control. He can be terrifying!"

"I've never seen him that way."

"Well, take it from me, it's no exaggeration. Still, you needn't worry. As far as he's concerned, you can do no wrong."

"I can't imagine why," David said humbly.

"Well –" Caro was smiling at him, teasing him a little. "Foreigners have a certain glamour for us all, I suppose. And then you're interested in history and have a retentive memory for poetry, as well as looking like a young Apollo, golden-haired, standing dreaming on the verge of strife –"

"*What?*" David looked at her, appalled, and she laughed.

"Don't say I've quoted something you don't know! That's Mrs Cornford on Rupert Brooke."

"I don't think I like it."

"Well, it all helps. Father's rather like that," she went on. "He gets runs on people."

David was at a loss to know what to say to this. It sounded fairly hopeful for his relationship with Trish, he thought, but on the other hand there was a rather temporary implication as if Mr Carne, having run on him, might just as easily run off.

"He – he's always very nice to me," he said. "I'm grateful."

"Mm." Caro tilted her head to look at him, teasing him further. "Who knows how long it will last? Now you mention it, I've seen him looking at you sometimes when you come back with Trish. Be warned, if he thinks you're playing fast and loose, he just might have a shot-gun at the ready. What *do* you two get up to, by the way?"

"Very little, as it happens."

For a moment Caro seemed to study him, still amused.

"I believe you," she said at last. "Poor little doughboy!"

She reached up and touched his cheek, a light, mocking pat, and for a moment – just for a moment – David felt a shiver of regret, a stirring of attraction; something told him she was more generous with her Alan than Trish was with him. But how disloyal could he get? For here was Trish at last, and she looked like an angel in a pink and white skirt and a thin white sweater that showed every curve. She carried a tartan rug, several towels, swimming gear. Pen followed behind with two baskets of food.

"'They went away for a year and a day, to the land where the Bong-tree grows,'" she shouted excitedly.

David, standing up, laughed at her. What a kid! Always flinging quotations at him and hugging herself when he could cap them, as if it united the two of them in a conspiracy against the others.

"'And there in a wood, a piggy-wig stood –'"

"Oh, do shut up," Trish said plaintively, reaching the bottom. "You two make me sick. Here, help me with these. It's much too cold for swimming really, but we might want to sunbathe. Isn't it the most glorious day in the whole world?"

"Glorious," David agreed, looking into her eyes and forgetting all about Bong-trees and piggy-wigs. "Beautiful," he added on a different note. It was clear to all that this was not a comment on the weather, and Trish rewarded him with a dazzling smile.

The breeze was light, the waves scarcely more than ripples on the surface of the sea. For a moment or two there was mild disorder as the boat made leeway, the sail flapping a little before filling. David longed to be at the helm of a *proper* sailing boat, his hand on the tiller, but when he looked at Trish he had no regrets. He edged a little closer to her.

"Hey," he said softly, knowing the others couldn't hear. "Did I tell you lately that I love you?"

She abandoned her air of remote detachment and turned to give him the kind of small, teasing, nose-wrinkling smile that drove him wild.

"Not lately, no."

"Well, you don't need to be told."

"Sure you don't prefer the ship's captain? You looked very friendly when we came down the steps."

"'Friendly' sums it up, I guess. You wouldn't want us to be unfriendly, would you?"

"I guess not." Trish's speech had become peppered with Americanisms lately, much to Pen's annoyance. She considered it gross affectation. "Just remember who loves you."

"Oh, Trish." David's heart, suddenly, was too full for words. He felt sorry for all the other GIs – those on duty, or ambling about the village, or making love to other, lesser girls. There was no one like Trish.

"Did you score?" Chuck invariably asked him when he got back to camp. Sometimes he lied in reply; sometimes he merely looked inscrutable, made some kind of a crack. At moments like this he didn't care. He was, here and now, wildly and gloriously happy, certain that the love he felt would last for ever, that the war was nearly over, that he would come through unscathed and would return to sweep Trish off her feet and back to Hannville.

There was never a more beautiful day. The sun was shining and there were only the smallest, most unthreatening clouds in the sky. Here, on the water, it seemed as if they were bathed in brilliance, small waves refracting the light into a million dazzling rays.

He would remember this always, he thought; and as he turned his head to look back at Roscarrow Beach and the rocky cliffs, he saw that Pen was looking at him. He acknowledged the look with a smile, but she turned away quickly, not smiling in response.

Had he done something – said something – to hurt her? If so, he couldn't remember it. He liked the kid, liked her a lot. She was bright and funny, and though she'd never have Trish's looks she'd probably be OK once she grew up and filled out and did something about her hair.

They had the cove to themselves, they found on arrival. It was an idyllic place – the loveliest beach for miles around, Trish told him. The pale, fine sand bore a drift of shells and pebbles and shiny seaweed. The blue-grey, slatey rocks jutting from the cliffs, had formed themselves into arches and spires and were hollowed into caves. They found a suitable one to use as a base and unloaded the dinghy, having first secured it to a convenient outcrop.

Trish dropped her various burdens and slumped down, leaning against a rock, face lifted to the sun.

"Bliss," she murmured

"What are we going to do?" Pen asked, engaged in taking off her canvas tennis shoes.

"*Do*? What do you mean, *do*?" Trish asked. "Don't be so damned energetic, child. That's the beauty of beaches, you don't have to do anything. You can just *be*."

"What do you want to do, Pen?" David asked.

"Well, explore, of course! There are all sorts of nooks and crannies here."

"The tide's coming in," Trish objected. "You could get cut off."

"Actually, it's on the turn."

"That's true," Caro confirmed. "Look, you can see it's gone down even since we've been here."

"Come on then, Caro," Pen pleaded. "Let's go and climb a bit."

"Not now. I want to flop. This is my one day of rest, remember."

"Gosh, you're so boring!"

"I'll come with you, Pen." David, having sat down beside Trish, got up again. Trish opened her eyes and sat up straight."

"Don't be silly, David. You don't have to."

"I'm curious to see what's round these rocks." And it would please Pen, he thought. It might make up for whatever it was he had done to offend her.

"You'd better roll up your trousers, then," Pen said. "There'll be pools."

She was right, David found; and in the pools were tiny, flickering fish, and sea urchins, and delicately coloured shells. Together he and Pen peered into them, enthralled with the life they could see within the shallow depths.

They wandered on, out of sight now of the others, the damp sand cool under their feet and between their toes. They explored a cave and tried its echo, and Pen was amused by David who hid from her in a crevasse and pretended, in a suitable voice, to be the ghost of Pop-eye, abandoned by pirates.

He was glad to hear the laughter, glad that she was enjoying herself. Maybe, he thought, he'd imagined the reproach in that look.

"We'd better get back," he said at last, thinking of Trish.

"I suppose we'd better." Pen sighed as she stepped across a pool that lay in their path. "Thanks for coming with me, David. It's not much fun on your own."

"It's been great," he said. "Honestly. I've had a ball."

"A ball!" Pen laughed at him. "Gosh, you Americans do say funny things."

"Do we? Well, let me put it this way. Gosh, I've had the most *mah*-vellous time!"

She didn't laugh, but looked at him with huge, searching eyes before turning to edge round a rock that stood in their way.

"Honestly?" she asked after a moment, looking over her shoulder to where he followed close behind her.

"Honestly. You're good company, Pen."

For a moment she clung to the rock without moving, her small face turned towards him and illumined with joy.

"So are you," she said. "I'll remember today for ever and ever."

Holy Cow, David thought, the penny dropping at last. The kid's got a crush on me. Embarrassed, but more for her than for himself, he looked down as if in search of a more secure foothold. By the time he looked up she was out of sight around the rock.

Trish, when he emerged through the archway of rocks into the first little beach where they had based themselves, was standing up and looking, with hand shading eyes, in the direction in which she might expect them to appear. She, it was clear, was not pleased.

"You've taken your time," she said accusingly, when they were within earshot. "We thought you'd drowned, didn't we, Caro?"

"I didn't," said Caro. She was laying a small cloth on a flat rock, and putting food of various kinds upon it; lettuce and tomatoes and hard-boiled eggs. "I thought they were exploring."

"We were." David put an arm around Trish and gave her a casual, placatory kiss. "It was terrific. You should have come, honey."

"It'll be much better after we've eaten, when the tide is out a bit further. That's when I was going to take you."

"You can take me again. I don't mind."

"I'll see if I feel like it."

Trish pulled away from him, stony-faced and David couldn't avoid the sight of Pen, exasperated, raising her eyes to heaven. He wished, fervently, that he hadn't seen that look on her face earlier, the look that revealed so much more than she must have intended. It made him feel uncomfortable, self-conscious. Perhaps, after all, he'd been mistaken; he certainly hoped so.

In spite of all the talk of food rationing, with the help of the products from Caro's market garden the girls had put together a satisfying spread. David had developed quite a taste for Mrs Carne's Cornish pasties, and ate heartily; short of meat they might be, but they were tasty just the same.

Trish remained a little cool throughout the meal, but though she pretended petulance for a few minutes when at last they were alone together, it was forgotten once he took her in his arms. There were times when he suspected that she engineered small tiffs simply to enjoy the kissing and making-up.

They had their arms around each other's waists when they returned to the picnic place. Pen and Caro were lying on their stomachs playing some complicated game with pebbles and squares drawn in the sand.

"I'd forgotten that," Trish said, collapsing beside them. "We used to do it when we were kids, David. Look, I'll teach you. It's a sort of complicated naughts and crosses."

Amicably, light-heartedly, they played the game; and the afternoon drifted on. Caro and Pen actually braved the cold to have a brief swim, but the others stayed on the shore – Trish through indolence, David because he had nothing suitable to wear. Full of contentment he lay on the sand beside her, raising himself on his elbow to brush her nose with a seagull's feather.

"You're beautiful," he said. "Wouldn't this be great if it was a desert island, just you and me?"

"You didn't seem to want to be with me this morning." Trish, it seemed, hadn't entirely forgotten his earlier desertion. "Honestly, I can't imagine why you think you have to obey Pen's slightest whim."

David laughed.

"What do you mean? I do no such thing."

"Well, why go off with her like that? You might have known I'd want to take you."

"You could have come. She was so keen, Trish – it seemed a shame not to let her have her way. It was no big deal. She's not much more than a kid, after all."

"Hm." She gave him a long, speculative look, but said no more since the others were running, shivering, up the beach towards them.

The warmth of early summer faded, and the sea turned to silver. It was, they all agreed, time to go home. They didn't talk much but sat quietly as the *Lady Sal* slap-slapped her way through the waves.

"The end of a perfect day," Pen said solemnly, as they tacked homewards, turning into the lea of the headland.

"No thanks to you," Trish said sharply, shattering what had seemed a contented silence. "How do you think David felt, being monopolised by you for hours on end?"

"Hey, that's not fair, Trish," David protested. She took no notice.

"He only went with you out of the goodness of his heart, you know, Pen. He thought you were pathetic – a little kid with no one to play with."

"You've got it wrong, Trish. I didn't say that."

"Oh, yes you did! You said she wasn't any more than a kid and that you felt sorry for her."

"I said nothing of the sort!" He looked towards Pen and saw her face was blank with pain, her eyes huge. "Trish is wrong, Pen. I enjoyed exploring with you. You know I did."

Pen went on looking at him, not speaking.

"Don't take any notice of her, Pen," Caro said. "She's just jealous."

"Shut up, Caro. It's nothing to do with you." Trish's cheeks had flamed scarlet.

"Well, lay off Pen, then, and don't let David see you for the selfish little bitch you are."

"Hey, c'mon, all of you. It's been a great day. Don't spoil it."

"You might have the decency to defend me, David," Trish snapped. David looked at her unhappily.

"There wasn't any call to hurt Pen," he said.

They were coming into the steps at Roscarrow now, and without saying more, David jumped ashore, fended the dinghy off the rocks and tied it up. Their belongings were handed over to him in silence, and Trish, her face flushed with anger, ran up the steps without a glance in his direction.

"I'll stay and help Caro," David called to her retreating figure, knowing how much stowing away was involved even with the smallest sailing dinghy.

"No," Pen said. "You go. I'll stay."

"Pen." He reached out and held her arm. "I don't know what got into Trish. We had fun, didn't we?"

Pen's head was bent, and her only reply was a quick, sideways glance, less a smile than a twitch of the lips. David let go her arm and hovered uncertainly for a moment.

"Are you OK, Caro?" he asked. "Can't I help?"

"You'd better go and mend fences," Caro said, looking as if the whole uncomfortable incident had amused her.

He picked up the food baskets, his shoes and his socks, and with the travelling rug over his arm climbed the steps, uneasily aware that he would have to run the gauntlet of the summerhouse. The Carne parents would surely have taken their accustomed places there by this time and must have guessed by Trish's manner that all was not sweetness and light, even if she had said nothing.

If they had, they weren't letting on, perhaps because there was a third person sitting with them – an old lady with a face like granite, wearing a dome-like hat with a small brim, embellished with fruit.

"Ah, there you are, my boy!" Caleb Carne's tone was as genial as ever, but he seemed more subdued. "I don't think you've met my mother. Come and be introduced."

"I'm rather sandy, sir. Maybe I should just take these things into the house and wash up." He smiled and nodded at the old lady to show his good intentions, however – a greeting that was returned by a basilisk stare.

"So you're the American I've heard so much about," she said.

"Trish's friend." Carne's voice, determinedly pleasant, seemed to David to be carrying a warning, as if he were trying to convey some kind of admonition to his mother, some stricture concerning kindness to the stranger in their midst. She chose to ignore it, however.

"They've done a lot of harm, the Americans," she said accusingly.

"They're doing a great deal of good in Italy, mother," said Mr Carne, still relentlessly cheerful.

"That's as may be. I'm talking about Porthlivick."

"Well, we're very fond of David. He's quite one of the family. You'd better run along, my boy, and make yourself respectable. Come back for some tea – and tell Trish to hurry down," he called after David as after another polite smile he continued on his way. "Her grandmother's anxious to see her."

There was no sign of Trish as he entered the house through the open front door. He went to the kitchen, putting down the baskets on the scrubbed table and dropping the rug over a chair. He washed at the kitchen sink, put on his socks and shoes, rolled down his trousers; and still there was no sight or sound of her.

He looked into the back sitting-room, and the front parlour, but drew a blank. Standing at the foot of the wide stairs, he called to her and it seemed to him that there was some muffled sound in response.

"Trish, you up there?" He went up a step or two. Upstairs was unknown territory, definitely off-limits. "Are you coming down?"

She had to be up there. He could definitely hear something. He ventured further, calling cautiously at intervals as he did so.

She was crying, small gasping sobs, and he followed the sound of them until he arrived at her bedroom where he found her lying on the bed, weeping into her pillow. The sight was more than he could bear.

"Aw, Trish, honey," he said, crossing the floor swiftly to sit on the bed beside her and attempting to pull her into his arms. "Easy, now. What is it? Don't cry like that. Please don't cry."

"Go away! I look horrible, and you'll hate me. You hate me anyway –"

"I don't! How could I? You know I love you."

"No you don't." She sat up, groped in a drawer in a bedside cabinet, and found a handkerchief with which she proceeded to scrub her eyes. "You think I'm silly and stupid, and you only want me for One Thing. You'd rather be with Pen, talking about books and poetry and stuff."

"You know that's not true."

"Isn't it, David? Isn't it? How can I trust you? I don't feel sure of anything any more! You Americans are all the same, everyone says so. We might as well finish now."

"Finish? You and me?" The unhappiness he had felt earlier was swept away in a rush of fear. Surely this wasn't the end? He felt as if he were fighting for his life. "I guess if you don't know now how much I love you, then you never will. I've never felt like this before, Trish."

"You can say such hurtful things sometimes."

"I never want to hurt you."

"That's what you *say!*"

"You mustn't be so sensitive. I'm crazy about you, Trish. There'll never be any other girl for me."

"You'll go away and forget me."

"I've got to go away, I know, but I'll be back. I want to marry you."

"You do?" Trish removed the handkerchief from her eyes. "Oh, Davey, I do love you so. You are being honest with me, aren't you? Cross your heart?" It was the baby voice once more. David had never been more thankful to hear anything. He reached out for her again, and this time she didn't pull away.

"Cross my heart," he whispered.

"Oh, Davey!" She lifted her mouth to his. "I can't bear it when we quarrel."

"Then don't let's."

"We won't. Not ever again."

They kissed; but mindful of their situation, David brought it to an end more rapidly than usual.

"We'll get hell if we're found like this," he said, reluctantly standing up. "You'd better get straightened up and come downstairs.

Your father told me your grandmother wanted to see you."

Trish pulled a face.

"I know just what she'll say. She'll go on and on about how only cheap girls go out with Americans."

"Say, that's not fair!"

"She doesn't like me."

"I didn't get the impression she was crazy about me, either. I didn't realise I was quite so detestable, though. Still, we ought to go –"

"Go on, then," she said resignedly. "Tell them I'm changing my dress and I'll be there in a minute. And you do mean it, don't you? We won't quarrel again, will we?"

"Not if I have anything to do with it."

*Had* they quarrelled? He pondered the question as he did what he was told and made his way back to the summerhouse, passing Pen and Caro on their way up. He supposed maybe they had; he'd certainly felt annoyance at the way she had misrepresented his words to Pen who seemed such a vulnerable little thing, so undeserving of hurt. Trish had been in the wrong there.

Then how come he'd ended up feeling like the guilty party? He shook his head, defeated by it all, but not caring too much just so long as the status quo had been restored.

Just so long as Trish still loved him.

# VI

To say that Laura thought constantly of Simon during her week in Paris would be overstating the case, for there were far too many other calls upon her attention for such self-indulgence. She was, it was true, only one quarter of the team entrusted with the task of introducing twenty senior students to the artistic and theatrical delights of the city, but even so constant vigilance was required.

Her charges were, on the whole, pleasant, intelligent and well-behaved young adults whose company she enjoyed; but inevitably there were problems. One individual, an inveterate dreamer, was constantly late. Another lost things, including her passport, and – eventually – herself, involving hours of worry and tedious interviews with the gendarmerie. Yet another had contrived to miss the bus at Fontainebleau so that he could spend more time beneath the trees with a delicious Brigitte Bardot look-alike. Several pairs were conducting love affairs of varied seriousness, and there had been a violent argument one night between two of the girls, the reason for which had never become clear though Laura suspected double-dealing on the part of one particular masculine charmer; all this in addition to the usual logistical problems inherent in getting a party of twenty to the right place at the right time.

Even when the students were in bed – hopefully their own – there was little opportunity for brooding, since the four custodians – one male, three female – tended to relax for a few moments of idle, uninhibited chat before staggering off to their own, much-needed rest.

Still there were times when the thought of Simon would come

unbidden to her mind; times when she was aware of a vague regret that they weren't together in this most magical of cities that Stella had ensured she knew so well. Times when a casual glimpse of a total stranger would remind her of the way he walked, the way he looked.

She didn't know quite what it was about him. He was tallish, slim, well put-together. He looked good in the casual kind of clothes he favoured, and as she had remarked that first time she met him, he had a nice, intelligent, amusing kind of face.

It wasn't that, though. Or not altogether. She couldn't, she supposed, ever be attracted to someone who wasn't intelligent and who hadn't the potential to be amusing. (Niceness was another thing altogether. She had gone overboard for one or two who were positively nasty; or at least, had ultimately proved to be so despite an initial ability to charm.)

What was it, then? Sex, she supposed. Chemistry. The chance arrangement of eyes and nose and mouth that for some reason appealed to her more than any she had seen for a long time. But there was more to it than that. Undoubtedly niceness had something to do with it; the feeling that here was a decent man who wouldn't exploit her or patronise her or dismiss her views and interests as being of less importance than his own. But, at the same time, he seemed a man she could respect, with his own strength and convictions.

She could do worse, she thought as she lay in her lonely bed; and immediately was furious with herself. It was the sort of thing her mother would say – a remark redolent of Victorian values, implying that no woman was complete without a husband of some kind – any kind being better than none at all. What utter rubbish, she told herself scornfully. A man might be necessary for sex – and for her, that was a real necessity; but she and her two female colleagues (two of whom were divorced, one single), without the company of the solitary male who had gone that night to visit a friend, had decided over a late-night bottle of wine that amiable though he was, his absence was a positive relief. Women usually had a far better time in the company of other women. Girl friends, they had decided – only very slightly drunk – were the ones that stuck by you, rejoiced in good times, comforted in bad. Were, in fact, more often *there* for you than the man in your life, who was most likely still at the office, or pub, or on the golf course.

"What about children?" Penny had asked. Penny was a mere babe of twenty-four, and rather attracted to the absent male.

Oh well, that was a bit different, they had agreed. Although then again, men weren't that indispensable, once they had performed their one, necessary function. The nuclear family was the exception these days, rather than the rule. A thing of the past.

Not to Simon. Laura knew with total certainty, even though the subject was one that had never been remotely approached with him, let alone discussed. This certainty made her the more wary of him, the more suspicious that he was not entirely a stranger to Victorian values himself beneath that right-on, politically correct exterior.

On the other hand, she was twenty-eight. Time was passing. One day she wanted children; wanted them very much. And it would be lovely if she could find someone to have them with who was admirable as well as sexy –

Oh, shut *up*! she ordered herself crossly. Apart from being guilty of thinking like her mother, she was jumping the gun, making assumptions she had no right to make, behaving as stupidly as some of the teenagers in her care. When she got back she'd play it cool. Leave it a few days before phoning. Be casual. Or was that merely playing teenage games?

Life, she decided, got no easier with age.

\* \* \*

Simon was contented. Laura was there at last, under his roof, sitting on his carpet, engrossed in her grandmother's diary:

It is as well I am not of an insecure disposition [Stella had written on 10th December 1939] since it has become abundantly clear that there is, even in the humblest capacity, no job for the likes of me; no job, that is, which can possibly be described as of national importance.

Even journalism suffers. Any critical appraisal of the government or its conduct of the war is generally deemed to be criminally unpatriotic these days, and in any case, the papers (both local and national) have shrunk as to be almost invisible. Even the weather forecast has disappeared, apparently regarded now as a military secret. So, guiltily frivolous but impelled by the sad fact that a woman must eat, I have resorted to *Lady Fair* (encouraged by Jane) and write things like 'Hats, and How to Buy Them', 'Make Friends with Mother-in-Law', 'Watch These Women!' etc., etc., and await the call from the Min. of Information who have promised to let me know once they feel there is a *niche* for me – their words, not mine! It makes me feel like a plaster bust!

To salve my conscience and to make me feel a little less useless, I am attending a first-aid course and have signed up to drive an ambulance should the expected air raids come to pass.

Today I received a letter from Mrs Evans suggesting that I spend Christmas with them. She is such a kind soul, and I wrote back immediately to accept the invitation. She says that Polly is happy and is eating and sleeping well, which is good news. Can't wait to see her. It will be wonderful to get out of London for Christmas. Have had no word about the Kayes' New Year's Eve party – normally such a feature of the festive season – but shall be surprised if a thing like a war makes them cancel. Magda is being dramatically brave and resolute as only Magda can be, and talks a great deal about Not Giving Way, which I rather think means that the party is on.

Sunday, 7th January 1940

A long lapse since my last entry, owing to lack of time. Much writing of sundry pot-boiling articles but spirits lifted immeasurably by commission from the *Gazette*, the first for ages – hooray! Social life also very active during the period leading up to Christmas. The general aim seems to be to make it a good one – who knows what the next might bring?

No raids yet. Many evacuees have returned to London, but I cannot think it wise. Besides, Polly is clearly ten times happier and healthier in the country. The Evanses adore her and would really hate to lose her. They are the kindest of people.

The Kayes' party went ahead as usual, enlivened by visit from an irate Air Raid Warden who said they had infringed the black-out regulations. Their lights were visible from one end of the street to the other, he maintained – adding 'and probably in Berchtesgaden as well' which seemed excessive, as the alleged blaze turned out to be one dim light in a little-used bathroom.

Magda instantly, and I feel sure erroneously, cast all blame on the hired help. 'The Butler Did It,' said a voice in my ear, and I turned to find that the voice belonged to someone I hadn't met before; a handsome looking devil who turned out to be none other than Caleb Carne, the author of a few saccharine novels, one of which I had the somewhat dubious pleasure of reviewing in the *Gazette*. I was not, as I recall, kind. Fortunately we were able to enjoy a pleasant conversation before we realised each other's identity.

Don't suppose I shall see him again, but despite his novels and my review, we warmed to each other. He's married, of course. They always are.

Sunday, 28th January

The date bears out my original contention that I am no diarist. The days go by so quickly there just isn't enough time. I always think I'll write a review of the week on a Sunday, but more often than not I have something else to do, or even if I don't I am like Clover in *What Katy Did* and can only say 'Forget What Did'.

Much snow has fallen, which naturally has turned to icy slush and walking anywhere is most unpleasant especially in the black-out. Polly writes that she has been 'tobogging' with Mr Evans and sounds in high spirits. They are so good to her. How much cleaner and more fun the snow is in the country.

Jane has been and gone and joined the NAAFI in a high-falutin' executive capacity. Except for ambulance duties (which so far have amounted to standing around and drinking endless cups of tea) I am reluctant to join anything much because of Polly. Apart from any considerations re cobblers and lasts, I can't submit myself to any organisation which might prevent me (a) going to see her or (b) having her home if the opportunity arises. If things go on like this, with no raids and nothing happening, I shall definitely go to Wales and bring her home for the Easter holidays.

Jane looks good in her uniform and is thrilled to have given up writing the cookery notes in *Lady Fair*. 'Fifty ways with a Carrot' cannot, she says, compete with devising nutritious meals for our fighting forces – and who can disagree? Everyone wants to find something useful to do. Caleb Carne is in the same position. He writes a 'Country Column' for the *Herald* and various things for the West Country papers, but never ceases to badger the Min. of Inf. for something worthwhile. He seems to have given up on the novels in despair. I was wrong, it will be readily seen, when I hazarded the guess that I would never clap eyes on him after the Kayes' party. He phoned a week later and we went out to dinner (behaviour roundly condemned, no doubt rightly, by Mrs Smiley each week on the back page of *Lady Fair*, the publication to whom we all owe so much. She holds firm views on women who accept invitations from married men!).

He is of all men the most infuriating; cocksure, childish, bumptious, arrogant and presumptuous. He is also charming, amusing, and tender, with the most endearing way of lighting up with enthusiasm when something takes his fancy. There are so many grey men. Cal is delightfully rainbow-hued, yet he is, in some way I can't quite fathom, vulnerable.

He touches my heart, despite the unspeakable books. How could he have written them? I now honestly believe him to have done so to please his mother who seems to be regarded by him with a mixture of love and loathing. Is this possible? And did they please her? Perhaps they did, but they certainly failed to please anyone else. Poor Cal!

Simon, pretending absorption in the papers on his desk, covertly watched Laura as she read. The relief of having her here, under his roof, was enormous. During the week she had been in France he had been resigned to her absence; it was only after Saturday, when he knew she was due to return, that the wait for her call had seemed interminable. He had cursed himself for not securing her phone number before she left. There were several L. Rossis in the book, but none in Notting Hill that he could see. Twice he had almost called Polly – had persuaded himself that this would be perfectly legitimate. The discovery of the diary must surely mean that he owed her a dinner which would be more than a price worth paying if it meant he could secure Laura's number.

Only the instinctive suspicion that this course of action might dish him with Laura altogether had stayed his hand; and he was glad now that it had, for today, Tuesday, she had phoned, and now, at four thirty in the afternoon, was sitting reading while he ostensibly wrote his New York column.

She seemed totally engrossed in her grandmother's diary, head resting on her hand, hair hiding her face, oblivious both to him and to the sudden shower that hurled raindrops against the windows. The heatwave had broken at last, the cooler weather a positive relief.

She looked up at him when she came to the end of the page.

"It seems intrusive," she said unhappily.

"Why do people write diaries?" Simon abandoned his pretence of work and left his desk to come and hang over the back of her chair. "I guess they must feel that eventually other eyes will see them."

"Is there any more?" Laura turned to the last page. "This finishes in September 1940."

"That seems to be it. Like she says, she's not a diarist by nature and clearly life and work became too much. Look, you can see how scrappy the last entries are. In July there's simply this: 'Unexpected approach by War Office. Something useful to do at last!' I suppose that was when she was asked to do this SOE thing. Pity there aren't any details."

"She wrote all about that period after the war in the notes I have at home. Nothing about Carne, though."

"Pity," Simon said again. "Look, the entire last half of August is simply 'Raids on East End. St Giles, Cripplegate bombed. Thank God I left Polly in Wales!' And so it goes on until the final entry on 30th September where she lets herself go a bit more."

Went with C. to visit old friend of his, (a Brigadier no less) now on embarkation leave [she had written]. Entire experience a complete disaster! We were decanted at Camden Town in mid-raid and told to wait for further train which never arrived.

Sundry crashes and bangs from above persuaded us to stay for what seemed hours and hours, on platform already crowded with shelterers. Hideous night made even worse by ghastly, raddled woman in knitted blue bonnet who insisted on giving us a blow by blow account of her particular 'incident' several times over and then encouraged us to join in the singing of *Roll out the Barrel* and sundry other ditties – an invitation that failed to appeal, either to us or to the rest of the gathered horde. Much bad language and ill-feeling resulted, causing me to wonder where Good Old Cockney Humour, so honoured in myth and legend, is hiding itself these days. How people can endure this kind of experience night after night passes belief; but they do.

"And that's really all?" Laura asked. "There isn't another volume in that box?"

"Not that I can find."

"It's not surprising. Her work with SOE kept her at it all hours of the day and night. It was a pretty stressful job. She got very emotionally involved with agents in the field – she writes about it in her notes."

"Laura, you *have* to write that book! I warn you – if you don't, I will. Hey, I must tell you – there's a funny postscript to that last entry. You've never heard Carne's tape, have you?" Laura shook her head. "Listen to this, then." He went to the other side of the room to run the tape back, then forward again. "This is it," he said softly, as the scratchy, squawky gabble gave way to Carne's voice:

Let me tell you about a woman I met the other night [he began]. A splendid, regal woman whose territory amounted to a square foot of railway platform, whose throne was an eiderdown of such antiquity that its original colour was debatable. I thought it was probably pink but my companion came down heavily on the side of puce.

It's true this queen didn't wear a crown, unless she was concealing one under her blue woolly hat, but there was no doubting her royal status. She told us that her house, bombed only the night before, had been a palace. She was modest about it. 'A little palace,' was how she described it, with roses on the wallpaper, and a red carpet she'd only just finished paying for on the never-never. There was a china dog on the mantelpiece, she told me, that she'd won on the pier at Southend at a hoop-la stall; and a vase which proclaimed that it was a Present from Clacton, and a picture of the two princesses with a little dog. All gone. All gone.

The repetition of these last words gave his colloquy a dying fall; but his voice took on a different, more cheerful tone as he continued: 'This queen decreed that we should sing; and sing we did, mutterings of discontent notwithstanding . . .'

He chatted on for another ten minutes, describing with mild but appealing humour this 'queen's' authoritarian rule, the anarchic fury of those who wanted to sleep, the barracking from the ranks, and ended – as his talks often did – with a tribute to the human spirit.

Laura was laughing.

"There you are," she said. "Proof, if proof were needed, that his little chats are really a load of bullshit, however well phrased. What a shyster!"

"He doesn't deny they were propaganda."

"His voice is beguiling, I'll say that for him. You know, I think Stella must have had a great influence on him, don't you? Their patterns of speech are very similar – which is odd when you think of the novels."

"Maybe she wrote them."

"What?" Laura was amused by the suggestion. "And let him get all the credit? You didn't know Stella! She was at one with Dr Johnson – no man but a blockhead ever wrote except for money! Seriously, though, her work was everything to her. It would have been against her principles to let anyone else pass it off as his own."

"She loved him."

"Well, yes; there's no doubt of that, is there? But she still wouldn't have – *coddled* him in that way. She was a feminist, for God's sake. And she was proud of her work."

"It wasn't a serious suggestion. Would you like some coffee?"

"Love some. Thanks." She returned to the diary as he went to the kitchen, continuing where she left off. "It was a funny sort of love, wasn't it?" she said when he came back carrying two mugs. "How old was she then? Thirty something." She screwed up her face in thought as she took the coffee from him, making the calculation. "Thirty-four, I think."

"That's what I made it. And he must have been forty-five. Why was it funny? Maybe all kinds of love are funny to someone else."

"She sounds oddly maternal, don't you think? Considering she was over ten years younger than he was."

"She was the successful one, don't forget – and I'm willing to bet she was far more sophisticated. She'd been around, lived in Paris, been to Spain – seen sides of life that Carne never had. Maybe she felt a little superior."

"Who wouldn't? It must have been a bit of a setback when she found out he was the author of those appalling books. I really do find the whole thing incomprehensible, don't you?"

"In what way?"

Laura hesitated a moment.

"She was so strong, so –" she made a small, punching movement with her clenched fist. "So sure of herself, somehow. I would have expected her to fall for someone equally strong. I don't see Carne like that. He seems a real pseud to me; a sort of all-things-to-all-men kind of person."

"Mm." Simon looked thoughtful. "Remember I mentioned to you that I asked him about his World War I record? If what I'd heard about his being in Intelligence was true?"

"And he said it was."

"Well, he kind of hinted in a nudge-nudge, wink-wink kind of way. Said he'd taken a vow of secrecy and still felt bound by it. I asked Mandy, my research assistant, to try and dig out a few facts for me, and she's just reported back. She actually found and spoke to some old guy who shared an office with Carne in Paris for the last two years of the war, and beyond – 1916 to the end of 1918. They were both attached to the Pay Corps, he said. There was never any question of Intelligence."

"Was this old guy *compos mentis*?"

"Absolutely, so Mandy said. Confined to a wheel-chair, but mentally on the ball. Totally believable."

"So what do you think of that?"

Simon hesitated.

"I suppose he could have been so far undercover that even the guy who shared his office didn't know; but I tend to believe that it was a kind of Walter Mitty-ish fantasy that he hinted at to impress people. He wouldn't be the first man to do so, would he? I mean, have a heart! Pay Corps! It's hardly heroic, is it?"

"There, what did I say! He was a con man," Laura sounded disgusted. "What on earth did Stella see in him?"

"You appear to discount physical attraction."

"*Moi?*" Her eyes over the coffee mug brimmed with amusement. "Never let it be said."

Simon felt a surge of desire so strong that for a moment he was conscious of nothing else. He drank a little of his coffee, steadied his breathing. Down boy, he warned himself. It wasn't time; he could feel it, was certain of it.

"Are you doing anything tonight?" He was pleased to hear that his voice was commendably calm. "I'm going to see Derek Jacobi in *Kean* – it's a special Press preview. You could come if you liked."

"Could I? Oh, I'd love to!" She had that eager, joyful expression that seemed to express more vitality than any one woman had a right to. "Are you sure it would be OK?"

"I'm sure," he said, hoping that her joy was not entirely confined to the prospect of seeing the play – that spending the evening in his company had something to do with it.

"I'm not dressed for anything like that," she said, looking down at her cotton skirt with its bronze coin-spots on a black ground, and her black, boat-necked T-shirt. "I should go home and change."

"Why? You look wonderful as you are. Don't go. It's a waste of tube fare," he added, mocking her with these practical considerations. "And time. If you go now, you'll catch the rush hour."

Laura, who had left her car behind because of parking difficulties, had to concede this last point.

"You're right," she said. "But you ought to be working – you said so yourself."

"Yeah – well, I do have to fax my New York column tomorrow, after I've added the bit about *Kean*. I'm almost through with the rest – it's just a question of tidying up. I can do it later."

"You might as well do it now. I'll just go on browsing through the box. I won't disturb you, I promise."

"Oh, yeah?"

He raised an eyebrow in amused disbelief. Hadn't she disturbed him from the moment of their first meeting?

It seemed incredibly natural to Laura to be sitting there on the mushroom-coloured, Grade A Wilton, occupying herself with Stella's papers, Simon working away at the other side of the room. She felt contented. Comfortable. Vistas seemed to open of days – years, even – spent in easeful harmony; which wasn't, if this vague feeling of excitement was to be trusted, as dull as it sounded. It was as if the time they had spent away from each other this past week hadn't been lying fallow; as if, in some supernatural way, their friendship had advanced, even *in absentia*. (She, like her mother, wasn't keen on 'relationship'.)

She hadn't been able to wait more than three days before phoning him despite all her resolutions – had known, the moment she woke up that morning that she couldn't possibly hang on any longer. To hell with being a strong, independent feminist, happiest in the company of other women – she wanted to see Simon and today was the day.

He'd sounded glad to hear her voice, eager for her to come round to read the diary. And here she was, and wonderful it was to be so. She looked up from the paper in her hand to find his eyes on her. They smiled at each other a little gravely, before each returning to their own preoccupations.

So much rubbish, she thought, as she looked through the collected trivia. And so old. Why had Stella kept it all – kept it for fifty years, no less?

She'd inhabited the same house all that time, that was why. She had never been compelled to have the kind of clearance forced upon other, more nomadic individuals, but had stuffed the lot into the drawers of that chest in the attic and forgotten all about it.

Methodically Laura sorted through it, putting anything she felt might be of use to her in one pile, rubbish in another, photographs in yet another. She'd keep the first and junk the second. The photographs she would give to her mother – and regarding Polly, would Stella's frequent references to her in the diary make her see that she had only sent her away with the utmost reluctance? Maybe, at last, Polly would see her mother in a different light.

They looked happy enough in the photographs; in one Stella was laughing down at Polly on a beach; in another they sat, lovingly entwined, on a garden seat. Most were of Polly alone, taken, it seemed clear, by the Evanses; evidence, one supposed, of Polly's continuing well-being on that Welsh hillside farm. Polly feeding a lamb, Polly riding on Mr Evans's shoulders, Polly in a swing-boat at the fair. Simon, glancing up from his word processor, saw her expression as she studied them.

"What is it?" he asked. "What have you found?"

"Just photographs of Polly. Those Evanses really loved her, you know. You can tell."

"I wonder what happened to them."

"No idea. Long dead and gone, I imagine." She picked up a Kodak folder, full of both pictures and the negatives, just as Stella must have picked it up from the shop over forty years before. "Hey," she said with a sudden sharpening of interest as she removed the photographs and looked through them. "I think this is probably one of Carne."

She held it out for Simon, and he left his desk to take it from her.

"Yes, that's him," he said. "He was a good-looking guy, wasn't he?"

"That's the outside of the house in Chiswick, so they weren't *that* discreet. And here's another of them together, by the river. I wonder who took it."

"Jane, the Carrot Queen, perhaps."

"Mm." Laura permitted herself a smile, but didn't speak for a moment. She was too engrossed in looking at another photograph of Stella and Carne together.

"They look awfully happy," she said at last, rather sadly. "I wonder what happened. Why he suddenly broke it off and didn't see her again."

"He was married, after all. Maybe his wife found out and put a stop to it."

"I suppose so. Bastard," she added, putting the photograph back into its folder and taking out another. "Stella was too good to be

149

treated like that. He said it was all over with his wife, that they'd been unhappy for years. She believed him. Well –" she sighed. "More fool her, I suppose. Only she wasn't a fool."

"I wonder who this guy is?" Simon said, picking another photograph from the pack and studying it with interest.

"Let's have a look."

The man in question was sitting with Stella on a rug under a tree amid the remains of a picnic, a mug in his hand. His thin dark face seemed cadaverous, no flesh on it at all. His black hair grew in a widow's peak on his forehead, a thin, dark moustache following the line of his lip. Laura shook her head.

"Haven't a clue," she said. "Could be anyone. Jane's boy-friend, maybe? Someone's taking the photograph, after all."

"He looks a touch Hispanic," Simon suggested.

"Hm. Flashy, anyway. You know, I bet that was taken in Richmond Park," Laura said, smiling. "Stella took me for lots of picnics there. It was one of her favourite places, and when she was old and ill I used to drive her round it sometimes, just for old times' sake."

"I've always meant to ask you; did you call her Stella when she was alive? My grandmother would have fainted dead away if I'd addressed her by her first name. Mind you," he added, "it was Augusta, so perhaps she'd have good reason."

"Stella insisted on it. Always, from as early as I can remember."

"She must have been a really unbuttoned kind of lady. Come on, let's see the other pics."

"They're not very interesting." Laura handed them over nevertheless. "Views mainly – and more Polly. Taken in Wales, I imagine."

"Pretty," Simon said. "The countryside, I mean, as well as Polly. It looks very like Cornwall – that's lovely too. Could that be the reason Carne couldn't make the break after all? Could he have decided that no woman in the world would make up for losing his summerhouse and his view? Not even Stella?"

Laura shrugged her shoulders.

"Who knows?" she said. "But one thing I do know; he did what was best for him."

"Best for his wife too, surely?"

"Best for him," she repeated firmly. Men do, she almost added; but, for once, managed to keep her mouth shut.

\* \* \*

Pen, shopping in Porthlivick, felt sorry for the holiday-makers, trailing despondently around the quay in their raincoats and kagools. It was, she thought, the height of misfortune to strike a bad week in a generally blazing summer – to be forced to listen, damply, to landladies' stories of last week's cases of sunburn and heatstroke.

"Shame, isn't it?" Mrs Laity of the bakery said to her; and Pen, knowing exactly what she meant even without further explanation, agreed. "Never mind," Mrs Laity went on. "It's got time to clear up again before your Dad's great day. The anthem's some lovely. We was up practising last night."

"I'm longing to hear it," Pen said.

Mrs Laity paused in the act of putting a large stone-ground loaf and a small white into a plastic bag.

"You don't do much to singing yourself, then?" she asked.

"I'm afraid I don't do anything to singing," Pen said, intrigued and amused as she had always been by this peculiarly Cornish way of putting things. "Except murder it, of course."

"Oh, get away!" Mrs Laity handed over the bag and accepted payment. "You'm always joking, Mrs Hambly. Your Dad had an 'andsome voice," she added as Pen turned to leave. "He was in the choir when I first joined; well, we'm both a bit older now, but I can still hear that tenor of his in 'Abide with Me'. Some lovely it was."

"Yes, it was, wasn't it? I always longed to be able to sing too, but my sister Caro was the musical one. She could sing – still can – and she played the piano too. We used to gather round and sing hymns on a Sunday night; can you believe it? I don't suppose anyone, anywhere, does that any more."

"Well, 'tis the telly, en it?" Mrs Laity said. "'Tis all different now. Tidn't the *fun*, say what you will, Mrs Hambly."

She's right, Pen thought; it had been fun, though admittedly of the homespun variety. Youngsters these days missed out on that kind of thing. Still, not all changes were bad. They'd never owned a car in the old days. All shopping had to be lugged up the long hill from the village, no matter how heavy. How on earth had her mother managed? Of course, tradesmen delivered then – but had they gone on delivering during the war, when petrol was in short supply? She couldn't for the life of her remember.

She remembered the singing, though; Mrs Laity's conversation had brought it all back to her. And as, thankfully, she stowed her shopping in the car, backed out of her parking space, and drove up the hill, she wasn't seeing the sodden holiday-makers any more. She was seeing David, leaning on the piano, singing as lustily as any of them.

Trish, she remembered, had been a bit embarrassed about it at first, thinking – suddenly, for she'd never apparently thought it before – that this family activity would make them seem naïve and unsophisticated in the eyes of this glamorous stranger. Appearing unsophisticated was the thing that Trish dreaded more than anything else in the whole world.

They were, of course. Totally unworldly, even Dad, with his clever, cultivated friends in London whom none of them had ever met. David didn't seem to mind it; in fact by this time Pen had come to the conclusion that even though he was an American and must, therefore, live a life of grandeur unimaginable to those who had spent their whole life in Porthlivick, he really enjoyed quite ordinary things – things like playing Monopoly and flying a kite. And singing round the piano. Actually he had seemed a bit taken aback the first time, but he'd gamely joined in and it hadn't taken long before he was as involved as anyone else, taking the bass part while Dad sang tenor, Caro alto, and everyone else held the melody. Even she had done her best. It wasn't that she sang off key, merely that her voice emerged in a childish squeak that was almost inaudible.

David knew hymns that they didn't. There was one about a garden; she'd never heard it before or since and couldn't properly remember it now, but it had a catchy little tune and she had loved it at the time. Loved David singing it, anyway.

The remembrance of it caused a sudden, piercing excitement – a tremor of the nerve-ends such as she had not experienced for years. You are a pensioner, she reminded herself severely. A senior citizen. It was a fact that appeared to have no effect whatsoever on the not unenjoyable flutter brought to the pit of her stomach by the thought of seeing David again.

Did he remember those days? *How* did he remember them? Her father's opinion was that he would have forgotten them all long ago; and strangely, in view of his one time affection for David, he had seemed astonished and a little put out that he was taking the time and trouble to come to Porthlivick. But Simon had been in contact once or twice and had said on the phone that David was looking forward to the celebrations – that they both were, and would be down in good time.

The rain had stopped and a watery sun was attempting to shine by the time she arrived home. Fred had just taken Mr Carne down to the summerhouse, Dolly told her. Mr Carne had been most insistent, though Dolly wasn't at all sure that it was wise. The weather, she said, wasn't what you could call *settled*, and anyway it was time for his bit of lunch.

"But you know what he is," she went on. "There's no arguing with him. He said he wanted egg sandwiches."

"Well, that's easy enough – I'll take them down to him. There was some of last night's soup left too. I'll heat that up."

"Was the village crowded?" Dolly asked, as Pen washed her hands at the kitchen sink before dealing with the lunch tray. "Poor souls! When you think of what it was like last week . . ."

Her father seemed quieter than usual, Pen thought, as she put the tray on the table in the summerhouse.

"Are you sure you're warm enough?" she asked.

"Of course I'm warm enough." His reply was testy. "I may be old, but I'm not made of Dresden china, you know."

"I know, I know. You're tough as old boots. Still, there's been quite a change in the weather."

"I've been thinking," he said, brushing off her concern. "This – this whatever it is they're preparing for me next month. I don't want it. It all happened so long ago."

"But people are buying your book *now*! You're famous all over again."

"Well, I don't want to be. Tell them to call it off."

"Darling, it's all arranged! People are looking forward to it. They want to pay you some kind of tribute."

"It's not necessary. I won't have it."

Pen dragged up a stool and sat at his feet, taking both his hands in hers.

"What's brought this on?" she asked, her voice soft and full of sympathy. "It's not like you to have an attack of nerves."

Carne moved his head uneasily, staring out at the sea, not meeting her eyes.

"It's not nerves. It's nothing to do with nerves. That's a stupid thing to say."

"What, then? You were pleased enough when it was first mooted."

"I can't be bothered, that's the truth of it. I'm tired. I'm not well enough." He was using his frail, fretful voice.

Pen bit her lip, frowning a little.

"Let's not do anything in a hurry, darling," she said after a moment. "You know how you go up and down; you could be fighting fit by next month – and in any case you can stay in bed for as many days as you want to, before and after. It – it would seem an awful slap in the face to everyone who's become involved in it. There's an augmented choir – all the churches have combined for it – and Gerald Pope has written a special anthem. And the Brownies and Guides are parading, and the Mayor and all the Council, and then there's the garden party afterwards. Trish and Caro are coming, and Hannah." Hannah was his favourite grandchild, the prospect of seeing her was bound to sway him, if anything could. "And lots of old friends," Pen went on persuasively. "All in your honour. It's quite a thing, really. They're even going to put the flags out in Fore Street – the ones they use for regatta week."

"I don't want it. What do I want to see the Mayor for? I don't know the Mayor."

"Of course you do; it's Maureen Mills –"

"A woman! That makes it worse."

"Don't be sexist! You sound just like old Life's-Work-Nobly-Done! She's a very good Mayor, but that's hardly the point. Porthlivick wants to honour you. You're their most famous son, after all."

"I can't go through with it. People looking at me, staring, whispering behind their hands."

"Oh darling, who'd do that?"

"There are still Yeos in the village, aren't there? There's not one of them who's ever wished me well. It's no good, Pen. You'll have to stop it somehow. Or if it goes on, it'll have to be without me."

"Well – " Pen stood up and began putting the plates on the table, shaking out a napkin to tuck into his collar. She sighed once more. The lady Councillor in charge of the matter would be furious. "I'll talk to Mrs Cartwright," she said, just to pacify him. But not for a day or two, she added to herself.

*   *   *

Simon, in his seat at the Old Vic, was operating on two completely different levels. On one, he was enjoying the performance, words forming themselves in his mind almost of their own volition: 'Who can forget *I, Claudius*? This is yet another masterly, exuberant performance from Jacobi – certain, surely, to transfer to Broadway' – and so on and so on.

Underneath was his consciousness of Laura, sitting in the next seat. Funny how, at the beginning of things, the touch of an elbow on a shared arm-rest could seem so erotic. She felt it too; he was sure of it. It was clear from her expression, from her smile, from the excitement in her eyes.

"Enjoying it?" he asked at the interval. They'd moved to the bar but by silent, mutual consent kept themselves to themselves, even though he'd exchanged nods of greeting with other journalists known to him.

"It's wonderful. *He's* wonderful – I'm not sure he's nasty enough, though. Kean was a horrible, venomous man, so I've always understood."

"I didn't know that."

"And physically quite small. It's well documented."

"Really? Well, it makes a good play, anyway."

"Oh, I agree."

What are we talking about? Laura asked herself. Our lips are moving and words are emerging from our mouths, and all the time our bodies are screaming out quite different things. He's

155

as aware of it as I am. The third bell rang and they returned to their seats, Simon's hand burning like fire under her elbow as he shepherded her back to their seats.

"Hungry?" he asked when it was all over and they were fighting their way to the street. "What do you say we take a taxi back to the flat and I'll fix you something? There's a pizza in the freezer."

"I've got a better idea," Laura said. "Why don't we take a taxi back to the flat, and you write your copy while I fix *you* something? I can heat up a pizza as well as the next man. That makes more sense, doesn't it?"

"I guess it does," Simon agreed.

And so, of course, it did; but sense, it seemed, was to stand small chance against their other hunger. With the door closed behind them, the rest of the world outside, they hesitated for only one brief moment as if to take in the heady fact that at last all the evening's restraints were lifted. Just one moment, one catch of the breath, and they were in each other's arms; no questions or doubts now, just need and longing and frenzied excitement. And oh – bliss, bliss, bliss, thought Laura. Oh God, how I want this man, want him so much.

His arms were still around her as they drew apart. Simon laughed a little shakily.

"You'll never know how close I came to doing that in the bar of the Old Vic."

"You'd have frightened the horses."

"Never mind the horses; I'm the one who's frightened."

And me, Laura thought, as they kissed again. For some reason I'm terrified; happy, but terrified. Why? Because this might be It?

"You've got work to do," she said at last, not a shred of conviction in her voice. She reached to run her fingers over his cheek and twine them in his hair. "And I've got a pizza to cook."

"Later," he said softly. "Do you mind? A very great deal later."

\*     \*     \*

The strangest thing about retirement, David thought, was freedom from the tyranny of time. Looking back, all his life seemed to have been governed by the clock. Trains, appointments, meetings – he'd always prided himself on being on the dot, had fretted when circumstances made him late. And further back too – schooldays, the Army, College. A life, you could say, of discipline and deadlines.

It was easy to feel a little lost without them, though such punctiliousness was acquired rather than inherent. Heaven knew, he'd kicked hard against discipline in his youth. He'd been regarded in the Army as something of a rebel at first, until he'd learned that the only sensible way to get through was to keep his head down and his nose clean, avoiding trouble wherever possible.

He'd been incredibly lucky while he was stationed in Cornwall, contriving, thanks to the good offices of various friends, to slip away to see Trish fairly frequently, with or without a pass. He and Chuck both. Chuck was dating a compliant older woman of twenty-five called Rita, whose husband was in the Eighth Army, currently fighting in Italy. He wasn't, like David, hopelessly in love ('Great legs, shame about the face,' he said). He was merely out for what he could get, but this made him no less anxious to skip camp at every opportunity. Together they had worked out a near foolproof exit and re-entry point just beyond the rocks. There was an unpleasant but thankfully short climb, leading to the cliff path, now as familiar to David as his own back yard. Here, at the top of the hill they parted, Chuck to follow another track inland to the farm cottage where Rita lived, David to carry straight on to the headland and Roscarrow.

He'd had no pass on the Sunday he met Caro. Trish wasn't expecting him; he hadn't thought he'd be able to get away, but the opportunity had arisen after all, and he was in no mood to waste a moment. No one knew when D-day would come, but the sense of expectancy was almost tangible. It would be very soon now.

On this occasion Chuck wasn't with him. Swiftly he climbed up the cliff to the rocky path and plunged into the cliff-top growth of stunted trees and brambles, ferns and foxgloves which effectively hid him from the camp.

As steeply as it climbed upwards for the first hundred yards, the path fell away downhill, clear of the trees now but dangerously close to the cliff, the sea with its embroidery of white horses blinking and winking to his left. There was no beach worth having here; just a grand tumble of rocks and stony coves. Someone, more appreciative of spectacular scenery than David on this day as he hastened towards his love, had placed a wooden bench at the bottom of the hill where walkers could rest to enjoy the view. He could see that a lone figure was sitting there as he came down the path, and as he drew nearer he recognised Caro.

He called out to her as he approached, and she turned from her contemplation of the wide bay to wave at him.

"What are you doing here?" she greeted him, surprise in her voice. "I thought you were on duty. Trish isn't home."

"Oh." He sat down heavily, weighted with disappointment. He hadn't seen her for three days.

"She went back with Mary after church. You've met Mary, haven't you? Trish's school-friend?"

"Sure." He spoke dully.

"She only went because Granny Carne was coming to Sunday dinner," Caro explained. "Which is why I'm here. I had to escape the second it was over – I just couldn't stand any more."

For the first time David looked at her properly and saw that she looked flushed and upset; might, even, have been crying.

"Any more what?" he asked.

"Criticism of Alan. She's worse than Father about the Yeos."

"But the family don't know you're still in touch with him, do they?"

"That didn't stop her. She went on and on about how wise I had been to finish with him and how terrible the entire Yeo family is, and what an awful, ignorant lout Alan is, and quite repulsive to look at – which isn't true, David!" She turned fiercely towards him, and now he saw that there were, indeed, tears in her eyes. "He's no film star, I admit. He's much too thin, like all the Yeos, but he's got a lovely smile and he's just the nicest –" She pressed her lips together and stared out to sea, angry all over again. "Anyway," she went on after a moment, "I love him, and that's all that matters. Who cares what that old bag thinks?"

"Is she really as bad as that?"

"Worse! Honestly, I had to get away before I said something really rude, because that would have landed Father in trouble. She blames all our sins on him, and says we've been badly brought up. Allowed too much freedom. That's a laugh, isn't it? Free-dom! As if I've been allowed to know the meaning of the word! Anyway," she went on, "she can say what she likes. Nothing can alter the way Alan and I feel."

"That's the important thing," David said.

"It is, isn't it? And I'm going to marry him, whatever they say. David –" She turned towards him once more and put her hand on his arm. He sensed that her mood had changed. She seemed eager now, full of suppressed excitement. "David, can you keep a secret?" He nodded, though without enthusiasm. Instinct told him that he would be better off not knowing whatever it was she seemed so anxious to confide in him. "Alan's in England." The excitement blazed from her eyes, all thought of her grandmother's jibes banished from her mind. "He's in Portsmouth. He docked a couple of days ago and phoned me at work."

"Well, that's great news, isn't it? You can relax now."

She made no comment on this, but tightened her grip on his arm.

"You know it's my twenty-first birthday on the 24th? Well, the moment that's over, I'm going to join him and we're going to get married. Just like that! He's getting a special licence."

"Without telling anyone?"

"Not a soul. And you mustn't tell, either – not Trish or Pen or anyone – especially not Trish. She can't keep anything to herself. You won't tell, will you? Promise?"

"Sure, if that's what you want. Caro, you really think this is the right thing? What about your Mom and Dad –?"

"I know they'll be upset; well, Father will be, and Mother will be upset because he is, not for any other reason. Oh, I hate doing it this way, truly I do, but if I tell them what I'm going to do, there'll be awful rows and Father will shout and everyone will be miserable, and it'll just go on and on and on until the time comes for me to leave; which I'm going to do anyway. Believe me, I've thought and thought about this."

"You don't think they'll come round, if they see you're determined?"

"Father will never come round. He hates the Yeos."

"How do they feel?" David asked.

Caro pulled a face. "Well, there's no love lost for Father, as you can imagine. Why would there be? He's done nothing but run them down for years and years. They don't seem to mind me, though. Alan says they'll forgive him for running away to get married – they just want him to be happy. If only my parents were the same!" She sighed and wrapped both arms around herself as if for comfort, and looked for a moment at the magnificent sweep of the bay. "You know," she said, "I was sitting here and looking at the view before you came, and thinking how lovely it all is. I can't imagine living anywhere more beautiful. A stranger would look at it and think that no one could possibly be bad or evilly-intentioned or small-minded, living in a place like this – but it's not true, you know. There's a dark side to Porthlivick. Rumours and gossip and back-biting, and long, long memories. I can't wait to get away."

"I guess all small places are the same."

"Perhaps. I only know Porthlivick. Oh, it's such a damned shame, David! If only people could forget the past."

"What's it all about, this – this vendetta? You said it wasn't just dirty tricks at the election."

"No." For a while Caro was silent, looking out at the sea. Then she sighed. "It's a lot more than that," she said. "Alan's father told him the whole story, and he told me. He made me promise not to tell Trish or Pen. It would upset Pen terribly, and Trish would go rushing around telling all her friends, and that wouldn't help our cause one bit. Well, nothing will, but there's no point in making it worse. I don't see why I shouldn't tell you, though. You'll be going away soon, and won't ever see any of us again."

David, still determined on a future with Trish, opened his mouth to argue; to say that in any case, he wasn't at all sure he could cope with any more secrets. But she had already embarked on the story.

Her father's grandfather, she told him, drank away all the profits of the fish-distributing business that Joseph Carne, Caleb's father, had expected to inherit, so that when he died there was nothing left but debts. Joseph by this time had married the village schoolteacher, now Granny Carne, and they'd had a son – Caleb.

"It was hard on Granny Carne because she'd expected better," Caro said. "The business was finished and they didn't have two ha'pennies to rub together, so that when William Yeo – that's

Alan's grandfather – gave Joseph a job as a hand on his fishing boat, they were very thankful. They were still hard up, but so was everyone else. The problem was that Joseph had inherited the family weakness and took to drink. Are you with me so far?"

"I guess so."

"Times really got hard. As you'll have gathered, I'm not exactly brimming over with love for Granny Carne – if she moaned as much then as she does now, who could blame the poor man for hitting the bottle? – but according to Father, they often went to bed hungry knowing that Joseph was at the pub drinking away the little they did have. She took in a few pupils, but no one had any money to spare so she didn't earn much. I can understand why Father's education meant so much to her; it was, really, all she had."

"And why he wanted to please her, I guess. I mean, she must have been the one secure thing in his life."

"I suppose you're right. Anyway – back to the Yeos. There was one night, so Alan told me, when old William Yeo and his son Walter – Alan's father, that is – were having a drink in the bar of the Anchor. Father was only a boy at the time – about twelve, I think – but Walter must have been eighteen or nineteen. It was a terribly stormy night, pouring with rain, with waves coming right over the wall of the outer harbour, like it does when it's rough.

"Well, the door of the pub suddenly crashed open, and there was Granny Carne with a shawl over her head. She'd come looking for Joseph. They told her he had been there but had left about ten minutes before, very much the worse for drink, insisting that he was going to make sure the boat was properly secure. They'd laughed at him, Alan told me, not taking him seriously because they knew that the boat was tied up perfectly safely in the inner harbour, and thought he was just putting on a show to impress them – you know, pretending to be the conscientious employee when everyone knew he was no such thing. They honestly thought he had no intention of going anywhere near the boat that night.

"Well, she was really angry, both with them and with Joseph, and stomped off into the night. Walter said afterwards that he got the impression she turned towards the harbour as if to continue the search for Joseph there, but he couldn't be sure. She maintained she went the other way, back home. Whichever was true, he wasn't found until the following day when one of the other fishermen discovered him floating face down in the outer harbour."

For a moment David looked at her, shocked.

"Are you saying they thought your grandmother had something to do with it?"

"That's what was said at the time. It was all just gossip and rumour. The police didn't take it seriously, as far as I know. Granny said she went straight back to the cottage where Caleb – Father, that is – was doing his schoolwork. She was there not two minutes after leaving the Anchor, so she couldn't have gone out to the quay, she said, and Caleb could vouch for it. I looked it all up in the local paper at the St Jory library after Alan told me; it was all reported there. They said it was Death by Misadventure, and it certainly seems as if it was more than likely. It was the worst night of that whole winter, and Joseph was undoubtedly drunk. But being Porthlivick, the whispers went on. Joseph had a bit of life insurance – it couldn't have been much, but there was no doubt that Granny was better off without him. And then –"

She paused and looked at him uncertainly, biting her lip, as if realising for the first time that this was not just a story but that these were real people she was speaking of, and her own people at that.

"Then?" David prompted her, totally absorbed, forgetting his initial reluctance to hear these old secrets.

"Well, then other rumours started up." She was looking down, rubbing her finger along the uneven edge of the seat and her voice was troubled. "People said someone had seen Caleb that night at the end of Fish Street. That's the little alley that leads from the square to the quay. He'd been noticed because it wasn't the sort of night for anyone to be hanging about, let alone a boy without a coat. Look, it probably *wasn't* him!" She looked up earnestly. "It was black as pitch and raining hard – anyone could make a mistake on a night like that. Both he and Granny said he never left home that night."

"But the gossip went on."

"That's right. Father was quite big and strong, perfectly capable of pushing a drunken man into the harbour. Some said they'd conspired to get rid of Joseph – that Caleb had been put up to it by his mother, that he'd put his head in the gas oven if she told him to. Others said that he knew what she was about and had gone running out to stop her. I can just imagine it! People are like that here. They like nothing better than malicious tittle-tattle – you know the sort of thing! Who was the father of whose baby. Whose wife is carrying on with whose husband. It's like Chinese Whispers – do kids play that game in America? You whisper something to the person next to you, and she whispers it to the person next to her, and at the end of the line the original statement is distorted out of all recognition."

David nodded, still silenced by the story. For a moment neither spoke, and Caro returned to tracing the grain of the wood with her finger. He cleared his throat.

"So – so your father blames the Yeos for these rumours?"

"Well, they were there, in the pub. He and Granny both thought they started the gossip and spread it round; and then, of course, years later when Walter and Father were standing against each other for the Council the whispers started all over again. That was some time in the early 1920s, so neither Alan nor I know anything about that at first hand. Walter swore then and he swears now that he was totally blameless – but nothing, apparently, would convince Father that it wasn't part of his election campaign. They had an almighty public row and Father swore he'd never speak to Walter again. And he hasn't."

"Didn't Walter make your Dad's life a misery at school? Pen said something about it once."

"No, no. I told you – Walter was quite a bit older. He and Father weren't at school at the same time. It was a cousin – Henry Yeo – who did the bullying. He was in the same class and plagued him unmercifully – and that I believe, absolutely! Henry's a nasty piece of work even now. Alan can't stand him and neither can the rest of the family. He's reckoned to have done quite well for himself, because he went into the Civil Service and works in London at some Ministry or other. Good riddance, everyone said – with the possible exception of Hilda, I suppose. She's his wife, but she came back to Porthlivick when the bombing started and she's been here ever since. Walter is as anti-Henry as anyone else, but as far as Father's concerned, they're all tarred with the same brush. So!" She lifted both hands up and brought them

163

down flatly on the seat. "That's why I'm going to run away and marry Alan without a word to anyone. You can surely understand it."

"I guess so."

"And you won't say anything?"

"Of course not. No," he added as she began to speak again. "Not even to Trish. I'm just sorry it has to be this way – sorry for you and your parents."

"Yes, well – they'll get over it. There's no need to be sorry for me, though. I'll have Alan. He's all I want."

Lucky guy, David thought, as he had thought before. Trish is all I want; but what'll be the end of it for any of us?

For some reason Caro's story had lit within him a small, flickering flame of disquiet. It seemed to him to underline the fact that life was full of uncertainties, that one could plan nothing, be sure of nothing; that a chance action could have an effect on generations yet unborn. Suppose Mrs Carne had sat quietly at home that night, resigned to the fact that her husband was drinking? There would have been no suspicion, no feud, no need for Caro to marry Alan in secret, no wailing and gnashing of teeth. The families could have been good friends, the wedding an occasion of rejoicing.

"I ought to get back," Caro said, looking at her watch. "Are you coming? I doubt if Trish will be home yet, though. Once she and Mary get together they lose all track of time – still, Granny Carne will be gone, with a bit of luck."

David looked at his watch too, and shook his head.

"It's gotten too late. I daren't risk it. I shouldn't have come at all, really." He stood up. "I'll see you before you go?"

"Of course! I can't go until after my birthday."

"Goodbye for now, then; and Caro – I'm so glad Alan's back home."

"For the moment," she said.

He could be the one to leave first, he thought on the way back to camp. Who knew when the call would come? Invasion was the word on everyone's lips. Strange to think that any day now all these tents would be gone, all these LCTs being used for real, all that firing practice proving its worth and Bow Beach quiet and empty once more, just as if the GIs had never made it their home.

Who'd remember them? Well, Trish, for one. And as soon as he was able, he would send for her to come to America. To him. And they'd be happy together, for ever and ever. It was crazy to feel depressed by Caro's story. Crazy to feel so chilled at the thought of old miseries and old feuds.

If only he could have seen Trish, he thought, everything would have been all right. He wouldn't have felt this need to touch wood.

# VII

Simon, familiar by this time with the West End, was nevertheless largely ignorant of Greater London – a lack which Laura took it upon herself to rectify. She took him to the old fishing village of Strand-on-the-Green where they strolled beside the Thames and sat outside a riverside pub.

"I'd no *idea*," Simon said appreciatively, looking at the cottages and the gracious houses that lined the bank. "I can't believe this is London."

"This is my patch," Laura told him. "Where I grew up."

They moved on to Kew Gardens and Hampton Court; and all the time they talked and talked, exploring with growing delight the beliefs and backgrounds and opinions that had shaped them. Even in the middle of the maze they stood for a full five minutes, locked in passionate discussion about – of all people – John Betjeman, whom somehow Laura had never linked with anything very passionate. It was only with the appearance of a couple in identical shell-suits who looked at them a little strangely that they came to their senses and embarked on identifying the elusive and tortuous path to the outside world.

They watched a game of cricket on Kew Green, in the end reduced to helpless laughter at Laura's attempts to explain the rules – only, she had to admit, sketchily grasped and little understood. And, because he knew she had a sentimental attachment to the place, he asked to be taken to Richmond Park, where she had so often gone with Stella.

It was there, watching her feed the ducks, seeing her smile as she turned to speak to him, that he knew without doubt that she was the woman for him. No matter that they had known each other for such a short time. No matter that there had been other girls before

– that he had imagined himself in love. This was different. This was going to last. His total certainty on this point was, at times, something that astonished him. Short the time may have been, but it seemed now that he could hardly remember when Laura wasn't there, at the very centre of his life.

Time and events moved on; and preoccupied as he was with his own emotions, not to mention the need to work, it was nevertheless impossible to ignore the smiling and implacable face of Saddam Hussein on the television. The world held its breath and worried over the fate of the hostages and the future of oil supplies, and how close Iraq was to having nuclear and chemical weapons.

George Bush ordered American troops to Saudi Arabia, and an international blockade was planned; nevertheless there was, after all, a hope that Jonathan Pryce might be able to play in *Miss Saigon* on Broadway, a vague possibility that Iran might lift the *fatwa* on Salman Rushdie, and a racist outburst in Stratford by a Frenchwoman protesting at the playing of a French king by a black actor. These were the things that engaged Simon's more professional attention, busy as he was with the gathering of material for his next *Soundings* report. Life, as he had said to his father, went on.

Which meant a trip to the Edinburgh Festival. He asked Laura to go with him, but she was forced to refuse. Other arrangements had already been made. She had promised to take Polly down to Sussex to stay with a friend, the sister of an ex-employer, and was, herself, then going on to Tunbridge Wells to spend the weekend with an old college friend on the occasion of her baby daughter's christening.

"You must meet Sally and John," she said to Simon. "They've been marvellous friends to me."

"I don't doubt it. But couldn't they spare you this weekend?"

"Not possibly." Laura was firm, if regretful. "I'm standing as godmother, so I have to go. Anyway, it's not for long, is it? I'll be home on Monday, and you'll be back – when, Tuesday?'

"Sure will. I'll call you Monday night, OK?"

The night before Laura and Polly left London, he took Polly out to dinner. He'd wanted Laura to come too, but she refused categorically.

"You said you'd take her," she said. "Not her and her daughter. There's a difference. She'll enjoy it a million times more if she can have you to herself. Anyway, I've already committed myself to listening to a poet in a pub."

Laura was right about Polly enjoying the occasion, Simon observed. She sparkled and fluttered and flirted; and, seeing her enjoyment, Simon had encouraged her – and on the whole was glad that, after all, Laura was not present. He would have found it inhibiting on several counts; not least because they had spent much of the afternoon in bed together and he felt quite sure that Polly would sense it every time he turned his besotted eyes upon her daughter. Because besotted was what he was. He didn't particularly welcome it. It complicated things. He hadn't yet had any more communications with *Commentary* since Greeley's visit, but he couldn't help thinking about the possibility of leaving London and how he would feel if it meant leaving Laura too.

It seemed presumptuous to think she might come with him. He couldn't, somehow, see her rearranging her life to suit any man, still less one who had only been on the scene for such a short time – her strength and independence were, after all, one of the many things about her that attracted and intrigued him. He would ask, though. How could he not, feeling as he did? Maybe, he thought hopefully, the offer would be delayed a month or two. Time was what they needed.

In the meantime there was the dinner with Polly. He raised the subject of Carne, and Polly was delighted to tell him all she knew, all over again, plus a few extra tit-bits he hadn't heard before that he stored away to be examined for their importance later. He had come round to the house several times while she was there for the school holidays, she said. He joked a lot, tried to make her laugh; she'd got the feeling that he was anxious that she should like him and was put out when she made it clear that she didn't.

"Why didn't you?" Simon asked her. She shrugged her shoulders.

"I suppose I just resented his presence, when I wanted my mother to myself. You know how children are!"

"But I get the impression he was a likeable man."

"Perhaps he was. I just didn't want Stella to like him more than me. You see, she was terribly busy, working all the hours God gave her with that job of hers. I didn't understand then how important it was. All I knew was that it took up all her time and energy, and I suppose I thought that if she had any spare moments, then she

169

should spend them with me. That was later in the war, of course, after the Blitz. I was at boarding school by that time, but still in Wales, not far from the farm. The Evanses used to come and see me and take me out to tea."

"What happened to them?"

"Oh –" she dismissed the Evanses with a shrug, screwing up her pretty little face. "I spent a few holidays with them, but mostly I came home. After I left school we kept in touch for a while. I was never one for writing letters, but my mother wrote to them for quite a number of years and used to send them things at Christmas. Lovely things. She had her faults, but she was a great present-giver. I remember signing the card she put inside. Then we heard that Mr Evans had died and Mrs Evans had gone a bit gaga. Senile, you know. Sad, wasn't it?"

Simon remembered the photographs – the loving, smiling faces of these surrogate parents. Yes, he thought. It was sad. But he also thought it highly probable that their sadness had started a long time before Mr Evans's death and Mrs Evans's senility.

"Laura told you about the diary, I believe," he said. He picked up the wine bottle.

"Oh – !" Ineffectually her fingers fluttered over her glass in a half-hearted attempt to prevent him filling it. "Really, I shouldn't – oh, well, it's not every night I come out with a handsome young man, is it? Not too much – oh, what a wicked boy you are! Yes, she did. And as you see, I was quite right about them being more than just friends, wasn't I? I know she didn't say so, not in so many words, but I gathered from Laura it was quite obvious. She always said I had nothing to go on, but I knew I was right. I overheard Stella saying something to her friend Jane once. Auntie Jane, I used to call her. She and my mother were friends. They'd known each other for ages, ever since Paris. Anyway, this particular night I came downstairs after they thought I was asleep. I had a tummy-ache or something. They were sitting together at the kitchen table, drinking tea, and I distinctly heard Jane say something like 'He adores you, Stella. It's obvious to anyone,' And *then* my mother said: 'There's the small matter of a wife and three daughters.' I knew they were talking about Carne when I heard that, because he'd been at the house the day before, and he'd been telling me about his daughters and how different they all were."

"How old were you?"

"Oh, about eleven or twelve, I suppose. Old enough to understand, anyway. I disliked Carne from that moment. They're both
as bad as each other, I thought. They couldn't care less about their
children. No wonder I was sent away."

"You were sent away because of the air raids!"

"Hm." Polly looked sceptical. "In the beginning, maybe.
Then there was this terribly important war job that came before
everything."

"What became of Jane?" Simon asked.

"She got married at the end of the war and went to live in
Devon or Somerset, or somewhere. Stella couldn't stand the man
she married. Evelyn, his name was. Well, he couldn't help that, of
course, but apparently he was a frightful snob and quite beastly to
Jane's old friends. An overbearing man, my mother said, who didn't
want Jane to have anything to do with anyone from the past."

"So they lost touch too."

"Yes, I think they did. I never remember hearing Stella talk about
her, anyway – not for a long, long time."

They had reached the coffee stage. Simon offered a liqueur, and
after some demur Polly accepted a Cointreau.

"Oh, I *am* having a lovely time," she said. "To tell you the
truth –" she lowered her voice and with a mischievous smile leant
towards him across the table, "I'm awfully glad Laura couldn't
come. There! Aren't I the bold one?"

"I told you, Laura wasn't invited. This is just between you and
me."

"You've been seeing each other though, haven't you? Oh!"
she laughed at his expression that had become, suddenly, a little
guarded. "Don't worry! She hasn't told me a thing except that you
went to the theatre together, and that came out by accident. And
of course, I know she went to your flat to get my mother's papers.
She doesn't tell me much, as a matter of fact."

"No?" Simon injected a note of surprise into his voice.

"Oh my dear, she did get so cross with me about that wretched
box! But never mind, we're friends again now. She's a wonderful
daughter, you know. I don't know what I'd do without her – which
doesn't mean I'm not anxious for her to marry and have a family
of her own – so long as she finds the right man, of course." She

leaned forward confidentially again, shaking her carefully tousled, ash-blonde head with rueful dismay. "I don't mind telling you she's had some real shockers! There was a poet once – unsuccessful, of course – with hair right down his back." (A poet in a pub, Simon thought, with a pang. Was that the one? Was she still seeing him?) "And then," said Polly, unaware of the pain she was causing, "there was a simply *frightful* social worker – terribly handsome, but such a phoney! He lasted quite a long time, but she saw through him in the end, thank heaven."

Thank heaven indeed, Simon thought but didn't say. He had, in fact, no chance to say anything. Polly's tongue was well and truly loosened.

"Laura was a great *marcher* in her youth, you know," she went on. "Ban this, ban that, save the whale, boycott South Africa. My mother egged her on, of course – even marched herself before she got too ill. Every year they went to Aldermaston. Stella actually knew Bishop Huddleston personally! But oh, there were some very strange types on those marches, I can tell you – but all that was a long time ago, of course. Laura's still concerned about all kinds of issues, but she's calmed down a lot since then. You mustn't take any notice of all that feminism. It can make a woman seem very *hard*, don't you agree? I've never understood it. But underneath it all, she's a very caring person. A wonderful daughter, who'll make some man a wonderful wife one day. And of course she's marvellous with children, a born mother."

"I don't doubt it," said Simon. "Actually, I come from a long line of wife-beaters –"

Polly looked at him for a second, pretty mouth rounded in astonishment. Then the little muzzle collapsed in laughter.

"Oh – *you!*" she said.

\* \* \*

"A gentleman," she told Laura approvingly afterwards. "Sit *down*, Fifi – be a good girl for Mummy, sweetie! She'll be all right in a minute, Laura. It's the novelty. I'll give her a biscuit."

Laura made no comment, but doubted the wisdom of this. It was the day after the dinner with Simon and they were on their way to

Sussex. Polly was agog to give an account of the evening, but the narrative was constantly interrupted by Fifi, who, installed in the back seat on a tartan rug, had yapped from the moment she had entered the car. It was, Laura felt, the last thing a motorist needed when coping with the traffic on the M25 but she was not at all sure it wasn't preferable to Fifi throwing up on the back seat, which she felt might well be her next move.

"A real gentleman," Polly went on, "with a lovely sense of humour. And not married! Can you believe it? (There's an itsy-bitsy sweetie, den! I really think she's going to bye-byes.) I mean, the nicest ones always are, it's one of the laws of nature."

"Mm." Laura was non-committal, her eyes on the road ahead.

"And a little bird tells me," Polly went on archly, "that he's interested in you. Or could be, if you play your cards right."

"What sort of cards did you have in mind?" Laura asked in a polite, remote way as she pulled out to pass an elderly Mini.

"Well –" Polly looked at her daughter sideways. She frowned, caught her lip between her teeth, sighed a little. "You know, darling. Just be nice. Don't feel you've got to have the last word all the time. (There! The little angel *has* gone to sleep, bless her!)"

"As if I would."

"Oh, *very* funny! When didn't you want the last word? You must learn how to treat a man, Laura. It's no good making them feel inferior –"

"Not even if they are?"

"What on earth do you mean? Simon Holt is simply lovely, not the least bit inferior."

"I wasn't actually thinking of Simon. I was speaking generally." Polly was in no mood to be deflected.

"I don't believe you could get anyone nicer. He's so – so *sympatico* – and so –" she struggled to find the right description. "So thoroughly decent. I mean, I feel sure it would be marriage or nothing with him. He's not the sort of man who'd play fast and loose."

"Play up, play up, and play the game," Laura said in a detached kind of voice, devoid of all expression.

"There, you see? That's what I mean." Polly pressed her lips together with exasperation. "You're always trying to be so clever-clever. So hard-boiled. I may not know much by your standards, but I know about men. All right, all right, I know just what you're going to say – how did I come to pick such rotters? Well, I was younger then. I've learned by my mistakes. You'd save yourself a lot of heartache if you learned from them too. Simon Holt," she went on firmly after a moment's pause during which Laura said nothing, "is good husband material – which, let's face it, darling, isn't something you come across every day, not at your age."

"I rather think the little angel is in distress," Laura said.

"Oh, dear! I'm afraid she's brought up the biscuit, darling, I *am* sorry! It's all over your nice seat. Maybe we should stop."

"I can't stop here. Just do the best you can with the tissues."

At least, Laura thought, it had stopped Polly talking about Simon and her own lack of marriage prospects; and when the temporary crisis with Fifi had been resolved, she resolutely guided the conversation into less controversial channels.

"What was the food like?" she asked. "Someone told me it's good at that place, but horribly expensive."

Polly, whilst recognising the ploy for what it was, still couldn't resist a blow-by-blow of the entire meal, and Laura sighed with relief.

It was midday when they arrived at the home of Beatrice Cameron, sister of a man whom Polly had looked after until he died, thus putting her out of the best and most comfortable job she'd ever had and forcing her into the arms of Mr Godwin.

Polly and Mrs Cameron, herself a widow of great refinement, had always got on well together. They both found much to deplore in British life – the manners of young people, the portrayal of sex on television, the lack of moral fibre in the nation as a whole, to name but a few of their mutual concerns – and enjoyed telling each other anecdotes to support these views.

They told anecdotes about their past lives too. Mr Cameron had been something quite high up in the Colonial Civil Service administering British law and order in some African outpost, so Beatrice had many an exotic tale to tell, usually involving native servants or the foolishness of naïve memsahibs newly out from England. Sometimes both.

Laura was pretty sure, bearing in mind Beatrice's refinement, that Polly's own life must, in the course of the telling, have been subject to some fairly radical editing. Beatrice, in Laura's judgement, was not the kind of woman to look favourably on flings

174

with Italian waiters, or babies out of wedlock. She only hoped that the friendship survived the visit of Fifi, acquired since Polly's last visit. Beatrice, she thought, was already eyeing the diminutive poodle askance, as if she feared the worst.

She welcomed them with great warmth, however, kissing them both fondly. It had become something of a tradition for Polly to spend a few days here each summer, and she paid her way with gushing enthusiasm. The garden: "Lovelier than ever, Beatrice. Just look how those hydrangeas have come on since last year! And the roses, what a marvellous blaze of colour – and not a weed or a green-fly in sight!" The house: "That foot-stool is new, isn't it? Laura, just look at this *petit-point*! Isn't it the most exquisite work you ever saw?" And Beatrice laughed and disclaimed and looked delighted.

"And how's the world treating you, dear?" she asked Laura smilingly as, to an accompaniment of Polly's cries of praise for her culinary skills, she handed her a plate of chicken casserole. "Do help yourself to vegetables, Laura. Still at that school of yours?"

"She's just come back from Paris," Polly said before Laura could speak.

"Aha!" Beatrice looked roguishly knowing. "Paris, eh? Do I detect a man on the horizon?"

"Not at all," Laura said hurriedly. "It was a school trip. This looks deli –"

Polly interrupted her,

"You're not so very far wrong though, Beatrice. There is a new man in her life – isn't that true, Laura? I was giving her a little pep-talk in the car. I shall never speak to her again if she lets this one slip through her fingers. He's a real charmer."

"Mother, please – !"

"You can't deny it, Laura. Honestly, Beatrice, if I were a few years younger I'd give her a run for her money, believe me. He really is a delightful young man."

"How lovely! I'm so glad for you, Laura." Head on one side, Beatrice beamed at her fondly. "There – didn't I say last year that you really shouldn't give up hope? You're still such a pretty girl, dear. I thought so when you came in. I thought, well I never, she doesn't look a day over eighteen."

"You're as young as you feel, Beatrice." Laura delivered the cliché with a smile as saccharine as Beatrice's own.

"That's as may be," Polly said severely, taking Laura's response at its face value. "But you're not eighteen any more, no matter how you feel, are you, darling? The years are passing, as I was pointing out on the way down."

"Polly, really!" Beatrice rolled her eyes in horrified amusement. "What a truly dreadful thing to say! Talk about tact!"

"There's a time to be tactful and a time to be frank."

"I wonder," Laura said, very sweetly and politely, "if you two would be good enough to wait to discuss my little foibles until after I've left? We old maids do get a little touchy in our dotage, you know."

"Oh, darling! You're not cross, are you?" Beatrice made a little-girl face to express her penitence. "It's because we care, you see. We can't bear to see you wasted, can we, Polly?"

"It's time I had some grandchildren –"

"Oh, yes indeed! And my dear, talking of grandchildren, I must tell you what little Harry said the other day –" Beatrice, seeing the opportunity, had grasped it with both hands. "He's only three, you know, but *such* a vocabulary! He came rushing up to me –"

Laura didn't hear what little Harry had said to his doting grandmother. She had to hold her knife and fork very tightly to stop her hands from shaking, and could only think of Simon. So far, thinking of Simon had been a pleasant occupation, to put it at its mildest; but now she felt sick and panicky, as if she were suffocating.

She managed, somehow, to get through lunch and left as soon as possible, making the excuse that she wanted to arrive in Tunbridge Wells before Sally had to leave home to pick her little girl up from school – a total lie, since Sally had warned her not to come before five thirty.

"It's always chaotic before then," she'd said on the phone. "But I give Oliver and Emma their tea about five, so they're fed and watered and relatively calm for the next hour. I'll be feeding Jess, but that's no bother. It's the other two who create all the mayhem."

It sounded, Laura thought, as if she were in for a hectic weekend; but she was unfazed by the thought. At least Emma and Oliver, five and two respectively, and Jess, now eight months old, were unlikely to hassle her about the need to marry and reproduce, and any noise was likely to be the sound of children at play, not the rushing of time's winged chariot.

She drove for a few miles, then pulled into a car park beside a stretch of National Trust woodland where she walked for a while, soaking up the tranquillity and the absence of human voices. The only sound was that of twigs snapping beneath her feet and the song of the birds.

At the end of the dim, tree-shaded path she could see a bright circle of light, as if ahead lay the promised land. It was, she found when she got there, a swathe of hillside bathed in sunshine, and below it a patchwork of fields and woods stretching on and on to the sea. She sank down on the grass and let the peace of it seep into her soul.

Be calm, she told herself. Be calm.

Why this feeling of panic? This sudden doubt?

None of it was Simon's fault. Nothing that her mother or Beatrice had said was anything to do with either her or Simon. It didn't touch the way they felt for each other. But what did they feel?

Lust – God, yes! There was that, all right. And friendship. She tried to recapture that contented feeling she had known that first day when they were both in the room together, busy about their own concerns. It had, for some reason, felt so good. But that was ten days ago – ten days that seemed like a lifetime. Much had happened in the interim. How did they view things now that time, and they, had moved on?

She didn't know. She was frightened again, really frightened. Her mother was right in one way; Simon wouldn't play fast and loose, whatever that meant. Marriage hadn't been mentioned. It was, after all, less than a month since the party where they had first laid eyes on each other, and only ten days since her return from Paris. Ten days wasn't *that* long, after all, even if you contrived to spend almost every minute together, but even so, commitment was undoubtedly implicit in all that had happened between them. Now, suddenly, she just wasn't sure he understood the sort of person she was.

She was, after all, what Stella had made her. Not her mother. Polly was more of an awful warning. It was Stella who had influenced her, been her role model – tough, independent, battling Stella, who had loved and lost but who maintained, at the end, that it had been for the best; that she would never have been the compliant wife that Carne wanted.

177

Simon hadn't suggested that she should become any kind of a wife, compliant or otherwise. Not yet. But he too was what others – in his case, his parents – had made him; kind and thoughtful, that was true, but conventional too. Marriage would be part of his long-term plan. Marriage and a family. And equally, he would expect his career to be paramount, his interests to come first.

He might say otherwise. He would respect her independence – to a certain extent. He would help with household chores, change nappies, ferry the children to school, take an interest in her job; but in the last analysis he would think the way Polly thought. He would expect Laura to be the helpmeet while he was the provider, the boss, the maker of decisions. That's what was so frightening. She wasn't ready for that and it was wrong to let Simon think she was.

On the other hand. . .

After a long time she stood up, dusted down her skirt. What was she to do? She couldn't walk away from him; not yet. The thought was unbearable, like walking into fire or falling on a sword. Besides, she could be wrong. She could be fooling herself in thinking he had long-term plans at the back of his mind. He might possibly regard this as no more than an interlude that had no relevance to real life – an exciting encounter in a foreign city, quickly forgotten once he was back on his native shores, and in that case she would be a fool not to enjoy the moment.

Things might work themselves out. This crazy yearning for him might lessen in time. Things didn't always last, after all, especially when they started off with as many fireworks as this had done – she'd had enough experience of life and love to know that; not that she had ever known quite such spectacular pyrotechnics.

Leave it, she cautioned herself. Wait. See how things go. Don't make a big deal of it, or take any notice of Polly. She's the *last* person. . .

But he still scares me stiff, she thought as she walked back through the wood to the car. Well, not him exactly, but the situation he's put me in. And I wish he was here with me right now. I want to see him, to have him smile at me and put his arms round me, make me feel wanted and cherished. . .

She laughed at herself; a short, derisive expulsion of breath. She didn't know what she wanted; that was the truth of it.

\*   \*   \*

The telephone rang just as Pen came downstairs having taken her
father his bedtime Ovaltine. She was glad to hear it. Whoever was
at the other end, the call created a welcome diversion from despon-
dency and apprehension, for she still had not brought herself to tell
Mrs Cartwright that her father, unlike Barkis, was not willing. Mrs
Cartwright sat on the Town Council, the position once so coveted by
Caleb himself, and was the organiser of the whole affair, the Grand
Co-ordinator of the parade and the presentation and the party, "The
three P's," as she jocularly put it to the committee involved.

She was, in her own right, a formidable lady and one whom
Pen avoided at the best of times. There was something about
her stature, her high colour, her jutting chin and her shark-like
smile that had always filled her with terror, and the prospect of
breaking the news of her father's change of heart had caused much
agitation and many a sleepless night.

Pen was not proud of this. She was aware that such fearful procrastination was ridiculous at her age. She should have
been able to confront Mrs Cartwright, putting her father's views
to her firmly and unequivocally – with great regret and sincere
apologies, of course, but brooking no argument. So far, however, she had not done so, hoping against hope that he would
reverse his decision as suddenly and inexplicably as he had made
it.

The call was from Caro.

"Oh, lovely to hear you," Pen cried. "I was going to phone you
a bit later on. How's everyone at your end?"

"Fine. Jilly and Nick are sailing round the Greek islands –
having a wonderful time, by all accounts. Rachel and Ben took
the children camping in France. They've just come back, brown
as berries. Richard's on some sort of course. Hannah's busy,
as always, and getting terribly excited about the wedding. She
and Mike are house-hunting –"

"What a welter of activity!"

"You sound a bit down. Anything wrong?"

"No. Well –" Pen sighed. "Allow me to rephrase that. Yes,
*everything's* wrong! Father's decided that this celebration thing
mustn't be allowed to go ahead. He can't face it, he says."

"Oh, my God! He doesn't change, does he? Whatever he can do to cause the maximum amount of trouble to the maximum number of people –"

"Well, he is very old, Caro. I keep reminding myself."

"It's nothing to do with being old. He's always been like that. Of course, he could easily change his mind back again."

Pen sighed again.

"That's what I keep thinking."

"Don't worry too much – I expect he will. He loves people to make a fuss of him really. I thought he'd be relishing the prospect of reliving his moment of glory."

"Well, I think he was until suddenly he had this change of heart. It's all because –" Because of the Yeos, Pen had started to say, but realised in time that the statement was hardly one to win Caro's sympathy. "Because he gets tired quickly these days," she said.

"Yes, I suppose he does, poor old love. Still, he could have said something ages ago, before everyone got steamed up about it. After all, he's had a long time to think about it. You really could *bash* him sometimes, couldn't you?"

"You could," Pen admitted. "And I really think Mrs Cartwright might, if he doesn't change his mind back again. She'll probably satisfy herself by bashing me."

"What does she say about it?"

"I haven't found the courage to tell her yet. I'm dreading it."

"You have all my sympathy. Listen, I know what'll make him go through with it. Tell him it will be one in the eye for the Yeos. No one ever held a celebration for them."

Pen finally came clean.

"It's the Yeos that seem to be worrying him," she said. "He says they'll whisper about him behind their hands."

Caro brushed this aside impatiently.

"Oh, for the love of heaven! Who's left to whisper? He's obsessed! There are none of Dad's generation left except poor old Hilda, and she's harmless."

"I have to say she doesn't look it. I saw her in the butcher's the other day. She looks more like a witch than ever."

"She always has, hasn't she? Remember how she used to moon about the cliffs all those years ago after Henry died?"

"You weren't here. It was after you scarpered."

"You told me about it. Anyway, she was still at it that time when I came home, after Rachel was born. Don't you remember how she loomed at us out of the mist and scared us half to death?"

"Yes – yes I do, now you mention it. What a memory you've got, Caro."

"I don't believe there's any harm in her, though – which is more than you could say for the late lamented Henry. He was a nasty piece of work if ever there was one."

"Hilda couldn't have thought so."

"Well no. But she must have got over her grief years ago – and anyway, whatever else Father was blamed for, he could hardly be blamed for that particular tragedy."

"No, of course not. No one ever did."

"You'll have to try to talk him round, Pen."

"You think I haven't?"

"Jolly him along."

"I've jollied until I'm blue in the face. But official celebration or not, whatever happens we'll have a family birthday party on the 15th. I thought of asking David and his son. You'll all be coming anyway, won't you? And Trish. She phoned the other night."

"David's definitely coming, then? Have you heard?"

"Yes, Simon phoned. He's supposed to be arriving in England at the end of the month, but of course they won't be down until the actual weekend. They've booked at the Marina. I wonder whether they'll come if the official doo-dah is called off?"

"It's us he's coming to see, not the Guides and the Brownies!"

"I suppose so," Pen said, sounding doubtful; but she found once she had put the phone down, that she felt happier. What did the silly old celebration matter, anyway? Suddenly she felt strong, optimistic and more than a match for Mrs Cartwright. She would talk to her tomorrow.

\*    \*    \*

Laura, not normally given to envying anybody, was nevertheless accustomed to leaving Sally with a feeling of vague regret regarding her own life. If such a thing as the perfect marriage existed, then Sally and John surely had it; or so she had always thought.

So Polly had always thought too. Sally's marriage to a bright, up-and-coming financial wizard had been held up time and time again as a shining example and one that Laura would be well advised to follow at the earliest opportunity.

She was thankful that Polly was staying a few more days with Beatrice and would be making her own way back to London by train, for her comments and exhortations on the subject would on this occasion have struck something of a sour note. For the first time, as she drove back to London, Laura felt uneasy and anxious about Sally. Things, she felt sure, were not as rosy as they had once been.

She couldn't put her finger on what was wrong but she hoped devoutly that it was temporary. Or the result of her overheated imagination. She didn't think it was that, though. Sally hadn't said anything – indeed, with a family party to prepare for, and the party itself on the Sunday after the christening, there had been little time for confidences – but Laura couldn't help noticing the distinct absence of eye-contact between husband and wife, a lack of warmth, the occasional edge in the voice. They had seemed like two barely-polite strangers.

What was it? Post-natal depression? Shortage of sleep? John's tendency towards workaholicism? Sally's boredom, now that she was stuck at home with only the children for company? She'd left Oliver with a baby-minder and gone back to part-time teaching when Emma started nursery school, but had given it up just before Jess was born. No, she'd said when Laura inquired. She wasn't going back – not for ages, anyway. She and John didn't want other people to bring up their children.

Was that it? Come to think of it, it just might be. John had been in the room when she had made that statement and for a second or two there had been, without another word being spoken, an oddly charged atmosphere, a faint echo of angry words. Well, whatever it was they'd work it out. No marriage, she told herself with perfect reasonableness, could possibly last without the odd rift. It didn't mean a thing.

She couldn't help relating the situation to herself, however. She had no idea how she would feel if she had children of her own. In theory, she thought she would want to oversee their early years; but who could tell? How would she feel if she was no longer a free agent, able to follow her own instincts, not in control any more, subject to someone else's rules?

John wasn't a tyrant. But on this issue, it seemed clearer and clearer to Laura as she put small pieces of the jig-saw together, he had taken the moral high ground and Sally had conceded.

She's unhappy because she's bored, and she feels guilty because she's unhappy because she's bored, Laura thought. Who needs that kind of hassle? Not me!

Her flat was the upstairs section of a converted late Victorian house not unlike the one in Chiswick now occupied by her mother – like houses all over London in fact. Sometimes she wondered how it must have been, living in London around the turn of the century. The place must surely have been one vast building site.

It wasn't a palace, or even a little palace, she thought, remembering the woman quoted by Carne. She loved it, though. She had a bedroom, a bathroom, a small kitchen, and one large living-room, the walls of which had been covered with particularly repellent lime-green paper when she moved in, but which she had stripped and painted white.

She'd wanted white walls as a background to the three modern paintings that seemed to dominate the room. The painters were unknown, unsung. She'd bought the pictures because she liked them – loved the shapes and the glorious, jewel-like colours which, on grey winter days, seemed to speak of warmer climes – of sun and richness and the kind of vibrancy that felt natural to her.

Simon had admired them. He had looked around at the room and thought how like her it was; how cool and unfussy, but exciting too, with its use of colour.

Stella's desk was the only piece of furniture of any monetary worth. It was covered now by the material Laura had brought back from Simon's flat. She had left the diary with him, but had carried away the photographs and the other papers she had deemed worthy of retention – foolishly, perhaps, she thought now as having looked at the unremarkable post that was waiting for her she made some coffee and brought it through to the living-room. Why had she bothered, she wondered, looking at it from across the room. There wasn't a great deal there that would add anything to the considerable material he already had by and about Stella, and heaven alone knew she was short of space to store it.

She'd go through it again, she thought. Harden her heart, throw more of it away. What the hell did it matter now that in 1958 Stella had made notes for an article concerning the need for an international agreement to halt tests of nuclear bombs? That she'd written a profile of U Thant, the new Secretary-General of United Nations in 1961, and of Indira Gandhi in 1966? It was all old hat, past history. Written on water, as Stella herself had been the first to admit.

No time like the present. She finished her coffee, applied herself to the task. U Thant was out; but Indira Gandhi stayed. It was a wonderful article. So, going back in time, was the article Stella had written just after the war concerning reconciliation and the plight of the dispossessed – the Displaced Persons, as they were called, with no home and no family and no hope.

At least, Laura thought, I can put things in chronological order, for she found herself even now reluctant to throw much away (my children might be interested, she told herself). It was when she was re-reading notes that Stella had made on the surrender of Paris to the Germans that she found the letter. It was caught up with a number of other scribbled notes and cuttings, all of which Stella had fastened together with a paper clip. The letter was several pages long, handwritten, on thin white sheets folded into four. It was clearly personal and looked as if it might possibly have attached itself to the other papers by mistake.

Curiously, she turned to the last page. It was from Jane, she discovered; Jane, who had become fed up with writing about carrots in *Lady Fair* and had joined the NAAFI. The paper was yellowing at the edges, the ink faded. It was dated 21st May 1940 and had been written from an address in Glasgow.

She was missing London, Jane wrote, though life was very busy and she didn't regret leaving *Lady Fair* for a moment. She hadn't met anyone congenial to have a laugh with yet – not, she added, that there was much to laugh about, was there? The news from France was terrible, with the Germans apparently having everything their own way:

I've only this minute heard about the capture of Amiens and Arras, [she wrote]. I can't believe it! Whatever happened to the Maginot Line? They say the Germans have driven a twenty-mile corridor from the Ardennes to the Channel. What can stop them invading us? I feel sick with horror at the thought of jack-boots marching up Whitehall and Piccadilly, just as inevitably they will soon march in our beloved Paris. And what can the Americans be playing at, leaving us to face them on our own?

How immediate it all seemed, Laura thought; the more immediate, somehow, because war was in the headlines again. How little man learned! And how sickeningly close defeat must have felt, that summer of 1940. Somehow, knowing the victorious end of the story, this aspect had never struck her before as forcibly as it did now.

She read on. Glasgow was enjoying sunshine that day, apparently, and Jane was hoping, some day soon, to get out into the glorious countryside, so far only seen from the train:

Talk of the countryside makes me think of Cal and his beloved Cornwall. I was glad to hear that they've at last found a use for him at the MoI even if it is, as you say, merely pushing bits of paper about. It may lead to something. I must say I agree with him that you should adapt your "patriotism" article for broadcasting. It was a wonderful piece – if Cal is in the Home Propaganda section he can surely put a word in for you? I simply cannot believe, as you suggest, that the BBC won't look at your work! All that fuss was a lifetime ago, another age! They surely wouldn't be so petty? Or would they? Worth a try, anyway.

There wasn't very much more, and what there was concerned people Laura had never heard of. She skimmed through it, returning, with disbelief, to the paragraph concerning Stella, the article, and the BBC.

She looked at it thoughtfully for a long, long time.

\*       \*       \*

It was Dolly who brought the news about Hilda Yeo.

"They reckon she must have been dead since yesterday," she said to Pen with the kind of mournful relish people keep for these occasions. "Mrs Laity called about seven last night with the Parish Magazine. She didn't get no answer so she went round the back and saw the milk still on the doorstep, and then she knew something was wrong so she called the man next door to break in through a window and there she was. Dead as a doornail, poor soul."

"She hadn't been ill, had she?" Pen asked. "I saw her just the other day and she looked much as usual. Pale, of course, but then she always was."

"They d'say 'twas her heart," Dolly said. "Always taking pills, Mrs Laity told me. And she was a good age, after all – eighty-nine. Must have been."

"Yes." Pen paused a moment in her preparation of her father's breakfast tray. "Yes, I suppose she was all of that. Poor soul, as you say." She poured boiling water into the teapot and covered it with a knitted cosy. "She can't have had a happy life, can she? Bringing up those children on her own –"

"And look at them now!" Dolly was tying an apron round her ample waist as she spoke. "Never come anywhere near her! That Leonard of hers is in London, up to no good if I'm any judge. Chip off the old block if you ask me. I'm not one to speak ill of the dead, Mrs Hambly, and goodness knows I wouldn't have wished Henry's death on anyone, but he weren't no good, say what you will. My old mother knew un as a boy, and she'd always say Hilda was better off without un."

Pen stood for a second, the tray in her hands, remembering the poor, distracted widow who had roamed the cliffs.

"Hilda must have loved him very much," she said.

Dolly crashed a heavy pan into the sink.

"Some women ent got the sense they was born with, Mrs Hambly."

And who am I to argue with that, Pen thought, as she took the tray upstairs. She told her father about Hilda as she settled him on his pillows and poured his tea. He liked to hear the news of the village, particularly news of deaths. Though he had mourned the passing of many old friends in the past, lately his main emotion seemed to be pride in his own longevity as others of his age group, and younger, fell away.

"Well, well; Hilda Yeo," he said several times. "Not too much milk, dear. Well, well; Hilda Yeo." He gave a snort of laughter. "Well, if there's any justice hereafter she'll go straight through the pearly gates with no questions asked. She had her share of hell down here, married to that rat."

"That's not a very nice thing to say!" Pen said reproachfully. "Anyway, her marriage didn't last very long, did it? Henry's been dead for the past forty years."

"Forty-six," said Carne.

"Forty-six? Yes, I suppose it must be. What a memory you have!"

Her father made no reply to this but she could see from his face that his reflections had for some reason lifted his spirits. When later Fred helped him downstairs he opted to sit in the drawing-room rather than go to the summerhouse, since the day was cool and rather misty. As was often their custom, Pen sat with him and together they attempted *The Times* crossword puzzle. It was clear after only a few minutes, however, that his mind was elsewhere on this occasion. Pen, failing to get any kind of response from him, looked up from reading out the clue to eight across to see him staring out of the window, a faint smile on his face, his fingers drumming on the arm of his chair.

"You're not concentrating," she said accusingly. He laughed and held up his hands as if in supplication.

"I admit it! Forgive me, my darling. It's simply that I was thinking," he paused and gave her his most charming smile. "I was thinking of all you've said about this birthday shindig. It would really be most dreadfully ungrateful of me to pull out now, wouldn't it? All those preparations you've told me about; the choir and the parade and the party and the flags. I don't deserve it, I'm well aware. I shall be frightfully embarrassed at all the fuss, but I realise now I can't disappoint everyone. Perhaps you'd better tell Mrs Thingummy it's on after all."

Pen looked at him narrowly.

Mine not to reason why, she thought, expelling her breath in a long drawn-out sigh of relief. Mine not to wonder what has caused this second change of heart. But I do agree with Caro; there are times when you could bash him.

"Mrs Thingummy never knew it was off," she said.

\*　　\*　　\*

187

"I don't think I want to know about this," Simon said unhappily, looking at the letter. "Maybe it doesn't mean what you think it means."

"Surely it's obvious what it means. Stella wrote the text of Carne's cosy little chats."

"There's no proof –"

"Since when did a good journalist close his eyes to the truth because it was inconvenient?"

"The way I see it, we don't know the truth and we've got no way of finding out."

"It's as clear as crystal to me." Laura, sitting close beside him, took the letter from him and read it once more, just as if she didn't already know it by heart. "It explains everything, Simon. Why the style was so different from Carne's novels, why he could never produce anything of the same quality afterwards."

"It's possible, but there's no proof."

"What about this letter? Jane is urging her to adapt for broadcasting an article on patriotism. And what do we find? Surprise, surprise, a talk about patriotism is broadcast all right, not by Stella but by Stella's boy-friend. It does, to say the least, give one pause for thought, don't you agree?"

"Of course I agree. Maybe they felt that with Stella's track record at the BBC she wouldn't have a hope in hell of it being accepted, so Carne submitted it under his name. Don't forget Carne was working in the Ministry of Information by this time. He might well have known what they were looking for in the propaganda line. It could have been a joke, for God's sake – a hoax! After all, it might have given Stella a laugh to think that anything she wrote was out, but that the same thing under someone else's name would be accepted."

Laura thought this over.

"OK, I'll buy that," she said. "It could have happened that way. But why didn't they come clean then? There are hundreds of talks in that collection – and Carne got all the credit, all the kudos. He's *still* getting it, for God's sake! You ought to expose him."

"Now, hold it right there," Simon said. "There are three things you've got to consider. One: we have no real proof that Stella wrote the text of that first talk, let alone any of the others. Two: as you rightly say, there are a lot of them extending over at least three years.

If she wrote them – and it's a big 'if' – she did it willingly. She could have exposed him any time she wanted to but she didn't."

"And the third thing?" Laura prompted him when he seemed to have come to a halt.

"Carne's an old man, honey. Ninety-five in just over two weeks time. What might this do to him? And to Pen –"

"You rather fell for her, didn't you?" Laura's smile was more a twist of the lips.

"I wouldn't put it that way. Sure, I liked her, but she's old enough to be my mother."

"You can't look at him – and her – cold-bloodedly, though. You're too personally involved."

"Mm." Simon gave a rueful laugh. "I've thought that myself from time to time. But even if what you say is true, you've got to think what effect exposure would have on the old boy; and here's another point for your consideration, Laura. It was Carne who made the broadcasts, remember? You've heard his voice. It was the delivery that mattered as much as anything else."

"I agree with that. I just don't see why he should have had all the credit. And I don't see –"

She stopped in mid-sentence, shaking her head. She got up and went to the window, hands thrust deep into her trouser pockets, while Simon looked at her unhappily.

"This has really upset you, hasn't it?" he said. She nodded, but didn't turn her head. He got up and went to her, putting his arms around her, turning her to face him. "She meant so much to you, didn't she?"

Laura nodded again.

"Ever since I saw the letter, I've felt – I don't know. Weird. As if I've trodden on a stair that isn't there. I know it's stupid. It's ancient history and I shouldn't take it all so personally. Stella took pride in her work but she wasn't really bothered about money or cheap acclaim, so heaven knows, I shouldn't be bothered about it either. It's simply that I've always believed that she was the most honest person I've ever known or am likely to know."

"She was generous too. Polly told me."

"Yes, that's true." Laura sighed and leant against his shoulder for a moment, feeling his hand on her hair. "She'd give a beggar her last penny –" she pulled away and looked up at him again. "But her work was something different, Simon. It was important on every level. All her life she practised what she preached – or I thought she did; that it was time women were taken seriously. Not as adjuncts to men, not as writers of gossipy bits on the so-called Woman's Page, not as some sort of under-class, but people in their own right. I thought she was strong and incorruptible. I just can't handle the thought that all the time she was pandering to her man as readily as any little suburban housewife. No better, really, than Polly. What happened to all those passionately held beliefs?"

Simon put his hands on her shoulders and looked at her four-square.

"You don't know that any of this is true. You could be building up a totally false picture. But in any case –" He paused and looked into her eyes, seeing her puzzled, hurt expression.

"In any case – what?"

"I guess she was in love."

"So integrity meant nothing? The beliefs of a lifetime were totally suspended?"

Simon continued to look at her.

"It wouldn't be that way with you, would it?" he said after a moment.

"Damned right it wouldn't," she said, turning back to the window.

# VIII

"Thank God for anniversaries," Cathy said contentedly.

David turned to smile at the woman who would always be his kid sister, no matter how many anniversaries had come and gone.

"You love it, don't you? Having all your chicks under the same roof again."

"I've got you too," she reminded him. "You don't visit as often as we'd like."

"Not as often as I'd like, either. Too bad Joe couldn't make it."

"I can't remember the last time the three of us were together. Still, it's great he's got so much work on hand. He says maybe at Christmas he and Dora might take a trip east."

"Yeah – he told me. Made like he envied me all my leisure, but I know he was just kidding. He always was a hustler, wasn't he? The one most likely to succeed?"

"You didn't do so badly yourself."

She turned her head to study him. It was an affectionate look for they had always been close, and she had worried about him these past two years. At one stage, in her extreme youth, her regard for him had been akin to idolatry; never, she had thought, would she meet any boy who would approach him in looks or character or general niceness. To her he had been without defect or blemish. That stage had long passed. She knew he had faults – who hadn't? – but the love remained.

She had liked Fay and had agonised for herself as well as for him and for Simon when she died. When David told her of his proposed retirement she was doubtful about its wisdom, just as Simon had been; but maybe he'd been right after all. This weekend she was glad to see that he appeared to have lost that awful, distant, distracted look he had taken on – the look that seemed to say that nothing, really, mattered very much any more. Lying beside the pool in the garden of the house in the Boston suburb where he had come to celebrate her forty-year marriage to Brian Lawley, she thought he looked relaxed and more at peace with himself than he had done for a long, long time.

"You're looking forward to this upcoming excursion down memory lane when you to go England, aren't you?" she said.

"Oh!" He laughed a little self-consciously. "I don't know about that. I'm certainly looking forward to seeing Simon."

"He's a good boy. Thoughtful. It was sweet of him to call last night. It meant a lot to me – Brian too."

"He's very fond of both of you. Always has been."

"He's always seemed like one of ours. Julie used to say she'd swap Simon for either of her brothers."

"Don't believe it!"

"There were times when she wasn't joking, I promise you. Is Simon going to stay in London, d'you think?"

"I don't know. He certainly seems happy enough there at the moment. I – I rather think there's a girl," he added. Cathy smiled at this.

"Knowing Simon, I'd be a little surprised if there wasn't."

"Mm. I kind of get the feeling this might be more important than most, though. Can't quite put my finger on why. A father's instinct, I guess – which I don't pretend is infallible!"

"An English girl? How do you feel about that?"

"If he loves her and she loves him I don't give a damn if she's English or French or a Shi'ite Arab. That's the least important thing."

"I wonder what your own English girl will turn out to be like after all these years – Trixie? Tracey? I've forgotten her name, though heaven knows you mentioned it enough in your letters."

"Trish?" David shook his head and laughed a little. "Did I mention her a lot?"

"Only about ten times on every page. Boy, were you smitten! Mom used to worry about it. She thought she was going to be landed with a daughter-in-law who would insist on afternoon tea and riding to hounds."

"I had dreams myself, I don't mind telling you."

"You wrote she was the prettiest girl you'd ever seen."

"Did I? Maybe I did. She was a doll, no two ways about it."

"I wonder what you'll think when you see her again?"

"After forty-six years I'll be astounded if we recognise each other. She's married to a Frenchman, Simon tells me. Lives in the south of France. He got all the news from Pen."

Cathy saw his smile.

"What's amusing you?" she asked.

"Nothing. Well, to be honest, I was just hoping she gives the Frenchman a better time than she showed me."

"What?" Cathy raised her head from the back of the lounger the better to look at him. "I thought she was everything that was wonderful – some kind of superwoman, not only ravishingly beautiful but full of virtue. I was so envious, you'd never believe."

David laughed out loud.

"You know what?" he said. "She was a pain in the ass! Pretty as a picture, sweet as sugar candy, but a Grade A pain in the ass. And I was probably equally so. Looking back, I think I must have come over like a kind of John-Boy Walton – so damned clean-cut it beggars belief. Youngsters today would laugh themselves sick."

"You mean she wouldn't let you have your wicked way with her?" Cathy looked amused. "Well, good for her!"

"Yeah, well, as mother of a daughter I guess you would say that. I can even say it myself, from where I'm standing; but then – oh boy! You'll never know how I suffered. I have often thought," he went on, shading his eyes to look up at his sister as she rose from her reclining chair and pulled on a pink cotton shirt, "that the joys of youth are much overrated – they were in our day anyway. Hey, are you leaving? I was kind of making up my mind to have a swim."

"I must go and get changed and see to things in the kitchen. Julie and family will be here in a minute – but don't you move, Dave. Brian will be out in a while, once he's finished setting up the bar."

"I ought to help," David said, not stirring. "Let me know if I can."

"There's nothing, really. We're a good team."

In every way, David thought as she left him. They'd had their differences, their difficult times, Cathy and Brian. It hadn't all been plain sailing in the early days. There'd been money problems, teenage children problems; a time, twenty-odd years ago when a drunken Brian had confided a tale of an office *affaire* that had gotten out of hand. Still, they had weathered everything together, and appeared to be surviving happily. The party tonight would consist of family and friends, all of whom genuinely loved them and wished them well. What more could anyone ask?

He ought to help, though. He ought to go and offer Brian a hand. Maybe in a minute. He felt delightfully sleepy, reluctant to move. These new pool-side loungers sure were comfortable. He must remember to ask Brian where he bought them – his own could do with renewal.

Imagine Cathy remembering what he wrote about Trish! Life was funny that way. You could forget something you heard yesterday, and still remember details from the past. Well, some of them.

And selectively remembering, David drowsed.

\* \* \*

Just as he knew that it must have rained that spring and early summer of 1944 even though he couldn't remember it, so he knew that Army life didn't consist entirely of slipping away from camp to be with Trish.

The Regiment consisted of three Battalions. They'd spent twelve weeks Stateside doing engineer training during which they'd been taught to use chisels and saws and rock drills and learned how to place and clear mines and booby traps – how to record where the mines had been set so that they could be removed and deactivated. They'd trained with weapons, in demolition and in road-building, in camouflage and bridge-building, and had practised these skills until they felt they could perform them blindfold. But still, on Bow Beach, as well as learning everything anyone could possibly want to know about the landing craft – the LCTs as they were called – they practised the same skills again. And as if that wasn't enough, there were drills and guard duties and guard duties and drills, and a sergeant who shouted and swore at them and generally made life a misery.

David knew that's how it was, but somehow, forty-six years afterwards, it was Trish that came to mind, and all the agony of loving her and wanting her and being denied.

He'd put every argument to her that he could think of, even descending to blackmail.

"I might die," he whispered hoarsely one afternoon when she lay supine in his arms, allowing him to fumble with the dozen small buttons down the front of her dress. Earlier she'd led him to the very end of the headland that lay beyond Roscarrow, down to a kind of ledge, wide and grassy, shielded from the rest of the world by gorse bushes and stunted hawthorn trees. The sun had brought out the coconut scent of the gorse. Beneath them, waves dashed themselves on the rocks.

"I'll soon be going into battle," he pursued, feeling at one with Henry V and Napoleon, and all those other soldier heroes of history. "I could easily be killed. Have you thought of that? How would you feel then?"

"Well, of course I'd feel very sorry, wouldn't I?" Trish said.

She sounded calmly matter-of-fact about it, completely untouched by the thought. Though she said she loved him, there were times when she seemed distant, luke-warm, as if she were merely sitting back and enjoying her power over him. But when such thoughts rose to trouble him, he remembered how she hated to share him with anyone. She grew silent and tight-lipped if she thought he was taking too much notice of Pen – if he joined in her quotation-swapping games with too much enthusiasm or laughed too heartily at her tales of school life. And once when returning from the village she found him down on the beach with Caro, she had been ridiculously upset, even though they had only been looking at the boat and talking of repairs. So she must love him, mustn't she?

They still hadn't Done It, though. It was really strange, he sometimes thought. The language that was common currency in camp was explicit, basic and filthy. It was language he had frequently used himself, though perhaps it didn't spring as readily to his lips as to some others on account of his sheltered, Episcopalian upbringing – but when it came to Trish, he couldn't even *think* it! It was as if she were some kind of pure, ethereal, spiritual creature, way above the

195

standards of normal womanhood, beyond the earthy instincts that plagued God's more lowly creatures.

So he avoided the more unambiguous words, referring only obliquely to his overwhelming desire even to himself. Eventually, surely, she would agree? After all, she appeared to enjoy his kisses, and not only on her lips. And she didn't appear to mind a straying hand in all kinds of intimate regions.

There was one night when he felt quite sure his efforts would be crowned with success. Adept now at avoiding every obstacle the Army could throw at him he had sneaked away from the camp at midnight, climbing up the cliff face to the path, bending double so that he was hidden by the gorse bushes. God knows what would have happened to him if he'd been caught. Looking back, he could only think that some kind of madness had possessed him – some suspension of common sense or logical thought.

A handful of gravel thrown at Trish's window had brought her downstairs, and hearts in mouths, giggling a little, enjoying the escapade all the more because of its illicit nature, they had fled to the summerhouse. They had piled cushions on the floor and lain there in each other's arms for an hour or two of love.

Well, sort of love. She had still managed to evade the final capitulation, but had been so sweet, so responsive, that, though driven into his usual frenzy of longing, by the time he had made his furtive re-entry to the camp he knew himself to be more deeply in love than ever.

Though no one, probably not even the Commanders-in-Chief, knew the date of the invasion, everyone was aware that it would be soon; and as if that wasn't bad enough, he had just learned that their time together was to be whittled away by three days during which he and the rest of the Battalion were to be sent to Devon to practise firing at moving targets. Three days!

"But you can't go! It's Caro's birthday on Wednesday," Trish had protested when, as they lay on the grassy ledge, he had broken the news. "We were banking on you joining us. Daddy's booked a table at the Marina."

The Marina was the big hotel on the cliff where some of the officers were billeted.

"You reckon if I told the Sergeant they'd let me off?"

It was a joke, of course, but a bitter one. He had a nagging, uneasy, inexplicable feeling that this afternoon marked the beginning of the end. There were only days left – perhaps no days at all. By the time the Battalion was back on Bow Beach the invasion could be only hours away.

"But you will be back for the dance on Saturday, won't you? Oh, you must be, David!"

"I'll try."

If he sounded perfunctory, it was because his mind was on other things. She had the silkiest skin, and smelled sweet like honey. Oh God, she had to let him –

"Everyone's going to be there," Trish prattled on, stroking his hair almost absent-mindedly. "It's Porthlivick's farewell to the GIs. There's an awfully good band coming from St Jory, and a whole crowd of us are going to decorate the Parish Hall and your Major said he'd bring some ham and stuff over so there could be refreshments. They've formed a Committee."

He didn't care about Committees or bands or anything but the insistent pulsing of his body and his desperate longing, a kind of screaming, desert-like emptiness in his soul that only possession of her could fill. Didn't she know? Didn't she understand anything?

Her kisses were as sweet as ever, and the small intimacies as enticing.

"Trish, please darling, please –"

Her hands were pushing him away.

"Honestly, what must you think of me? Stop it, Davey! I'm not that sort of a girl."

It wasn't going to happen. Not even here on this little plateau with the waves booming away below them which surely must be the most romantic place in the world to make love to a girl; and not even now, when soon he would be going away to war. Wearily he turned from her and lay on his back, folding his arms under his head. Sudden, shaming tears pricked at his eyes.

"What time do you have to get back?" Trish asked.

"My God!" David sat up and looked at his watch. "I must go. I'm going to be late."

The afternoon was over. They climbed back to the path and said goodbye with a long, lingering embrace.

"I do love you, Davey," Trish said.

"Do you?" She'd said so often enough, and sometimes he believed her; today, however, there was a stony sadness at his heart.

"Silly, you know I do. Oh Davey, you must be back for Saturday! Promise you'll try? I'll die if I have to go to the dance on my own."

The knowledge that she would go to it anyway, with or without him, increased the stoniness.

"If I don't make it, it won't be my fault," he said. "You seem to forget I'm a soldier. I do what I'm told."

She stood on tip-toe and kissed his nose.

"Well, I'm telling you to hurry back."

For a moment he stood looking at her, his finger gently rubbing her cheek. She was still the prettiest girl he'd ever seen. His love for her seemed to constrict his throat, overwhelming him with emotion.

"I'm so crazy about you, Trish," he whispered. "You will wait for me, won't you? We will be together one day?"

"Of course! Now run back to camp. You'll be in trouble."

Still he lingered.

"Promise you love me?"

"Of course I do, silly! All my friends envy me like anything. I shouldn't tell you this because it'll make you conceited, but my friend Mary says you're the best-looking GI on Bow Beach."

He gave a mirthless grunt of laughter.

"Does she have a white stick and a seeing-eye dog?"

"Go on!" Trish acknowledged the quip with another brief kiss and a push on his shoulders. "You'll be shot at dawn."

She stood and waved as he went down the path. He turned at the first bend, and she was still there to give a last wave. There was, he told himself, no reason for this doom-like feeling of sadness, but it was there just the same. Was it a premonition of some awful disaster? Maybe he wasn't going to make it after all. Maybe there'd be a bullet with his name on it, like they said.

No – it was wrong to be morbid. It was all Trish's fault, he told himself, fighting the sadness with anger. There were words for girls like her –

But oh, how he loved her! He wished he didn't have to go away.

He wished this bloody war was over. He wished he were ten years older, with a Chevy Convertible and money in his pocket, wooshing round Carter's Bend on his way to Hannville Lake. And most of all, he wished that Trish would –

But what was the use? She wasn't going to. He might just as well face it.

\*     \*     \*

Laura was about to go to bed, alone for once and in her own flat, when the thought suddenly struck her. She looked at her watch. Almost eleven thirty. Simon had gone to a reception given by an official at the US Embassy, but he might be home by now. How long did such functions last? She had no idea.

She dialled his number, just in case, and pulled a face when his Answerphone came on the line; however, the message hadn't run its course before he interrupted and answered in person.

"Sorry – just come in. *Laura!* I didn't expect to hear from you tonight." Maybe not any other night either, he might have added. They'd parted the previous day, not on bad terms, exactly, but gloomily, coolly, as if all the uncertainty about the Carne scripts was like a cold wind, blowing them apart.

"Listen," Laura said now, a note of eagerness in her voice. "How do we know she's dead?"

For a moment he thought she meant Stella and he frowned in bewilderment; then the penny dropped.

"You mean Jane?"

"Who else? We just assumed it, didn't we, and with absolutely no reason. I mean, look at Carne – ninety-five! Stella was seventy-nine when she died five years ago, which would make her eighty-four now. A mere stripling compared to him. Jane could easily be around still. People are living longer and longer."

"That's right." His answer was enthusiastic, and not only at the thought of the population's increased longevity. It was good to hear Laura sounding cheerful and positive again. Yesterday he had the distinct impression that however great the injustice, he was somehow being blamed not only for Carne's sins, but for her grandmother's failure to live up to her high ideals as well. "So all

199

we've got to do is to find her. Does Polly know her last name? She told me she married a man called Evelyn."

"Yes, I've heard that tale too. I've never heard the surname, though. I'll phone and ask her tomorrow. I seem to remember she told me that she went to Jane's wedding with Stella, so she ought to know."

"Don't get your hopes up. It was a long time ago."

Polly said exactly the same thing when Laura phoned her at Mrs Cameron's house the following day.

"I suppose she could be alive," she said. "She was a bit younger than Stella, I think, but as to her name – well, darling, I haven't a clue. I did go to the wedding, you're right there, but I was a mere tot at the time. I never called her anything but Auntie Jane."

"But if you went to the *wedding*, Mother –"

"It's no good getting cross. Do you realise you only call me Mother when you're cross?"

"I'm not cross, Polly dear, but do think!"

"I am thinking." A silence ensued, while Polly silently pursued this somewhat unusual activity. "Her maiden name was something like – Stratford. Only it wasn't that. There was a shop in Richmond High Street with the same name when we were living there, but I simply can't remember – *Stratton*! That was it. Stratton."

"And her married name?"

"Darling, it's no good. I remember her husband was called Evelyn, which I thought was quite extraordinary. Mrs Evans's name was Evelyn, you see, so I never thought of it as a man's name. But what the rest of it was I didn't register. I didn't take to him much, that I do know."

"When was she married? Can you remember that?"

After more thought and much calculation, Polly decided that it must have been in the summer of 1945, around the time of VE day.

"Yes, that's right," she said, with growing certainty. "The wedding must have been literally just before VE day because there was a street party very soon after and I wore the same dress to it. Pink, it was, with a white frill on the bodice and round the hem. I *adored* that dress! We bought it at Daniel Neal's especially for the occasion."

"If it was just before VE day you weren't such a tot as all that," Laura pointed out. "You must have been at least thirteen."

Polly, who always seemed to suffer from amnesia whenever the subject of age was mentioned, denied this absolutely.

"No, no, darling, you're quite wrong! I was no more than ten, if that –"

"But you're sure that it was around VE day?"

"Absolutely. Why?"

"Because if I have some idea of the date of the marriage, I can go to St Catherine's House and look it up. Then I'll know her married name."

"Yes," Polly said. "Yes, of course. What a good idea."

"And I think you said she went to live in Devon?"

"I believe so. Somewhere down that way. It could have been Somerset. Why are you so anxious to know all this?"

For a second Laura hesitated, as always chary of telling her mother too much.

"We thought, perhaps – that is, I thought – that if she's still alive, she might have something to contribute to Simon's piece about Caleb Carne."

Polly was instantly full of enthusiasm.

"Darling, what a splended idea! And you're going to help with Simon's research? Oh, how lovely! I mean, I'm sure he'll appreciate it, and it will help you get to know each other –"

"That's *not* what I'm doing it for!"

"No, of course not, darling. Well, heaven alone knows if Jane's alive or dead, but I wish you the best of luck in tracking her down. Of course, she always seemed fairly old to me. I remember thinking at her wedding that she was terribly ancient to be a bride – I thought I'd *die* if I didn't find a husband before I was her age – but in retrospect she could only have been in her early thirties. Younger than Stella, anyway, so she could well be alive and kicking. On the other hand, she might not have stayed with Evelyn Whosit, might she? She might have a different name by now. Some of us have, after all."

Momentarily Laura's spirits fell a little, but she soon recovered. OK, she thought. Even if this proves to be a wild-goose chase, it's better to be doing something than nothing. Almost anything was better than sitting and wondering about what really happened all those years ago and why Stella did what she did.

"Can you think of any other friends from those days?" she asked Polly. "I know there were plenty that came later, but none that I can think of who go back that far."

"No –" Polly was thinking again. "I can't remember any. Of course, I was away all the time –"

Oh *God*! Laura groaned inwardly.

"Put another record on, Mother," she said.

Maybe she had only herself to blame for this undeniable feeling of let-down, Laura thought, after she had put the phone down. Maybe no woman, not even Stella, should be put on a pedestal; but she had known her intimately, she reminded herself. Talked to her. Imbibed her philosophy of life – in which bolstering the ego of incompetent males played no part at all.

St Catherine's House yielded the information she sought without a great deal of trouble. Jane Gwendoline Stratton, aged thirty-one, was married in London on 5th May 1945 to Evelyn Reginald St John Porteous, aged thirty-nine. So at least she now knew that she was looking for a Mrs Jane Porteous. Determinedly Laura discounted the theory that Jane might have remarried, for whatever reason. For the moment she would assume that Jane and Evelyn had stayed married. People did, after all.

Finding the name was easy enough; finding Jane's whereabouts, Laura could see, was going to prove a great deal more difficult. She went though the telephone directories for Devon and Somerset and made a list of all subscribers called Porteous – thankfully quite few – and afterwards, back at her flat, she tried ringing them. Not one gave her a positive result. Some who answered were regretful, one was brusque to the point of rudeness, one was inclined to chat; but none had any knowledge of either Jane or Evelyn Porteous.

There was, from two others, no reply at all. She'd have to try later, Laura thought – but drearily, with none of her previous enthusiasm.

"There has to be a way," she said to Simon when, still later, she went round to his flat for dinner. "Can't your Research Assistant at the *Gazette* do anything?"

"Hmm." Simon looked dubious – more concerned, it seemed to

Laura, with mixing the salad than with her efforts to find Jane Porteous. "I can't see Mandy taking kindly to that. I can ask her, of course."

"Other than that, we could advertise. Or use some sort of enquiry agent."

"Look –" Simon glanced at her warily. Her face wore a look of determination, setting off a whole carillon of warning bells.

"Something tells me," she said accusingly, "that you are less than whole-heartedly committed to this line of enquiry. Am I right?"

"I'm not sure it'll be very helpful, no. Sure I'd like to talk to Stella's friend, but all these methods of finding her would take time. My copy has to be in by the end of the month. That's four days from now. With my father arriving tomorrow, that doesn't give me much time to change anything."

"So it's just going to be a whitewash operation, is that it?"

Simon refused to rise to the biting note in her voice.

"My job was to write a profile of an old man whose brief moment of wartime glory lifted the spirits of ordinary British people, publication of which is timed to coincide with the fiftieth anniversary of the Battle of Britain which also happened to be the old boy's ninety-fifth birthday."

"I know all that!"

"I was just reminding you. I find it hard to imagine writing the kind of exposé that you seem to have in mind. So what if he did have a little help from your grandmother? She didn't appear to object, did she? Why, in God's name, should we?"

"Because –" Laura began; then sighed. "I don't know," she went on, much of the fight going out of her. "I don't know why this should have upset me so much."

"I do." Simon abandoned the salad and reached out to take her hand. "At least, I think I do. You've identified so much with your grandmother all your life. I guess that he who violates her work, violates you."

Laura laughed shortly.

"That sounds a bit over the top, but you could be right. Sort of."

"C'mon, let's go eat," he said. "Forget all about it, just for a few minutes."

Simon had prepared the dinner with great care, and in addition to making the salad he had grilled steak, bought a *baguette* and a bottle of Beaujolais. It was all delicious and she felt regretful that she couldn't enjoy it more – that she couldn't do as Simon had instructed and forget all about Carne and Stella and the whole puzzling business.

"The thing is," Simon said, also not forgetting it but not letting the matter affect his appetite either, "the way I look at it, she wasn't violated. Anything she gave, she gave willingly."

"I know." Without enthusiasm, Laura cut her steak into small pieces. "Don't you see that's almost worse?"

"I know, I know. She was untrue to her principles. You said."

"For goodness sake, you said forget all about it! Talk about something else! Tell me the buzz. What's going in your latest *Sightings* piece?"

"Mostly Edinburgh Festival stuff. God, I wish you'd been there! There was this incredible duo –"

She tried. She laughed in the right places, and put in the odd word; but she knew it was all too obvious that her spirits were low. Finally Simon seemed to run out of things to say and the silence between them lengthened. She looked at him apologetically.

"I'm sorry, Simon," she said.

"For not appreciating your steak? So you should be."

"I am appreciating it. It's lovely! Actually," she went on after a moment, "I was apologising for being such a bore."

"You know something?" He poured more wine into her glass. "I'd rather be bored with you than have the earth move with anyone else."

Her laugh had a contrite note.

"Oh, Simon –"

"Not, I hasten to say, that I'm averse to the earth moving."

"I'd noticed. Simon, tell me – can you really ignore that letter from Jane? Just leave your article the way it was, as if nothing's happened? Won't it nag at you for ever more if you do?"

Simon looked at her. He saw the clear, expressive eyes and the full curve of her lips that touched him like none he had known before. He wanted to please her; hated to think he was failing her. Suppose she got up and left? Didn't want to know him any more? Still, he had to tell her the truth.

"Look," he said. "Be practical. There's such a thing as libel, you know. As I keep on saying, Jane's letter doesn't prove a thing, whatever your gut feelings are telling you. If I say that Stella Morel might – just might – have written the text of Caleb Carne's talks, do you think for one moment the *Gazette* would print it? They wouldn't dare, not without one helluva lot more proof than we're likely to get in a month of Sundays. As it is, the article's on the long side and they'll probably edit half of it out of existence."

Laura appeared to think this over, her head bent. Then, as if with deep regret, she sighed and slowly rose from the table. Fearfully Simon watched her. I've blown it, he thought. She's going. It's over. I've failed her. She wants nothing more to do with me.

But she was only picking up the plates and making for the kitchen.

"Do we wash the dishes first?" she said over her shoulder as she swept past him.

Simon laughed, relieved and thankful.

"After," he said.

\*     \*     \*

Later, when they lay in each other's arms, they were quiet. He wondered what she was thinking, and thought he knew.

"You mustn't mind so much about Stella," he said at last. "She did what she wanted to do."

"Unless –" Laura paused for a long time. "Maybe he had some hold over her," she finished.

"Well, of course he did! She loved him, didn't she?"

She was looking up at the circular canopy over the bedhead with its hanging folds of gold and turquoise. She had laughed at it before now, and made scurrilous speculations regarding the type of elderly bachelor who would bother with such ornate draperies. She wasn't laughing now, however, just looking up as if she wasn't seeing it at all.

"Doesn't it frighten you?" she asked after a silence. "Love, I mean. Commitment. Promises. People behave so oddly when they're in the throes of it. How often does it last?"

"Often enough to make the experiment worthwhile, I guess."

"Your parents were happy." It was a statement, not a question.

He had told her about his parents. "But you know what they say," she went on. "One loves, one turns the cheek. Which one of your parents turned the cheek?"

"That's too glib!"

"Maybe." She eased herself out of bed, began to dress. "It's time I went home."

"I wish you wouldn't. Why don't you stay?"

She seemed in such a strange mood, he didn't want to let her go.

"Not tonight, Simon," she said and went on dressing.

Eventually he got up too and pulled on his trousers.

"Well, when can we see each other again?" he asked her.

"You'll be busy, you and your father."

"Not that busy."

"I shall probably be fairly occupied myself."

"Oh? What have you got planned?"

She didn't answer for a moment, and when she did, she sounded purposely vague.

"Oh, this and that. A bit of research. I want to try and have a go at Stella's biography. I haven't done nearly as much these holidays as I'd hoped."

"My fault."

She grinned at him.

"That's right. All your fault."

He looked at her uncertainly. Her mood seemed different now, altogether more positive and purposeful, but he asked no questions. She was at the rococo dressing-table by this time, combing her hair, laughing once more about the owner of the flat, saying how she simply had to meet him one day – she was beginning to have fantasies about him. She thought he probably looked like one of the gilt cherubs that supported the mirror, plump with a little pursed mouth.

"Am I right?" she asked. "I'm sure I am! He must be too precious for words."

"You're not far out. Look, I'll call you tomorrow. I want you to meet Dad."

She smiled at him in the mirror, vaguely and fleetingly.

"That'd be nice."

Simon looked at her suspiciously.

"What are you up to, Laura? What's on your mind?"

"Absolutely nothing." She turned and smiled, and getting up, came over to put her arms round his neck. "I'll see you soon."

"Come to dinner on Wednesday."

"No, not Wednesday. It's Polly's birthday, and I've promised to take her out somewhere – if, that is, she can bear to leave that bloody dog! She says the trip to Sussex has upset Fifi's nervous system and she doesn't like to leave her. Would you believe it, she's scouring Chiswick for a dog-sitter! Hey –" She looked up at him as if something had just struck her. "I've thought of a marvellous idea! Why don't you and your father come to dinner at my place on Wednesday, then Polly can bring the blasted hound with her. Not to mention the fact that dinner with two men will be a far bigger treat than going out with just me. She'll be in her seventh heaven. How about it? Could you bear it?"

"Sounds great," Simon said, kissing her. "C'mon – I'll walk you to the Fulham Road and we can pick up a taxi there."

"You're a nice man, Simon Holt," she said, her arms still around his neck.

"That sounds real exciting!"

"Mm. That, too."

Which was comforting; but he still thought she was up to something.

\*    \*    \*

Unable, as always, to sleep in flight, David thought about Caleb Carne. He was determined to get some answers from him. He was more than halfway across the Atlantic, however, before he made up his mind that no good purpose would be served by telling Simon about that night on the cliff.

The matter was one which had troubled him a lot of late. He had opened his mouth to mention it the other evening when Simon called, but had thought better of it and closed it again. For one thing it was too long and too complicated a story to tell over the telephone; and for another – well, he'd been around journalists too long not to know that his son might be fundamentally incapable of ignoring it. And what good would it do to bring it up after so many years?

Not a damned bit, and that was the truth. Strange things

happened in wartime. It was best to accept that fact and forget it – the Lord alone knew he'd forgotten it for all these years, along with a hundred other incidents. He'd never given it so much as a passing thought, not until Simon mentioned Carne and everything came flooding back to him. Since then – well, the whole damned thing had begun to haunt him. Still, that was his problem, nobody else's. Telling Simon wouldn't help, and might do a lot of harm.

It wasn't, after all, as if Carne was a nobody. He had been in the public eye then, and apparently was again. Any revelations about his character or behaviour would be classed as news. It would be splashed across the tabloids. Reporters would camp on his doorstep. People – in Britain, no doubt, just as much as in the States – liked nothing better than tearing down the heroes of yesterday.

And for what? For nothing, probably. Carne's explanation had probably been the true one. And even if it were not, there was nothing to be gained now in exposing it.

Would Carne even remember it? And if he did, how would he feel when he saw David again?

Forty-six years! One hell of a long time, by any count.

Best forgotten, he thought. Yes, best forgotten. And, briefly, he slept at last.

\*    \*    \*

It was late by the time the taxi brought Laura back from Simon's flat. She flung her handbag down on the table and went straight to the shelf that housed the telephone directories, pulling one down to leaf urgently through its pages – just as she had longed to do from the moment when, staring idly at the canopy over the bed, the idea had come to her.

And there it was! She stared at the entry, disbelievingly. After all these years! Was it really possible? But there it was, there was no mistake. Kaye, Victor. 129 Brook Place, Stamford Brook, London W4.

What was it that Stella had written about him? Something to the effect that he was handsome, or debonair, or – urbane, that was it. And he smoked a lot. But even so, it would appear that he hadn't succumbed to lung cancer or emphysema or anything else but was still around, possibly still a major cause of air pollution. Oh, blessed Victor Kaye!

He must have known all of them quite well. Stella had met Caleb Carne at his New Year's Eve party, after all, and had spoken of going over there with Jane on the first day of the war. Would he remember?

She phoned the number the next day, reining herself in to wait until ten o'clock which seemed the earliest hour at which one could decently phone an old man who must surely take his time about getting up in the morning. Hope was alive again as she dialled; but all she heard was the bell ringing on and on in an empty house.

She tried several times during the day, always with the same result. Victor Kaye, it appeared, was not in residence. Well, it was the holiday season; she'd keep trying. But when her next attempt achieved only the same result, she took pen and paper and wrote a letter:

Dear Mr Kaye

I have been trying to trace the whereabouts of a Mrs Jane Porteous, née Stratton, and wonder if you are by any chance able to help me.

Mrs Porteous was a great friend of my grandmother, Mrs Stella Morel. Their friendship dated back to pre-war days, but, very much to my grandmother's regret, they drifted apart after Mrs Porteous's marriage.

Sadly, my grandmother died five years ago, but for various personal reasons I am anxious now to get in touch with Mrs Porteous. Since I gather from my grandmother's diary that you were a mutual friend (she wrote that she took Jane to see you and your wife on the first morning of the war), I am writing to you in what I fear may be the rather vain hope that you are still in touch with her; or failing that, that you may be able to pass me on to some other friend from those far-off days who might know her present address.

I hope that this is not too much of an imposition and shall be most grateful for any information you may be able to give me.

Heaven along knew if it would bear any fruit; but it was worth a try. She signed it, stamped it, and went out then and there to post it in the postbox at the corner of the street. That done, she phoned Polly who was delighted to hear of the party arranged for her birthday.

"My dear, how *lovely*! If Simon's father is half as nice as he is, I shall adore meeting him. Oh, it's wonderful to be back in civilisation!"

"Didn't you enjoy your little holiday?"

"Oh, of course!" Polly was as overtly enthusiastic as ever, but Laura knew her too well not to detect the note of reservation in her voice.

"Did Beatrice object to Fifi?" she asked, apparently hitting the nail squarely on the head at the first attempt.

"Well, yes, she did, actually. I told you on the phone, didn't I, that the poor darling is a bag of nerves? It's hardly surprising! Beatrice was for ever shouting at her, 'Don't do this, don't do that, get off the cushions, don't dig up the plants' – honestly, it was too much! We're both delighted to be back home, I can tell you. I took her out for a walk on the green right away, and it was such fun for both of us to meet all our doggy friends."

"About Wednesday night –"

"What should I wear? Fairly casual but smart, I imagine."

"You'll look lovely, as always."

"I want to do you credit. That little navy two-piece always looks stylish, don't you think? It's the sort of thing you can dress up *or* down –"

"That'd be fine. Listen, if you can get yourself over here about seven thirty, I'll take you home. Can you manage that?"

"I am," said Polly with dignity, "not *quite* senile yet."

\*　　\*　　\*

She didn't, Laura saw, look in the least senile when she arrived at the flat on Wednesday night; in fact it was clear that she had taken even more trouble than usual with her appearance. The hair was newly teased and she had rejected the little navy two-piece in favour of a stylish black silk dress which, though gravely over the top for an informal supper, was nevertheless becoming. Laura began to feel rather sorry for Simon's father on whom, it was clear, Polly was ready to mount a sustained assault. She herself was wearing her best pair of black trousers and a cream-coloured Parigi blouse with a low neck and full sleeves that cost more than she cared to think about.

What to wear had been the least of her problems. What to cook had occupied her mind more – plus one other question: Why had she suggested this party in the first place?

Like so many other things in life, it had seemed a good idea at the time. Entertaining normally held no fears for her. There were a few simple dishes that she prided herself on doing well and which she had no qualms about serving to the circle of friends who from time to time partook of them; but did Simon's father come into this category? Having blithely issued the invitation without too much thought, later consideration assured her that he did not.

Friends were phoned, advice sought. Laura despised herself for the panic and failed to understand why she was feeling it. It wasn't like her. Who cared if she made a good impression? She was as bad as Polly, operating by Polly's standards.

Well, it was all too late now. For good or ill, she was serving iced curry soup, followed by *coq au vin*, followed by late strawberries and cream – which in all conscience was straightforward enough. She still worried about it, though.

"Something smells wonderful," Polly said, once she had enthused over the blouse Laura had bought her for her birthday. "Can I do something? Set the table?"

"All done," Laura said. "But you can keep bloody Fifi out of my way –"

"She'll be as good as gold once we're all sitting down. She's just excited about coming out – and of course, she's never been the same since staying with Beatrice. I told you, didn't I, how Beatrice seemed to take against her –"

"Yes," Laura said briefly, engaged in setting out soup bowls in readiness. Polly nevertheless told her again and was in the middle of a story regarding Fifi and a bag of manure when the door bell rang.

"I'll go," Polly said; and did so, leaving Laura to catch her breath and realise that, much to her fury, she was still ridiculously nervous. She wanted Simon's father to like her, that was the truth of it. It wasn't the right and proper thing for a confident woman to worry about, but the fact remained: it mattered. She didn't, at this moment, have the leisure or the desire to examine why.

And here they were. She emerged from the kitchen into the tiny passage, just as Polly was ushering them into the living-room, fluttering her eyelashes at Simon's father – who was, she now saw, worth the odd flutter if you liked that sort of thing, by which she meant groomed and tanned and white-haired and typically American, rather like a thinner-faced Cary Grant.

Simon kissed her, briefly. Introductions were made, platitudes spoken. The flight, David said, was unremarkable – and yes, he'd been suffering from jet-lag. It was always so much worse travelling from west to east rather than east to west.

"But I'm glad I came. I'm delighted to meet you, Laura," he said. "It was worth every mile. I've heard so much about you."

Why do people *say* that? Laura thought, savage behind her smile. There isn't any intelligent reply one can make to it. And boy, what a smoothie! Still, he was clearly well-intentioned. Knowing it was Polly's birthday, he had brought her a box of expensive chocolates, while Simon produced a silk scarf.

Polly, whose vivacity had gone into overdrive, thanked them effusively and repeatedly, while Laura stood by, trying hard to subdue her panic. Simon gave her a surreptitious wink and she calmed down a little.

"What can I get everyone to drink?" she asked. "There's wine or gin or lager –"

Everyone opted for wine. Fifi leapt about and was spoken to severely by Polly, without any effect whatsoever.

"I'll murder that animal," Laura said through clenched teeth as Simon followed her into the kitchen, where she had gone to attend to the vegetables.

"Don't worry about it," he said. "Don't worry about anything. I've missed you. Have you been OK?"

"Yes, have you?" She wondered, as she tipped the mange-tout into boiling water, if she should mention anything to him about Victor Kaye, but decided against it. Time enough to say something if she received any response – besides, she wasn't at all sure, after what he had said the other evening, that he would approve of her trying to kick sleeping dogs into life. "You only have to do these for a minute," she said worriedly. "I should have waited until we'd finished the soup."

"They'll be fine! Put them on a dish over hot water."

"Is there no end to this man's talents?" Laura enquired of no one in particular. "Go on – tell your father and that little social butterfly out there to get to the table. Soup's up."

Fifi tended to dominate the conversation throughout the first course; not in person, as it were, but through Polly, who once more went through the traumas suffered at Beatrice's hands.

"You don't think, perhaps," Laura said in a neutral kind of voice, "that a little *training* –"

"Fifi's perfectly well trained," Polly said indignantly. "She responds to kindness, that's all. Just look at her now! What dog could be better behaved?"

Fifi had, indeed, subsided quietly under the table though Laura had no real hope that she would stay there. At least, with luck, the conversation could now be guided into other channels.

Deliberately, she waited until the coffee stage before she introduced the subject of Caleb Carne – not a difficult thing to do since the plight of the hostages in the Middle East and the desirability or otherwise of war with Iraq inevitably arose, like a spectre at the feast that couldn't be ignored. But at last they turned to other matters – to the theatre scene generally, and Simon's work in particular.

"I'd love to know what you thought about Caleb Carne back in 1944," Laura said to David. "I expect Simon's told you he had a wartime *affaire* with my grandmother. Did it surprise you?"

"Not altogether." David sounded reflective. "I don't mean I had any inkling of it at the time – not at all! The idea never entered my head. But looking back, I can see that he and his wife were chalk and cheese."

"What was she like?"

"Mrs Carne? To look at? She was kind of heavy –"

"Fat, do you mean?" Polly asked.

"Well – solid. Statuesque. Dark hair coiled up on top, and a swarthy kind of complexion. She was a quiet woman, not easy to know. Kind of –" he screwed up his face in thought. "Brooding, I guess you could say."

"Not given to light conversation?" Laura suggested.

"Indeed not. Not given to light anything. She adored Carne, though; there was no doubt about that. Everyone else came a poor second to him."

"Quite right too," Polly said approvingly. "That's how every good wife should be."

She's presenting her credentials, Laura thought with amusement; and catching Simon's eye realised that the same idea had occurred to him.

"Even her daughters?" she asked. "They came second too?"

"Even her daughters. But as I said before, she wasn't an easy woman to know. She seemed placid – even dull – but there were times when one was aware of hidden fires. I have to say, she was always very kind and hospitable to me."

"What were the daughters like?" Laura asked.

Suddenly boyish, David grinned at her.

"They were something else," he said.

"Especially Trish, I gather," Simon added.

"Oh, Trish was lovely. Beauty queen material –"

"And you adored her?" Laura asked, smiling at him.

"To distraction! I even penned the odd sonnet."

He'd be easy to like, Laura thought; and with this realisation the fluttering of her nerves stilled at last. She caught Simon's eye and exchanged smiles once more. It struck her how nice it was, to have someone to exchange smiles with.

"Laura darling, you never gave me those photographs," Polly said. "Those you found in the box of Stella's things. You showed them to me, but you put them back in the drawer and I didn't take them after all."

"I'll get them now," Laura said. "David might be interested to see them." It was symbolic of her new ease, that she felt able to call him by his name like this. She went to her desk and took out the packet. "There," she said, selecting the photograph she was looking for and handing it to him. "There's Carne and my grandmother outside her house."

He extracted horn-rimmed spectacles from an inside pocket, put them on and looked at the photograph with interest.

"So it is!" he said, smiling. "That's just how he looked when I knew him."

Laura handed him another.

"And there they are again in Richmond Park. And this is one of Stella with her friend, Jane. I don't suppose you ever knew her, did you?"

"No. Simon's already asked me. I had no knowledge of either of them."

"Are there any of me in there?" Polly asked. "I used to love having my picture taken – that's why there are so many of them."

"So what's changed?" Laura asked her teasingly as she turned towards Simon, offering him more coffee.

"Oh I absolutely hate it now! I can't bear to see all my terrible wrinkles and crow's-feet. Really, I think I must be the most conceited woman alive, because whenever I see a picture of myself I think that surely I must look better than that –"

David was missing his cue; so was Simon, come to that. Surely *someone* ought to be assuring her that she looked wonderful, no matter what the camera said? But Simon was talking to Laura about this article-thing that he was writing, saying that he thought the paper was going to use the picture of Carne and his family, rather than the wedding photograph. And Laura was listening to him as she poured him a second cup of coffee. And David – *such* a nice, easy kind of man to talk to, and absolutely chock-full of charm – David was staring at one of the photographs with the most peculiar expression on his face, almost as if he'd seen a ghost.

"What is it?" she asked him. "Is it someone you know?"

"No, no, not at all," he said hastily. "Just – just . . ."

His voice trailed away uncertainly. Polly looked at him in some concern, and then craned a little to see which picture had engaged his attention. It was the one of Stella and the strange man they had decided must have been one of Jane's boy-friends.

"But you said you never met them," she said.

"I was right." He smiled at her, no uncertainty in evidence now, as charming as ever. "I never did." Briskly he shuffled all three photographs into a neat pile and put them down on the table. "May I have some more of your delicious coffee, Laura? It's very good

– in fact it's been a wonderful meal altogether. Tell me – I meant to ask before we sat down – who painted those three pictures? They're absolutely stunning!"

She had imagined it, Polly thought. Perhaps he'd had a twinge of indigestion. That was probably it. She only hoped that Fifi hadn't nipped his ankle. It wasn't something you could bank on.

# IX

They'd sat and talked for a while over a last Jack Daniels when they got back from Laura's flat.

"She's quite a girl, your Laura," David said.

"The Right Stuff?" It was a family joke; the term used by old Grandfather Holt when pontificating about politicians and captains of industry and other pillars of society. David smiled as he acknowledged it.

"The Right Stuff," he agreed. "A man would have to be serious about a girl like that."

"I guess this man is. However –" Simon paused, and didn't continue.

"She doesn't feel the same way?"

"I have no idea how she feels. Oh – she likes me! We make beautiful music together – but that's hardly the same as a lifetime commitment, is it?"

"No." David looked at him thoughtfully. "I guess you haven't known her so long, at that." He gave a grunt of laughter. "Though God knows what that's got to do with it. I think I knew within the first five minutes of meeting your mother that she was the one for me. Different from all the rest."

"Laura's different, all right."

David continued to look at him with affection and concern. "God, life is complicated for your generation, isn't it? You know what? You have too many damn' choices! For us it was easy. If a guy and a girl wanted to live together, then they got married. Period."

"Yeah, yeah. And grass was something you mowed and pot was something you cooked in. And you could get a good chicken dinner for a quarter, spend a day at Coney Island and still have enough cash left over to go round the world."

"Barefoot, naturally."

Simon grinned at him.

"Could be you're jealous," he suggested.

David laughed as if in agreement, but then shook his head.

"No, I don't think so. Call it conditioning if you like, but your mother and I met and fell in love and got married – and there's not one damned thing I'd change about that. We had thirty-four good years. All I'd say to you is this: if you know what you want, then go for it. The time goes so fast."

Easy to say, Simon thought, thinking of all the conflicting signals that Laura put out; all the dislike of dependence of any kind, all the determination to make her own way, be her own person, leave space. Not that he was knocking it exactly; just felt a little helpless in the face of it.

And then there was the possibility of his return to America. He'd heard nothing more from *Commentary* and hadn't mentioned John Greeley's approach to his father; but he did so now, and they talked it over until their drinks were finished and both decided to call it a night.

David was tired, still mildly jet-lagged, but sleep stubbornly refused to come to him. Until this moment he had deliberately shut the thought of that photograph out of his mind. It had, surely, to be some self-hypnotic illusion; a figment of his overheated imagination. All the talk of Carne had triggered his subconscious, making him see things that couldn't possibly have existed. For why on earth would that man be picnicking in a park with Laura's grandmother?

He had to be mistaken. Surely, he had to be. But as he turned his head restlessly on the pillow, this way and that, unable to get comfortable, the image seemed to grow larger and larger, filling the space beneath his closed eyelids.

It *was* the man. However unlikely. He couldn't mistake that face, last seen upturned, glimmering palely in the darkness. The lean, dark face and thin moustache; the black hair, growing in a widow's peak. Who the hell was he, and what had he been doing there, at Roscarrow? He hadn't thought of him for years; but he knew now that he had never forgotten him, and never would, not as long as he lived.

An enemy, Carne had said. A threat. Yet here he was, picnicking in a park with Carne's mistress – caught with a cup half raised to his lips, smiling for the camera.

What was the truth? Had too many years passed ever to know? Too much water over too many dams?

Too much water; water everywhere – cold and black and menacing. And that poor, pale face! He'd got to stop thinking of it or he'd never sleep again. Think of something else.

Simon and Laura. He liked her; and Simon loved her, that much was clear. He could be in for a lot of hurt. Loving made you vulnerable, no doubt about that. Which, inevitably, seemed to lead back to Roscarrow and Porthlivick and that night just before D-day.

And Trish . . .

\*　　\*　　\*

He'd come back in time for the dance, but only just. The Battalion had, for reasons best known to those in authority, been forced to spend five days in Devon instead of the three they had all expected; five precious days out of the meagre store left to him, every minute as long as an hour.

Back in Porthlivick the feeling that they were in the last days had gained strength. The Germans were retreating in confusion in Italy. Nobody believed that the invasion was more than days away; some thought they wouldn't even last until Saturday, the night of the dance in the Parish Hall – the dance that was Porthlivick's farewell to the GIs.

"It's like in *Vanity Fair*," Pen said to David when he presented himself at Roscarrow that Saturday evening and was waiting in the sitting-room for Trish to come downstairs. "Haven't you read it? It's one of our set books at school. There was a dance on the eve of Waterloo, and there they were, dancing the night away, never realising what horrors awaited them'–".

"Well, thanks," David said.

Pen looked at him, aghast at her own want of tact.

"Oh, David! I'm so sorry. I didn't mean –"

"It's OK, Pen. Don't worry about it." She looked as if she was about to burst into tears, and he was moved to put an arm around her shoulders and give her a squeeze. "I'm going to be all right. Believe me!"

"You'd better be." She did her best to smile, but it was a poor effort.

"Aren't you coming tonight?" he asked her. She shook her head.

"I'm too young. Anyway, I don't really want to. I'd only be a wallflower."

David didn't argue with her. He knew from experience that there would be other even younger girls at the dance – there always were; but they'd be painted and permed copies of their elder sisters, not in the least like Pen who was still so much the schoolgirl, with her straight hair and boyish figure and bookish interests. He smiled at her with affection.

"Your time will come," he said. "Say, how was Caro's twenty-first on Wednesday? Did I miss a good dinner?"

"It was all right." Pen seemed, David thought, markedly lacking in enthusiasm, suddenly a little ill at ease. But he had no time to pursue the thought, for Mr Carne, apparently newly back from London after one of his broadcasts, breezed into the room like a hurricane.

"You'll not be long with us now, my boy," he said. "There's a *tremendous* air of expectancy in town. *Such* excitement! You can cut it with a knife. Lord, I wish I were twenty years younger –"

Any minute, David thought, he would be crying 'God for England, Harry and St George'; but whether this prediction would have come true he was not to know, for here was Trish, looking as fantastically beautiful as ever in a kind of dark rose-pink dress with a lacy yoke. It was all he could do not to take her in his arms then and there – it was, after all, six days since he had last seen her – but he managed to restrain himself as she twirled in front of him.

"Do you like it? Do you like it, Davey? It's new! I actually bought it new –"

"With my coupons!" Pen muttered darkly.

"I'll pay you back, I swear. It's not as if you need anything just now, after all."

Pen gave a derisive laugh.

"I need *everything*! I haven't a rag to my back!"

"Now admit it, darling," Carne said pacifically. "Your sister looks a picture. Isn't that right, David?"

"It is, sir." David's voice was low, almost reverent. He felt he had never, ever, seen anything as wonderful as Trish in that pink dress. To think that she was *his* girl – that he was the one who would walk into that hall tonight with her on his arm!

Hand in hand they walked down the hill to the village. Trish was in a prattling mood, but David didn't mind. He couldn't talk much about his activities anyway, and was perfectly content to smile down at her as she rattled on.

She prattled about the library, where Saturday was always a busy day; and she prattled about her friend Pansy, and how the wedding looked as if it was going to be postponed. And she prattled about the dinner at the Marina.

"We had a lovely time," she said. "It was too bad you couldn't be there, Davey. Some of your officers were at the next table."

"Maybe it was just as well I wasn't, then."

"Why do you say that? They were perfectly sweet!"

"Sweet!" He laughed at the very possibility that any officer could be such a thing.

"They were, honestly. Do you know one called Pete?"

"Do I know –? Have a heart, Trish! Would I know an officer called Pete? They're all called 'sir' from where I'm standing."

"Well, he's quite young. Nice looking. Dark-brownish sort of hair and dark eyes."

"That could describe a couple of them. You seem to have inspected him pretty thoroughly, whoever he was."

"Well, they came and joined us, you see. One of the waitresses told them who Father was. The older one, the Major, had actually heard one of his broadcasts and came over to pay his respects. So then Father said it was Caro's twenty-first birthday and would they have a drink to celebrate the occasion. It was all great fun."

"I bet."

"No, don't be cross! You're not jealous, are you?"

"Of course not. I don't have any reason to be, do I?"

"The Major's coming tonight to make some sort of speech and a couple of the others said they might look in too, as it's a sort of special occasion."

Great, David thought, without enthusiasm. That'll sure add to the fun. But he said no more since they had by this time arrived at the bedecked hall, and Trish was greeting friends and being greeted in turn. The place was stiff with uniforms and all the girls had dressed up to the nines, despite the rationing that they grumbled about constantly. Chuck was there with his woman; you couldn't really call her a girl, David thought. Without make-up she'd look a lot older than the twenty-five years she admitted to. She was inches thick with the stuff, and her straw-coloured hair was black at the roots.

The band was pretty good, he had to admit. They were playing 'Boogie-woogie Bugle Boy' and already the floor was full of jitter-bugging couples. He stood watching them, waiting for Trish to come back from the cloakroom. Heaven alone knew what the girls got up to in there; it seemed to swallow them up for hours.

But at last she came, just as the band moved into her favourite 'String of Pearls'.

"Our tune," she said to him, smiling up as he led her on to the floor. She's right, he thought with a sudden pang. I'll never be able to hear it without thinking of her, and of this strange, frightening, bitter-sweet waiting time.

They joined a small crowd of Trish's friends and he danced with some of them; but although he chatted and laughed with them, always, as if he had some kind of quivering antennae, he was aware of Trish – knew where she was, who she was dancing with. They caught each other's eyes over the shoulders of their temporary partners, and smiled as if to reassure each other that soon, once more, they would be together.

There was beer to drink; but it was served by respectable ladies of the village, mothers of the girls who were dancing, and no one had too much or overstepped the bounds of good behaviour. And when a noisy band of soldiers who had too obviously been fortifying themselves at some of the local pubs before attending the dance erupted into the hall, two of the fathers stepped up to suggest that they might, perhaps, have mistaken the nature of the party.

At first they seemed inclined to argue and there was a moment or two of tension; but then they decided to behave themselves and gave no more trouble. The reason for this became quickly evident. The officers had arrived – three of them, including the Battalion Commander, Major Goldsmith.

The band played a kind of fanfare to introduce him and everyone on the dance floor stood still, looking expectantly towards him. He was a large, burly man with a face like a slab of raw meat. It was a face that looked as if it smiled only rarely; but the gallant Major was doing his best now, grinning hugely to right and left, shaking hands with various of the organisers as he made his way up to the platform and moved centre stage.

"We call him Khan," David whispered to Trish. "Short for Genghis Khan."

"He was the one who came over to our table to talk to Father the other night. Look – there's Pete. That one standing on the right, by the steps."

David looked and he saw the man known to him as Lieutenant Bronowski. He was, as Trish had said, quite young; not more than twenty-two or twenty-three. And he was, as Trish had also said, almost indecently good-looking.

The Major launched into a speech directed towards 'You wonderful people of Porthlivick who have welcomed us into your homes, taken us to your hearts'.

David didn't hear the half of it. He was only aware of Trish, standing on her tip-toes, peering around the couple in front, trying to catch Lieutenant Bronowski's eye; she was even waving her hand, for God's sake! He dug her in the ribs with his elbow.

"For Pete's sake, Trish –" he said and was mortified when she giggled, because of course, it *was* all for Pete's sake, and there was Pete himself standing just across the room. And now he had seen her and was flashing his smile in her direction. David always thought he seemed to have more teeth than anyone else. Every last one of them now seemed to be signalling his pleasure in seeing Trish.

"And wherever we go," the Major droned on, "no matter where

the future years may take us, there will always be a little piece of our
hearts that belongs to Porthlivick, and always a place at our tables
for any of you dear folk who might, one day, cross the Atlantic.
So, friends, we give you our thanks –"

He was winding down at last, and was applauded politely; but
the audience was not yet to be released from its bondage. Norman
Nankivell, the Mayor, who had until this moment been standing to
one side acknowledging the speech with a modestly inclined head
and a faint smile, now took the Major's place and thanked both
him and everyone else in sight: the ladies who had performed
wonders with the refreshments; the band who had come all the
way from St Jory; the Committee who had decorated the hall;
the Americans who had added so much to the colour and gaiety
of life in Porthlivick these past months.

"He's *awful*," Trish whispered to David. "He always goes on and
on and on."

"He must stop soon. There won't be any time left!"

David was acutely conscious that the seconds were passing,
passing – just as if he had an hourglass there in front of him
and could see the grains of sand falling faster and faster until
there were no more left. He made a resolution. When at last
these cretins stopped talking and the band started playing again,
he wasn't going to dance with anybody else but Trish. Time
was too precious to waste. Trish was the only person in the
entire hall who mattered to him.

But when at last Mr Nankivell had thanked everyone and retired
from the stage and the music had started again, it was not to him
that she turned. Unseen by David until that moment, Lieutenant
Bronowski had somehow approached by a circuitous route and was
standing just beyond his left shoulder.

"Excuse me, soldier," he said, flashing his smile in David's
direction. And to Trish: "May I?"

She gave him her most dazzling smile.

"Pete! How lovely to see you again." And off she drifted, held
close in his arms.

It would have to be a slow one, David thought bitterly. They
were cheek to cheek! It was torture to watch them, yet somehow he couldn't turn away, couldn't do the sensible thing and
ask some other girl to dance.

She was looking up at the handsome lieutenant, laughing, preening a little, proud to be dancing with an officer – and such an attractive one at that. The sight of it caused a physical pain in David's stomach; he didn't know how to bear it. But when other couples came between and blocked his sight of her, he couldn't bear that either.

He went over to the trestle table that served as a bar, but all the beer had gone. Chuck and his woman had left – gone over to the pub, very sensibly, the moment the officers had arrived. David thought of going too, but knew that he couldn't. Besides, the dance would be over soon and Trish would come back to him. He was a fool to make so much of this, he told himself. Hadn't she danced with several other partners before this? And hadn't she always come back to him? After all, she couldn't have turned the Lieutenant down, could she?

It was no good, though. He knew that Lieutenant Bronowski – Pete – wasn't like the other partners. You had only to remember the way she'd greeted him – the joy in her voice when she'd spoken his name, that extra-special smile she'd given him. He was sweet, she'd said. And look at her now! She was yearning up at him, dancing so close, hanging on his every word. This time there were no smiling glances over the shoulder in David's direction. And, oh God! Even though this set of dances was finished and the band had fallen silent to scattered applause and were now turning the pages of their music and talking among themselves, she wasn't coming back to him as on every other occasion. She was standing in the middle of the floor listening to the lieutenant attentively with her head slightly on one side; *engrossed*, for God's sake, nodding solemnly at his words of wisdom, before gracefully arching her neck to peal with laughter in response to his wit.

The band broke into a waltz, 'I'll be loving you – Always'. Once more, as if there had never been any question about it, she moved into his close embrace.

David took himself and his pain outside and breathed deeply of the night air. He couldn't take any more, couldn't watch his love, his Trish, ignoring him while those tiny grains of sand fell so remorselessly.

In the passage at the side of the hall, other couples were kissing, embracing. He moved away from them, back to the front of the building beside the door, and leaning against the wall, closed his eyes.

'I'll be loving you – Always.'

The strains reached him in his agony, and made everything worse. They'd danced so often to this; had sung it to each other; had meant every word. Well, *he'd* meant every word, though he couldn't, now, answer for Trish.

There were always three dances in a set. When this one came to an end, there'd be two more; and when he heard the band move from 'Always' to 'Stardust' he knew he was destined to stay outside for another fifteen minutes since he couldn't bring himself to go in only to be confronted by Trish and the Lieutenant dancing another slow number.

Only when he heard the roar of the 'Hokey-Kokey' was he able to return to the hall. It brought him no comfort. Trish and her partner might be only two of a large circle, but any observer could see by the way they were laughing and fooling about that they were together, a pair, conscious only of each other.

He saw them leave the floor hand in hand. Saw them join the other two officers. She was dancing with the Major now – well, he wished her joy of that! He guessed his small-talk wasn't up to much – and indeed, Trish's smile did look somewhat fixed. Relief was at hand, however. The band switched from a slow and smoochy number to 'Don't Sit Under the Apple Tree' – with all its memories of the first time they had danced together. The Major appeared to throw up his hands in surrender and amid laughter, handed her over once more to Lieutenant Bronowski.

He might as well go back to camp right now, David thought dully. She had no interest in him. He'd leave it until this dance was over, and if she still didn't come back to him –

But wait – what was this? The band had finished this particular number and it looked as if the officers might be leaving. Their transport had arrived and the Major, it seemed, was anxious to be gone. The Marina Hotel was marginally closer to the village than Bow Beach, but officers couldn't be expected to walk home, not like the enlisted men.

Lieutenant Bronowski held both her hands in his. What was he saying? That he wished he'd met her months ago? That he'd call her tomorrow? That he'd be seeing her every minute that was left to them? Together they walked to the door – then the Lieutenant, apparently in answer to an urgent summons from the others, waved his hand and was gone. For a moment Trish stood there beside the door in her pink dress, smiling a little. She turned her head slowly, chin slightly elevated, as if checking to see who had witnessed her triumph. Only three officers; only *one* handsome one; and she had snaffled him under the eyes of all-comers.

Her eyes finally focused on David; and very slowly, a petulant little half-smile puckering her lips, she walked over to him, the full skirt of the pink dress billowing this way and that.

"*Really*, Davey," she said in the baby voice. "I'm very, very cross with you." ('Vewwy, vewwy cwoss'.)

He stared at her.

"*You're* cross with me! How do you make that out?"

"You just stared at us. All the time! Wherever we danced, there were two big Davey-eyes mooning at me."

"I was outside most of the time."

"We just couldn't escape them. Pete thought it was terribly funny, but it just made me uncomfortable."

"You didn't look uncomfortable. You looked as if you were enjoying every moment."

"Well, there you are – you *were* watching!"

"What did you expect me to do? Go home and leave you to it? Trish, you were dancing an hour and a half with him."

"Was I?" She fluffed her hair nonchalantly and looked around the hall. "I wasn't counting."

"Doesn't it mean anything to you that this might be our last night?"

"Well, you say that, but nobody knows for sure. Unless, of course, Mr Churchill makes a habit of confiding in you."

"Let's go, Trish. Let's go home."

"No! This is the last waltz anyway. Come on, Davey – we might as well. They're going to play 'Auld Lang Syne' afterwards."

They danced, but didn't speak. 'Who's Taking You Home To-night' – couples all round were singing the words to each other. Some looked tense and sad – aware, as David was, of time running out; some kissed as they danced; some were laughing, joking, fooling. Trish and David were like strangers, brought together by accident; and when the dance ended and they looked into each other's faces, David knew a moment of real fear because Trish's eyes were cold, with no reflection whatever of the intimacy they had shared.

"Oh, Trish," he said miserably. "Honey, I –"

"Come on!" She was brisk managerial. "Form a circle."

There seemed a kind of lump in his throat, composed of anger and unhappiness and fear. It was the dreariest thing he'd ever known, walking round in the huge, heaving, chanting, cross-handed circle, holding Trish's left hand in his right, that of a total stranger in his left, knowing deep within himself that everything had gone, none of his dreams would come true. Up and down, up and down:

'For *auld* lang syne, my dears. For *auld* lang syne.'

What did it mean? Why did people do it? There seemed no sense in it, no sense in anything.

On the way home they quarrelled. He hadn't meant to. He'd made up his mind, when Trish had disappeared to the cloakroom to get her jacket, that he wouldn't reproach her again. He'd almost managed to convince himself that he'd behaved churlishly, that Trish had felt compelled by circumstances to dance with the handsome young officer – *all those times*? Never mind, never mind. Forget it, it was over. He had her to himself now. Any more recriminations would only spoil the short time they had remaining to them.

She decreed otherwise, however. She wanted a fight; was spoiling for one – and all the way home she needled him. Nothing, it seemed, was right about him now. He was too serious about her, wanted to smother her, couldn't bear it if she so much as looked at another man.

He pulled her to a halt, and turned her to face him.

"You're my girl, Trish. Aren't you? You've said so often enough."

"A girl can change."

"Are you seeing him again?"

"Who? Pete? I might. He's got my telephone number. Of course, being an officer he's got lots of responsibilities –"

"Oh, sure!" David's voice was savage. "He's also got a flashy uniform and a jeep at his disposal. Who am I to compete with that? I thought we were in love –" He was mortified to hear the sob in his voice.

He turned and strode on, not touching her any more. It was a dark, cloudy night, but hot and humid, and the scent of the honeysuckle in the hedge that bordered the lane seemed overpowering. They passed the church and the cottages and turned down the track towards Roscarrow. Neither spoke. Could he have imagined all that sweetness, all that tenderness?

She would turn to him soon, he thought. It couldn't end like this, in silence. But still, as they approached the solid block of darkness that was the house, she said nothing.

They went towards the side door that was always left unlocked; and as they did so, a figure detached itself from the shadows.

"Oh, Trish! Oh, David!" It was Pen, her face very white in the darkness. "I've been waiting for you –"

"What's happened? What's the matter?"

"It's Caro, Trish. She's gone. She wanted me to catch you and tell you before you went in." Her whisper had a hysterical edge to it. "You mustn't tell anyone, it's a secret –"

"Don't be an idiot!" Trish grabbed her by the shoulders. "How can it be a secret? A secret from who?"

"From Mother and Father, of course. She's left a note for them, but she doesn't want them to know until morning. She told me to warn you in case you looked into her room tonight and found out she wasn't there. You mustn't say anything – you won't, will you? Promise?"

"Has she gone to Alan?"

"Yes. They're going to get married. But you won't split, will you?"

"All right." Trish sounded casual, not really affected by the news. Then she laughed. "Gosh," she said. "What a rumpus there'll be in the morning. Caro – a Yeo! Father'll go mad."

"Oh, Trish! We might never see her again. I know she loves Alan and had to go – but isn't it terrible?"

Pen was clearly upset, tears not far from the surface.

"You will see her, Pen. Of course you will," David said comfortingly. "Don't worry. Your Mom and Dad will forgive her."

"What on earth do you know about it?" Trish sounded annoyed that he had ventured an opinion.

"Nothing, I guess." At this, Pen turned to look from Trish to David and back again. Even in the midst of her grief it was clear to her, as it would have been to anyone, that something had happened between them. "I'd better go."

For a second, however, he stood there. He raised his arms a little, made an imperceptible movement towards Trish, but she turned from him and opened the door, disappearing into the house. For a moment Pen stood with her mouth open.

"What's got into her?" she asked, forgetting for a moment the drama of Caro. David shook his head, not able to answer. "What's the matter?" She took his arm. "David, what is it?"

He took a long, shuddering breath, and leaned back against the wall of the house, looking up at the night sky. Leaning against walls seemed, he thought miserably, to have taken up a considerable amount of his time that evening.

"I guess it's all over," he said. "Me and Trish."

"I don't believe it."

"It's true. I think she's met someone she likes better."

There was a short silence from Pen as she digested this.

"That officer. That Pete man." It wasn't a question. She knew. When David didn't answer, she moved and took his arm again as if to comfort him. "She's mad! I saw how she was at the Marina, but I never thought it was more than a brainstorm. He's not nearly as nice as you. Oh, David – don't be unhappy! You mustn't be! It couldn't have lasted, could it? You're going away soon, anyway."

"That only makes it worse."

"I know. I'm sorry. I was only trying to –"

"Don't worry. I guess I'll live." His voice was strained. In fact, he wasn't at all certain on this point.

"You must. You *must*! I'll die if you don't."

"You're a sweet kid." She was holding so tight to his right arm that he had to bring his left across in order to touch her hair.

"David –" she hesitated for a moment, then began again, the words coming out in a rush. "David, I know I look like a kid, but I'm not one. Not really. I'm a year older than Juliet was."

He gave a little breath of laughter. What a character! Caro gone, he and Trish split up, and still she thought of Shakespeare! Juliet, would you believe?

"So?"

She took a deep breath.

"I'm not too young to love you, David. I've loved you from that time I saw you in the church. I think I always will. Oh, don't worry about it! I know you don't feel like that about me, but I just wanted to tell you before – before –"

"Before I go to face my Waterloo?"

"Well –" she was embarrassed now. "Sort of."

"Pen – believe me, I think an awful lot of you. It's a pity you're not a year or two older."

"I still wouldn't look like Trish."

"No, you'd look like Pen. And that's a pretty good way to look. Believe me."

"Do you really think you'll be going soon?"

"I'm sure of it."

"I shall miss you."

"I'll come and tell you goodbye. That's a promise." He pushed himself away from the wall. "I've got to go, Pen."

"Try not to be too sad about Trish."

"I'll try. And – and thanks. You're lovely." He bent and kissed her cheek. "You're just the sweetest kid."

Pen, watching him go with her hand held against the spot that he'd kissed, thought his last remark unfortunate in the extreme; but the rest was wonderful, something she'd never forget. She was aware that, sooner or later, she would blush with shame at her declaration of undying love; but for now, she was glad she'd made it. How could Trish be so beastly to him, just when he was going into battle? How could she let him go like that?

It was a question that echoed and re-echoed in David's mind, its tone changing from one moment to the next. Sometimes he was angry; at others, he despised his self-pity. Sleep took its time coming to him that night, but when it did he slept peacefully, without dreams, so that in the morning the awful truth hit him with a rush, its strength renewed. Never again would he hold Trish in his arms. Never again feel her lips on his, or the sweet silkiness of her skin. How could he bear it?

Perhaps it was as well that they were so busy the following day. They were confined to camp; no passes allowed. No one yet knew when they would move or where they would move to, but clearly they were in the last hours. Equipment was checked and rechecked. No one doubted for a moment that they would soon have use for it.

Chuck was taking bets, the next twenty-four hours carrying the shortest odds.

"I told Rita, 'this is it, baby,'" he reported to David when they were side by side in their Army cots that night. "'This is goodbye for ever,' I said. And do you know what she said?"

"No idea." David's voice was flat, without interest.

"She said 'why didn't you bring me some extra gum?' How d'you like that? 'Is that all I mean to you?' I said. 'Ain't I worth no more than half a dozen sticks of gum? Don't I have feelings?'"

"We're not real to them," David said. "I guess that's it. We dropped in out of nowhere, and we're about to drop out again, leaving no trace."

Chuck laughed.

"Don't know about that," he said. "Guess one or two of the boys have left a few souvenirs. Morry Cohen's girl's in the family way."

David didn't answer. There'd been no danger of that, at least, he thought grimly. Not that there would have been anyway – he wasn't as irresponsible as all that.

Oh God, how it hurt, this rejection. Had it been his fault? He'd wanted her so; had he pressed her too hard? He longed to have the last months back again, do it all over again, only better. He wouldn't press her. He'd settle for any terms, just to hold her, just to have her lovely face turned to his, glowing with the love he had thought she felt for him.

And the more he thought about it, the more it seemed to him that he had been at fault, all the blame his. If only he could see her one more time – just tell her he was sorry, that it was only because he loved her so much, that he'd agree to anything just so long as he could know that one day they would be together.

He'd go to her. The idea came to him after Chuck had fallen silent, when all around him were sleeping. He'd done it before and he could do it again. He'd creep up the rocky path and along the cliff, and throw a handful of gravel at her window. And then she'd come down and he would tell her that he was sorry, that he'd been wrong.

He dressed hastily in khaki slacks and sweater and stealthily slipped out of the tent. The waves were pounding on the beach only yards away. He paused and listened, but could detect no other sound. For a moment he hesitated, familiarising himself with the dark and the shadows. There must be guards, but he couldn't see them. Swiftly, without a sound, he moved from shadow to shadow, until he could see the rocks rising sharp and jagged in front of him, pools around their bases.

He didn't know why he should feel so much more nervous this time than the last; except that the last time it had been a clear, starry night and he had been able to see without difficulty. Now there was only a fitful moon and scudding clouds, a strong wind blowing. It was confusing, worrying; however, he looked around once more, took his chance, and ran.

Once behind the rock he felt safer. This was more like home ground, he'd trodden this way so often, but he did wish the visibility was better. There was the cliff to climb before he achieved the path; if anyone was inspired to shine a torch – but no one did, even though a false step sent a shower of stones rattling down to the beach beneath and for a few moments he was forced to cling to the cliff, immobile, not daring to breathe.

He felt the worst was over once he reached the path. It was just a question of bending double to keep out of sight until he reached the higher growth. Once in its shelter he felt safe and could straighten up; but it was an uneasy kind of night, he thought. More than once he whipped round, feeling that something or someone was following him, thinking that he could see a human figure out of the corner of his eye; but it was only the wind shaking the branches of the stunted trees so that they cast strange, leaping shadows, and once the sudden, startled flight of an owl.

He climbed as swiftly as he could up to the top of the hilly path between the trees, then took the downward slope at a run. It would take eight minutes to get to Roscarrow; he knew – he'd done it often enough.

He passed the seat where he had sat with Caro, and breathing hard, climbed up the long slope that led away from it. This was the steepest part, and always seemed endless. Here, at the top, a smaller path led off to the left, towards the steep, spiny headland (and the grassy ledge, where so recently he and Trish had lain together). Roscarrow was along the path to the right.

And now he saw that something was wrong, or at least not the same as on the other occasion, for there was a light in that direction, and as he approached it he saw that it was streaming from one of the downstairs windows, just as if there was no such thing as the blackout.

What did it mean? It was well after midnight, when he might have expected the occupants of the house to be asleep in their beds. Perhaps someone had left it on by mistake; or perhaps – and here his heart leapt – perhaps Trish had, like him, been unhappy and unable to sleep, and had come downstairs to make a hot drink, and forgetting that the curtains were drawn back had switched on a light.

He approached the house cautiously, wondering what to do. If someone was about, it was clearly impossible to throw gravel at Trish's bedroom window.

The wind was getting stronger, bringing with it a few spots of rain. It brought the sound of the waves too; and as he stood and watched, the light from the house grew dim and blazed again, as the branches of the trees between him and the house tossed and dipped, momentarily obscuring his sight of it.

For a moment he stood and watched, irresolute. He'd come so far, risked so much; he had, by this time, managed to convince himself that Trish would be as anxious as he to kiss and make up. He couldn't just abandon the plan and go back to camp without seeing her. There wouldn't be another chance.

He took a few steps nearer the house. He was inside the hedge that marked the boundary now, and all around him were the clumps of rhododendrons, swaying a little, making the shadows dance. He edged round the bushes; was almost, now, at the top of the steps that led to the beach. How strange and unfamiliar everything looked! He had seen this garden many times – would have said he knew his way about it – but it seemed different now. That bush, for instance – he would have sworn it was half that size, not nearly so broad across –

His heart came into his mouth as part of it moved and turned and revealed itself as a human figure.

234

"David?" His name was spoken in a hoarse whisper, the tone one of surprise. "David, is that you?"

For a moment he froze, on the point of denying it, of turning and running. But it was far too late. The figure had approached him and revealed itself to be Mr Carne. He knew a moment of panic. How could he possibly explain his presence at such an hour? He could find no words to begin.

"David – thank God –"

It was then that David saw that Carne looked odd and unfamiliar, wild-haired and wild-eyed, his shirt open at the neck.

"Sir? Is something wrong?"

"I need your help."

"What's the matter? What's happened?"

"Thank God it's you! Come with me."

"Where to, sir? Where are you going? What about this light?"

For a moment Carne looked towards the house and made a movement as if he would go there, but then he gestured with his hand as if to sweep that matter aside, as if other matters were far more important.

"Never mind that. Come with me." He went towards the steps, then turned impatiently. "For heaven's sake, come, boy! I need your help. Desperately."

David gave one despairing look towards the upstairs window where, he assumed, Trish was sleeping peacefully, but the urgency in Carne's voice impelled him to follow without further questions, though his head seemed to swim with them.

Halfway down to the summerhouse Carne turned on the steps and gripped David's arm.

"What have you heard about my work in London?" he said, his voice low and intense.

"What?" For a moment David was too confused to answer. "Your – your work?"

"What have you heard?" Carne's grip was painfully tight, and he gave David's arm a shake. "Have the girls told you?"

"They – they said you're a broadcaster." Had he gone mad, David wondered?

"Nothing else? They didn't hint that I was involved in secret, security work?"

"N – no. That is, Pen did say once that you were in Intelligence in the last war –"

"They don't let people go, my boy. Once these people have you, they keep you. Believe me. What you're going to see now is all part of it. Ask no questions. Just give me your help, and you'll be doing your country and mine a great service."

It sounded like all the bad films David had ever seen rolled into one; but he had never seen Carne like this, so frantic and urgent. He let go David's arm, and continued down the steps to the summerhouse. The double glass doors were locked, but he produced a key, fumbled in the lock and opened them cautiously.

All was in darkness inside. Carne flicked several times at a cigarette lighter; fruitlessly, at first, then suddenly it flared into life. He held it up in front of him, and for a moment David could see nothing amiss. Everything seemed exactly as it always was, except that the square cushions that belonged to the chairs – those same pillows that he and Trish had spread on the floor – were piled up to the rear of the room.

"Behind the cushions," Carne said, still whispering. His breathing sounded strange; laboured and ragged. He took a few steps forward and pulled the cushions away from the wall, still holding the lighter.

It was then that David saw the face; pale skin, staring eyes, thin moustache, thin nose, dark hair in a widow's peak. He froze with horror – felt its icy fingers wrap themselves round his heart and his stomach and his throat so that he couldn't move, couldn't speak.

"We've got to get him away from the house," Carne said. "You'll help me, David. You'll help me, won't you?" And bending, he began, one by one, to throw the cushions to one side so that the whole figure was revealed; the dark suit, the thin, shiny shoes.

At last David found his voice.

"How – how did he – ?" he began hoarsely.

"It was an accident. He slipped. On the steps. But he had no business here – I must get him away. He's an enemy. We must get him away from the house." Carne was almost sobbing in his urgency now. "Away from the house!" he said again, as if obsessed. "Come on, David! Help me, help me. I've rigged the boat. The man's evil. A spy. I mustn't be connected with him.

236

I'm – I'm under cover. It's a national emergency. Come on! You're a soldier. You must help me."

And as one in a dream, in a nightmare, not believing that this was real – that this night with the pounding waves and the gusting wind wasn't part of some wild fantasy – David bent and grasped the dead man's shoulders, and together they heaved him out of the corner, out of the summerhouse, down to the beach below.

"Away from the house," Carne muttered, over and over, his breath sawing in his throat. "Away from the house. Get him into the boat. Get his feet in – get his *feet* in, for the love of God! He mustn't be seen – not here, not with me. We'll go straight out and drop him over the side. Come on, come on, push the boat off – get *in*, boy!"

And, normal thought suspended, David did as he was told.

# X

Caleb Carne seemed, miraculously, to have taken on a new lease of life. Far from being the feeble, querulous old man who had not felt strong enough to withstand the rigours of the celebrations prepared for him, he seemed now to be taking a positively robust attitude towards the whole affair.

That this had something to do with Hilda Yeo's death, Pen did not doubt. It was just as if a cloud that had hung over him for years had somehow lifted. She didn't pretend to understand it fully. She had learned the macabre facts behind the feud many years ago, but couldn't understand why they should have any importance at this particular point – why her father should react with such triumphant zest to having outlived all his hated adversaries. Poor Hilda was, after all, only a Yeo by marriage – not even in the picture when the controversial death of Joseph Carne had taken place.

She ventured a few questions but was greeted with a smiling and rather smug silence and in the end she left the matter alone, treating it as she had always treated her father's aversion to the Yeos – as an aberration, corroding but essentially childish, something unlikely to be modified at this stage in his life. She suspected his chief emotion was one of sheer triumph; he was alive and the last of that generation of Yeos was not. He'd emerged the winner.

If only this triumph would result in a little more charity towards the next generation she would positively welcome it, for his relationship with Alan had never been more than a kind of armed neutrality – though heaven alone knew, he'd been an exemplary son-in-law. As well as proving himself a devoted husband and father, he had founded a small engineering business after the war which had prospered mightily, and for many years now he had been

239

able to keep Caro in a far more luxurious manner than she had been accustomed to or, indeed, had ever expected. Pen looked forward to seeing them on Saturday for the birthday celebrations, together with Hannah, the proprietor of successful livery stables and the youngest of their four children.

Trish would be arriving some time on Saturday too – by which train she wasn't yet able to say. She had promised to phone Pen from Paddington to let her know when to meet her at St Jory station.

It was a busy period for both Dolly and Pen. Rooms long unused were being prepared, and Pen was forced to make an unscheduled trip to St Jory to buy new sheets, for though there were plenty in the linen cupboard several had disintegrated virtually at a touch.

Mrs Cartwright, in her position of Organiser in Chief, made a personal visit to check arrangements. Pen, she said in her smilingly authoritative manner, wasn't to worry about a thing. All was in hand.

"Everyone's being very kind," Pen said, feeling guilty because she found the woman so irritating – wondering if, perhaps, it were a kind of jealousy. Perhaps secretly she longed to be a self-assured manager of other people's affairs. Was she, perhaps, a bossy-boots *manqué*? She suppressed a smile at the thought, and hoped Mrs Cartwright hadn't noticed it.

On Saturday, Mrs Cartwright continued, trestle tables and chairs would be brought to Roscarrow and made ready as far as possible for the celebrations that would take place after the parade and church service on Sunday morning. A small platform was to be erected on a site selected earlier, and a profusion of pot plants was being brought to create a colourful bank around its sides. Here the Town Band would play while the buffet lunch was in progress; later their places would be taken by Mr Carne and the town dignitaries. Speeches and a presentation would then be made, this latter taking the form of a large oil painting depicting the harbour of Porthlivick, carried out by Wesley Clore, a famous painter of the St Ives school. It had, said Mrs Cartwright, a most beautiful gilt frame – she herself had been instrumental in choosing it – with a most tasteful plaque inserted on the lower edge saying that it was given to Caleb Carne 'by the people of Porthlivick on the occasion of his 95th birthday: 16.9.90'. And underneath, the words: 'With Proud Thanksgiving'.

"Again, my choice." Mrs Cartwright thrust her head forward proudly, smiling her shark-like smile.

"How very thoughtful of you," Pen said. "I'm sure he'll be most touched. People have been so kind."

"We had money left over, so we've bought two state-of-the-art reclining chairs for the famous summerhouse. It seemed the most practical thing –"

"How very kind," Pen said again, wishing she could think of some other way of expressing her appreciation.

"My dear Mrs Hambly, it's the least we can do for our most famous son. Of course, we've had to restrict the Roscarrow guest list to those who contributed, otherwise you'd have had the world and his wife here. The *hoi polloi* will have to put up with the church service. The front pews will, of course, be reserved for the Mayor and the councillors on the left and your family on the right. You are all right for transport, I take it? Or should I arrange a car? You're quite sure? Well, do try to arrive sharp at eleven, by which time everyone else will be in place. The vicar tells me that his sermon will be based on the text: 'After the fire, the still, small voice'. I think that's rather lovely, don't you?"

Pen, not sure that this sounded remotely applicable to her father, smiled non-committally and changed the subject.

"About the catering –" she said.

"Absolutely nothing for you to worry about, Mrs Hambly." Mrs Cartwright, abandoning the soulful expression she clearly deemed applicable to the discussion of spiritual matters, smiled confidently once more. "The caterers will put in an appearance quite early on Sunday morning. All they need is the use of your kitchen. Most of the food will be ready-prepared."

"Suppose it rains?"

"The weather men have predicted sun, so we can only hope and pray – however, we have made arrangements for a marquee to be held in readiness."

"You seem to have thought of everything," Pen said.

Mrs Cartwright beamed. "All part of the service, Mrs Hambly. We do want to make it a great day for a great man."

Pen experienced a pang of guilt. They all meant so well; she was wrong to let her personal antipathy to Mrs Cartwright get in the way of her appreciation.

241

"And he's enormously grateful, I assure you," she said. "You will remember, though, that he is a very old man, won't you? I mean, when it comes to speeches, they shouldn't be too long –"

Moderation in all things was guaranteed – a promise that Pen rather doubted, for though she rose to take her leave at that point Mrs Cartwright ran through the arrangements twice more before achieving the front door and was embarking on a third reprise as she stood on the top step. She was, however, interrupted by the ringing of the telephone bell which caused her to take her leave at last, much to Pen's relief.

She, expecting the electrician to ring to arrange a time to fix the washing machine which had chosen this inconvenient moment to break down, was momentarily puzzled by the voice on the phone.

"It that Pen?" it asked.

"Yes. Who's that?"

"It's David. David Holt. Hi – how are you?"

"*David!*" Pen's voice, once she had regained her breath, was weak with surprise. "How lovely to hear from you! When did you arrive?"

"Last Monday. It's great to be here. I'm really looking forward to seeing you – and your father, of course. Are you both well?"

His voice sounded just the same, now that she was able to hear it properly. It seemed astonishing to her now that she hadn't recognised it instantly.

"We're fine. And looking forward to seeing you too. You're going to stay at the Marina, I gather."

"That's right. Simon booked a room for Saturday and Sunday, two rooms in fact. One for me, and one for him and his girl-friend. But Pen –" He hesitated a moment. "Look – you'll say if this isn't convenient, won't you? I know how busy you'll be this coming week –"

"Not as busy as all that. I've just had the organiser of the whole affair here and she assures me I haven't a thing to worry about."

"Would you mind, then, if I came down earlier? Like, say, tomorrow? It'll give me more time to see the place and to see you – and also I feel it would be kind of tactful to remove myself from London for the moment."

"Oh? Why's that?"

"You met Simon, didn't you?"

"I did. I thought he was charming."

"Thanks. I'm pretty fond of him myself. The thing is that he's just been offered a job back in New York and he and his girl-friend need a bit of space to talk it over, settle things between them. This past weekend I've felt very much superfluous to requirements. How about it, Pen? Would I be in the way down there, too? I've already asked the Marina if I can have the room early, and they say it's fine with them. The season's virtually over, apparently. So what do you say? I wouldn't get in your hair, I promise – but it would be great to see you."

"Yes," Pen said. "Oh yes, David, I'd like that too. Do come. Can I meet your train?"

"I wouldn't dream of putting you to so much trouble, but do come to the hotel for dinner with me tomorrow night. Would that be possible?"

"I – I should think so." Either Dolly or Fred would come in, she felt certain. "Yes, I'm sure I can arrange it."

"Wonderful! I'll call when I get to the hotel."

"I'll look forward to it."

After he had gone, Pen replaced the receiver and stood staring blankly into space. Slowly her gaze moved upwards until she met her own eyes in the mirror above the hall table. What would he see? Not the girl he had once known, that was certain – which, in many ways, was no bad thing. Some changes had undoubtedly been for the better. But what would he think of the overall image? With her fingertips she traced the lines around her mouth, thinking how much she hated the tiny puckers on her upper lip. Americans had cosmetic surgery. Americans had silicone implants.

And then she laughed. She was doing it again; glamorising everything to do with the States, feeling inferior, just as she had when David was here before. Surely by now she had learned that not all Americans were as seen on TV?

Dinner. *Tomorrow!* The reality of it suddenly hit her with a high-octane mix of joy and nervousness and exhilaration. Would he remember that confession of undying love? Probably – but so what? He wouldn't make anything of it, any more than she would make anything of the fact that he'd never come to tell her goodbye, as he'd solemnly promised. They were both mature enough to laugh at it now.

They'd parted as friends, that was the important thing, and as friends they could meet now. There was, she thought happily, no sell-by date on friendship. So often it outlasted so-called love.

With that, she thought of Simon. Love, she guessed, would be a serious thing with him. Treat him well, she begged the unknown girl. Love him back.

And she thanked heaven, as she made her way to the kitchen, that all those kind of complicated affairs of the heart were far, far behind her. Age, she thought, had some compensations after all.

\*     \*     \*

"It's an offer you can't refuse," Laura said, not for the first time. "Your career comes first."

"Before what?" Simon asked. "Before happiness? Before you?"

"Don't say that! You're shifting the responsibility on to me."

"I'm not! I know it's my decision; but I have to take everything into consideration, don't I? I love you, Laura."

"Oh, Simon!" She had been putting knives and forks away. Now she slammed the drawer shut with an air of exasperation and came to sit opposite him at the kitchen table where he was slumped dispiritedly, head between his hands. For a moment she looked at him, lip caught between her teeth. Then she reached out and touched his face with her finger tips. "Look," she said. "Don't think I'm not grateful –"

He looked up at that, with a furious expression.

"Oh, for God's sake! *Grateful?* What the hell are you talking about, Laura? Gratitude hardly comes into it."

"No, I know. I'm sorry. I didn't mean that, exactly."

"You mean 'thanks, but no thanks'."

"Simon, I don't know what I mean. It would be the easiest thing in the world to say that I love you too; maybe I do. I love being with you. I feel more for you than for any other man I've known. But that doesn't mean I feel ready to give up everything here – my job, this flat, my independence. Anyway, how can I? I'm about to embark on another school year –"

Simon looked at her bleakly. The discussion had gone on all weekend, on and off, whenever they were alone together, and he could see no happy resolution to it. Marriage was out for the moment; he knew her well enough to know that. She shied like a frightened filly at the merest mention of the word. And without marriage, without the necessary piece of paper, she would be an alien in America and therefore unable to work. The thought of being dependent on him – on anybody – was total anathema to her. It was an impasse.

"As I see it," he said, looking at her almost coldly, "there are three choices. Either I have to give, or you do, or we walk away from each other. Simple as that."

"You can't pass up this opportunity."

"I don't want to, I admit; but neither do I want to lose you."

"If you refuse it because of me, you'll end up hating me."

He shook his head wearily.

"It's late," he said. "And we're getting nowhere. I'd better go."

"Oh, Simon." Laura looked at him miserably, and he gave the ghost of a laugh.

"You keep saying that!" He got to his feet, pulled her up and held her close, rubbing his cheek against her hair. "My sweet, I can't lose you. It mustn't happen."

Her arms went round him too; but she sighed unhappily and made no promises.

"Is it still on for next weekend?" Simon asked after a moment. "You'll come to Cornwall with me, won't you?"

"If you want me to."

"If? You're crazy! Of course I want to you to. I shan't go if you don't come."

"Then I'll come. I'm curious, I confess."

He held her away from him, looked into her face.

"About Carne?"

"That's only natural, isn't it?"

"You're not up to anything?"

"Like what?"

"Like throwing a spanner in the works?"

"I haven't got a spanner to throw, have I? Don't worry, Simon! I've other things to worry about right now."

Still he looked at her, trying to divine what was going on in her mind. Why should he feel so sure that Stella, dead these past five years, had so much to do with Laura's indecision? It made little sense to him, but he was well aware that there was some kind of connection.

"Sleep well," he said. "Remember I love you. That's not something that's going to change. See you tomorrow."

\*     \*     \*

What would Stella have advised?

Laura found herself unable to guess. Once she had regarded her grandmother as a kind of High Priestess of the Sisterhood – a standard-bearer, ahead of her time.

She had made an early, impetuous marriage which had been over, she had confided to her granddaughter, long before Jean Morel had been killed in Spain. She had won respect for her work. She had lived to rejoice at the election of a woman Prime Minister; and to bemoan the fact that having been elected, she had done nothing for women in general. She had campaigned for equal pay and conditions; for child-care in the workplace; for an allowance for women who chose to stay at home. If Laura had sought her advice in those days, she would have been quite certain that it was untainted by Polly's Law – that any man was better than none.

Now, she felt sure of nothing. The High Priestess had allowed Carne to take the credit for work that she had done; had deliberately, in Laura's eyes, downgraded herself by pandering to a man with no real talent – a man who traded on his charm, cheated on his wife, and would very likely have cheated on Stella herself eventually, if things had worked out differently. As it was he had strung her along and in the end let her down. Had she, then, capitulated? What were those who came after to think?

That night Laura slept only fitfully, all the arguments going round and round in her head, her mind growing ever more confused. Was she 'in love' with Simon? She thought about him in his absence; loved being with him, loved going to bed with him, so if that was love then she guessed she was in it.

If only they could have stayed like this for a while! Everything had been going so well, so happily. Life had been wonderful from the moment of their meeting, full of love and excitement and mental stimulus. She might not have written much of the proposed biography, but she'd seen plays she wouldn't have dreamt of seeing without Simon; gone to exhibitions she might well have missed. She'd met all kinds of people she would never have known; had laughed a lot and talked a blue streak. It was a pretty sure guess that sooner or later they would have moved in together. Marriage might have followed eventually, perhaps. Or perhaps not. Either way, it would have been no big deal.

But this preposterous idea of giving in her notice at the West London Collegiate, of moving lock, stock and barrel to New York without a job or any prospect of getting one, was something else. It just wasn't on.

Of course, if she married him she'd be an American citizen and could take her chance in the job market along with everyone else. But what kind of reason was that for getting married?

Someone has to keep the faith, she said to Stella's shade. Someone has to live wholly and freely, not tailoring every move to suit the man in her life. Not pursuing love as if it was the one important thing.

What was it, anyway, this strange emotion that was said to make the world go round? How did anyone know it would last, or was more than a fantasy, encouraged by poets and pop-stars? How many married couples of her acquaintance showed any trace of it, now that the glamour had worn off?

They were questions with no answers. Towards dawn she seemed to sleep more peacefully, and when she woke she found that, miraculously, the questions had stopped plaguing her and in their place was a kind of calm – not a happy calm, more the arid stillness of the desert; but calm nevertheless.

Stella had loved with all her heart – had experienced no doubt. She had given one man everything. Even so, in the end, how had she summed up her life?

"I see now it was all for the best," she had told Laura. "It would never have worked."

Laura could almost hear her voice as she said it; could see her face – strong and handsome and serene as it had been in later life. The message was too insistent to ignore.

The wonderful summer was over. Simon was going back to New York. She would miss him – couldn't, at this moment, imagine what her life would be without him – but in the end it would be all for the best. Total dependence, the only alternative, was something she couldn't contemplate.

The post arrived after she had got up and gone to the kitchen to make coffee. It brought a letter in a square white envelope addressed in an unfamiliar hand. A London postmark. She stared at it, her brain not yet functioning at full speed; then suddenly she came to her senses and tore it open.

As she suspected, it was from Victor Kaye, and she read it with growing excitement and disbelief. It was dated Monday 10th September:

Dear Ms Rossi

I have been away on holiday and returned only today to find your letter awaiting me.

I must first correct a misapprehension on your part. It was my father, also called Victor Kaye, who was your grandmother's friend. He was divorced from my mother, Magda, in 1943, and brought me up on his own until his early death in 1950, by which time I was doing my National Service. After this I went out to Kenya to work on a coffee estate, and though thereafter I leased this house to tenants, I retained ownership of it and in retirement have now returned to live here.

I have fond memories of your grandmother, who was inordinately kind to a rather lonely schoolboy. I remember having several meals with her and her little girl in Chiswick during school holidays, and being taken for picnics and various excursions.

Regarding your query about the whereabouts of Mrs Jane Porteous, I am indeed still in touch with her, in fact I spent last weekend staying with her in the Cotswolds. My father was her cousin (I rather suspect that it was she who brought your mother to our house in the first instance rather than vice versa). She was widowed some five or six years ago whereupon she gave up the farmhouse where she and her husband had lived all their married lives and moved into a cottage in the village. I have already contacted her by telephone, and she tells me that she would be delighted to meet you and to talk with you about the old days. Losing touch with your grandmother was a great sadness to her, too. I well remember what good friends they once were. Her address is Rose Cottage, Upper Swinshot, Nr Cirencester, Glos, phone: 0285 00399.

It occurs to me that the little girl I mentioned must be your mother! I hope she is in good health. May I ask you to pass on to her my very best wishes?

He was, he finished, hers very sincerely. Oh, bless his heart, Laura thought, putting her other problems to one side for the moment. Bless his dear, old fashioned, pedantic heart. She'd phone Jane up at once.

Devon, indeed! Well, it was all a long time ago, as everyone kept reminding her, and anyone could be forgiven for getting it wrong. Even Polly.

\*    \*    \*

Simon went with his father to Paddington.

"I envy you," he said as they stood on the platform waiting for the train to arrive. "It must be beautiful down there right now. Remember me to Pen, won't you?"

"Sure will. Son, I hope everything works out with you and Laura. Don't close any doors permanently, will you? Try to hang loose."

"Don't worry. I'm not about to scare her off."

"Give her time."

"I'll give her anything she wants. At least she says she's coming down to Porthlivick with me on Saturday. Maybe Cornwall will work some kind of magic."

"As I recall, it's a pretty magical kind of place. Look, you don't have to wait, Simon. I know you've got work to do. There's no point in hanging about."

Simon looked at his watch.

"Actually, I did want to catch the British Library before lunch. I'm meeting an editor at one –"

"Go on, then. I'm big enough and old enough to find my own seat. Good luck."

If ever anyone needed it, then I sure do, Simon thought, leaving David on the platform and making his way to the Underground. He had, as he had said, made a resolution to give Laura all the space she needed – but he had to leave London for New York at the end of September, which gave him less than three weeks to put his case. It wasn't long, and was getting shorter all the time.

It was three thirty by the time he got home, and the Answerphone was winking at him. Laura, he thought at once. They hadn't made any firm arrangements for meeting that day but it was understood that they would have dinner together; she would phone him, she had said. And indeed it was her voice he heard when he pressed the playback button.

"Simon? It's eleven thirty, Tuesday. I'm sorry you're not there. I was hoping to speak to you. Look, I'm going away for a few days. Don't worry, I'll be in touch, and I'll be back for the weekend, I promise. Please don't worry! I know you will, but there's no need. I just think it best to get away for a bit. See you soon. Take care. Bye."

He smashed his fist on to the table and swore mightily. How could she *do* this to him? So little time left – and not one word of her whereabouts! Where the hell could she have gone? Who might know? Mentally he went through the list of her friends that he'd met and realised that though he knew their first names, he was sure of nothing more. Polly, then? He stretched out his hand to pick up the phone, but at the last moment decided against it.

What about his resolution to give her all the time she wanted? She did say she'd be in touch. She did say 'see you soon'. Give her space, he cautioned himself, forcing the panic down. Don't crowd her. And above all, don't involve Polly until it's strictly necessary.

A pity, really, that his father had decamped so tactfully. It was all a bit of a waste now. Still, he wasn't at all sure that tact was the entire reason for his unscheduled departure for Cornwall. The desire to see Pen had something to do with it, he felt sure; and Carne too, perhaps. But mostly Pen.

\*     \*     \*

The train was fast and made few stops. It was when they pulled into Exeter station that David heard it first – that West Country burr that he couldn't describe, couldn't replicate, yet recognised immediately. He was at once transported back to the days of his youth; those wartime days that had lifted him out of his familiar surroundings and dumped him into the alien and ultimately terrifying world of the Carnes.

How much did Carne still remember? Surely even the oldest of men would be unable to forget a night like the one they had spent back in 1944.

He had hung a couple of fishing lines over the bow.

"In case the coast-guard's looking," he said. "Go straight out. Keep away from the headland."

Those were almost the only words spoken. It was cold. David wasn't dressed for the sea and was shivering; so, apparently, was Carne, for they'd only been out a short while when he pulled a couple of oilskins from a locker and threw one over, putting on the other himself. But he didn't speak and neither did David, though his head roared with panic and outrage and a thousand questions.

It wasn't right – how could it be right? It wasn't enough to say that this was in the national interest. If it was so, then the Army should have been called, or the police; it shouldn't be up to a Private in the American Army to carry out this dirty work. For it was dirty, it was horrible – obscene! That was a man lying there, a member of the human race, dead, with a wound at the back of his head. Incurred when he fell on the steps, Carne said. Well, maybe he was telling the truth – maybe this was a spy. It was perfectly logical to think that there were spies about at this time, trying to find out when and where the invasion would happen, but even so, he shouldn't be the one to take him out to sea and dump him overboard like a load of garbage. Even spies had trials, judges, legal representation and, if guilty, were shot by those whose job it was to do so. This wasn't right. It didn't make sense. None of it made sense.

He could get into terrible trouble if it all became known. *When* it all became known. He couldn't, somehow, imagine Carne speaking up for him. What would the Army have to say about it? Worse – how could he explain his presence at Roscarrow when he should have been back at camp?

The sea became rougher as they left the shelter of the headland, the waves picking up the small boat and flinging it down again, spray drenching them both as well as the uncomplaining passenger. Water was flooding into the hull, and Carne began pumping. No leisure now to think about anything but keeping the little boat afloat.

Carne shouted, but the wind took his words and hurled them away.

"What?"

Carne waved an arm to signal the futility of speech.

"Getting back'll take hours," David shouted. His own precarious situation had now taken precedence over everything else. So great had been his horror at what Carne had asked him to do, so great his disbelief that he was actually doing it, this aspect of the affair had seemed of comparatively little importance. But now the possibility – probability – of trouble back at the camp almost paralysed him with panic and he felt physically sick. He had to get back before his absence was discovered. God alone knew what would happen to him if he didn't. He squinted at the luminous hands of his watch and couldn't make out if it was nearer two or three o'clock. He had no idea how long it was since he left the safety of his tent.

And in this panic he forgot about the man and his membership of the human race. All he could think of now was the necessity of finishing this gruesome task, getting it out of the way. It was wartime – this spy, or whoever he was, was just as much of a casualty as he or any of his buddies might be in a few days' time. He was dead and wouldn't suffer any more. Let him go, and forget him.

Carne was shouting again and waving his arms. This, then, was the moment; this the chosen place.

\*    \*    \*

The Cotswold stone was a warm shade of honey-gold in the sunlight. Why, Laura wondered, hadn't she heard of Upper Swinshot? Pictures of Bourton-on-the-Water, and Stow-on-the-Wold and Lower Slaughter adorned calendars all over the country; Upper Swinshot, however, remained unsung.

"And thank God for that," she said to herself as she drove slowly down the main street where the tops of chestnut trees already displayed the golden sheen that proved autumn was on its way. There were cars parked around the green, and several more outside the one shop that, as far as she could see, represented the commercial centre of the village. But in spite of the undoubted beauty of the place there were no coaches, no evidence of mass tourism.

She was looking for Rose Cottage. Jane, on the phone, had told her that it was on the High Street side of the green, three doors down from the Red Lion.

"It's the easiest place in the world to find," Jane had said. "But not always the easiest place to park. It depends on the time of day, and whether trade is good at the pub."

At four in the afternoon she found both cottage and parking place without difficulty. She got out of the car and looked around her, appreciating once more the timeless charm of the village – the graceful houses and the profusion of flowers in gardens and baskets and window-boxes.

Rose Cottage was not large, but it looked loved, the rose that gave it its name clambering in profusion over the door which was resplendent with a shining brass knocker and letter-box.

Laura knocked, and the door was opened by a small, rather plump, white-haired woman whom she recognised immediately from the old photographs, in spite of the passage of years. She had bright shrewd blue eyes in a face that was lined and russet-coloured, rather like an old, withered apple. A merry face, Laura thought, with a smile that was unchanged since those pictured days. The hair wasn't so very different either. Then it had been fair, cut short and curling crisply all over her head. Now it was white, but the style was much the same.

"Mrs Porteous?" Laura said, smiling.

"Laura! Come in. I can't tell you how glad I am that you've come. Let me look at you. Oh, you're so like Stella!"

"People say so."

"People are right. D'you know, I've missed her so –"

"She was there, in Chiswick, all the time –"

"I know, I know. Come and have some tea and I'll tell you all about it. Or perhaps you'd like to go up to your room first? It's up the stairs on the right."

"I feel guilty about imposing on you. Are you really sure it's convenient."

"My dear girl, I couldn't be more delighted. We've got so much to talk about, haven't we? And I do love having visitors. As it is,

I'm restricted to talking to the cat ninety per cent of the time. You'll make a most refreshing change, I assure you."

She was warm and friendly and seemed sincere, but Laura couldn't help wondering, as she washed her hands in the tiny white bathroom that led from the tiny white bedroom, why, if she had missed Stella so much, had she never phoned or visited or written?

"I suppose," she said, trying to be fair as, downstairs once more, she accepted a cup of tea, "it's all too easy to drift apart from old friends. There are people I knew at college –"

"I know. One swears to keep in touch, but it's so easy to let things slide. Stella and I met in Paris, before the war. Thinking of it now, it seems like another world. We thought we were so *avant garde*, so daring – drinking *anis* and smoking Gauloises, mixing with artists and writers, never with a penny to bless ourselves! Then, during the war, we were almost like sisters – even closer than that, judging from some of the sisters I know. But we had rather a bitter quarrel –" Jane broke off, her blue eyes a little wary. "I don't know how much you know about your grandmother's life," she said after a moment.

"Quite a lot," Laura said. "She told me about Caleb Carne."

"Did she, indeed?"

"Was he the cause of the quarrel?"

"Not entirely." Jane stirred her tea, her brows drawn together as if she were trying to bring the past into focus. "It was Evelyn, just as much. My husband. He could never get on with Stella – didn't approve of anything she stood for. He was a real throw-back to the Victorian age, you see. A woman's place was in the home. Full stop."

Laura laughed.

"I can imagine how well that went down with Stella."

"To be honest, it didn't go down too well with me! We argued a lot, Evelyn and I, but in spite of it I knew he was the man for me. We thrived on argument. We had two fine sons, and a lovely home just down the road from here – an old farmhouse dating from Tudor times. I loved it. Stella thought I'd copped out – forgotten my principles for a comfortable existence; and I thought –" she paused, sighed, shook her head. "How brash one is when one's young. Who was I to give her advice?"

"Didn't you like Carne?"

She considered the question for a moment, smiling a little, remembering.

"Yes, I did, actually. He had a kind of innocent, childlike enthusiasm for all kinds of things that was intensely likeable. One laughed at him a little, but it was always affectionate laughter. And of course, he was very handsome. I could see what Stella saw in him, but I was convinced she was wasting her time – that in the end he would break her heart. I was quite certain he would never do what he always promised – ie., leave his wife and marry her. And what Stella wouldn't admit is that she would never have forgiven herself if he had! She tried to subdue all her feelings of guilt about an *affaire* with a married man. She told herself how unhappy he was, how his wife didn't understand him – all that kind of thing – but I know it was on her conscience."

"And you pointed this out to her?"

"I did. It was all part of the quarrel that blew up over something quite trivial that Evelyn did or said. It was before we were married. I was posted back to London by that time and Evelyn was on leave. We had a kind of tacit agreement, Stella and I, that we wouldn't react to his more infuriating statements, but somehow this day we did. Maybe the weather had something to do with it, or the time of the month, who can tell? It was a sultry, stormy kind of a day in late summer and the three of us were sitting out in the garden of the Chiswick house. Evelyn made one of his crass remarks about pre-war politics. I can't even remember what the issue was now, but the most fearful row broke out and he walked out in high dudgeon, dragging me with him.

"A few days later Stella and I met, ostensibly to smooth things over. There was no need for *us* to quarrel, we said, no matter what Evelyn thought; but then Stella took me to task about forgetting my principles sufficiently to marry him, I stood up for him, and before we knew it all kinds of home truths were coming out. Talking of principles, I said, how did she square her conscience when it came to carrying on an *affaire* with a married man? Cal would never leave his wife, I told her. He'd go on promising the earth, but he'd never fulfil his promises. I was brutally frank – I can't tell you how I regretted it afterwards – and she stormed out of the restaurant like an enraged prima donna."

"Really? Stella? I can't imagine it!"

"Oh, she could be quite a drama queen, could Stella. I thought then and I still think that it was the truth of what I said that made it so unforgivable; she did have a conscience about Carne's marriage. She tried to persuade herself that love conquered all things, but she couldn't really quieten that still, small voice. We made up the quarrel, smoothed things over. Both she and Polly came to our wedding, but things were never quite the same again. Too much had been said."

She sighed a little and shook her head, as if even now she would manage things differently if only it were possible.

"After I was married and Evelyn demobbed, we came here to take over the family house and farm. Meetings between Stella and me became much more difficult, for practical reasons as well as everything else. Longer and longer times elapsed between seeing each other – then, of course, the children came along, and the farm was a tie. I never got to London, she hardly ever came here – and when she did, she and Evelyn invariably managed to fight. Finally even Christmas cards stopped."

"I was with her a lot in her last illness. She talked about you very fondly."

"Did she? Oh, I wish I'd seen her! After Evelyn died I found myself thinking about her and I made up my mind to write to her. You perhaps won't believe this, but I swear it's true – I'd even begun a letter when I saw the report of her death in the paper. I was so sad to think I'd left it too late. How wasteful we are of time, when there's so little of it."

"Tell me –" Laura hesitated a moment or two. The question she had travelled all the way from London to put to Jane Porteous suddenly seemed almost too momentous for speech. "Those famous talks of Caleb Carne. Did Stella write them?"

"Oh, dear!" Jane laughed, the blue eyes almost disappearing in a network of wrinkles. "With all this renewed acclaim he's getting, I wondered if anyone would bring that up. The answer is yes – sometimes. A bit. She certainly wrote the first one. She tried to sell it to the BBC but they wouldn't look at it under her name, so Cal tried it – as a joke more than anything else. Anyway, they leapt at it. Afterwards when he was commissioned to do a whole series – well, they talked things over, of course, and I daresay she had quite a contribution to make."

"I'm sure it was more than that! Have you read Carne's books? They're not at all the same style. And it wasn't a style he ever recaptured, was it? It doesn't seem fair that he should get all the praise."

Jane looked at her for a moment with a slightly amused expression.

"More tea?" she asked.

"You seem to take it very lightly."

"No more lightly than Stella did, believe me."

"But it was her *work* –"

"She never saw it that way. Anyway, it wasn't all her work, more of a joint effort. She used to run through the talks with him – make changes here and there, tell him what words to emphasise. It amused her – made her think she was putting one over on the BBC."

"But it seems such a betrayal of all her principles."

"Bloody principles," Jane said, unexpectedly. "Here, let me give you a refill. And you've hardly eaten any of your cake. It's very good, I promise you. I haven't many talents, but I can cook.

"Principles," she went on when she had poured more tea, "make extraordinarily cold bedfellows – as I feel sure I pointed out to Stella during the fatal argument when she accused me of not having any. It's so easy to pick and choose them for other people, don't you find? It's not nearly so easy when it's one's own turn. Look, Stella didn't sell out. She had an awesomely responsible job after the fall of France. I expect you know all about that. She had little time to herself, and she became far too emotionally involved with it all. Her health suffered, but she never gave up or took leave, except to have a few days with Polly now and again. Vetting Carne's broadcasts was a kind of diversion – a little light relief. And if she did add or subtract a little to the text of the talks, she never believed for one moment that her part was the greater. Have you heard Carne's voice? Then you'll know the importance of it. I've seen her listening to him with tears pouring down her cheeks, moved beyond bearing, even though she knew exactly what was coming next."

"It seems quite extraordinary."

"They were extraordinary times." Jane looked at her curiously as, finally, she ate her piece of cake. "We did what we could, took our pleasure where we could. Why does it matter so much?" she asked gently at last.

Laura shook her head as if in defeat.

"I don't know," she said. "But it does. I just feel I need to understand her – need to know why she appeared to jettison all her feminist principles to prop up the self-esteem of a third-rate writer. I looked up to her so."

"Rightly," Jane said.

"It maddens me to think of Carne having so much acclaim."

"Do you imagine she wouldn't be glad that he's making a little money in his old age? He didn't make much at the time."

"She was always generous." Laura drank her tea, set the cup down carefully on its saucer. "No," she said after a moment. "I mean no, I don't imagine that, and yes, I expect she would be glad. It just seems unfair that she got no credit. As far as I know Carne's never said a word – never hinted for a moment that it wasn't all his own work, and that seems wrong to me."

"Is it a wrong you intend to right?" Jane asked. Laura took her time in replying.

"I don't know what to do," she said at last. She sighed. "Quite honestly, I don't know what to do about anything."

\*     \*     \*

Pen, entering the hotel through the swing doors, saw David coming down the stairs that led to the main foyer and knew him immediately. Her heart was fluttering in a ridiculously immature kind of way, just as if she were fifteen again, instead of sixty-one, but at least she knew enough not to show it any more. She paused for a moment and took a few deep breaths, watching him from a distance. It wasn't fair that he should have changed so little! Forty-six years was forty-six years, after all.

And now he was coming nearer and had seen her; had paused as if to make certain, was walking towards her with a tentative smile as if he was still not entirely sure. Then the smile became more assured.

"Pen!" He held out both hands towards her. "It is Pen, isn't it? You haven't changed a bit."

"Nonsense." Laughing, she presented her cheek for his kiss. "That's not true – and bearing in mind that I was a gauche schoolgirl when we last met, not even complimentary!"

"It's so good to see you. I feel as if all this is a kind of dream –"

"Me too. You know, you're the one who hasn't changed."

"A likely story! Come on, let's have a drink to celebrate."

A little self-consciously, they surveyed each other afresh once seated in the cocktail bar of the hotel.

"Where do we start?" David said. "There's so much I want to ask you. I know from Simon that your father's in good form, but Trish and Caro – how are they and what happened to them?"

He listened attentively as she gave a brief outline of the years between; of Trish's marriages and divorces, of Caro's successful marriage. He laughed about the Lounge Lizard and said that he was sorry not to be meeting him, and pronounced himself pleased about Caro and Alan and their delightful family.

"But you," he said when they had moved to the dining-room. "Your life hasn't been a bed of roses. I'm sorry it worked out that way."

"I had eighteen years of happiness." Pen gave him the quick, mischievous grin that assured him that he'd been right when he had said she hadn't changed. "It may surprise you to know that before your arrival in Porthlivick in 1944 Philip was my hero. I'd known him all my life – he was the son of our local doctor – but he was a lot older than I was and had been away a long time. I was about ripe for another crush when you came on the scene. I was just off to Art College when he came home. He'd been in hospital for months and was still weak from his experiences in the prison camp. He looked like a skeleton, but that made no difference. I fell for him all over again."

"I forgive you. Do you still read poetry?"

"All the time. I paint too."

"Are you better at doing the sea, now? You had difficulties with it, I seem to remember."

"Oh, I've conquered that little problem. Believe it or not, I sell things! People actually part with their hard-earned cash."

"Clever you! How else do you spend your time?"

"No, it's your turn. I was so sorry to hear about your wife, David. Simon told me how happy you were."

"Yes, we were. Like you, I'm thankful for what we had. I just hope –" he broke off and she looked at him curiously. "I just hope

259

Simon sorts his affairs out as happily," he finished. "He's going through a bad patch at the moment. He's going back to New York very shortly. He's crazy about this girl – Laura – but he's not at all sure that she'll agree to go with him."

"I liked him so much. He reminded me of you."

"He looks like Fay's side of the family."

"His manner, I mean. Poor Simon. I hope he doesn't have to suffer the way you did over Trish. Did it take you a long time to get over her?"

David laughed.

"Do you know, I can't remember," he said. "Isn't that a terrible confession? I remember thinking my heart was broken, but so many life-and-death things happened just afterwards."

"Yes, of course they did."

Did she know about the man in the summerhouse, then, and the hideous way he was disposed of? No – how could she? She meant D-day, the Normandy landings, the battles. Carne had been desperate to keep the whole thing quiet then and it was his guess that he'd continued to do so. And unless she mentioned it first he had no intention of bringing it up.

Carne, now; that was a different thing altogether. Somehow over the next few days he would have to find the opportunity for a heart-to-heart talk with the guy. He wanted to know the truth, was determined to seek it out.

"Do you remember that day when we sailed to the beach and you and I went off exploring?" he asked, concentrating on happier matters.

"And Trish was cross? Jealousy has always been her downfall – either because she's feeling the pangs herself, or inspiring it in others."

"She was so pretty."

"She still is. It just takes a lot longer now."

"That day was the first and only time I had the pleasure of meeting your grandmother. She was sitting in the summerhouse when I came up the steps and she had a few choice words to say about GIs."

"I don't doubt it. If she said anything nice about anyone it was a red-letter day." Pen's smile died as she remembered. "Poor Father. He did try so hard to please her, almost always without success. When I was very small I thought she was a wicked witch. I was terrified of her. In my mind she always seemed to be surrounded by a kind of black cloud."

"I guess she'd had a hard life."

"So had lots of other people. They weren't all as bitter and malevolent as she was. Let's not talk about her. Tell me about the work you did, David. Advertising, Simon said."

David laughed.

"Believe it or not, those days seem almost as distant as wartime," he said.

But he warmed to his theme; told her about the business, the house, the boat. Conversation with him was, Pen found, as easy as it had ever been, but inevitably memories formed a great part of it – memories shaped by the years, their hard edges softened. Laughter came easily.

"Oh, it *is* nice to see you again," she said, taking his arm as, finally, the evening at an end, he walked her home. "It's funny how those old days come back to you once you've set the memory process in motion, isn't it? Do you remember singing hymns round the piano? You must have thought us terribly naïve!"

"It was fun. I enjoyed it."

"I've been trying to think of that hymn about gardens and roses that you used to sing."

"I remember it well," David said; and sang it to her as they walked along, jazzing it up a little so that they walked in time to it almost as if they were dancing. "My God," he said, laughing, as he came to the end of it, "it's many a year since I heard that."

But Pen, her smile suddenly a little tremulous, said nothing; she just hoped that somehow it would be possible to remember the happiness of this night when once more life had returned to normal, as return it must. She was under no illusions about that.

\*    \*    \*

Laura only intended to stay with Jane for one night. She wasn't, she always thought, very good at staying with people; was, perhaps, too selfish to make the necessary adaptations.

There was, however, an unusual feeling of ease at Rose Cottage; an absence of pressure. For the first time in what seemed a long while, Laura was conscious of a slow relaxing of tension. London, Simon, the decisions she had to make, all seemed a world away from Jane's garden where she spent the next morning sitting in the late sunshine. She wasn't reading, though she had a book open on her lap; she wasn't, she realised, even thinking very much. Just being.

Jane, busy in the kitchen, looked out of the window and saw her. Something, she was aware, was troubling her guest. Surely not just this old business of Stella? There was an air of strain about her, of unhappiness, which hardly seemed justified by any unanswered questions from the past.

"You don't have to rush away today, do you?" she asked, when she took coffee out for both of them. "I wanted to take you over to the farm this afternoon. Deborah – that's my daughter-in-law – just phoned. I told her you were here and she said she'd be pleased to see us. You'd like her, I think, and the house itself is definitely worthy of inspection."

"I'm sure it is," Laura said. "It's awfully kind of her, and of you, but –"

"You look like someone who needs a break from London," Jane said. "Do stay another night or two."

Laura hesitated a moment; made up her mind.

"Only if I can take you out to dinner tonight," she said, and Jane smiled, all the lines on her face slanting upwards.

"It's a deal," she said. "I can recommend the Red Lion."

Later, when she had finished her coffee, Laura roused herself sufficiently to walk around the village. She called in at the Red Lion to book a table, wandered up to the church and entered its cool, dim depths. For a while she stood in the aisle facing the altar, looking up at the round window above it with its blazing stained glass, red and blue and gold and green.

What am I to do? she asked; but though she waited, head lifted, she had no divine revelation and expected none. Any decision would be hers, and hers alone. She was conscious of calm, however, and a feeling that she was perhaps in the right place, doing the right thing. Waiting.

I ought to phone Simon, she thought, as she went back to the cottage; but she made no move to do so, either then or later. She felt a strangeness in the atmosphere, in herself; a langour, as if the air she moved through was heavy, weighting her limbs.

"Don't go yet," Jane said the following day as they lingered over breakfast.

"I don't want to be a bother –"

"You're not! I love having you. Truly, I mean it. Do you know Cirencester?"

Laura smiled at this apparent *non sequitur*.

"No," she said.

"Then come with me this afternoon. I've got a dental appointment, and must do some shopping. It's a lovely little town, well worth seeing."

"If you're sure –"

"I told you, I like having you."

"Then I'd love to stay. Thank you."

She helped clear away the breakfast things and did the washing up; but this done, Jane insisted she spent another lazy morning in the garden. After a while she brought out two mugs of coffee, holding, somewhat precariously, a large, leather-bound photograph album under her arm.

"Look what I've dug out," she said, putting the mugs down on the garden table and handing the album to Laura. "I think you might be interested. There are a lot of Stella. And your mother."

The photographs were all stuck into neat, decorative corners and underneath were little captions written in white ink. 'Jane, Stella and Polly, New Forest, 1938'; '*Lady Fair* Xmas Party, Frascati's, 1938'; 'Trip to Brighton, Whitsun 1939'; 'Magda, Vic and Victor, Stamford Brook, Summer 1939.'

The faces smiled from the photographs, their clothes and hairstyles placing them squarely in their period, making them appear unreal, not the living, breathing, emoting people Laura knew them to be. Little Victor, in flannel shorts down to his knees and a tuft of hair sticking up at the back of his head; he had grown up to be the ex-coffee planter now resident in Stamford Brook, who wrote rather wordy, pedantic letters. And here was a picture of Caleb Carne standing by himself under a tree, smiling a little shyly towards the camera, one arm half-lifted, about to speak. He had, she saw, indeed been handsome; still was, according to Simon.

She turned the page. A lovely picture of Polly; she really ought to have advertised something, Laura thought. She should have been a model. Too late, too late! More picnics. How they seemed to go

263

in for picnics in those days – and never one without a dozen photographs to commemorate it. Here was that same picture of Jane and Stella that she'd seen among Stella's possessions, and following it the photograph of Stella and the cadaverous looking man.

'Picnic in Richmond Park, Summer 1943' was written, stretching across the page to serve as a caption to both of them.

"I knew this was Richmond Park," Laura said. "This man isn't Evelyn, is he?"

"Shouldn't think so. Which man?" Jane craned to look across the width of the small table that divided them. "Lord, no! That's not Evelyn. I'll have you know he was a highly attractive fellow!"

"Who was this chap, then?"

Jane screwed up her face as she tried to remember.

"My goodness, now you're asking. He was one of those people who flit in and out of one's life without leaving a trace. Stella's friend, I think. No – wait! I remember now. Cal and Stella were always very discreet and hardly ever seen in public together, but the three of us went out to a pub for a drink one night when I was in London on leave. This chap happened to be there, and he came across to say hallo. Cal was furious, because it turned out they both came from the same village. So much for discretion and skulking round corners! Poor Cal made everything much worse by going bright scarlet and introducing us as colleagues at the Ministry of Information. Actually, it's all coming back to me. He couldn't have been less convincing! I'd never seen him so angry as he was with Stella that night. They had the father and mother of all rows. I soon made myself scarce, I can tell you."

"Why was he angry?"

Jane frowned in a veritable agony of thought.

"I think it was something about a room. This man was being thrown out of his, or was looking for one for a friend. Honestly, I can't remember – but Stella apparently knew someone who might have one to let and gave him her phone number for him to contact her. Accommodation was very difficult to come by in those days. I suppose Cal was jealous. Afterwards Stella was sorry she hadn't listened to him because this chap turned out to be a real pain in the neck. He kept phoning up and pestering her. What he was doing on this picnic with us I can't imagine, but there's the proof. She must have had a rush of compassion for him."

"We thought he was probably your boy-friend," Laura said.

"We?" Jane cocked her head in an interrogative manner.

"Simon and me. I told you about Simon, didn't I?"

"This is the man who's written the profile of Caleb Carne? You've told me that much. Is there more?"

Laura laughed ruefully as she turned another page.

"Much, much more!"

"Hmm." Jane looked at her thoughtfully. This was it, then. Man trouble. How little changes, she thought. "Do you want to tell me?"

For a moment Laura hesitated. She closed the photograph album and put it down on the table at the side of her chair, lining it up very deliberately as if it were important to get both edges exactly parallel.

"I think I do," she said at last, rather wondering at herself. "If you don't mind."

"Maybe this calls for more coffee –"

"I'll get it."

Laura got up and went inside to the kitchen, feeling, as she waited for the kettle to boil, as comfortable as if she were in her own kitchen. It was something she couldn't quite account for. It must be Jane, she thought; her talent isn't only for making cakes.

"It was a strange sort of Cornish name," Jane said, as Laura brought the refilled mugs back to the garden.

"What was?"

"That chap. The man in the picture. Can't remember what it was, though. Now, what's all this about Simon?"

# XI

Her father, Pen learned on her return to Roscarrow after her dinner with David, had been restless and fretful.

"Isn't he well?" she asked Dolly anxiously.

"I don't think 'tis that, Mrs Hambly. He didn't complain of no pain nor nothin'. Just couldn't seem to get off, like."

Pen went to his room and found him still awake. She made tea, and sat on the side of his bed to drink a cup with him as she gave an account of her evening with David.

"It's really amazing," she said. "I'd have known him anywhere."

"When is he coming here?"

"Tomorrow morning. Coffee time. He's looking forward to seeing you." Carne sipped his tea dourly, without comment. "He seems to remember those old days with great fondness," Pen went on, hoping to please him.

Carne lowered his cup and looked at her. He's so old, Pen thought; and was struck with sudden panic at the sight of his frailty – of the trembling mouth, the sparse white hair that sprouted at the neck of his striped pyjamas, the mottled skin. Where had all that vigour and confidence gone?

"I don't know that I can be bothered," he said.

"I'll make sure he only stays a few minutes." She smiled at him reassuringly. "He'll understand. You've got to husband your strength for the weekend."

"What did you talk about, you and David?"

"Oh, you know. Old times. His life in America. Simon. You remember Simon, his son? That nice young man who came to interview you? He's going back home very soon."

Carne said nothing to this, but continued to listen as she expanded

267

on the evening, and to look at her as he sipped his tea. Once he lowered his cup, this time to give a rusty, mirthless heave of laughter.

"Good thing the Lounge Lizard isn't coming this weekend," he said. "Trish'll have a clear field. Might have been pistols at dawn."

"Are you ready for sleep now, do you think?" Pen asked him, acknowledging this flight of fancy with a polite smile, but making no comment. "I'm pretty tired myself."

"Yes, yes, I've finished." He handed her the cup, settled himself back on his pillows. "Take yourself off. I shall sleep now, I expect."

She kissed him goodnight and took the tray downstairs. She was tired, it was true, but not at all inclined to sleep. It was the fancy meal, eaten so much later than she was accustomed to, she told herself. And the wine, of course. Without any doubt, that accounted for the fact that as hour followed hour she remained wide awake, going over every moment of the past evening. At her age it would be foolish indeed to imagine it could be anything else.

But he surely wouldn't fall for Trish all over again?

That's it, isn't it? she said wryly to herself. Nothing's changed. Past your sixtieth birthday you may be, but beneath that ageing exterior beats a heart as vulnerable as any girl's. You're still jealous of Trish – of her gaiety and her smooth, expensively nurtured skin, and her fashionable clothes. No fool, she told herself, like an old fool.

All that nonsense she'd fed herself about friendship!

Well, it wasn't entirely nonsense. She and David *had* been friends – and still were, as tonight had shown. To entertain even the smallest scintilla of hope for anything more was ridiculously childish. Immature. After all, what did she know of him, really? They had talked mainly of old times, not of today's issues. He might be a hanger and a flogger for all she knew. Or a racist. People were. There was a man on the telly the other night in some *vox pop* programme explaining why he didn't want his daughter to marry a Pakistani. "You see, I'm a racist," he'd said, with as little shame as if he'd said he was a Baptist or a cyclist.

Maybe David was like that.

Oh, *rubbish!* Of course he wasn't Anyway, he could be a flat-earther or a fully paid up member of the Klu Klux Klan without it making the slightest difference to her. Her life was here, at Roscarrow. The most she could hope for were a few happy, entertaining days – days that she would be able to take out and relive once he had gone.

*     *     *

Laura, on the way to Cirencester, felt strangely divorced from all the problems that had so recently beset her, just as if she had stepped out of everyday life into some blissful never-never land where ordinary concerns were put on 'hold'. For the first time in her adult life, she even felt removed from world events. At lunchtime she and Jane had chosen to eat their snack inside so that they could watch the one o'clock news on television. It was only with the appearance of the weather man that she realised that she hadn't taken in a word of it – that all the talk of sanctions against Iran and UN resolutions had washed over her without trace.

Even the imminent approach of the new school term, due to begin the following Wednesday – a week later than the Comprehensive in the village next to Upper Swinshot, since the West London Collegiate was a private school and made its own rules – failed to disturb her calm. She had, the previous day, seen children pouring off the school bus beside the village green and had suffered a momentary stirring of conscience at the thought of the preparations she should undoubtedly be making. The moment had, however, been fleeting, and her conscience quickly quieted. School belonged to next week, and next week seemed a lifetime away.

Once in Cirencester Jane parked the car and they went their separate ways. The town was busy, bustling, and the atmosphere one of friendliness. People smiled at one another and appeared to have time to chat.

No doubt, thought Laura, it was the good weather that was the cause of this. Sunshine brought out the best in people; but even on the dullest day the town would have been full of charm, and she explored it appreciatively and was inspired to do some shopping on her own account. She bought a book to give to Jane – one that she had mentioned the previous night – and the tape of Carne's talks, now in the shops. Her eye was caught by a black linen suit with a dashing black and emerald shirt displayed in the window of a fashionable boutique, greatly reduced in the End of Season Sale.

269

She tried it on, was captivated, and bought that too. It would be exactly right, she considered, for the Carne party on Sunday. And with that thought came a *frisson* of pleasurable anticipation, and the first charge of energy that she had felt for days.

"You know," Jane said as they drove homewards, "sitting in the dentist's chair, I had a thought."

"Oh?" Laura turned from her peaceful contemplation of the countryside and smiled expectantly. "About what?"

"Stella. You know you told me that she said to you in her later life that she regretted nothing, that marriage with Carne wouldn't have worked?" Laura nodded. "Well," Jane went on, "in my view, that's a load of cobblers. If you'll pardon the expression."

"Well, that's what she said, I assure you."

"Oh, I'm sure she did! Maybe it's what she brain-washed herself into thinking. After all, she was hardly the kind of woman who would sit around wringing her hands, bemoaning the fact that her life was ruined. However, it's certainly not what she thought at the time. If Caleb Carne had been free, she would have married him like a shot, and my guess is that they would have been as happy as most other couples. Happier. They were complementary to each other. Carne supplied something that Stella lacked – warmth and emotion and a certain spontaneity."

Frowning a little, Laura thought this over while Jane, stuck behind a farm tractor, slowed to a snail's pace.

"You make it sound as if she were cold," she said after a moment. "Which she wasn't – not at all!"

For a moment Jane said nothing. She was watching for her opportunity to pass the tractor, her face screwed up with concentration, and at last was able to do so, zooming past with a triumphant wave to the driver.

"She was about men," she went on, continuing the conversation. "Not issues or causes – she was fired up about them, all right – but sex was different. She'd been scarred by her marriage and was fearful of love. Infinitely cautious."

"But was Carne the man who could liberate her? Leaving aside the not inconsiderable fact that he was already married, I mean. Was he really the man for her?"

"She came to think so. He wasn't perfect. He'd been scarred too, by his ghastly mother and by poverty and by heaven alone knows what else – but she loved him. And according to you, went on doing so."

She paused at a T-junction, forced to wait before making the turn.

"So," Laura said when they were on their way once more. "You think she was rationalising when she said it never would have worked. Just making the best of a bad job."

"Yes, I do." Jane's tone was positive. "Life's a journey, after all. You can hang around on a station bemoaning the fact that you've missed the train, or you can get out and hire a car or hop on a plane. Stella wasn't one to hang around. She might have been hurt – she was hurt, I can vouch for that – but she dusted herself off and went out looking for the next challenge. Work-wise, I mean, not sex-wise."

Laura laughed.

"You have a vivid way of putting things," she said. Then her smile died, and she was silent for the half a mile that remained before Jane pulled up in front of the cottage and switched off the engine. Then she spoke.

"I'm fearful of love too, Jane. And infinitely cautious – just like Stella."

"You identify with her too much."

"That's what Simon says."

"You can't pattern your life on Stella's. She had great strengths, Laura, but she had weaknesses too. You have to experience things for yourself, work out your own salvation, just as we all do. Stella was fearful because Jean Morel was a cold-hearted fanatic who treated her badly. I know – I met him. He was a handsome devil with the most incredible green, black-lashed eyes. Now I come to think of it, they weren't unlike yours. I'd rather forgotten he was your grandfather!"

"Maybe he has a lot to answer for."

"I can't detect any other likenesses, thank heaven. He had no thought for anything or anybody apart from The Cause. By all accounts he was as much like your Simon as I'm like Marilyn Monroe. You know," she went on after a moment, "from all that you tell me, I think my analogy of a journey was very apt – more true for Stella than for most, perhaps. You speak of her being serene and wise; well, she always had plenty of nous, but I would never have called her serene." She frowned as she searched for the apt description. "She was more – oh, I don't know! Volatile. Enraged. Flying off in different directions. If she became serene in later life, then she'd changed quite a bit from the Stella I knew."

"Really?" Laura turned to stare at her, hardly believing it.

"Really. She must have travelled a long way, you might say, and learned from her experiences en route – which, I suppose, is the secret of a successful life."

"You said she was fearful. She doesn't sound fearful."

"Of love, I said. Of commitment. That was your green-eyed grandfather's legacy. It didn't last long after she met Carne. You know," she went on, "maybe you should write her biography. God knows she had an eventful enough life."

"One day I will," Laura said, keeping secret the fact that she had tried and had come up against a brick wall. Was this, she wondered now, because she hadn't known her grandmother at all?

They'd had tea in an Olde Worlde teashop in Cirencester and now, back at the cottage, Jane decreed it high time for something a little stronger. She prepared the drinks while Laura attempted to phone Polly. There was no reply; and Simon too was unavailable. It was as if the entire outside world had shut down for a spell, leaving her unmolested in this little window of time.

They listened to the Carne tape as they sipped their drinks, the once famous voice filling the small sitting-room.

"It's the way he tells them," Jane said when it was finished. "You have to admit it! You know, it's rather eerie, sitting here listening to Cal – with you sitting opposite, looking so much like Stella."

They had talked more of Stella then; and later, after dinner, Jane had recounted stories of the times when she and Stella had been so close.

"I'll never forgive myself for allowing us to drift apart the way we did," she said sadly; then pulled herself together and sat up straight. "Though, dammit all, it wasn't entirely my fault. Stella could be difficult, you know. But oh, I did love her! I've never known anyone else remotely like her."

"Nor have I," Laura said softly.

Before she went to bed she phoned both Polly and Simon once more, but this strange lack of contact with the outside world was still in operation and once again there was no reply from either. She left a message on Simon's Answerphone. He wasn't to worry, she said. She'd decided to drive straight down to Cornwall on Saturday and would see him at the hotel on Saturday afternoon. Couldn't exactly say when.

"Miss you," she said at the end of the message. It wasn't entirely true, but in this strangely detached state nothing seemed real to her, even herself. The brief moment of energy, even excitement, she had experienced in Cirencester had somehow gone, it appeared. However, it seemed a kind thing to say. And she had a feeling that once this numbness wore off, it might very well be true.

✳   ✳   ✳

Caer Plas was exactly as David remembered it, even to the cow pats. Nothing had changed; well, perhaps there were a few more houses far away towards the east – but all the essentials were the same. The rugged coastline, the gently heaving sea, the wheeling sea birds, the expanse of folded hills and valleys, meadowland and woodland.

Here he had stood and longed to be with Trish, all this beauty wasted on him. And here had Caleb Carne declaimed those stirring lines from Shakespeare. All is forgiven, he thought now, almost ready to declaim in his turn.

"Tell me again about the fort that was here," he said to Pen. "I've forgotten."

This time he was fascinated by the story, and asked for more.

Earlier he had sat in the summerhouse, taking coffee with Pen and Carne. The old boy had seemed distant, a little odd in his manner, rather glum, which Pen had explained afterwards was due to the fact that he'd had a disturbed night and was tired.

Was that true, David wondered? Or was he worried that his visitor had come to ask questions about what had taken place the last time the two of them had met face to face so many years ago, right here on this spot – though thankfully in a place that looked very different from this one. The old summerhouse had been taken down, replaced by this far more weather-proof, permanent-looking structure, with modern, sliding full-length windows and a pitched slate roof.

The aspect before it was as lovely as ever, and as unspoiled. The high cliffs were the same unscalable barrier they had always been.

"I've been so grateful to you, all my life," he said to Carne, putting the dark memories to one side for the moment. "From you I learned more about Arthur and his knights than I'd ever have known. And Tristan and Isolde. And those old Cornish saints."

Carne gave a grunt of laughter.

"I thought they'd gone in one ear and out the other. My stories usually do."

"Oh, I remembered them."

"I wish I could!" Carne was staring out over the bay as he spoke. His voice quavered a little. "I remember so little these days. Old age is a terrible thing."

"You can remember the things you want to, Father," Pen said, gently teasing.

"Occasionally, my darling. Occasionally. A curtain lifts from time to time, but for the most part all is dark."

"I was absolutely stumped on five down this morning," Pen said off-handedly as she poured a second cup of coffee for David.

"'Estrange more than ever'? My dear child, it's positively infantile! What could it be but 'sever'?"

"My case rests. You are not yet for the funny-farm, old boy."

"You give him a tough time," David said afterwards, as they toiled up the slope towards Caer Plas. "You always did, you girls."

"He thrives on it. How do you think he's managed to keep going for ninety-five years?"

"It's a great age, isn't it? Would one want to live so long? I suppose," he continued, answering his own question, "one would, given a devoted daughter such as yourself to see to one's every need."

"We keep each other going," Pen said. "It will be like losing a child when I lose him."

The child she never had, David thought; and felt a swell of sympathy and affection for her – for the shyly eager young girl she had once been, who, with grace, had become this dutiful, tranquil woman.

✳    ✳    ✳

"Miss you," said the message.

Back late from the theatre, Simon swore. Still no contact number! He had no idea where to find her, where she was hiding out. He really would phone Polly now, he decided. Well, not now – it was late. Tomorrow would have to do. What the hell was Laura playing at? It was three days since she'd taken it into her head to disappear without trace. He was beginning to have grave doubts that she'd make it to Cornwall for the weekend, in spite of the message.

But it was wrong to lose hope, he told himself, his naturally optimistic nature struggling to reassert itself. Laura was missing him, wasn't she? Hang on to that, he thought wearily. Hang on to that.

\*    \*    \*

On Friday morning Laura woke to bright sunshine, feeling unaccountably happy and expectant, as if something good was about to happen. It was, she remembered, rather like the feeling she had known as a small child on the occasions when she had gone to stay with Stella, long before she had made her permanent home with her. It seemed to her that she had been thinking of Stella all her sleeping hours – not dreaming, exactly, but conscious of her in a tangible way as if the stories and conversations and tapes of the previous day had somehow evoked her presence.

And as she lay in her bed, smiling at nothing, she knew without doubt that the strangely lethargic mood of the past few days had gone for good. She felt the charge of energy again, just as she had the previous day, only this time she knew it wouldn't leave her as suddenly as it had come.

She felt normal at last, and wanted to leap up and shout aloud with the joy of it. Suddenly she craved physical action – wanted to stretch her limbs and breathe lungfuls of fresh air. Would Jane, she asked at breakfast, care to accompany her up Swinshot Beacon? The wooded hill that overshadowed the village seemed, suddenly, the place to be. Jane, however, declined the offer.

"Dear child, I can walk all day on level ground, but my days for hills are over. Besides, I have a few urgent jobs in the garden. But you go, there's a marvellous view from the top. Well worth the effort."

She was right, Laura found, as she made frequent stops during her ascent to turn and look at the panorama behind her. Now, as she strode upwards through groves of beech trees with their leaves faintly turning gold, through bracken and past clumps of blackberry bushes glistening with fruit and hedges feathery with old man's beard, she felt more alive than she had been for days – more conscious of shapes and textures and scents, all her perceptions heightened. Though she was grateful to Jane for these few peaceful days, knowing exactly how much she owed to her unlooked-for but unstinting hospitality, she was glad now of the solitude – almost mystically aware that although her feelings about Simon were unresolved the waiting was nearly over.

On the lower slopes she had passed a woman with a dog coming down the hill, but since then she had seen no one. At the top she sank down on the grass, feeling remote and powerful and god-like, as if she had dominion over all the world. Before her stretched an undulating patchwork of fields and woods, all the way to the mistily purple hills in the far distance. Though aware that nothing was the same in the agricultural world any more – that there were now such things as a Common Agricultural Policy and Set-aside and all manner of wrangling between farmers and politicians, to her layman's eye and from this distance the countryside looked as peaceful and beautiful and satisfying as it had always done; perhaps more so, in the light of the world's unrest.

Timeless, she thought. Unchanging. Tyrants came and went – wars and rumours of wars. They made no difference to those hills that had stood for century upon century, and would stand into the next millennium and the one after that. And then suddenly, apropos of nothing, like a rocket exploding in her mind, there came a single thought.

*Stella!*

She would have said that all the way up the hill she had been thinking of other things, concentrating on the beauty of her immediate surroundings; for the first time since waking from her Stella-filled sleep, she would have said, her mind had been leaping in other directions, propelled by the evidence of autumn all around her into the next school term, the new syllabus, the Christmas play.

But now, suddenly, between one thought and the next, she felt filled with the certainty that Stella was somewhere near, just

out of sight; and with that certainty there came the most exquisite burst of excitement – an excitement so great that she
was forced to catch her breath.

It was as if all the talk – all Jane's reminiscences, all Laura's
own memories, all the words spoken by Carne on the tape, had
suddenly coalesced to form a great, white light that illumined
Stella's life and character – as if those pages of leaden prose
that she had in her desk at home had turned themselves into a
Technicolor, all-singing, all-dancing production that had somehow
become encapsulated in a shining bubble that was now lifted above
her head for inspection, waiting to be transformed into the book she
had always wanted to write; a book that would be worthy of Stella.
Inspiration? Hardly, thought Laura, who shied away from what she
considered pretentiousness. But what else would you call it – this
sudden visitation of confidence? This overwhelming assurance that
this task and this task only was what she had to do, and that she
had it in her power to perform it with drama and conviction?

Ideas and angles flooded into her mind. She hugged her trousered
knees and rested her chin on them. She'd begin not with the
humdrum facts of Stella's birth and education – those could be
sketched in later – but with all the passion and politics of Paris in
the 1930s. Jane, who had seen some of it and had heard more from
Stella's lips, had already told her much and would tell more.

She had, she acknowledged, so much to thank Jane for in addition
to her hospitality. It was Jane's analogy of Stella's life as a journey
towards serenity that had somehow set her alight; Jane's memories
that had suddenly brought Stella to life, not as a paragon of all
the virtues but as a real, living, breathing, talented woman who
had worked and loved, made mistakes and paid for them – a
wonderful woman who had not been born with the wisdom of
the ages, but had learned it along the way. And my God, Stella
thought, what a way it had been!

Oh, I can't wait to tell Simon, she thought. And laughed aloud
at herself for this instinctive, instant response; for it *was* instinctive,
she realised, and totally irresistible. She would tell Jane of her plans,
of course; it would seem churlish not to, and in any case she would
want to ask questions, suggest subjects for notes. But it was Simon
with whom she longed to share this revelation, just as if the project
was a gift to lay before him – something to exult in, something

that belonged as much to him as it did to her. Nobody else would do. Only Simon would know what she was feeling, understand her excitement. Just Simon. Oh God, how she wanted to see him!

And as she smiled at her thoughts she was filled with happiness, because if there was one thing she felt certain about, it was Simon's constancy. No doubt she'd worried him by dropping out of sight. He would have stamped around and sworn at her, and she was genuinely sorry for that – upsetting him had not been at all the object of the exercise. He wouldn't bear a grudge, though; she knew that as surely as she knew the sun would rise. He would turn to her joyfully, with all the love and passion and support of which he was capable.

And oh, how she needed it! Others might shake their heads and accuse her of undue haste – say she was foolish and feckless, and ask how could she possibly know that this was the one man for her?

She knew, that's all. She had known, if she were honest, from the first, even if she'd been too scared to admit it. Well, she wasn't scared now. Everything, suddenly, seemed so simple, so straightforward. Life without Simon wouldn't be any life at all.

\*    \*    \*

David, driving the car he had rented from a firm in St Jory, brought Pen back to Roscarrow on Thursday evening. They'd spent the afternoon on Bodmin Moor, marvelling at the ancient stones that were known as The Hurlers, at Bronze Age hut circles, at Dozmary Pool into which, it was said, King Arthur had thrown Excalibur and from whence came the arm clothed in white samite, mystic, wonderful.

"What a day! I'm in a kind of daze," David said. "I've never in my life been so conscious of the past – of the *seamlessness* of everything! It's an odd feeling."

"I can't honestly guarantee the bit about Excalibur," said Pen, regretfully.

"Don't spoil it! I believe every word. Where are we going tomorrow?"

"Oh, David, I can't go anywhere! I'm sorry," Pen said. "You

know I'd love to – there are so many places I want to show you, but I must stay at home and cook things for the freezer. We're going to be such a crowd at Roscarrow for the next few days, it'll make life a lot easier if I've got ahead of myself, food-wise."

"When are they all leaving?"

"Trish and Hannah – Caro's daughter – are going on Monday. Caro and Alan are staying for a few more days, but they're no trouble. Far from it!"

"Look, I'm committed to going back with Simon on Monday. Fay's Scottish cousin is down in London for a few days and we've arranged to meet. But I was thinking –" he hesitated for a moment and glanced at her shyly.

"Yes?" Pen prompted him.

"Maybe I'll come back. If you wouldn't mind, that is?"

"Of course I wouldn't mind!"

"I don't want to be a drag –"

"A drag? Oh, David! How could you be –"

When she smiled like that, David thought, she looked exactly like that eager young girl he had known.

"I'll have to talk to Simon, see what he wants me to do about the flat. I said I'd close it up for him – and there was talk of my going to Scotland. I'm not sure how it'll all fit in."

He won't come, Pen thought, her heart sinking. It won't happen. Still, she went on smiling.

"You know you're welcome."

"Thanks. Look, Pen – I don't want to be any kind of trouble or disturb you in any way, but could I come over and have a chat with your father tomorrow morning? I expect he'll be in the summerhouse as usual, won't he?"

"He certainly will. Thanks, David. He'd appreciate that. He loves visitors."

"About ten thirty?"

"That'll be fine."

At last, David thought as he drove away, he'd have a chance to see Carne on his own, talk about that last night, check out his memory and maybe get some answers. But in the middle of breakfast the following day he was called away to take a phone call. It was Pen to say that her father wasn't, after all, feeling up to receiving visitors that day, and in view of the fact that he needed to rest, she thought perhaps –

"Don't worry," David said. "I'll give it a miss. It doesn't matter a bit."

"You are coming over for a birthday drink tomorrow night, aren't you?" Pen asked. "The clan will have gathered by then, and I know everyone will love to see you. Simon and his girl-friend too, of course. About six thirty?"

"Thanks, Pen. We'll be there," David said – wondering, as he put the phone down, whether he had been a little too sanguine about accepting this invitation for Simon and Laura. The last word he had heard from Simon was that Laura had gone to ground, but had promised to make her own way down to Porthlivick on Saturday. He had detected that his son was far from pleased about this arrangement.

Meantime he had the whole of Friday to fill. Much as he would have liked to spend the day with Pen, the prospect of his own company failed to dismay him and he drove first to Bow Beach. The vast majority of tents and caravans had packed up and gone, and only a handful of holiday-makers remained.

At first sight, much had changed since the days when he was camped there. On the east end of the beach where he parked the car there was a village which in his day had consisted only of a scattering of cottages. It had grown, he saw now, out of all belief, with dozens of small white houses fanning out from its centre.

He turned his back on it and walked up the other way, towards the rocks and the cliff that he had scaled so often. This too had changed, for someone had constructed steps where in his day there had been only the rough cliff face; and when he climbed them and reached the path, he found that this, too, was reconstructed to make access easier.

A good thing, he supposed. People had more leisure now to walk these incomparable coastal ways, and it was right that they should be encouraged to do so – but perversely he was glad when he found that the path deteriorated as he went further along it, resembling more the track he had known so intimately all those years ago.

He climbed up and up, and steeply down; and there was the wide swathe of springy turf and the seat where he had sat with Caro when she had told him the Carne family secrets. No – he corrected himself as he sat down. This wasn't the same seat. That had been no more than a bench. This was a more comfortable affair with a back and arms; placed, so a plaque informed him, in memory of Mrs Edith Nankivell, who had so often enjoyed, in life, this spectacular view.

The name stirred memories – made him conscious, once more, of past and present merging in a way no other place had ever done. And once more he sat there and thought about times that had gone.

Carne was avoiding him. He felt sure of it. The old man hadn't forgotten a thing – he knew perfectly well what he and David had done together and was afraid, even after all this time, that it would be brought out into the light of day.

He'd never questioned David's presence on that May night, but had merely accepted it as if it were a gift from heaven. On the way back to shore, after they'd dumped the body, he had said not a word, but had sat with his head bowed, staring at nothing, one arm steadying himself on the bow of the boat, his face haggard and streaming with spray. Only as David had jumped ashore and fended off the boat to prevent it bumping against the steps had he spoken.

"Caro's gone," he'd said, lifting his head. "Did you know?"

He hadn't waited for David to reply, but had left him to tie up the boat. At the top of the steps David had found him standing dumbly, once more staring into space, a shambling figure with bowed shoulders, almost unrecognisable. At David's appearance he had passed a hand over his face – wearily, as if he were exhausted.

"You've done a good night's work," he said, his voice rough with strain. "The Allies – your country – would be proud of you. Say nothing –"

For a second David had looked at him. He tried to speak, but no words emerged. He made a move to leave, then remembered the oilskin and peeled it off, flinging it to the ground at Carne's feet. And then he had taken to his heels and fled.

He'd got away with it. The chances were a thousand to one, but no one had seen him. Once in his cot, he had experienced a nervous reaction, shivering uncontrollably, his heart hammering; the next day he'd looked and felt ill. His nerves had flown to his stomach.

"You ought to go sick," Chuck urged him. "You look like the underside of a fish's belly."

"I'll be okay," David said. "It's only a hangover. Must have had too much beer last night, I guess."

Chuck looked at him with sympathy but said nothing. He'd heard word about Trish's behaviour at the dance and had put two and two together. It was, in his book, only natural that David should have hit the bottle.

The next day they moved out.

David, looking out at the waters of the bay in September 1990 gave a brief, rueful laugh. He must, he thought, have been the most willing soldier in that entire invading force.

Damn it to hell, he *would* get some answers! Even though so many years had passed, old though he was, Carne owed him that much.

\*    \*    \*

Simon was not happy. He had made a mistake – maybe a fatal mistake. He was convinced of it. Sure, an editorial position on a prestigious New York magazine wasn't something to be ignored, but there would be other chances – he would make other chances! He had that much confidence in his ability.

There might, however, never be another chance with Laura; and now he knew that this mattered more than anything.

Tomorrow he would be seeing her, and he would tell her. I have sorted out my priorities, he would say. I am staying with you. If you want me.

Perhaps she didn't. Perhaps this absence meant that she had decided against him, turned her thumbs down, consigned him to outer darkness.

But 'Miss you' she had said. Suddenly inaction seemed intolerable and London claustrophobic. He might just as well throw a few things into a bag and go down to Cornwall right now so that whatever time she arrived the following day, he would be there, waiting for her. And as always when he had decided on a plan of action, his spirits rose. Everything was going to work out just fine, he told himself.

Maybe.

＊　　＊　　＊

Laura, having bade a fond and grateful farewell to Jane, set off soon after breakfast on Saturday. She had been fearful that the extraordinary moment of revelation on Swinshot Beacon would turn out to be nothing more than a flash in the pan – that she would wake up the following day to find that there was nothing left of it but a faint and regretful memory and a feeling of inadequacy – but she had been proved wrong. The excitement was in no way diminished, and she was in high spirits as she drove down the M5 on her way westwards.

The longing to see Simon, to tell him her news, was as great as ever; and there was another, slightly lesser, piece of news that she was looking forward to communicating to him too. Finally, after several thwarted attempts, she had managed to contact Polly by telephone. The reason, it was explained, that she had been out so much was because a new man had come into her life.

"And I have you to thank for it, darling," she said to Laura. "If you hadn't got in touch with Victor –"

"Victor Kaye? You've been out with him?"

"Several times. He's so terribly sweet – *such* a gentleman – but of course rather lonely because he doesn't know many people in London having lived abroad so long. He remembered me from our childhood days."

"Yes, he said in his letter; and of course, when I phoned him back, I told him you were still living in Pomfret Road. The crafty thing! He didn't say he was going to look you up."

"Well, that's what he did. And we've been out to dinner, and to the theatre, and yesterday we had a lovely little trip down to Brighton. He bought me a simply super prezzie from a shop in the Lanes; a little Victorian brooch. Wasn't that sweet?"

"What about Fifi? Has she adjusted to being left alone at nights?" Laura's question sounded guileless, but she smiled to herself as she spoke.

"Since you mention it, she does seem more on an even keel these days. And Victor is mad about dogs, and frightfully knowledgeable. He's going to take her in hand, he says. Train her."

"That's good news."

"So, darling, I'm really very much in your debt. Imagine Victor being Jane's cousin. I don't think I ever knew that – or if I knew it, I'd forgotten. D'you know, he was at the wedding, and he even remembers that dress I told you about! The pink one with frills? He said he remembers thinking I looked like a little flower. Isn't that amazing?"

"Amazing," Laura agreed. "I'm so pleased you're having a good time, Polly."

Victor, Jane assured her when this conversation was reported to her, was indeed the perfect gentleman. A little quiet and inhibited, perhaps, and something of a dreamer, but with his heart in the right place.

"He never married," Jane said, "because I rather gather he was madly in love with his boss's wife for years and years. I don't know the ins and outs, but from the hints he dropped it all sounded very Kenya-ish, and rather as if the woman in question would have benefited from a good horse-whipping. I should think your mother will do him a power of good."

"And vice versa," Laura agreed. "But Polly says they're Just Good Friends, so we mustn't look too far ahead. That's the sort of thing she does with me."

She remembered, however, Polly's giggle as these words were spoken and was glad that she had something to giggle about.

The journey was uneventful; for once, no hold-ups or contra-flows or other annoyances. She stopped for lunch at a Motorway Service Station, crossed the Tamar by mid-afternoon, and, marvelling at the beauty of the countryside on either hand, kept straight on until a signpost marked 'Porthlivick' to the left sent her down narrow, twisted lanes with high hedges on either side.

She stopped the car when she reached the place where she could look down on the harbour and for a moment or two sat and gazed, spellbound. The sun, which had been fitful all day, came out at this point, and she felt she had seldom seen a sight that was more pleasing than this – more satisfying in its composition and completeness. The discovery, when she drove on to the village and finally located the hotel, that its windows over-looked the harbour and she could see this same scene from the other side, put the final touch to her assurance that all would be well.

Leaving her bag in the car, she went into the hotel; all was quiet, with no one at the reception desk. She looked around and discovered David sipping tea in the hotel lounge, and was surprised to learn that Simon had already arrived; had in fact been in residence since the night before.

"But he's just gone down those steps to the harbour to take some photographs," David said. "The sun came out and he suddenly realised that it might be his last chance to get Porthlivick with the tide in – which is, I'm here to tell you, one hell of a lot more scenic than Porthlivick with the tide out. Why don't you join me for some tea? He'll be back soon."

"I think, perhaps, I'll go and see if I can find him, if you'll excuse me," Laura said.

David grinned at her.

"He'd like that," he said.

The steps he had indicated led down from the hotel grounds to a small street – hardly more than an alleyway – lined with tiny, flat-fronted cottages, painted white and pink and pale, pale green; and a few yards along, another street, even narrower, sloped steeply downwards. Here, at the end, was a wall, and looking over it, Laura found that she was only a few feet above the inner harbour and could view it at close range, rather as if it were a stage set.

Fishing boats rode at anchor; she could read the names of them. There were the *Mary Rose* and the *Lady Anne* and the *Sea Maiden*. All female, she noted, and wondered why this should always have been so. Sentiment, or a recognition of a woman's true worth? No prizes, she thought, for guessing the answer.

And then all such abstract thoughts were swept from her mind, for from the gap in the harbour wall that separated the inner from the outer harbour had sauntered Simon, unaware of her presence, stopping to choose his subject, to take one picture, and then another.

The depth of her joy astonished her. It seemed to well up inside her, flooding her with tenderness for him. I love him, she thought;

oh God, how I love him. How could I possibly have been in doubt? All the time – how utterly astonishing!

She still, she realised, felt scared; but it was the pleasurable scariness of the Ferris wheel and the Chair-o-Plane – an exhilarating experience that she wanted to embrace with excitement, not watch others enjoying while she hung back in fear.

He was getting closer now. He looked serious, absorbed in what he was doing – and so damned *sexy*, she thought, the excitement growing. What was it about him? She'd always liked him in those particular jeans and that blue sweater. She took pleasure now in watching him, unobserved; in pretending that she was a stranger seeing him for the first time.

It was a pleasure impossible to sustain. Eagerly she hung over the wall and called his name. He looked up and saw her; and instantly his absorbed expression turned to one of delight and she knew that she had been right – that nothing had changed, he still wanted her.

There was a slope leading from this level to the harbour. At the same time as she turned to run down it, Simon swung into it and ran up towards her. They were laughing as they met, their arms outstretched to hold each other, hug each other.

Simon was the first to speak.

"It's going to be all right," he said. "I'm not going."

Laura drew back a little and looked into his face, astonished.

"Rubbish!" she said. "Of course you are. And I'm going too."

＊　　＊　　＊

Not immediately, she explained, and he accepted, once the initial elation had subsided. She'd have to put in her notice, work out the term.

"But by Christmas I can be with you," she said. "If that's all right."

"That's all right. That's pretty damned all right. I'll settle for that," Simon said. "What made you finally decide?"

"Oh, Simon!" Laura put her arms round his neck once more and held her cheek against his. "It's all mixed up; it just suddenly seemed right. And I've got so much to tell you. All about Stella, and the book I want to write – it suddenly seemed – oh, just *there*, I can't explain it any better. I'm on *fire* with it!"

His eyes were alight with love and the sheer relief of knowing that the uncertainty was at an end.

"I know the feeling," he said; and suddenly Laura remembered how she felt that day in his flat, when they had both been absorbed in their separate occupations yet had seemed so at one with each other. It was going to be like that, she thought happily. She working on her book, he working on *Commentary*. Together.

"I knew you would," she said.

# XII

David, looking at Simon and Laura across the Roscarrow drawing-room where they were engaged in conversation with Pen, felt a sensation that was part affection, part amusement, part envy; they were so much in love that it seemed to surround them like an aura. Any onlooker could feel the effort they were making not to touch each other.

Though neither had yet attempted to tell him what had been decided or by what process that decision had been achieved, it was clear to the most casual observer – which David most certainly was not – that a happy solution had been reached. It came as a great relief to him, for he knew how troubled Simon had been; had known, too, that he had resolved to give up the new job in New York if Laura had remained opposed to joining him. They had discussed it minutely on Friday night, and while such a decision went against the grain with David – the concept of man-as-hunter not as readily cast aside by him as by his son – he had agreed with Simon that there were other things more important than ambition.

But now, it seemed, no such self-denial was going to be necessary. Everything, he thought, as he looked across the room, was coming up roses. For everyone? Well, for Simon, anyway.

"One glass of red wine, as ordered," Caro said, joining him beside the fireplace, filled at this moment by a huge, autumnal display of leaves. She smiled at him warmly as she handed him his glass; matronly now, and grey-haired, but essentially much the same. "David, it's good to see you!"

David took the glass and thanked her.

"I'm glad to see you too, Caro. It all worked out, then, I'm happy to know. I left in mid-drama, if you remember. I am going to meet Alan, I hope?"

"He'll be here in a moment. He's gone to see if Father needs any help. He's a forgiving soul," she added. "Even after all these years Father can never really forget he's a Yeo, but Alan resolutely ignores the whole ridiculous business."

"I've met your daughter. She's lovely."

"She is rather, isn't she? A bit like Trish, do you think? She's getting married soon; the last one. We've got five grandchildren. How about that?"

"Congratulations! I envy you. I'd enjoy grandchildren."

Caro indicated Simon and Laura with a nod.

"Maybe you won't have too long to wait."

"Hey –" David gave her a warning look. "Hush up! Don't jump the gun, whatever you do. I've schooled myself not to make those sort of remarks."

"Da-*vid*!"

His name, spoken in a voice that seemed to throb with all kinds of nostalgic undertones, caused him to turn towards the door. A woman stood there, smiling, her reddish hair beautifully coiffured, her face more enamelled than made-up, her eyebrows plucked into thin arches. There was a plump, well-upholstered look about her.

"Trish," he said faintly, not sure even now. The hair and the eyebrows and the added weight made her seem totally unfamiliar. "It is Trish, isn't it?"

She tilted her head and smiled at him and he saw that of course it was Trish and wondered how he could have had a moment's hesitation. She was expensively and fashionably dressed, and the hand that she held out to him was encrusted with rings.

"How extraordinary to see you like this," she said. "I couldn't believe it when Pen told me you would be here! Caro, darling, do get me a drink because I intend to take David over here to a quiet corner so that he can tell me all his news."

Her voice had changed too, since he had last heard it. It was more mannered, a little over-emphatic – more upper-crust, maybe. She'd gone a long way from Porthlivick. Married three times, so Pen had told him.

"You first," he said. "I guess your life has been a lot more interesting than mine. Action-packed, you could say. Three marriages, I hear."

Trish pulled a face, trilled with laughter.

"My dear, we'd need more time than we have this evening to go through all *that*!" She seated herself in a small armchair, and patted the seat of the one close beside it in invitation. "Let's just say that I've had my moments – but now, thank God, I've sailed into calmer waters. Raoul is an absolute poppet – retired, of course, but still with interests in the diamond industry. Such a pity he couldn't be here tonight. He had business in Paris. We have a lovely place in Antibes, a lovely life." She sighed with dramatic relief, and raised her improbable eyebrows. "Peace at last, one might say. Tell me, is that your son over there? He's not very much like you, is he? I heard about him from Pen. Strictly between us, my dear –" she leaned towards him confidentially, laughing a little, inviting him to share the joke, "I think she rather fell for him when he came down to interview Father. Poor Pen! She leads such an uneventful life."

"She seems happy."

Trish shrugged her plump shoulders.

"Maybe. It certainly wouldn't suit me, I can assure you of that! It'll be in tomorrow's *Gazette*, won't it – that article he wrote?"

"That's right."

"I can't wait to read it. I think Father's quite nervous."

"Why should he be? He didn't say anything indiscreet, did he?"

"I don't suppose so for a minute. You know Father! He loves to play to the gallery and I've no doubt he put on the usual performance. But you can't trust journalists, can you? They can twist one's words, make a story out of nothing."

"I'm sure Simon wouldn't do that – and it is a reputable news-paper, after all, not a cheap tabloid."

"Well, we'll all know the worst tomorrow."

"Here comes your father." David got to his feet to greet Carne as he came into the room. The old man was smiling, dressed in a pearly-grey suit with a pink bow tie, clearly in good spirits.

Pen, watching his progress towards his chair, breathed a sigh of relief and relaxed a little. No one would think him pathetic now. He looked as different from the diminished, vulnerable old man that he became in his low moments as it was possible to imagine.

Hannah, raising her glass, initiated a chorus of 'Happy Birthday to You', in which everyone joined.

"Well met, friends all," he said, smiling to right and left. "I decree that the celebrations begin here! David, how nice to welcome you to Roscarrow once more. I appreciated your birthday present – how did you know that was my favourite tipple? I suspect you may have benefited from inside information! Many thanks, my boy, many thanks. And of course, this is your son. We have met, have we not? I'm so sorry, my boy, I fear I have momentarily forgotten –"

"Simon." Smiling, Simon offered his hand. "Many happy returns, sir. This is my friend, Laura Rossi."

"Welcome, welcome, to you both."

If either of them expected any sudden recognition of Laura, any memory of Stella to show on his face at the sight of her, they were disappointed. He patted each of them on the arm in a benevolent manner and subsided into his usual chair, beaming around the room.

"Shall I get you a drink, Father?" Caro asked.

"Don't worry, my darling. Your good man is seeing to the matter." Benevolence all round was, it seemed, going to be the order of the day. "Ah, here he comes. Well done, Alan, my boy –"

David glanced towards the door as Alan appeared and felt a jolt that was almost physical. The newcomer gave Carne his drink and turned, smiling, to be introduced to the strangers among them.

"Darling, this is David," Caro said to her husband, taking his arm. "David, meet Alan, at last."

"How do you do?"

"Glad to know you, Alan."

David felt almost sure that he had given no sign of his shock. He had managed to smile, had surely sounded normal; but even so he was glad when Alan went on to greet Simon and Laura.

He had seen that face before. No, no – not that face – how could it have been that face? One very like it, then. Thin, dark, with hair growing in a widow's peak. Alan was clean-shaven, without the Clark Gable moustache as worn by that other man. He was older too, with greying hair, but in all other respects the likeness was astonishing.

Involuntarily, he looked towards the old man in the seat by the window, and immediately their glances locked. Carne's face was inscrutable, his mouth slightly open, the glass of whisky held motionless in his hand. It was a moment frozen in time. Conversations continued around them. Caro was saying something about the noontime flight of Spitfires over Buckingham Palace to mark Battle of Britain day; someone else remarking that the Desert Rats were once more back in the news – they were being sent, it seemed, to Saudi Arabia. And all the time he looked at Carne, and Carne looked back; then, suddenly, the old man moved, turned away, raised the glass to his lips and the spell was broken. David became aware that Trish had taken hold of his arm.

"I've just had the most marvellous idea," she said. "Why don't you come and have a few days with us in Antibes? It's quite lovely there at this time of year . . ."

\* \* \*

Pen allowed her smiling glance to pass over them as she watched from the opposite side of the room, her face showing none of the tremor of apprehension she felt in her heart. It was all going to happen again, she could see. Trish had put on weight but she knew just what clothes to wear to flatter her figure and looked, as always, marvellous. She'd always had lots of style – and since her marriage to Raoul, she had the money to indulge it.

She'd always had sex-appeal too. Maybe that wasn't what people called it these days, but whatever term was now in vogue, that's what Trish had, and it hardly seemed reasonable to expect David to be impervious to it. He had, after all, loved her once.

Simon's girl-friend had that mysterious commodity too, in a different kind of way. At first sight Pen had thought her a little intimidating – a typical example of the modern, self-confident career woman that one saw so little in this rural part of England. After only a few minutes conversation, however, she realised that she had been mistaken. Laura might be self-confident, but she was warm and outgoing, easy to talk to – and clearly Simon loved her. It was her guess that she loved Simon too.

Lucky them, she thought, rather bleakly.

\* \* \*

"It's kind of you, Trish, but I don't think I'll be able to fit Antibes into my schedule."

David hadn't got a schedule; didn't have any particular date by which he had to return to the States. Still he had no intention of visiting Trish in the south of France, for instinct told him that such a visit had no hope of being a success. Trish, he realised, had grown into the kind of woman he had never liked very much; plump and pampered and slightly bitchy, with a life that revolved around the beauty parlour and the Bridge Club. Or if not the Bridge Club, something very similar, something wholly self-indulgent.

Why wasn't she grovelling at Pen's feet in gratitude for taking on the burden of Caleb Carne? For Christ's sake, someone ought to give her a break – didn't they realise what a tie it was? How her entire life was tailored to his?

He didn't care too much for the overwhelming scent that Trish had dowsed herself in, either. In any case, he was in no mood to consider any such invitation at the moment. His mind was too full of this incredible turn of events.

Who, then, was that man?

He thought of the photograph, seen so recently at dinner with Laura. Had she spotted the likeness to Alan Yeo? Had Simon? They were both chatting to him at this very moment; he would, he thought, give much for a quick word with them.

". . .we could, perhaps, call on you," he heard Trish say.

"What –? I beg your pardon –"

"I don't believe you've heard a word I've said, David! Really, that's not very flattering, is it?"

"I'm sorry, Trish –"

"Raoul and I hope to be in New York in the spring. I was saying how nice it would be if we could call on you."

"Yes, of course. That would be great. Will you excuse me? I must go and have a word with Pen."

She, he saw, was sitting on a stool, rather on the outskirts of the small group around her father. Hannah was perched on the arm of his chair. Simon and Laura stood together in the window, Alan facing them, engaged in conversation, Caro nearby.

Pen stood up when he approached, seeing he was intent on speaking to her.

"I can't ask you to come down to my level," she said, smiling.

"Don't think I couldn't! Pen, an idea has struck me. If Caro and Alan are staying down here for a bit, couldn't you come back to London with me? We could take in a few shows, visit some galleries."

"Oh David, I don't know –" She'd gone rather pink, David noticed. He hoped he hadn't embarrassed her. Too bad if she was having to search for excuses, like he'd been doing with Trish just now.

"Well, think about it." He patted her arm; friendly, avuncular, not wanting to scare her, adding – so as to make things absolutely clear – "There's a great little hotel just round the corner from Simon's flat. We could get a room for you there."

"It's a wonderful idea. I'm sure I'd enjoy it very much. But it seems – I mean, Caro's come down all this way and I don't see much of her – I wouldn't want her to think –"

"Talk to her," David said gently. "They have holidays, don't they? It's only fair that you should have one. Say – here's an added bonus – an offer you can't refuse. You could use Simon's return rail ticket! How about that? Something tells me he'll be driving back with Laura. Promise you'll think about it?"

"I promise," Pen said.

*       *       *

Over dinner, back at the hotel with Simon and Laura, David probed a little.

"I thought Alan Yeo seemed familiar," he said. "As if we'd met before."

"Funny you should say that!" Laura's response was immediate. "I thought at first that I'd met him before somewhere, too, but I couldn't nail it down. I think he must be very like someone I've seen on television – that sort of narrow, dark face is a definite type, don't you think? Usually villainous," she added.

"I thought," David said after a moment, his voice casual, deliberately low-key, "that he resembled that unknown man in the photograph you showed me. The one picnicking in the park with your grandmother, Laura – you know the one." He looked from one to the other of the faces opposite him. "That didn't strike either of you?"

"Ye-es!" Laura drew out the word with the air of one upon whom light has dawned. "Yes, of course! You remember him, Simon?"

"I can't honestly say I took a lot of notice –"

"Well, I did. Jane had another copy of the photograph and she told me about him."

"She *did*?" David stopped being low-key. "What did she tell you?"

"That he was someone Caleb Carne knew – someone from Cornwall. Jane couldn't remember his name. She said it was something odd and Cornish."

"Yeo," said David.

"Could have been. Maybe it was Alan's father. Odd to think that he might have known Stella. But not outside the realms of possibility, I suppose."

"So Carne's two lives met at some point after all," Simon said. "That could have been awkward for him."

"Jane said he and Stella quarrelled about it," Laura said, remembering. "They met in a pub, quite by chance, and this man – the one in the photograph – was looking for a room. Stella thought she might be able to help him and gave him her telephone number. Carne was furious about it – and afterwards Stella was sorry too, because he became an awful pest and wouldn't leave her alone."

"Does this have any significance, Dad?" Simon asked him.

David hastened to brush any such idea aside.

"No, no, of course not. It's just interesting, don't you think? Makes you realise that the past is nothing more than a whole heap of interlocking circles. Don't forget that I was around when Caro ran away from home to marry Alan. I have a kind of long-standing interest in them."

"Maybe this is what Carne had against Alan," Laura suggested. "That his father had not only seen him with Stella in London, but had had the temerity to pester her afterwards."

"We don't know it was his father," David said. "It's all guess-work. Just because there's a certain similarity we shouldn't jump to conclusions. Anyway –"

Carne's dislike of Alan went back a lot further than that, he was about to say, when suddenly he thought better of it. Least said, soonest mended, he thought; and here came the first course to take all their minds off the past. The smoked salmon looked good.

"It's probably best to forget the whole thing," he said, taking up his knife and fork. "There's no point in raking up old enmities."

Easy to say – but he hadn't convinced himself. He still wanted answers.

\*     \*     \*

"How long since the three of us were together?" Caro asked.

"Jilly's wedding? One of your children's weddings, anyway," Pen said.

"Not Jilly's," Trish said. "We didn't get over to that."

"Well, it must have been Ben's then. You were wearing a kind of sky-blue, floaty creation, Trish."

"With a marvellous feathered hat? That was definitely bought for Ben's wedding. I saw it in Paris on the way over and couldn't resist it. I remember it well – I've never, in my entire life, had a hat that cost so much!"

It was late and nursing mugs of tea they had retired to their old play-room where the gas fire still popped and spluttered, just as it had always done. Their father had gone to bed some time ago; Alan and Hannah were in the sitting-room, watching television.

"This is like old times," Trish said. Pen cocked a sardonic eyebrow towards her.

"You reckon?"

"Well, things have changed, I know that, but here we are – the same girls in the same place."

Caro groaned.

"Some girls! I feel about ninety tonight. We left Harrogate at crack of dawn. That's the trouble with Cornwall. You have to travel so far to get here."

Pen shot her an anxious glance. She had intended putting David's suggestion to her tonight, but this hardly seemed to augur well for the outcome.

"You are all right, aren't you, Caro? You're keeping well, I mean?"

"Lord, yes; just tired," Caro yawned. "As I've every right to be. We all ought to go to bed. Tomorrow sounds as if it's going to be quite a day."

"Funny about David being mixed up in all of this, isn't it?" Trish said. "I wonder if it was sheer coincidence, or if he put his son on to writing this article?"

"Why should he have done?" Caro asked.

"He might have thought it a clever wheeze to get in touch with us again. You know – trying to reawaken an old love, now he's on his own again."

Caro stared at her, and began to laugh.

"*Honestly*, Trish, you take the biscuit! You think that the article in the *Gazette* is David's attempt to woo you all over again? You can't be that egocentric!"

"Can't she?" Pen sounded cynically amused. "Forget it, Trish," she went on. "Simon used David's somewhat tenuous connection with Father to get the commission to write this article – he admitted that much to me. You can't blame him. He needed the work. He gets paid very little by the magazine that he's accredited to and he makes up the difference by freelancing."

"That's fair enough," said Caro.

"If David had wanted to get in touch with us that much, he could just have written, surely?"

"All right, all right, it was just a thought." Trish smiled to herself, however, unconvinced by her sister's derision. "I just hope that son of his does Father justice, that's all. He's not as handsome as David was, is he? Still, there's probably a lot more *to* him."

"What do you mean by that?" Pen was outraged, but did her best not to show it.

"Well –" Trish laughed and shrugged her shoulders. "David was always too nice – too much of a gentleman. I've always liked my men more – well, more aggressive, I suppose. He's aged a lot, didn't you think?"

Caro laughed again.

"No more than the rest of us, and less than some. He doesn't look nineteen any more, but I'd say he looked pretty good for a sixty-five-year-old."

"I know someone who'd agree with you there, eh, Pen?" Trish turned a sweet and knowing smile on her sister. "I believe he's bowled you over again, just like he did before. You rather like your men nice and gentlemanly, don't you?"

"Don't be ridiculous!" Pen got to her feet, collected up the empty mugs. She would abandon any idea of tackling Caro tonight, she decided. The day had gone on long enough. "I'm tired too, and I'm off to bed," she said. "Goodnight, both of you. See you bright and early in the morning."

The caterers, she remembered, were coming at nine thirty. Tomorrow would be another long day.

\*     \*     \*

David, standing on the terrace of the Marine Hotel, could hear the distant church bells. He hadn't been at all surprised when neither Simon nor Laura joined him in the dining-room for breakfast. It had been clear to him from the moment he had seen the way they looked at each other yesterday that all they really wanted to do was to fall into bed together, and this goal having finally been achieved, it seemed unreasonable to expect them to rise and shine like normal, everyday folks.

He, on the other hand, had rushed down to buy the *Sunday Gazette* and had read Simon's article over his bacon and eggs. Simon, he knew, had felt less than satisfied with it, but he had thought it masterly – a truly rounded picture of a complicated but attractive figure. He looked forward to congratulating Simon on a job well done.

But where the hell was he? His understanding was beginning to wear a little thin. True, it would take them no more than five minutes to get to the church, but the bells seemed to him to be chiming with an added urgency that made him anxious. Any minute now he would call the room – tell them that they could do what they liked, but he was leaving and they could make their own way.

"Good morning."

Relieved and smiling, he turned at the sound of Laura's voice.

"Hi – you made it! And don't you look good? My, that's a super outfit."

"Do you like it? I bought it specially, when I was in the Cotswolds. One of those bargains you couldn't afford *not* to buy."

"It's great. And Laura –" he paused a moment, wanting to say something, not wanting to say too much. "Laura, you're great too. I couldn't be more pleased about you and Simon."

"Thanks. I'm pretty pleased myself."

"He's a lucky guy. I've never seen him happier. For a few days there, I think he lost hope."

"Hm." Laura leaned on the wall beside David. "I was like a Rottweiler, defending my independence."

"But now you're not?"

"I imagine I'll always be pretty independent – that's the way I'm made – but suddenly other things seemed even more important. More fun too! Someone to share things with –"

"That's it!" David's agreement was immediate. "That's absolutely it. And you're right, it's one helluva lot more fun." As this week had reminded him. "Say, Laura, have you read Simon's article yet?"

"Yes. We had the paper delivered to the room. It's good, isn't it? Having met Carne I'm glad we didn't blow the whistle."

"Aha – you've fallen under his spell too!"

"I wouldn't say that. It's more a case of keeping faith with Stella – doing what she would have wanted. Anyway, I feel –"

She paused, and David looked at her curiously.

"You feel what?"

"Oh," she shrugged. "Less personally involved, somehow. Less angry about the whole thing. Mind you, I shall probably start a few hares in this book I intend to write."

"Fair enough. That's what hares are for." But what would Pen think? Impossible to look that far ahead; impossible to look a week ahead, though he'd been working on it, making plans. "Where is Simon, for God's sake? We ought to be on our way."

"He'll be here in a couple of minutes. He forgot to shave, would you believe?"

"I'll believe anything!"

Laura surveyed the view before them.

"This is really something, isn't it? I keep thinking I'm in a foreign country. Brittany, or somewhere like that."

"The Cornish and Breton languages were once practically identical," David said. He turned his head and grinned at her. "Not a lot of people know that. There was a whole heap of comings and goings between the two countries at one time. Traders, saints, you name it."

"Pen's been instructing you, I perceive."

"That's right."

"She's a nice lady. I liked her a lot."

For a moment he said nothing, his attention apparently riveted on the harbour below.

"Yeah," he said softly at last. "Me too."

\* \* \*

The organ was playing softly as they entered the church. It still smelled of history, David thought – was still much as he remembered it, except that now it was almost full, with the seats at the side full of small, uniformed figures, their whispers and wriggles quelled by the stern glances of their Captains or Great Owls or whatever they were called these days.

They found an empty pew halfway down on the right-hand side and took their places. From where he sat, David could see the tomb that Pen had been so fond of; the one of the couple in Elizabethan dress with the little dog.

The flowers were magnificent; he recognised chrysanthemums but not the others. However, in spite of this autumnal magnificence, it was daffodils he thought of, and a young girl struggling with a huge vase, who turned to look at him with wide, startled eyes.

A small commotion at the back of the church and a stirring chord or two from the organ heralded the arrival of the Mayor in all her regalia, together with her Councillors, preceded down the aisle by a smirking Rover Scout holding aloft a Union Jack. Behind, after a suitable interval to allow the official party to settle themselves, came the Carne family. Pen was holding her father's arm as they came down the aisle – as she must have done, David thought, when she was married. Was she thinking of that day? Trish and Hannah walked behind them, Caro and Alan bringing up the rear. They were ushered into the front pew; they smiled their thanks, all but Carne himself kneeling momentarily to pray.

David saw Pen smile slightly at her father as she took her seat beside him. She looked calm, but rather serious; he wondered what she had prayed for. Whatever the day holds, he thought; whatever answers I am able to get from Carne, either now or later, I must never hurt her.

The processional hymn began. The choir – men and boys in white surplices, women in dark blue – moved down the aisle in their turn led by a burnished cross. The service had begun.

\*     \*     \*

Afterwards the congregation milled about outside and Pen, seeing David, went across to him.

"It was all right, wasn't it?" She was smiling widely now, clearly relieved. "The vicar does tend to go on a bit, but he was fine today – said all the right things. And wasn't the anthem lovely? The choir-master wrote it specially for the occasion."

"It was a wonderful service, all of it. Your father must have been pleased."

"Yes, I think he was. He was pleased with Simon's article too. I must get him home now."

"Have I got time to show Laura your forebear's tombstone? I have a hunch she might appreciate it."

Pen laughed delightedly as she took her father's arm.

"Fancy you remembering that! Take all the time you want. See you back at the house."

The garden of Roscarrow had been transformed with small tables and chairs and one long trestle table on which, as they arrived, trays of food were being laid. Black-clad waitresses circled with trays of sherry or soft drinks. The band on the flower-decked platform played a selection from *HMS Pinafore*.

David, not sure how it happened, found himself standing next to Trish.

"My word," she said, surveying the scene, "they have gone to town."

"Just shows how much they think of your father. I – er – gather that your fears were unfounded. Simon's article met with approval, Pen tells me."

"I haven't actually read it myself – but yes, Father seemed quite pleased. Relieved, I thought. Maybe he suspected that Simon was going to reveal a whole lot of dark secrets from his past that he's kept hidden for years." And she laughed in amusement at the wholly ridiculous nature of this idea.

"He's not that sort of journalist."

"I don't trust any of them on principle." She took his arm and smiled up at him. "Don't mind me, David, I'm only joking. Do let's sit together for lunch. Afterwards I've got to go up on the platform with all the nobs, but I can please myself until then. Come on – we've hardly had any chance to talk."

It was not what he would have chosen, but Laura and Simon were already sitting down with an unknown couple and appeared deep in conversation, and Pen had steered her father to what was clearly a place of honour where they had been joined by Caro and Alan and several unknowns who he assumed were town dignitaries.

"Sure," he said. "How about here? And how about a sherry?"

"Wonderful," she said, and rewarded him with a dazzling smile which she turned on two ladies who made as if to share their table. "Do you mind?" she said. "I'm keeping these places for various relations."

Abashed, the ladies retreated.

"I know those two," she said, in answer to David's amused glance. "They're frightfully nosey. They'd be listening to every word that passed between us, and by this evening the whole of Porthlivick would be in possession of a highly-coloured version."

David laughed and shook his head at her.

"Still the same old Trish," he said.

It was later, as they ate their way through the surprisingly good cold buffet, that David saw an opportunity to satisfy at least some of his curiosity regarding Alan Yeo.

Trish was speaking of Hannah, Caro's daughter.

"Everyone says how like me she is," she said. "Which may not be saying much," she added, falsely modest, "but is a great deal better for darling Hannah than if she'd looked like Alan, you must admit."

"It's a funny thing," David said, "but I feel I've seen Alan before – yet I couldn't have, could I? He was never around when I was here. He was away at sea."

"That's right. Caro was always mooning about over him, wasn't she? The poor darling! They were star-crossed lovers, and no mistake."

"Maybe it was his father I saw."

"Maybe. Not that he looked much like Alan. He was fatter and broader – at least he was when I last saw him, at Ben's wedding. Ben is Caro's son."

"You're telling me Alan's father lived to see his grandson married?"

"Certainly he did. He was a ripe old age when he died. Late eighties, anyway."

So much, David thought, for the idea that he could have been the man dumped at sea. This particular shot in the dark had clearly been off-target.

"And *we* all witnessed," Trish continued amusedly, "the unlikely sight of Caleb Carne and Walter Yeo not only attending the wedding of their joint grandson, but actually exchanging civil words. It was a wonder the heavens didn't fall."

"They actually made up the quarrel, then? That's good news."

"Oh, I wouldn't go quite so far as that – but at least they talked to each other without coming to blows. You know, I always thought Father was completely wrong when he accused Walter of dirty tricks at the election. He always said that Walter spread slander –"

"I remember the story."

"I think it was much more likely to have been Henry, Walter's younger brother. He was a nasty, sly sort of chap – now he, come to think of it, was very like Alan. Not that Alan's nasty and sly, I didn't mean that. I'm really very fond of him. I mean that Alan takes after Henry in looks."

"What happened to Henry? Is he still around?"

"Good Lord, no. He died during the war. Drowned."

David's throat was suddenly dry.

"In action?"

"No, it was an accident. All rather mysterious, actually. He worked in London at the time and apparently was expected home for a few days' holiday. He arrived at St Jory by train, that much was verified, but no one ever saw him again until his body was washed up about a month later on Merrick Beach. You remember – we went there in the boat."

"Yes."

It seemed the ultimate horror, somehow, that the body should have come to rest there in that beautiful place, sullying it for all time despite all the tides that must have washed it.

Trish's narrative was continuing, unabated; clearly this was a *cause célèbre* in the history of Porthlivick, something that had been recounted with ghoulish delight many times over.

"The night he arrived was wet and dark. They think he must have missed the last bus to Porthlivick. Taxis were in short supply in those days, so probably he decided to walk. He must have taken the short cut over the cliffs and missed his footing. It's the only explanation."

"Yes." David couldn't have said more if his life depended on it.

"There were some who said it could have been foul play – there wasn't, after all, much love lost for the man, but his body was pretty battered by rocks and eaten away by fishes and things by the time it was washed up, so there was no way of telling. It was a pretty gruesome spectacle, by all accounts – we have sharks off here, you know." She punctuated the narrative by giving him a wide smile. "I'm not putting you off your lunch, am I? His poor wife nearly went demented. She was weird at the best of times, but she took to haunting the cliffs looking like the Angel of Death."

"Yes." David put down his fork, took a breath. "Trish, will you excuse me for a moment, please? I have to go inside for a moment. I'm sorry –"

"I *have* upset you! Oh, poor David – I didn't realise you were so squeamish!"

"I'm OK. Don't make a fuss, please."

Urgently he left the table. He blundered inside the house – anywhere, away from everybody. He went to the bathroom, washed his hands, splashed cold water on his face, telling himself that it was ridiculous to feel so upset about this long-ago tragedy. Somehow it seemed so much worse now that the man had a name.

Pull yourself together, he told his reflection in the glass, breathing deeply. He hadn't killed the man, after all. Carne had.

Someone rattled the door. He took another few breaths and opened it, smiling in apology as he passed the woman who waited outside. He felt calmer now, able to cope. Downstairs he bumped into Pen emerging from the dining-room, a glass of wine in her hand.

"Oh David, do me a favour," she begged him. "Father can't drink that stuff they're serving out there. Would you be an angel and take this over to him? It seems I'm wanted in the kitchen for a moment."

"Of course." He took the glass from her. "Pen, have you spoken to Caro –?"

305

"Not yet. There simply hasn't been time! But I will, I promise."

"Please," he said.

Something in his voice seemed to cause her to look at him with more attention.

"Are you feeling all right, David?"

"I'm absolutely fine," he said heartily. "Say, this is a great party, isn't it?"

"Fingers crossed!" Pen, suiting the action to the words, disappeared towards the kitchen.

David emerged once more into the garden and made his way towards the table where Carne was sitting. And as he approached, he saw that Alan and the officials who had been sitting with him had left the table and were now standing to one side, clearly discussing how best to arrange the chairs on the platform for the second part of the programme, the presentation and speeches. Someone else, in passing, was bending down to speak to Caro. Carne, for the moment alone, was beaming round at the assembled company – massive, composed, benevolent.

David checked a moment, before continuing on his way, threading his way through the tables. The band, he noted with one part of his mind, was playing a selection from *South Pacific*. The strains of *Happy Talk* floated towards him; not, he felt, the most appropriate accompaniment for what he intended to say.

At last he reached Carne, and stood before him.

"Sir," he said, just as he would have done as a nineteen-year-old private in the Army. "I've brought you this, at Pen's request." He put the glass down on the table. He could hear Caro laughing with her friend in the background, and the band playing merrily on.

Only Carne had any significance for him – Carne, and the sudden shrewd look of comprehension in his eyes, the dying smile.

"Thank you, my boy," he said. "Very good of you."

"When are we going to talk, sir?" David asked.

"Talk? We have talked, have we not?"

"Not about that last night." He spoke quietly, but Carne seemed to have no difficulty in hearing him. "For my own peace of mind I need to know the truth. I don't pose any threat to you."

For a moment Carne stared straight ahead, his mouth pulled down, his lower lip tremulous. Then a look of great weariness came over his face and he looked up at David at last.

"Later," he said. "Later."

\* \* \*

Alan came back to the table, Caro turned to include David in the conversation, and there was no chance to say more. Not, he thought, that there was anything more to say; in fact as the afternoon wore on – as laudatory speeches were made, the picture presented, the great man applauded – he began to feel some compunction that he had raised the subject at all.

He sure chose his moment! He should have waited until all this had died down and Carne had recovered from what must be an exhausting experience. But Trish's revelation had shocked him, his time was limited – it was easy to make excuses for himself. In any case, he thought, Carne had made no promises. 'Later' could mean anything he chose it to mean.

After the presentation, Simon and Laura made their farewells and left.

"You've seen nothing of Cornwall," Pen said in dismay. "Do you really have to go so soon?"

"I'm afraid so," Laura said. "I must get back to London. The new school term starts on Wednesday, and I've got things I must catch up on."

"Me too," Simon said. "You know I'm going back to New York very soon. We'll be back though. You can depend on it."

"I hope so." Pen smiled at them both, a little shyly. "And I do hope you'll have a wonderful life together," she said. "Forgive me if I'm speaking out of turn."

"You're not," Simon assured her. "And we intend to. Thanks."

"They're a lovely couple," Pen said to David as they drove off.

"They sure are. Pen, have you asked Caro –?"

"I will, I swear it, after I've seen Father into bed. He's about to go up – he's absolutely exhausted, and I've persuaded him he's done enough. I expect most people will drift off now, anyway."

So that was it, David thought. By 'later', Carne had meant some unspecified time in the future – this year, next year, sometime, never. Maybe he was even hoping that death would catch him first! Well, there was no more he could do.

By the time he returned to the garden, Carne was saying his

farewells, assuring an officious-looking woman in a red hat that he had had a wonderful day, that her arrangements couldn't have been bettered.

"Not a single hitch, my dear Mrs Cartwright. I am so grateful for all your efforts and I shall treasure that wonderful picture. We'll have to find a worthy place of honour for it."

"We're all grateful." Pen, still smiling but looking far more tired than her father, was urging him away. "Come along, Father. You will excuse us, Mrs Cartwright?"

"Of course, of course." Mrs Cartwright stepped back a little, cast a triumphant look around her, and found herself face to face with David. "What a wonderful man," she said earnestly. "An example to us all."

"Indeed he is," David agreed; and determinedly moved away, suddenly longing to be alone.

His steps took him to the slope that led to the summerhouse, and after a moment's hesitation he walked down it. It was locked, as he expected it would be, but there were a table and two chairs on the terrace and he sat down, closing his eyes and lifting his face to the weak sunshine. They'd been lucky with the weather, he thought. It had held up well. The afternoon was almost over now and maybe he should think of leaving with all the others; he was determined to hang in there, however. He wanted Pen's answer.

Was Carne a wonderful man? Maybe, he thought. He's a survivor anyway; but whether any of us know what he's really like is quite another matter. Which Caleb Carne was the real one? The sentimental novelist? The jocular father? The lover of an avowed feminist? The man who inspired millions, but at the same time cherished a feud that, in the end, proved fatal?

And with this thought came another which he had somehow managed to forget over the years – incomprehensibly, it now seemed. There had been those who thought that Carne had murdered his father. Were they, then, in the right? Had it been easier for him the second time around?

"Oh, David, *there* you are!" Trish, it seemed, had tracked him down. "I've been looking for you everywhere. I thought you must have gone, but Pen said you might be here."

"It's kind of peaceful –"

"Forget the peace! Father wants to see you. Pen's settled him in bed and given him his tea, but he says he hasn't had a chance for a chat."

"That's true." David got to his feet. "Thanks, Trish – I'll go up right now."

So this was it, he thought. The moment of truth. High noon at the OK Corral.

He'd never been in Roscarrow's main bedroom before. It was a large room, he found, containing a big brass bed and heavy, Victorian furniture, all of which looked perfectly at home, completely in keeping. A velvet-covered armchair was beside the bed, and across the room was a wide, mahogany chest on which stood silver-backed brushes and framed photographs of all three daughters when young. A larger picture of Emily Carne staring expressionlessly towards the camera had been awarded a table to itself.

Carne was sitting up in bed, sipping tea, clad in striped pyjamas; on the table by his side was a tray set with a teapot under a flowered cosy, milk, an extra cup.

"Help yourself if you want one," Carne said, indicating the cup with a jerk of his head.

"Thank you."

David did so, thinking with some amusement that the revelations, if revelations there were to be, would be made in true English style, accompanied by the drinking of tea. Well, at least it covered a moment of awkwardness, gave them both something to do with their hands.

"A great day, sir," he said. "One you'll remember."

"For such time as is left to me. Sit down, sit down, boy!"

"This boy," David said, amused, "is sixty-five. I haven't been a boy for a long time." He sat down in the chair nearest the bed. "And I find, in my old age, that I need some answers."

"So I gather."

"Am I going to get them?"

Carne said nothing for a moment, but turned to put his cup back on the tray, taking his time. He sighed, settled himself against the pillows."

"I'm very old," he said miserably.

"I know that. But you've a good memory, especially for the past. I repeat what I said downstairs. I don't pose any threat to you. I just want to know the whys and the wherefores."

The old man had been staring up at the ceiling but now he lowered his head and looked directly at David.

"Don't think it hasn't haunted me too," he said, in his tremulous voice. "It was a dreadful night, the worst of my life. But I paid for it, you know. I gave up everything because of it – all the fame, all the future."

"And Stella Morel?"

The white head lifted from the pillows.

"What do you know of Stella?"

"That you and she had an *affaire*. That you were jealous of Henry Yeo –"

There was a strange wheezing noise, and David realised, with some surprise, that Carne was laughing.

"Jealous of Henry Yeo? You're mad! I was never jealous of that blackguard in my entire life. I despised him, hated him –"

"So you killed him."

"No, no, no! You've got it entirely wrong. It wasn't like that at all."

"I don't buy the story that he slipped on the steps."

"What?" Carne's face creased in a frown.

"That's what you told me."

"Did I? No, no – that was wrong. I had to say something, after all." Like telling me Yeo was a spy, David thought; like telling me I'd done a service for my country. How readily these lies had tripped from his tongue!

"Maybe it would be as great a relief to you as it would be to me if you told the truth after all these years," he said with deceptive mildness. "How did you kill him?"

"I didn't. I never did. Tell me, David, how well do you remember my wife?"

"Mrs Carne?" David stared at him. " She was – quiet. Not easy to know. Always kind to me, though."

Carne's gaze was fixed on a point on the ceiling some way beyond David's head and he held the bunched top sheet in his two hands, holding it tightly as if it gave him support.

"Banked-up fires," he said hoarsely. "That's what she had inside her, David. Banked-up fires. People thought she was placid, without emotion, but it wasn't true, particularly where I was concerned. I didn't even realise myself the depth of her feeling for me until after

310

we were married – long after. It was the reason we came back to Cornwall. She hated Oxford. She felt she was losing me – that I didn't speak her language any more. You understand? She became – a little unbalanced about it all. She wanted babies – a son, most of all, but when the girls came she was cold towards them – they felt it, I know, and I did my best to make up for it."

"So what happened that night?"

Carne paused as if to gather his strength, looked at David once more.

"You were right about Stella Morel," he said. "I don't know how you learned of her, but I loved her. We'd been together, more or less, throughout the war, whenever we could manage it – but there was need for discretion, you understand. It wasn't only because of my wife, my family commitments. There was my work, the BBC – it would have been disastrous if anything had leaked out –"

"But you met Henry Yeo by chance."

"How do you know all this? We met in a pub by the river. I knew he was working in London, but our paths had never crossed; then, suddenly, there he was. I was with Stella and a friend of hers. I tried to pass them off as colleagues – perhaps I tried too hard and only succeeded in appearing guilty. He wasn't fooled! He hated me as much as I hated him and he made it his business to find out about me and Stella – he knew exactly what it would do to me if it came out.

"Then, one night – *that* night – just after Caro had run away with another of that bloody clan, he came to the house. It was late. The girls were in bed – Emily and I had been sitting up, talking endlessly about Caro. We were both upset – she, I think, more angry because I was angry, rather than because she was worried on Caro's behalf. Perhaps I do her an injustice . . ." His voice trailed away, then picked up again.

"She had just gone to the kitchen for something or other. There was a ring at the front door and I went to answer it. Yeo was standing there, grinning at me like a death's head. He pushed his way inside, said he had something to say to me."

"Blackmail?" David asked softly.

"Yes. He wouldn't leave, said I had to hear him out, so I went into the sitting-room and he followed. He stood there, said his piece – said he'd ruin everything for me if I didn't pay up. He said my name would be spread across every newspaper in the land – and of course, it would have been. I was famous then.

"We argued, raised voices – he didn't hear Emily come behind him. She was a big woman, you remember, and powerful. She had a heavy brass tray in her hands and she must have caught his general drift before ever she came into the room, because she didn't hesitate a moment. She crashed it down on his head and he fell as if he'd been pole-axed."

He stopped then, dropped his chin on his chest, closed his eyes. David lifted his hand towards him, then let it fall.

"You know," Carne said, looking up at David once more. "You were right. It is a relief to speak of it. Sometimes, when I least expect it, it plays over –"

"I know," David said. "I do understand. It's the same with me."

"We tried to revive him, but he was gone. We didn't know what to do. We should have called the police, I know, but how would that have affected Emily? She was easily upset at the best of times. I had to spare her – I just knew that we had to get him as far away from the house as possible. We managed to get him down to the summerhouse together, then Emily came back to clean up here. He bled profusely – the corner of the tray had somehow caught him –" he fell silent.

David reached out to touch him.

"Look," he said. "I honestly didn't want to distress you, but the whole thing is something that played on my mind lately and I really needed to know. Forgive me, won't you?"

Carne nodded, sighed, smiled at him briefly.

"Well, you know it all now," he said. "Nothing was ever the same again. Emily had a nervous breakdown – people thought it was because of Caro, but it wasn't, of course. She was ill, distressed, and I promised I would never see or communicate with Stella again – that I'd stay with her, down here in Cornwall, give up all prospect of the new broadcasting career I'd hoped for. I had no option. I was never sure what she might say –"

A knock at the door followed by the entry of Trish caused him to break off short.

"I hope I'm not interrupting any boys' secrets," she said roguishly. "I'm doing my ministering angel bit! Everyone's gone, peace has been restored, and we wondered if you would like anything in the way of liquid refreshment."

Her father smiled at her a little tremulously. David, who had felt considerable guilt at causing so much added strain on a day which the old man must surely have found exhausting, was thankful to see that, though clearly tired, he seemed calm and at peace.

"Well, now," Carne said softly. "A small Scotch wouldn't come amiss, since you're so kind. How about you, David?"

"I think I'm going to spirit David away downstairs, Father. You're exhausted, I can tell. You really ought to rest, you know."

"Perhaps you're right, my darling." He held out his bony, knotted old hand towards David. "Thank you for coming up, my boy. It's been good talking to you. I've enjoyed it. We must talk again."

"I hope so, sir." David took the hand, held it a moment. "I'm so glad to have had this conversation."

"He always thought a lot of you," Trish said, as they went downstairs together. "The blue-eyed boy, we used to call you. Do you remember?"

"Indeed I do." David grinned at her. "I remember everything."

She gave him a coquettish smile.

"Steady on! You'll have me blushing in a minute. Go on, every-one's in the sitting-room –"

\*   \*   \*

Nothing, ever, the same again.

The old man's head fell back on the pillows, his once-handsome face sagging into the folds and furrows of age, his mouth hanging open as if in a silent cry of pain, the pain with which this truth had dawned on him, after the happenings of that night; the dreadful, inexorable, knell-like sound of the words as they hammered in his brain. Nothing, ever, the same again.

Such a lot to lose!

The power, the praise, the *certainty* that at last he had found, in his broadcasts, something that he could do better than anyone else had done it before him; a dream fulfilled, you could say – a dream that was nurtured in a drab cottage with his carping mother whom he could never please, and in the little grey school where he had been the butt of other, lesser boys.

Such a lot to lose!

Respect. Fame. A future. And Stella. Most of all, Stella. It was Stella who had filled his head throughout those frantic, panic-stricken hours – the thought that he might be accused, sentenced – *hanged* for God's sake! That his private life would be scrutinised, their love mulled over by morons, made dirty, when in fact it had been the one good thing in his unsatisfactory life.

She had been all he had ever known of gaiety and tenderness and understanding and generosity of spirit, her love and wisdom and practical help miraculous gifts he could only accept with astonishment and gratitude. Even now the thought of her had the power to calm him, suffuse him with a melancholy joy for what they had, for what they lost.

All he did, he did for her; yet, in the doing of it, he had shackled himself to Emily for ever. How the gods must have laughed! Were laughing still, perhaps, at the sight of an old man, with tears in his eyes, mourning the past – and after such a day, when surely he should be full of triumph.

He turned his head on the pillow and looked, dimly, towards the blurred shape that he knew was Emily's photograph.

"You would have hated it, Em," he said. "So many people. So much talk. All so – very – very – tiring." Even in his mind, the words were slurred. "So very – very –"

His eyelids were drooping. He was nearly asleep. It must, he thought hazily, be imagination, but he seemed to see Emily's photograph clearer now. And though he knew her sombre expression by heart, it seemed to him that she was smiling at him; not the shy, sweet smile that had captivated him when he had first known her as a girl, but a smile with a hint of triumph behind it.

Well, why not? he asked himself, not knowing whether he was awake or dreaming.

She won, after all.

\*     \*     \*

"We've just flopped," Pen said as David and Trish went into

the drawing-room. "What a day! I can't quite understand why it should have been so exhausting."

"It's all that smiling and thanking people," Caro said. "Being pleasant is about the most exhausting thing I know. But it did go off well, didn't it? Come and flop too, David. Alan's getting drinks."

"We were talking about Grandfather's presentation picture," Hannah said. "We were all rather surprised by it."

"I suppose we should have known what to expect from Wesley Clore," said Pen. "That's the sort of thing he does. It just doesn't seem the sort of thing Mrs Cartwright would choose. How little we know people!"

The picture in question had been put to stand on top of a bookcase until a more permanent home could be found for it, and David studied it for a moment. It was modern, semi-abstract, the colour slashed on to the canvas, yet in some magical way it was clearly Porthlivick on a fresh, windy day.

"I like it," he said. "In fact I'd go further. I think it's wonderful."

"We're split," Hannah told him. "Aunt Pen and Mum and I are definitely pro, but Aunt Trish is anti and Dad has yet to register his vote."

"Oh, I'm pro," Alan said, coming in the room at that moment with drinks on a tray. A small, round, wooden one, David was thankful to note. "What does Caleb think? That's the important thing."

Hannah removed a glass of whisky from the tray.

"I'll take Grandfather's up, shall I?" she said. "I'm sure he liked the picture. I heard him enthusing about it to Mrs Cartwright. He said she couldn't have chosen anything he liked more, and he honestly sounded as if he meant it."

Trish gave one of her trilling laughs.

"Oh, Hannah! When will you learn?" But Hannah had gone, and it was left to Pen to put the question.

"Learn what, Trish?"

"Don't be naïve, Pen. You know Father as well as I do, and you know perfectly well that he can look anyone straight in the eye and tell the most outrageous tales just as convincingly as if they were holy writ. Not to put too fine a point upon it," she went on, leaning forward to take her drink from the tray, "I would go so far as to say the old rogue has been a liar all his life."

"Nonsense!"

"What a thing to say!"

The voices of Caro and Pen blended in defence of their father; but Trish was laughing, sticking to her guns.

"It's the Celt in him. He can't help it. He's given to romantic flights of fancy."

David found himself staring at her, suspicion and outrage giving way, at last, to a certain rueful amusement. Was that all it had been, then – a romantic flight of fancy? Had he been well and truly fooled by a master?

It was possible. He could, himself, think of at least two equally plausible scenarios right now, without really trying. On the other hand, there had always been something a little odd and unfathomable about Emily Carne. Something disquieting about that dark, opaque look of hers; something that made you think that, like an iceberg, nine-tenths of her was hidden. Caleb's reference to banked-up fires rang true. It was easy to imagine her calmly listening to Henry Yeo blackmailing her husband, and deciding, without a trace of indecision, what she had to do.

Forget it, he told himself. It was ancient history; over, dead, finished. Surely, here and now, on the brink of another war, there were things more worthy of concern?

There were other things far closer to home that were occupying his mind right now too. Simon and Laura, for example. And Pen.

What was he going to do about her? There were no easy solutions, the future was by no means clear. He didn't even know if she'd spoken to Caro yet.

"Grandfather's asleep," Hannah said, coming back into the room. "Anyone want an extra glass of whisky?"

"Just put it down. We'll get around to it," her father said.

"Poor darling!" Pen's voice was full of loving concern. "I knew he was exhausted."

Caro leaned across and squeezed her arm.

"You're awfully good with him," she said. "I hope I manage so well –"

David looked across at Pen, caught her eye, saw her smile.

She's asked her, he thought; and Caro's said yes. He smiled back with uninhibited delight, not caring who saw it, raising his glass in her direction, toasting the prospect of a few days in her exclusive company. He recognised a feeling of happy anticipation that seemed to have been absent from his life for some time.

Just a few days. It wasn't much, but it would do for now.

Oh yes; it would do very nicely for now.